THE SHADOW OF THE SYCAMORES

DORIS DAVIDSON

THE SHADOW OF THE SYCAMORES

BLACK & WHITE PUBLISHING

First published 2004
by Black & White Publishing Ltd
99 Giles Street, Edinburgh
Scotland, EH6 6BZ

Reprinted 2004

ISBN 1 84502 012 X

A CIP catalogue record for this book
is available from the British Library.

Cover illustration by Kate George

Printed and bound by Nørhaven Paperback A/S

THE SHADOW OF THE SYCAMORES

PROLOGUE

1870

Even realising that his predicament was of his own making, Willie Rae felt at odds with the whole world. Surely he could be excused for drowning his sorrow at his wife's death? Of course, he *had* done a good bit of celebrating yesterday evening for the birth of his first son but he could hold his liquor, always could, and Mister High-and-Mighty John Gow was worse than him, blethering like a daftie and him the Kirk's Session Clerk.

'Are you sober enough to carry out your job?' Willie asked suddenly. 'I dinna want things going wrong.'

'I'm as shober as you!' came the indignant response, which was not saying much for he needed the bar counter to keep him upright.

'We'd best get on wi' it, then.'

Walking unsteadily to the door, neither man was aware of the ludicrous spectacle they made. 'The blind leadin' the blind,' as joiner Tam Mavor remarked to his brother, sitting beside him on the bench nearest the fire.

'The blind drunks more like it,' sniggered Geordie, the local carrier.

'You're right there,' nodded Ben Roberts, London-born landlord of The Doocot wherein they were drinking and, as resident in the small town of Ardbirtle for little more than seven years, still considered an incomer, even a foreigner. 'But you can't blame Willie, can you? This must be his fifth child.'

Tam shook his head, 'My Jean says it's his thirteenth.'

Even Geordie's eyes widened in astonishment at this statement. 'Thirteen? As much as that? Surely no'?'

'Right enough – though the other twelve was lassies. There's only . . .' Tam broke off to count the survivors on his fingers. 'There's Jeannie – she's ages wi' my Jessie so that would make her twelve – and Bella, after her Ma – she'd be ten, maybe – and . . . eh . . . Kitty – she must be six or seven – and Abby, Abigail, I suppose – she's just two.' He paused again to check his memory and then continued, 'So that had been . . . um . . . eight that died as infants.'

'Poor things,' his brother said mournfully, then reverted to his previous thought. 'Thirteen? That's a terrible lot for ony man to gi'e a wumman.'

Ben blew into the tumbler he was drying and gave it another rub with the towel. 'His missus can't have had as many headaches as my Sophie,' he said, wistfully.

Steadying himself after almost overbalancing on a large stone, John Gow said, 'Have you and Bella decided on a name?'

'Bella decided.' Willie's brow furrowed now. For the life of him, he couldn't remember what his wife had said last night before she died but it would come to him.

They tottered along in silence, the tall well-built blacksmith with a shock of brindled hair and the short tubby Session Clerk whose bald pate made him a target for the youths of the town to laugh at. Each man had to concentrate on putting one foot past the other without tripping, although it was hardly any distance from the hostelry to the church.

When they went into the vestry, Willie muttered, 'You'd best register the death first, eh?'

'This one hasn't died as well? I thought you said you had a son . . .'

'It wasna the bairn that died this time.'

John Gow sat down on his chair with a thump. 'Oh, Willie, you're surely not telling me Bella's dead? Eh, man, I'm truly sorry to hear that.'

'Aye.' The widower wiped away the tear that had edged out in spite of his efforts to stop it. 'I dinna ken what I'll do without her.'

2

The death duly recorded, John turned and said to the other man, 'Now for the bairn. What's his name?'

Having been dredging his pickled brain in the hope of recovering the instruction he had been given, Willie had a flash of inspiration. His mother-in-law, living with them to help her daughter through her accouchement, had lifted the infant to feed him before he had left the house this last time. 'Come to your Gramma, my poor, motherless, wee Chookie,' she had crooned to him. Willie felt a surge of triumph. That must be the name the two women had chosen.

'Chookie?' repeated the Session Clerk, his eyebrows in danger of shooting off his forehead altogether. 'What sort of name's that?' He scratched his head for a moment, then burst out, 'Wait! Chookie? That sounds Russian to me. Your Bella was well educated was she not? She had seen the name in a book more than likely.' His expression changed. 'It's not the kind of name I would have chosen myself, mind.'

Ignoring this, Willie puffed out his chest with a look of relieved pleasure. 'Aye, my Bella was real clever, God rest her soul.'

'So how is this Russian name spelled?'

'How would I ken? You're the Session Clerk – it's up to you. Surely you've come across it afore?'

'To be honest, Willie, I have never heard it before, let alone seen it written down, but I will give it my best try. Let me think.' Taking a sheet of paper from the top drawer of the desk, he wrote a few versions before looking up uncertainly. 'C-H-O-O-K-I-E doesn't look the least bit foreign, not even C-H-O-U-K-E-Y.'

He bent his head as if praying for enlightenment, then said, almost to himself, 'It has just come to me – there is a Russian composer, Tchaikovsky, and he begins T-C-H.' Writing down these three letters, he regarded them speculatively. 'Yes, that looks good. Now the oo sound. The Russian currency is the rouble, spelled O-U, so now we have the Tchou . . . but we need the 'key'. To be authentic, the name should end in just a Y or an I. Let me see.'

He studied this final version, mouthing each syllable separately before sliding the paper across 'What do you think?'

Willie took a quick squint but he had had little schooling and none of the items made any sense. 'I'll leave it to you,' he mumbled, congratulating himself on remembering the name at all. His mother-in-law had never had a good opinion of him but she was bound to be pleased about this. A few moments later, he signed his name laboriously and rose to go.

Isie McIntyre, a thin woman of medium height with abrupt, bird-like movements, shot out her hand as soon as he went through the door of Oak Cottage. 'I hope you minded my Bella's dying wish,' she grunted, fixing Willie with her beady eyes.

This baleful glare always made him feel as if she considered him dirt under her feet, but he handed her the document with a clear conscience. The old besom could not find fault with him over this. It was her own choice, though he could bet that she wouldn't have known how to spell the name herself.

It took the woman some time to digest the information recorded on the certificate – she was not a fluent reader and, although John Gow was renowned for his copperplate handwriting if for no other talent except his capacity for strong drink, it was more difficult to understand than print. Then she let out a shriek of outraged anger that curdled Willie's blood, it was so unexpected.

'What's this heathen name supposed to be?'

'It's what you s . . . s . . . said,' he ventured, timidly.

'I never said . . . that! I dinna even ken *how* to say it.'

'It's Tchouki,' he mumbled, frantically wondering what had gone wrong.

'Tchouki? Where on earth did you . . . Bella wanted the bairn cried after her father, my dear, dead husband.'

Recalling the many rows he had witnessed between her and her dear, dead husband, Willie wisely made no reference to them. 'Tchouki's what you said to him when you lifted him oot o' the cradle,' he mumbled, 'so I thocht . . .'

4

'Me?' she screamed. 'I've never heard tell o' such an . . . outlandish name afore. Sounds African or Indian or something.' She sank down on a chair with her hand on her heart as comprehension dawned. 'Ach! You daft, drunken beggar! Chookie, Chookie's what I cry to my hens when I'm feeding them and I sometimes say that to the bairn and all for he's a dear wee chickie to me, poor motherless mite.'

Reminded thus of his wife's death, Willie's eyes brimmed with tears. 'I'm sorry, Isie. I couldna mind what Bella said and I thocht . . .'

'Thocht?' she yelled. 'Thocht? What do you use to think wi', may I ask? Your brain's pickled wi' the whisky you pour down your thrapple, and that John Gow's none better! Fancy thinking Chookie was a real name!'

'He said it's Russian,' Willie declared, on the defensive, 'and he ken't how to spell it.'

'He wouldn't want to admit he didna ken so he made up that story and you believed him. Ach, Willie Rae, you're worse than a bairn. You canna mind one thing I say to you.' Taking another glance at the offending document, she shook her head and said, grimly, 'So you'll take this right back to the kirk an' you'll tell John Gow to change it. Your son's not a foreigner . . . though it might be better for him if he was. God help him having you for a father!'

'What have I to get it changed to?' Willie tried not to sound aggressive, though he felt like throwing the interfering bitch out on to the road. He would have to depend on her to look after things for a while yet.

'See?' Isie cried, triumphantly. 'You've forgot already.' She gave a prolonged frustrated sigh and reached up to the mantelshelf to take something from behind the little alarm clock, noisily ticking the time away. 'Bella wrote it down for you, even though she was dying, she ken't she couldna depend on you. So you'd best take it wi' you this time. The first name's Henry – that's my poor man – Bruce – that's my maiden name – McIntyre – that's Bella's maiden name – and William – for you though you dinna deserve it. That's what his name should be. Off you go, now, and dinna come back till you've got it sorted out.'

'I'm kind o' hungry,' he muttered but her heaving chest and lowering brow made him pick up his tweed cap and hurry out. Who did the woman think she was, he asked himself, as he went along the road. She thought she knew everything, but she knew damn all. It was no wonder Henry McIntyre had given up the ghost. He'd been scunnered with her dictating to him like that. But, once he got over Bella's death, *he* would lay down some rules. Isie would have to knuckle down and do what *he* told her and she'd better have meals ready for him when he wanted them. She wasn't going to rule the roost. She wouldn't tell him when to change his socks . . . like she did that very morning.

'I can smell your feet from here!' she had sneered, looking at him across the table with her nose screwed up, and him in the middle of his porridge. He couldn't help having sweaty feet. It proved he was a man, didn't it? Not that anybody needed more proof of that, he thought proudly. He had fathered thirteen bairns – a baker's dozen in fifteen years – and, if his Bella hadn't died, he'd have fathered a good few more, for she hadn't reached her thirty-fourth birthday, poor lass, and he was only thirty-six.

Busy with his thoughts, he reached the church gate before he knew where he was and slowed his pace to a nonchalant saunter. It wouldn't do to let John Gow suspect that this change was not his own idea.

The Session Clerk was still tidying up his papers in the vestry – Willie's journey home and back plus his confrontation with his mother-in-law had taken but a mere twenty minutes – but where the inkwell had been there now stood a tall bottle of Black and White whisky. 'Oh, it'sh you again, Willie? I did not expect you back. What can I do for you this time? Nothing has come over your son, I trust?'

'No, he's still fine but it's like this, John.' He drew a chair up to the opposite side of the wide desk. 'I was . . . thinking, it's maybe nae such a good idea for my only son to have a foreign name. Folk'll maybe think my Bella . . .' He gave his head an abrupt shake as if to ward off the unwelcome supposition. 'No, you'd best take out the Russian name and write in . . .' He resorted to passing over the slip of paper he had been carrying.

The Session Clerk frowned as he read out, 'Henry Bruce McIntyre William Rae? That's an awful long name for the infant.'

Willie smiled sheepishly. 'You ken what a wumman's like.' He explained the origin of the moniker and added, 'So if you'll just take your penknife or whatever you use and scrape out the foreign name and write that in, I'd be much obliged.'

A second small glass had mysteriously appeared and was being filled to the top. 'We will have another drink to the newborn,' Gow enunciated carefully, as he held it out. 'You must be very proud to have made a son after . . . um . . . so many females. How many of your girls are still alive?'

Willie did not regard this question as indelicate but he had to think for a moment before he could answer. It was not something that came up very often in conversation. 'Eh . . . Jeannie, Bella an' . . . Abby.' He looked bewildered for a second. 'Oh, I've forgot Kitty. She's a wee moosie and it's easy to forget her. So that's four.'

'The boy is your thirteenth, if I remember correctly, so that would be . . . eight that died. My, my! Poor, poor Bella. She was such a bonnie young thing at one time, I remember. You know, I would not have minded . . .' Halting in some confusion, he looked at the two empty glasses. 'It is time for another toast.'

Glasses filled, he held his aloft. 'To Bella, the poor dear departed. May she find more happiness in heaven than she did here on earth.'

'To Bella,' Willie echoed, obediently, not knowing how to take Gow's last few words.

It was some time later before the Session Clerk got back to the business in hand. 'I am truly sorry, Willie, but I cannot do what you asked of me.'

'What was I asking?' The extra drink had not helped Willie's memory.

'You asked me to change the name on this birth certificate but it is against the law to change what has been written on a document of this type. And it is not just the certificate I would have to change – there is the register, as well. Do you see? That would be a double crime and I could be put in jail for it.'

Willie was struggling to keep a grip on his senses. 'But . . . but . . . Govey Dick, John, Isie McIntyre'll tear me limb from limb if it's left like this and she'll never let me forget it. Is there nae something you can . . . ?'

The other man held the empty bottle upside down over his own glass to shake out any remaining drops. 'You should have thought about it properly before you came here in the first place.'

His tone irritated Willie but Gow was not a man to argue with – particularly not after having drunk almost half his whisky. A compromise was called for.

* * *

So it was that Tchouki Henry Bruce McIntyre Rae got his name – there was no room on the certificate for the William – and Isie McIntyre got the upper hand of her son-in-law. Willie held no grudge against John Gow but their long and frequent drinking sessions were perforce reduced almost to the point of non-existence over the next few years.

PART ONE

1878-1890

CHAPTER ONE

1878

Having spent six whole hours at her old aunt's bedside waiting for her to die – not out of any compassion for the feeble ninety-year-old but to ensure that no one else got at her tin money-box – Nessie Munro was not in the best of humours. Somebody had forestalled her, probably one of her cousins. There were only a few pieces of silver left – a shilling, two florins and a half-crown – and, when she lifted out the partitioned tray to take out all the guineas and sovereigns that she believed lay underneath, all she found was Auntie Kirsty's birth certificate. Her hopes had been dashed! Instead of living comfortably for the rest of her life on her aunt's money, she would have to find a man rich enough to keep her in a manner better than she had been accustomed to. There weren't many of them around! She'd been looking for years.

In her anger, Nessie lashed out with the whip, making her pony, a shelty, buck violently and she had just got her breath back when it set off at the double. She had to hold on for dear life now, her very teeth rattling in her head. When the animal tired, it came to such an abrupt halt that Nessie went flying out of the trap on to the road. She skidded along the gravelly surface and came to rest in the ditch. 'God dammit!' she roared, never having been one to consider blasphemy an unpardonable sin. 'God dammit to hell!'

Checking that she was still all in one piece, she moved her limbs gingerly but everything seemed to be working. The only harm she had come to, as far as she could tell, was a bleeding hand, where it had come in contact with the stones – and there was blood seeping through her right stocking so her leg had been scraped and all.

She stood up, dusted herself down and limped over to see if the trap was damaged in any way. Finding nothing untoward, she had a look around to take stock of her whereabouts. Not far ahead, three spires rose at different heights into the sky and she knew that she was not far from Ardbirtle which, despite being such a small town, boasted three kirks. At this end was St John's Episcopal, the Roman Catholic St Mary's stood at the far end and the Parish Kirk, for the ordinary folk, was about the middle of the main street. It had the highest spire.

Only five more miles and she would be home, she thought thankfully. Looping her skirts over her arm, she climbed up to her seat again, testing the reins gently, for she did not want a repeat of the mad dash.

Her shelty took only two steps and stopped, nichering as if in pain. She got down again, her heart sinking when she lifted his right hind leg. However it had happened, the shoe had worked loose and buckled and was now lying diagonally across the hoof. Although she had a short temper, Nessie was also a woman of resourcefulness. 'It's all right,' she soothed, 'we've not far to go but we'd best cry in by the smiddy.'

Taking the rein, she walked in front of the poor animal, hoping that the spits of rain would come to nothing, but, as she should have known, this was a bad day for her. Before they had even reached St John's, it was teeming down.

The smiddy was empty, the fire barely glowing, so work had likely finished for the day, but she was desperate. There was a notice at the side of the door, however. 'If smith urgently required, go through gate and knock at back door of Oak Cottage'.

This Saturday, his mother-in-law having taken his three oldest daughters with her when she went to air her own house, Willie had just returned from a furtive visit to The Doocot when he heard the rain battering against his kitchen window. He could have bidden a while longer, he mused, for Isie hated getting wet and wouldn't come out in this but he didn't feel like going out in it either. Abby and Henry were bedded and it was a treat to sit at the fire without Isie harping on about something. He unlaced his boots and took them off, holding his feet up to the heat and smirking at the steam that spiralled up from them. She was never done complaining about his sweaty socks.

He was relaxed, legs stretched out, when someone rapped on the back door. He tutted in annoyance, got to his feet and yanked the door open, expecting the caller to be a man needing his services and was quite taken aback to see a woman standing on the step. Bedraggled though she was, he couldn't help but admire her.

'Aye?' he asked, cautiously.

'Are you the smith?' Her voice was low and soft.

'That's me. What can I do for you?'

He took her inside out of the rain and, while she described her 'accident', he let his imagination run riot. He could picture himself taking the pins from her thick chestnut hair, making it fall to her shoulders or farther so that he could run his fingers through it. He could see himself putting an arm round her waist . . .

'Will you manage to do it today?'

'Eh?' Willie dragged his mind back to reality.

She gave a shy smile. 'Will you manage to shoe my shelty?

Positive that his mother-in-law would not be coming back that night, Willie chose his next words carefully. 'Is somebody expecting you home?'

'Nobody.'

Their eyes locked, both mature enough, wordly-wise enough, to know what was going to happen. The mutual attraction had been instant . . . and overwhelming.

If Isie McIntyre had been aware of what was going on in her absence, she would have braved the thunderstorm that rumbled on for most of the night, the lightning flashing, cascades of water descending from the skies. Always afraid for her chest, she also had her granddaughters to consider so she eventually told Jeannie and Bella to sleep in the spare room, while she took Kitty into her bed.

Their late night resulted in none of them stirring until five past ten on Sunday morning. There was no food to make any breakfast but Isie insisted that they all washed their faces in cold water and that the girls raked their fingers through their tangled locks to make them look presentable. As for herself, it would have taken too long to replace all the hairpins that had fallen out so she just gave the top of her grey head a few pats, jammed on her black bonnet and tied the ribbons under her chin.

They had to watch their steps once they went outside, for great lochs of water covered much of the road and it was ten minutes to twelve before the sorry-looking quartet trailed into Oak Cottage, skirts soaked up to their knees. Hours too late!

There was no sign that anything out of the ordinary had happened. The shelty had been shod, its owner had gone on her way satisfied both in mind and in body, for fate had been kind to her after all, and because Isie and her three grand-daughters had to change into dry clothes, Willie's rather hang-dog expression went unnoticed.

In less than four weeks, Nessie Munro became Mrs William Rae, her first task being to tell Isie that she wouldn't be needed there any longer. 'You're welcome to visit,' she went on, making it sound almost like a dare.

When Willie feebly protested at this, his bride snapped, 'Please yourself but I'm not stopping if she's to be here. It's not as if she hasn't a home of her own to go to.'

He had often wondered why Isie never sold her house but guessed now that she must have foreseen this very eventuality.

Willie Rae's remarriage, seven long years after his first wife's death, caused quite a stir in the town. Being the blacksmith, he was well known, particularly to the men who owned horse-drawn vehicles of some kind, and being a tall, muscular, handsome widower, he had been eyed hopefully by all the unattached females. Willie, however, had had no eye for any of them. He had believed that the fire had gone from his loins since his beloved Bella had passed on, stamped out, perhaps, by his mother-in-law.

It was as if the old besom had made a pact with God to prevent him from enjoying himself, Willie had sometimes thought, but it was different now. Either Isie had done something to incur the good Lord's wrath or the deity had simply taken pity on *him* – though he didn't care how it happened. It *had* happened and his nights would no longer be lonely.

The marriage had also made a drastic change to the lives of Willie's three eldest daughters. Neither Jeannie nor Bella could stand their new stepmother and handed in their notice to the local shops where they had served. Defying their father, they left to find work in Aberdeen and Kitty, newly turned thirteen, went with them. Not one of the three made any attempt to pay a visit home – all, in fact, said that they couldn't afford the fare. Even after six whole months, Willie still swore that he couldn't understand why they'd been so anxious to leave home and so 'sweir' to come back but his acquaintances could have told him.

'I was surprised he put up wi' his mother-in-law for so lang,' commented Tam Mavor when their old crony had scuttled out of The Doocot one evening. 'And, to my mind, that Nessie's a deal worse than Isie McIntyre.'

His brother nodded. 'God kens what he thocht he was at, taking her for a wife.'

Ben Roberts snorted loudly. 'I bet he only thought of one thing but I wouldn't be surprised if he got more than he was asking for with Nessie.'

Geordie ran his stubby fingers through the remaining wisps of his cotton-wool hair. 'He surely wouldna object to getting' *mair* than he asked for?'

'You're as bad as he is.' The landlord's top lip curled up in a sneer. 'Do you not get enough yourself? Is that it? Are you jealous of Willie?'

Geordie's lined face registered deep outrage at this. 'Me jealous? About him and Nessie Munro? I wouldna touch that wumman wi' a greasy pole!'

'Not with a pole but . . .' Ben gave a lewd cackle. 'By God, there's plenty of her to touch and she's not bad-looking . . . if you look at her properly.'

'If you look at her quick,' was Geordie's sarcastic retort.

It seemed as though Tam had stopped paying attention to the conversation. He was so intent on burrowing in his left ear with his cranny but he had been thinking of another side to Willie's marriage. 'It's his bairns I'm sorriest for. That two youngest havena had much o' a life since they got her for a stepmother. Isie McIntyre maybe ruled Willie wi' an iron rod but she looked after his bairns as well as Bella would have done hersel'. That laddie hasna grew a inch since Nessie took ower the reins – or didna take ower, it should be, for it's poor Abby that does the work. He must be near eight but my Kirsty's bigger than him and she's nae five yet.'

'He was the last o' the litter, of course, and runts never grow big.'

From under his shaggy eyebrows, Tam regarded his brother with distaste. 'If you canna say onything sensible, Geordie, keep your big mouth shut.'

With no proper schooling himself, Willie Rae had made sure that his son – on the register as 'Tchouki (known as Henry)' – attended school every single day. A healthy boy, he had a quick, receptive mind and was an exemplary pupil, which endeared him to his teacher, a forty-something-year-old spinster whose life had been spent trying to impart at least the rudiments of the three Rs to unwilling, uninterested children.

Because Miss Meldrum, who would take them as far as the Qualifying class, made no secret of how she felt about Henry's abilities, he soon became the butt of snide remarks, 'Top o' the class! Teacher's pet,' being the most repeated, to which he usually responded, 'Better the teacher's pet at the top than a dunce at the bottom.'

There was no rancour in any of the repartee, however – just boys being boys and they all remained good friends.

It was when they finished the sixth grade, as far as they

could go at the Junior School, that the watershed came – the parting of the ways. Those who passed the examination, which qualified them to continue their education, transferred to what was known locally as the Big School at the other end of town but those who failed had to remain where they were.

Only five girls out of seven and, besides Henry, nine boys out of twelve made the transition in 1882. The others had to face the taunts of the incoming class – until they could legitimately leave. Luckily, Maxwell Dalgarno and Cameron Ellis, Henry's two closest friends, moved up along with him. Unfortunately, the problems and temptations of adolescence – at first just joked about – were soon to disrupt the friendship.

The Big School was not as cosy as the one they had left. Instead of the fat round stove in the middle of the room, there was a fireplace on one wall, designed to heat only the teacher. Instead of the illustrations of poems and stories they had grown used to, the walls were covered with huge maps – The World, with British colonies marked in pink; The United Kingdom, shires shown in varying colours; two of Scotland, one showing the counties and towns and the industries for which they were noted (Glasgow for shipbuilding, Dundee for jute, jam and journalism and so on) and a physical map with contour lines marking heights above sea level.

Under the windows, glass higher that any pupils could reach, stood four waist-high cupboards for storing textbooks, new jotters, paper, boxes of chalk, white and coloured, bottles of ink, sheets of pink blotting-paper, boxes of pen nibs – anything that was best kept out of sight. On top of the cupboards lay piles of jotters that had been marked. A tall easel held a large blackboard, the top area so high that Miss Meldrum, their last teacher, could never have written on it, even if she stood on tiptoe.

The rest of the floor space was taken up by five rows of eight desks, each with its own inkwell, which the pupils took turns to fill, a groove for pen and pencil and a hinged lid that apparently could only be closed with a tremendous clatter. Apart from the jotters in current use and perhaps a wooden

17

pencil case holding a rubber and a rag for cleaning a pen nib – they had left slates and slate pencils behind in the junior school – the contents of the boys' desks might include a matchbox holding a spider to scare the girls at playtime, a bag of marbles, a Jew's harp or mouth organ and so on. In the case of the girls, the desks would be more likely to harbour a small doll and its clothes, paper scraps to exchange and collections of fancy buttons or ribbons.

Pupils from the schools in Drymill and Corrieben, two nearby villages, also had to transfer to Ardbirtle Senior – only parents who wished, and could afford, to have their children educated further sent them to Ellon Academy. So there were new friends to be made, teams to be chosen for football or hockey in winter and cricket or netball in summer. There were, of course, new girls to pester, pigtails to tie together, blotting-paper pellets soaked with ink to be catapulted with a ruler. These pleasures, however, were the cause of arguments between Henry Rae and his very best friend, over one particular recipient of their blushing attentions. After letting it pass until his anger boiled up, Henry exploded one day as they walked homewards. 'Maxie Dalgarno, would you stop pestering Millie Reid? Can you not see you're scaring her?'

'She only makes on she's scared,' the other boy defended himself. 'She likes it.'

'She does not!'

'She does sut!'

'She does not!'

They squared up to each other, fists flying, and, when Cameron Ellis tried to separate them, his right cheek took a blow not meant for him. It had developed into a three-way fight by the time Mr Shinnie, the headmaster, cycled past them unnoticed. Their scrap soon petered out due to lack of breath in all cases.

When they arrived at school the following morning, they were surprised to be ordered to report to the dominie, but Mr Shinnie spent no time in explaining why. 'Line up!' he barked, lifting his leather tawse to shoulder height. 'Right hands out!'

His next words were delivered one at a time as he swung the three-tongued weapon down on one palm after the other. 'I . . . was . . . shocked . . . to . . . see . . . pu . . . pils . . . of . . . this . . . school . . . braw . . . ling . . . in . . . the . . . street.' He stopped for a moment, having given each boy five stinging strokes, then glared at them malevolently, his nostrils flaring. 'Do you understand me?'

Right hands tucked under left arms in agony, they chorused, 'Yes, Mr Shinnie.'

Rested, the man raised the tawse once more. 'Hands out! No, no, my fine fellows! The same hands as before. I . . . will . . . not . . . tolerate . . . such . . . behaviour!' Ignoring the silent grimaces of pain, he finally flung the instrument of punishment down on his desk. 'I trust I will not have to summon you here again!'

They said not a word as they hurried along the corridor and up the stairs but their white faces and obviously painful hands when they tried to write told their classmates why they had been late.

The three were the centre of attention during the half-hour dinner break. Quite a crowd of boys gathered round them, wanting to know more.

'Did he gi'e you the strap?'

'How many did you get?'

'Was it awful sore?'

Heroes in all eyes now, their pain was forgotten. 'Seven each,' boasted Henry.

Mouths gaped as Maxie added, 'On the same hand and we hardly felt them.'

Having had time to think, Cammie pouted, 'It wasna fair, though. I shouldna've gotten the strap. It wasna me that was fighting.'

All heads turned to him now. 'What was they fighting about?'

'About a . . .' Cammie began but Maxie butted in.

'We was arguing about being biggest. I said it was me but Henry said it was him.'

19

This caused much hilarity – Henry was at least two inches shorter than Maxie – and, in the argument that developed between other pairs of boys over who was the taller, things got back to normal in the tarred playground and dinner pieces were gobbled before the headmaster came out to ring his handbell for afternoon classes.

Going home was not as much fun that day as it normally was. There was a new constraint between Henry and Maxie. And Cammie, still outraged at being embroiled in a fight that had nothing to do with him, refused to speak to either of them.

This state of affairs eased off a little after a few days but they never got back to being quite as close as they had been before – not even when Millie Reid, the reason for their quarrel, bestowed her affection on the top boy who had been in her class at Drymill.

Henry and Maxie remained friends but it was a delicate, tenuous friendship which neither did anything to revive.

CHAPTER TWO

1883

On his way home from The Doocot, Willie's thoughts were in a slightly maudlin state although he certainly hadn't drunk much. Even one dram seemed to have him feeling sorry for himself these days, that was the trouble. He had made a poor bargain, getting wed to Nessie Munro. She didn't really care anything for him. She had led him to believe she did, but she had just been on the lookout for a man to keep her and had plumped for him. She had thought, with him having his own smiddy, that he was a wealthy man so she hadn't got a great bargain either, now he came to dwell on it.

Their life together did have its compensations, of course, for she was a buxom woman who needed a man as much as he needed a woman. Unhappily for him, she held him to ransom at times, refusing him his rights if he did anything to annoy her. What was more, she picked on poor Abby, made her do all the chores and the cooking, while she, herself, stravaiged about the town with her friends. Strangely enough, she wasn't as hard on Henry so that was one blessing.

Nessie wasn't his only problem, though. His eldest daughter, Jeannie, twenty-four now, had been married for four years and was living in a tenement in Aberdeen's George Street with her husband Pattie – a long streak of uselessness, to Willie's way of thinking, not that he'd seen much of the man – and their daughter.

Bella, two years younger, was also in Aberdeen. She was also married but had beaten her sister by having two girls. Her husband seemed to be a hard worker, moving them out of their first home – a room-and-kitchen on the top floor of Black's Buildings – within a year of their wedding. In her very occasional letters, Bella wrote proudly of their cottage in Holburn Street, 'a lovely area away from the dirty centre of the town', and their garden, 'big enough for the girls to take their friends in to play'. Willie's only comfort from all this was that neither Jeannie's man nor Bella's had managed to make a son so they weren't as good as he was.

Kitty was still single at eighteen. After working for a time in a draper's shop in Aberdeen, she had found quite a good job in a hotel in Glasgow but was always too busy working – or so she made out – to come home.

Taking his silver watch from his waistcoat pocket, Willie gave a start. He hadn't realised it was that late and he had best get a move on. There would be hell to pay if his wife got home before him.

Fourteen-year-old Abby Rae picked up another of her father's socks and slid her left fist inside. She didn't know how he did it but he always managed to get great holes where his big toes had poked through. It was just a matter of weeks since she finished knitting this pair and there was more darn than sock already. Giving a long sigh, she bit off another length of the wheeling wool and threaded the big eye of the darning needle.

Henry's twelfth birthday was less than a month away and he had taken to going to the mart as often as he could, looking for a job, and she was really worried that he might get a fee. None of her sisters cared what happened to her. Jeannie and Bella had their own families to worry about now, God knows when they were here last, and Kitty said she couldn't afford the fare to come home more than once or twice a year.

A lump of self-pity obstructed Abby's throat for a moment. If Henry went away, she'd be left here on her own every day with Nessie! It would be worse than working for a mistress, not that she'd ever had that experience. She'd had little schooling since her father's new wife moved in and she hadn't been allowed to take a job when she was old enough. She'd been kept at home supposedly to look after her brother, though a hundred and one chores had fallen on her as time went by and

22

she hadn't had the courage to complain. Nessie wasn't the kind of person you could complain to. She was big, both lengthways and roundways, with a chest on her that would knock you flat if she turned round on you quick, a backside that made her long black skirt wobble when she walked, hair that was a yellowing-white like her teeth and her eyes . . .

Abby shivered. She couldn't really describe the woman's eyes. They were the darkest she had ever seen, almost jet black, and there was something in them that scared her, as if they held a threat. And yon big hands of hers always seemed to be ready to clout you round the lug if she wasn't pleased, and it was difficult to know what it was that displeased her. Just the same, it was good to be able to sit quietly like this, knowing the woman had gone to visit her sick mother in Corrieben. Father had taken the chance to slip out for half an hour, for a breath of fresh air he said, but he'd likely be having a quick drink with his old cronies at The Doocot.

Henry was out as well – she was sure he was up to something. Nessie didn't seem to mind *him* going out, Abby thought resentfully, but, the minute *she* said she would like an hour off, there was an almighty row. As far as she could see, the only way she would ever escape Nessie's clutches would be to get wed to some suitable man as soon as she was sixteen. But how could she meet any men, suitable or not, if she was tied to the fireside like this?

Abby jumped nervously as the back door rattled but it was only her brother. 'You'd best wash yourself and get up to your bed afore Nessie comes back,' she warned him, noticing that his eyes were dancing with excitement.

He lifted his shoulders and tapped his nose, grinning secretively. 'No, I've got something to tell Father and I want her to be here and all. I canna wait till morning to see her face.'

Abby's stomach started to churn. She knew by his smug expression that, whatever he wanted Nessie to know, it was something she wouldn't like and Nessie in a bad humour was . . . 'D'you have to tell them tonight?'

'Aye, I have.' His smile broadened even further. 'Ach, I'm

bursting to tell somebody. Jim Legge wants me to start at Craigdownie on Monday.'

It was worse than she thought. Telling Nessie that would be like throwing a lighted match into a barn full of hay – or worse, into a barrel of paraffin. 'You're not twelve yet, Henry, can you not just wait a while afore you . . .'

'Craigdownie's one o' the best farms there is. If I say no this time, I'll likely never get another chance.'

'But it's miles and miles – you'll have to bide in.'

'There's a bothy for the single men.'

'You're not a man yet and, any road, *she'll* not let you go.'

'She canna stop me. She's not my real mother.'

'Father could stop you. He *is* your father.'

'So he says.'

His sister's chin dropped with pained shock at such a statement, her serious brown eyes were in danger of popping out of their sockets. 'God'll strike you dumb for saying things like that, Henry,' she managed to whisper. 'Of course he's our father.'

'Yours, maybe, but . . .'

'You're surely not hinting that Mother was . . . that she had another man? You're mad to even think it. She'd four of us to look after even before you were born. What time had she for other men?'

Henry stopped, looking rather abashed. 'I'm sorry, I was just teasing you – but it was a stupid thing to say.' Little did he know that he had almost voiced a suspicion that was festering in the mind of Mary Jane Gow, whose husband had revealed his part in the secret of the boy's real name when he was lying on his deathbed less than a month ago.

The sound of the back door opening again stopped what was fast developing into a quarrel and Abby tried to calm her rattled nerves as her father tiptoed into the kitchen. 'She's nae back yet?' At Abby's head shake, he sat down on his usual chair by the fire, laid his tweed cap on the fender-stool and held his hands out to the heat. 'It's that cold outside it'd freeze the words afore they left your mouth.'

24

Henry winked at a flustered Abby. 'I've some good news, Father, but I want to wait till Nessie comes in.'

Looking up at the wag-at-the wa' clock Nessie had brought with her when she moved in, Willie said, 'She shouldna be long. She aye comes in dead on nine.'

No sooner had he said this than the clock gave a wheezy whirr and a little bird popped out to herald the passing of another hour. It had only given four hoarse 'cuck . . . oos' when they heard Nessie's heavy feet approaching the front door.

'My,' she said breathlessly when she burst in, 'you're fine and cosy in here. Think yourselves lucky you didn't have to go out. My hands and feet are like to drop off me.'

'Abby's got the kettle boiling for some tea,' Willie prompted his daughter, who dutifully rinsed the teapot into the slop pail kept handy for such purposes.

Sensibly waiting until his stepmother's hands and feet had thawed a little, Henry took up his stance centrally to the fire and Abby cowered her brown head down into her knitted jumper in dread of what he was going to say – or, rather, of what would happen once he said it. Thankfully, he made it short and to the point.

'I'm going to Craigdownie on Sunday, for Jim Legge wants me to start work first thing on Monday morning. Isn't that good news?'

He cast an apprehensive glance at Nessie now, waiting for her to erupt in anger, but was astonished to see her thin lips curved slightly upwards for a change. 'Well, now, that *is* good news, isn't it, Willie?'

The wind taken out of his sails, the arguments he had prepared remaining unsaid, Henry was even more surprised by the look of shame on his father's face. 'Aye, Nessie, it is that,' he mumbled.

The boy couldn't believe it. 'You mean, you're not saying I canna go?'

Nessie pursed her mouth for a moment. 'It's time you learned how to look after yourself. You'll be bothying, I take it?'

'Aye, but we'll get our food in the farm kitchen.' He felt

cheated. He had expected to put up a stand for the right to go and his stepmother was practically telling him she'd be glad to see the back of him. 'Father?' he asked, pleading for some show of affection, for a sign that he'd be missed – but the middle-aged man avoided his eyes.

It was Abby who cried, 'No, Henry, you're not old enough to be . . .'

'Not old enough?' Nessie barked. 'It's time he was earning a living and not leaving it to me and his father to feed and clad him. Speaking of that, wouldn't you say it's time you took a job and all?'

This did make Willie react. 'No, no, Nessie. I agree with you that the lad should start learning how to fend for himself but let the lassie be.'

His wife's brows plunged down. 'See here, Willie Rae, I've been wed on you for a good few year now and not one single night have we had by ourselves. We should be able to do what we like, without wondering if the bairns'll hear us.'

'But she's just fourteen and never been away from . . .'

'It's time she was out in the world meeting folk. How d'you expect her to find a man? Or do you want to be keeping her for the rest o' your life? If that's what you want, it'll be without me!'

'No, Nessie!' His ruddy face had paled. 'You'd not leave me, would you?'

'Try me. It'll be just me and you or it'll be you and your precious lassie.' She turned round and stuck her face close to the girl's. 'Is that what *you* want, eh? Would you like me out o' the road so your father can come to your bed and . . .'

'That's enough!' Willie shouted his outrage at this insult. 'She doesna understand what you mean and, if I was any kind o' man, I'd throw you out for saying it.'

Nessie smirked suddenly. 'But you're not any kind o' man, are you? You're a man that needs a woman like me, a woman that needs a man, isn't that right? Eh?'

It was the truth and he dropped his head, too shamed to look his children in the eyes.

'Never mind them, Abby,' the boy soothed as he led his

sister up the stairs, 'you can come to Craigdownie with me on Sunday if you want. I'm sure they'll have a job for you an' all.'

But Abby was not to be comforted. 'I canna bide here now,' she moaned. 'She wants rid o' me. She'll go on and on at me and punch me and . . .'

Somewhat self-consciously, Henry sat down on the bed beside her and slipped his arms around her. 'I'll tell you what. We'll pack some things and go to Gramma. How about that?'

'They'll hear us going out.'

'We'll wait till they're sleeping.'

Her face was miserably white but there was something she had to find out as they waited. 'Henry, why did you say Father wasn't your real father?'

He gave an embarrassed grin. 'I didna really think he wasn't. It was just . . . you four were girls.'

The doubt in her eyes clearing as an explanation struck her, Abby whispered, 'But Gramma once said Father had been dying to get a son and he'd just got daughters.'

'I thought he couldna make a son. That's why I said he wasn't my father.'

'No, you're wrong, Henry. He was that desperate for a boy, he'd no thought for anything else. No thought for Mother, really . . . not till after . . .'

'I can't remember what she looked like,' he said, sadly.

'You were only hours old when she died – I don't remember much myself. I ken Gramma didn't have much time for him but she said he really *had* loved Mother. He near went mad when she died, blaming himself and getting so drunk she thought he might do away wi' himself. That's why she was so hard on him.'

'So Gramma never thought it was funny him getting a son after so long?'

'No, she said it was just one of those things and it was, Henry.'

'Aye, I suppose it was. Wheesht, here's them coming up now.'

He kept his arm round his sister as the feet went along the landing, having to hold his breath when his father said, 'I'd maybe best look in to see they're all right?' and letting it out at Nessie's hissed, 'They'll be sleeping, just leave them.'

Not until the house was as silent as the grave did Henry make a move and, within ten minutes, brother and sister were creeping through the back door, each carrying a pillowcase stuffed with clothes.

One knock on her street door was enough to have Isie McIntyre pulling back the heavy curtain at her bedroom window. At her age, she didn't need as much sleep as she used to. 'Abby! Henry!' she exclaimed when she saw her unexpected callers. Forcing her stiff joints inside an old woollen cardigan to hide her well-worn wincey nightgown, she shuffled to the door to let them in, tutting when she saw their drawn faces properly.

Henry took over as spokesman. 'We've run away – so would you please let us bide here, Gramma?'

Gathering that something was far wrong at Oak Cottage, Isie decided that now was not the time to ask questions. Her grandchildren were obviously far too upset to answer any and it was long past their bedtime. 'It's a good thing I aired out my spare bed yesterday,' she smiled. 'You can sleep there, Abby, and Henry can ha'e the couch in the parlour.'

Recognising from their looks of despair that they needed the comfort of being together, their grandmother ignored any thought of the impropriety of boy and girl, one in her teens, sleeping in the same bed. They were still only bairns, after all; young innocents, what harm could they come to? It would be all right – for one night, at least. Then she would have a try at being peacemaker, in the hope that they'd go back to Oak Cottage.

Despite having assured herself that nothing untoward would happen between them, Isie took a quick peep into her spare room after she had cleared up in the kitchen and was relieved to see Henry with his hand protectively on his sister's shoulder, both sound asleep. Poor wee lambs, she thought, as she went through to her own bed.

A big pan was hottering on the range when the two youngsters made their appearance in the morning, looking, Isie was pleased to see, rather better than they had the night before. 'Now then,' she said, briskly, as she poured the breakfast into three deep bowls, 'you can tell me your story once we've supped this porridge.'

Nothing was said until the bowls and the enamel mugs of milk were empty, then she raised her eyebrows encouragingly to the boy. 'Come on then, Henry.'

Some moments later, as he came to a gulping halt, Isie was having to bite her tongue to stop her from voicing her opinion of their father for not standing up for them. It was terrible to think that Willie Rae had sided with that uncorseted mantrap against his own flesh and blood. But what was inside his breeks had aye been more important to him than what was inside his head, even when he was wed on her poor Bella – the filthy pig.

But it was these two hapless creatures she had to consider now. If she could afford it, she would gladly keep them for good but what she made from the washing and ironing she took in wouldn't stretch to feeding two extra mouths.

'The thing is, Gramma,' Henry went on suddenly, 'I'll have to go to Craigdownie today, for Jim Legge said I'd to start first thing Monday morning.'

Isie had almost forgotten what had led to the row at Oak Cottage and couldn't help being pleased that there was one less for her to worry about, although she was instantly ashamed of herself. They were of her flesh and blood and all, poor things. 'Well now, Henry, if you dinna like it there or if things dinna turn oot the way you want, you're welcome to come back here. We'll manage somehow or other.'

Old enough to be aware of his grandmother's poverty, the boy hurried on. 'I'm going to ask Mr Legge if there's a place for Abby and all. She's done near all the housework for a few years now and she can sew and knit and darn and patch . . .'

'Oh, Henry, stop!' The girl was red with embarrassment.

'Aye, laddie,' Isie nodded, 'you'll not need to lay it on ower thick. That would put them right aff. Besides, there's nae hurry.

29

She'll be fine here wi' me for a few . . .' She broke off as a perfect solution struck her. 'I'm nae getting any younger, I'll be sixty-five in June so I'll be glad of her company – and her help. Eh, lass, what d'you say? You could take in some sewing or mending and we'd manage fine.'

Shy Abby, having secretly dreaded the day when she would have to go out to work amongst strangers, sat back thankfully. 'Oh, Gramma, I'll work as hard as I can for you.'

Henry felt free to smile now. He had been worrying about Abby, about what would become of her if he couldn't find employment for her, but this was something he had never expected. Jumping up, he bounded over to his grandmother and flung his arms round her. 'Oh, Gramma! I've aye loved you best – better than anybody else – except Abby,' he added, bringing his sister into his embrace.'

Even knowing that he had an extremely long walk ahead of him, his heart was singing as he set out for Craigdownie and, as the saying goes, fortune favours the brave. He had been on the road for hardly twenty minutes when the carrier caught up with him, drawing the hefty Clydesdale to a halt.

'Aye, Henry.' Geordie Mavor was an old friend of the boy's father, although neither frequented The Doocot as often as they had once done. 'Where might you be heading for on a Sunday in sic' a hurry?'

'I'm starting at Craigdownie the morrow morning,' Henry said proudly.

Geordie was suitably impressed. 'Craigdownie, eh? Jim Legge's a good boss, I've heard, a fair man, as long as you keep to his rules. Orra loon, I suppose?'

'Aye and I'm prepared to work hard for him. He'll not find any fault wi' me.'

'I'm pleased to hear that. Now, you've a good bit to go yet, so how about coming up beside me? I'm nae going as far as Craigdownie – just to Meikle Birtle to gi'e my brother a hand wi' his flitting – but I'll drop you aff as near as I can.'

'Oh, thanks, Geordie,' Henry said as he happily scrambled up on to the big cart.

The journey was lengthened by the various detours Geordie made to deliver odds and ends his wife was sending to her sisters but this didn't bother Henry. As long as he reached his destination in time to have a decent sleep before starting work the next day that was all he needed. At least he was travelling on four wheels – maybe a bit hard on his backside but a lot easier on his feet.

CHAPTER THREE

Being the orra loon – the odd-job boy – wasn't exactly as Henry Rae had envisioned. By the very name, he had known that the jobs would be dirty but he spent nearly all his time up to his elbows in muck *and* with his semmit sticking to his back with sweat. That in itself wouldn't have been quite so bad if his sleeping quarters hadn't been so awful.

On his first day, Mr Legge had explained that there was no room in the bothy for him and he would have to sleep in the hayloft. 'It's fine and cosy up there,' the farmer had gone on, 'and it'll only be till old Watson admits it's time for him to retire. Once he goes, young Charlie Simpson'll get that house and he and Betsy can get wed.' Noticing the uncertainty on the boy's face, he had added, 'You'll get his place in the bothy, d'you see? A month or so at the longest.'

'Just a month or so?' Henry had felt much better then.

But he had been in the hayloft for nearly eight months now and there was no word of the first horseman retiring. It was reaching the point when Henry dreaded climbing the rickety ladder to the space under the roof, though he wouldn't have minded it if he'd been on his own.

It was his unexpected nightly companions that he was afraid of – the dark grey shapes that inched nearer to him if he lay still but scuttled out of sight if he moved. He was terrified that, in their obvious hunger, they would eat him alive when he was sleeping. In daytime, he could tell himself that the first bite would rouse him so there was no need to be scared. But, in the night, with darkness all around him and his heart beating as if there was somebody inside it pounding to get out, it wasn't so easy to be brave.

The other drawback to being the orra loon was the lack of company when he was working. Only very occasionally was he put on to help one of the other men and none of them seemed very friendly anyway. In the kitchen, he'd to sit at a small table in a corner on his own and conversations went on without a soul speaking to him. One of the young maids brought him his porridge and milk in the mornings and handed him his dinner piece to take away but the only one of them who had a smile for him had just left for a better job. The others, including her replacement, were either too scared that they'd be teased or too shy.

He was sitting one morning, by himself as usual, when he noticed that the farmer was deep in conversation with the man called Watson. Henry, of course, could hear nothing of what was being said but he could see that the old man was a bit upset and wondered what had happened.

The mystery was solved later that day. The boy had been detailed to clear a big drain in the byre and it was such a revolting job that his stomach was heaving in complaint when Jim Legge came in and stood for a while just watching him.

'There's bad news and there's good news,' the farmer said after a moment.

'Aye?' muttered Henry, cautiously. Bad news was something he didn't want, even if it was followed by good.

'Watson got a letter from his daughter in Fife this morning. Her man was working a tractor when something went wrong and it overturned on him. Poor man, he was trapped underneath.'

'Was he badly hurt?' Henry shuddered to think what might have happened.

'Killed instantly, the letter said. So she wants her father to go and help her run their wee croft and he's leaving on Saturday. It's short notice for me but, on the other hand, as you know, I've been expecting him to retire.'

'Aye.' Now, with an idea of what was coming, Henry didn't want to sound pleased.

Legge looked at him speculatively. 'Ach, lad, I thought you'd be quicker on the uptake. I said there was good news and all. Charlie Simpson'll be moving into Watson's house once it's cleared out and you'll get his place in the bothy. Not only that, it means a shift up, as well. You'll get Charlie's job as second horseman and I'll need another orra loon.'

Henry could hide his excitement no longer. 'That's great, Mr Legge! I wondered how much longer I was going to be . . .' He halted, colouring in confusion.

The man smiled sympathetically. 'You wondered how much longer you'd have to sleep up there with the rats? You maybe thought I didn't know but I was once an orra loon myself – when my father ran the place.'

It took three weeks for the cottar house to be emptied – after which Jim Legge allowed Charlie Simpson and his bride-to-be to go in to clean it out. David Watson had lived alone since his wife died seven years before so things had got in a bit of a mess and a lot of work had to be done on it.

The wedding took place in the farmhouse. Mrs Legge had helped the cook to prepare masses of food and, when the knot had been duly tied in the parlour, tables were carried in and covered with plates of cold sliced beef, pork and lamb, tureens of broth and lentil soup, dishes of vegetables, pies of various kind and hot casseroles.

Jim Legge waited until everything was in place before he cried, 'Come on, then, folk. Get stuck in! The quicker you shift this lot, the quicker we'll get on to the next lot.'

The 'next lot' was a selection of tempting puddings – pastries, sponges, jellies, trifles, caramelised oranges and much more. Most people ate so much they began complaining they were too full. As Mick Tyler – a carroty-haired, skinny youth who never minced his words – said, 'My belly's that fu', it's like to burst.'

After the tables were cleared of food and set round the walls to hold the whiskies, port, cider, ginger ale and porter, there was a great rush, with the men almost knocking each over in their need for a drink.

The ladies in the company stood by and watched with forced smiles or deep frowns, knowing that their men would get drunk no matter what they said so it was best to say nothing – until the next morning. Then the sparks would fly! The younger people, male and female, were just out to enjoy themselves while they had the chance and, at last, a fiddle and an accordion struck up, the bride's father and his brother going at it full tilt, and the dancing began.

Never having seen anything like this before, a mesmerised Henry stood beside Mick and Frankie Ross marvelling at the intricacies of the Dashing White Sergeant, the Eightsome Reel and the Strip the Willow and thinking dejectedly that he would never remember how to do them.

Between these truly exhausting dances, there were, of course, a few Scottish waltzes and polkas that, although still somewhat boisterous, were not quite so physically tiring.

'Och, Henry,' Mick said, suddenly, 'it's a wedding, nae a frunial. Tak' a wee drap o' whisky, for God's sake. It'll maybe put a smile on your face.'

Henry gave his head a shake, determined not to taste even a drop. That way lay temptation. One drop would give him a taste for it and he'd end up like all the other men, grinning like an idiot, face scarlet, eyes not focusing properly.

'Come on,' urged Frankie. 'It'll make you want to grab a lassie roond her waist and get in among the dancing.'

Mick forced a small glass into the boy's hand. 'Get that doon you, Henry. It'll put lead in your pencil.'

The two youths doubled up with laughter but Henry laid the glass resolutely on the table. 'No, thank you. I'm not going to start drinking.'

As the evening wore on, more and more of the men grew too drunk to dance and, by midnight, only a few couples were taking the floor. By ten to one, the two men who made up the band were incapable of providing any music and the celebrations were forced to come to an end.

But Mick Tyler's odd remark lingered in Henry's mind for most of what was left of the night.

Clearing up after breakfast the following morning, Janet Emslie wondered why Henry Rae was still sitting there when the other men had gone out to work. There was something about this boy that raised motherly feelings in her breast, not just because he was such a wee thing. He was good-looking and all. His dark hair was quite curly and his green eyes always seemed to have a mischievous twinkle in them; his round cheeks were healthily rosy and his mouth was usually turned up in a smile. More than one serving-lass had said he looked like an elf and one, whose father had taken his family from Ireland, had said he reminded her of a leprechaun, always enjoying himself. He hadn't looked as if he was enjoying himself last night, though, and he certainly wasn't smiling this morning.

'Is something worrying you, m'dearie?' The cook regarded him sympathetically.

Henry's face reddened. 'Can I ask you something – if you dinna mind?'

'Ask what you like.'

'It was something Mick Tyler said last night.'

Now Janet understood. Mick was a good worker but his mouth would be none the worse of a good wash out with disinfectant sometimes. Like a sewer, it was. 'Go on, bairn. Nothing Mick could say would shock me.'

'Frankie wanted me to try a drop whisky and Mick said it would put lead in my pencil. What does that mean?'

She couldn't hold back the laugh, though she could see he was put out by it. 'It doesna mean a thing,' she gasped at last. 'They were wanting you to . . . take up wi' one o' the lassies.'

'But I still canna understand,' the boy persisted, his eyes wide and serious. 'How can I put lead in my pencil when I havena got a pencil? And, if I had, what am I supposed to write?'

His earnest, pleading expression made her straighten her face, though it needed a great effort, and the explanation she gave, in the down-to-earth words she had learned through years of working with men, left him in no doubt as to what Mick had meant. Clearly overwhelmed with embarrassment when she ended, he rushed outside.

Feeling that he was blushing from the crown of his head to the soles of his feet, Henry looked for a quiet place to think and, passing the byre it came to him that the kye wouldn't be taken in for the milking for hours yet. Casting a surreptitious glance around to make sure that nobody saw him, he scuttled inside and plopped down on the straw-strewn floor behind the door. As he should have known from previous experience in the cows' domain, the stink was overpowering. His stomach was heaving already and he'd be sick in no time. He couldn't concentrate here.

Sneaking out again, he remembered the dairy. It, too, would be empty for hours yet. It was the cleanest place on the whole farm but he'd have to take care that the milkmaid didn't come in and find him there. Again, he took up his position behind the door – it was the safest place.

Hesitantly, he went over what the cook had told him, the strange words she had used and had explained by patting his front and her own. What Mick Tyler had called his 'pencil' was really his . . . No, he wasn't even going to think the word – his Gramma would go daft if she knew what Janet had been saying to him. It wasn't decent to discuss things like that. And it surely couldn't be true? Was that really how bairns were made, like the cook had warned him? He could never do anything like that.

In fact, he would never as much as touch any woman, except the one he took as his wife – if he ever took a wife, which he wasn't at all sure about. It seemed to him that wives weren't all the same and a man couldn't be certain of getting a good one. He'd known of some fine wives and some bad – his father had had one of each. Mrs Legge was a good wife to the farmer, always laughing – he'd never seen her angry, though the kitchen maid must try her patience at times, she was so slow and dim-witted.

What was it that made a woman a good wife, though? It couldn't be a good figure – that was one thing. They came in all shapes and sizes, from tall and skinny Ina Sim, the ploughman's wife, to Gramma, thin, too, but cuddly with it, to the farmer's wife, who could only be classed as fat and it was a puzzle how Jim Legge could get his arms round her – though he must have managed at one time. Then there were women like Janet Emslie, not fat as such, just well padded all over, but her breasts didn't swing when she walked like Nessie's. Were they what had attracted his father enough to make her his wife?

Henry felt uncomfortable thinking about breasts. They hadn't figured in his thoughts before but Janet had said that fondling breasts was part of the lead-up to the taking. Intrigued by this and doing his utmost to picture it, he was startled by the sound of footsteps but the dairymaid walked in without noticing him in his dark corner. She stood for a minute or two, side on to him, thinking about a lad maybe, and he found his eyes drawn towards her bosom, swelling gracefully up from her waist – two perfectly-sized, well-rounded, pointy-finished . . . breasts.

It was as well that the girl moved now, before his thoughts got out of hand. He kept still as she set about making the churns ready for the butter-making and washed out the pails ready for the five o'clock milking, before it dawned on him that the din she was making would be excellent cover for him to make his escape.

He had no chance to dwell on what he had seen, however, until he was safely in his chaff bed in the bothy and the other inhabitants had finished their men's rowdy talk. He had never looked purposely at any girl before, only at their faces, but breasts had been in his mind in the dairy – that was why he had noticed Louie's. They weren't big and horrible, like his father's wife's, nor as round as Janet's, but she was still a young lassie, about the same age as his sister, so they were likely still growing. He had never noticed Abby's, he was so used to seeing her, but the dairymaid's looked pretty firm, though he wouldn't know for real unless . . . he fondled them.

Becoming aware that his wandering thoughts were having a most unusual effect on him, he reined them in, afraid of what might happen if he allowed the lead he could feel gathering in his 'pencil' to get out of control. Maybe it wouldn't go away until he 'took' a lassie. Maybe.

Trying to think of everyday, mundane things, he lay awake for some time but, when sleep finally overtook him, his dreams were of breasts – big, small, pointy, half-formed, of blouses being unbuttoned but never as far as to reveal the treasures lying below.

In the morning, some more of Janet's words came back to him. 'Some men, you see, just use a woman but a decent man only touches her like that if he loves her.'

Was that what a man did . . . used a woman? It wasn't a very nice thing to do so Henry silently vowed that no woman or girl would ever say that he had used her. He would never touch a woman like that unless he had made her his wife first and, if a girl was expected to be pure on her wedding night, as Janet had also said, so it should be with the man. So it would be with him.

On Christmas Day, Jim Legge made a surprise announcement at the breakfast table. 'This has been a right good year for us and I'm that pleased with the work you did during the harvesting, I'm giving you all a day off. Not at the same time,' he added, seeing some puzzled expressions. 'The lads in the bothy and young Harry, our new orra loon, will get this Saturday coming and the rest of you, you'll get yours the week after. Janet, you and the lassies can decide among yourselves who'll be off this first Saturday and who'll be off the next. If there's no problems with this, I'll do it every year so it's up to yourselves.'

Their day off was the sole topic in the bothy that night and it was decided that those who were off on the first Saturday would go to the New Year Dance that was to be held in Corrieben.

'You should come, Henry,' Mick coaxed. 'You're bound to

meet a lass that's mair than willing and, wi' a few drinks inside you, you'll nae care if she's the right ane for you or no'.'

Accustomed now to being teased about his refusal to drink alcohol as much as for his oft-voiced intention of keeping himself for the girl he married, Henry gave a guffawing laugh. 'I'd rather bide here and read. I'll get peace wi' you lot awa'.'

After a moment's consideration, Mick put forward a more acceptable proposition. 'Well, you can get a len' o' my bike if you want to go and see your sister.'

Henry jumped at the chance of seeing Abby again but, with little experience of bicycles, the almost ten-mile-journey was hard going for him. His welcome at the end of it, however, made up for every sweating minute, although his grandmother's hugging made him hotter than ever.

'Oh, laddie!' Isie breathed when he broke away. 'I'm that pleased to see you.'

'Me and all,' said Abby, keeping hold of his hand. 'We've been wondering how you were getting on. Do you like it at Craigdownie?'

'It's not bad,' Henry said, diplomatically, and gave them a brief description of the varied jobs he had to do. When his grandmother asked about the bothy, he didn't tell her where he had slept for his first few months. And he only spoke briefly of the cramped quarters in the small stone building with the sod roof, the chaff mattress on the wooden board for a bed and the constant chatter that wouldn't let him sleep for hours. 'But Janet's a good cook,' he went on, not wanting them to feel sorry for him. 'You should see the size of her porridge pot and the soup pot and all.'

'How many does she feed?' Isie wanted to know, thankful that she'd never had to cater for large numbers.

'The married men go hame, of course, but there's ten in the bothy, counting me and Harry the orra loon, Mr and Mrs Legge and Georgina, that's their daughter, the cook, a kitchen-maid, a housemaid and . . . um . . . a dairymaid. That's seventeen.'

The pink tinge that had flushed his cheeks at the mention of the dairymaid made Isie say, 'And have you got yoursel' a lass yet?'

His colour deepened further. 'No, I've hardly spoken to any of them.'

'Early days,' she smiled, 'you're nae fourteen yet.'

It seemed to him that the time was right to ask something that very occasionally bothered him. 'Gramma, was it my fault my mother died?'

'Na, na, bairn! It was your father's fault. He was aye coming hame drunk, you see, and getting on top o' her and putting another bairn inside her belly.' She stopped, aghast at what she had said. 'I'm sorry, lad, I shouldna speak like that in front o' you but it's the God's honest truth.'

Apart from realising that this statement corroborated Janet Emslie's lesson in human biology, something struck Henry as odd. 'But there's just five o' us, Gramma – that's not a lot.'

She shook her head mournfully. 'Five living but there was a lot mair than that.'

'How many were there altogether?' Henry persisted.

'There was thirteen. So you see, it was a lot.'

'Thirteen?' Both the young people gaped at that.

'The rest died – some wi' pneumonia when they was infants, some wi' galloping consumption when they was toddlers and some died afore they was born, poor souls. They was a' lassies and all.'

The boy glanced meaningfully at his sister who muttered apologetically, 'Henry thinks Father's not his real father.'

Isie bridled. 'For ony sake, loon! What gave you that idea?'

'I didna really believe it at first but now . . . Do you not think it's queer that he had twelve lassies? It's like he couldn't make a son.'

Isie nearly choked laughing. 'The Lord preserve us! You think your mother took up wi' anither man?' she gasped. 'There was nae other man, Henry. Willie Rae was mair than enough for her. If she hadna died an' you hadna been a laddie, he'd likely have made a lot mair.'

'But, Gramma, that's terrible. I ken it's what the man does

to the woman that makes the babies but how could any man make a woman have thirteen?'

'Not all men are like your father, mind that Henry. If you keep your breeches buttoned, you'll nae get in trouble and, once you're wed, think on your mother afore you tak' your pleasure wi' your wife.'

'I'll remember that, Gramma, but why d'you think he'd to make thirteen afore he got me? It's an awful lot.'

'It was God's will.'

'Was it God's will my mother died and all? He can't be a very good God.'

His grandmother heaved a long, shivery sigh. 'Maybe God just took pity on my poor Bella . . .'

Her abrupt stop, her hand on her chest, made both young people jump up in alarm.

'Gramma!' Henry cried, taking her free hand and massaging it. 'What's wrong? What is it? Tell me.'

But Isie was past telling anybody anything.

Henry slept with Abby that night again – or to be more precise, he shared her bed because sleep did not come to him. Even knowing that he might lose his job, he simply could not leave her on her own at such a time and he was plagued by the worry of what the future would hold for them. Doctor Michie had offered to let his father know what had happened but he had pleaded with the man not to tell anybody.

'You need a man here, Henry, lad. The burden of arranging a funeral and all the other things that have to be done after someone passes on is too great for a boy your age to carry. Whatever went wrong between you should be forgotten and I'm sure Willie would want to attend to what has to be done. She was his mother-in-law, wasn't she? And she looked after the family for some years after your mother died.'

The boy couldn't deny this. 'But he threw her out when he took another wife.'

'Threw her out? Surely not. Asked her to leave, perhaps?'

'It was Nessie Munro's fault but my father didn't stop her.'

'Ah, well, my boy, a man does not argue with his bride.'

Recalling the doctor's expression when he left, Henry knew what would happen and he wasn't in the least surprised when his father walked straight into the spare bedroom without knocking at seven the next morning, with Nessie following in behind him – her obvious reluctance becoming outrage when she saw the boy with his arms round his sister.

'Would you credit that, Willie?' she shouted. 'They've been . . . you know, with their grandmother lying lifeless in the next room!'

'Haud your wheesht, wumman!' Willie snapped. 'They're only bairns, for God's sake!' Striding over to the bed, he took his bewildered children into his arms, soothing them as they burst into tears.

Before that day was out, all arrangements had been made for the funeral, most of Isie's neighbours volunteering to bake or cook something for after the burial. Willie had registered the death with John Gow's replacement utterly sober and without a thought to the last shambolic time he had been there. (Willie's second marriage had been conducted and registered at Nessie's own kirk in Corrieben, five miles away.)

A steady stream of Isie's friends and acquaintances and the keepers of the shops she had used called over the next few days, each with only complimentary things to say about her, each stressing how much they would miss her. Abby and Henry were overwhelmed by it all and it was not until after the funeral, after all the mourners had left, that they were alone with their father and stepmother. Nessie was so quiet, so receptive to all that was suggested, that it was glaringly apparent that Willie had given her a good talking-to but Henry was not in a forgiving mood towards either of them.

'You'll have to come home now, the two of you,' Willie said, not as an order, more of a tentative question.

Before Henry could say a word, Abby astonished them all. 'No, Father, I'm not going home with you. Gramma let me do what I wanted, within reason, and I've discovered I can make a living with my sewing – not a great living but all I need. I'll soon be sixteen and I'm able to look after myself. And Henry's welcome to come back and bide wi' me if he's lost his job.'

Clearly rattled, Willie got noisily to his feet. 'I could take you both back, you ken,' he ground out. 'You're still minors till you're twenty-one.'

Ignoring him, Abby turned to her brother. 'What about it, Henry? Will you come and live here with me? You could get a job somewhere near and, if you wanted to get married sometime, there's plenty room.'

He was torn between compassion for her and his own need to be independent. He wanted to make something of himself – he wanted to have a wife and bairns . . . but not in a house he would be sharing with his sister. He didn't, however, want to upset her tonight and especially not in front of the other two. 'I'll have to think about it, Abby,' he said, softly, and then turned to his father. 'But I'll definitely not be going back to your house. Never! Like Abby, I've had a taste of freedom and I'm not going to put myself in that position again.'

After a curt 'Suit yoursel's, then!' Willie pushed his now simpering wife towards the door and Abby turned tearfully to her brother, who held her until all the emotions she'd had to hold back that day had flooded out, then he made her sit down until he explained how he felt. 'I don't like leaving you here on your own, though,' he added after he made it clear that he wouldn't take up her offer of a home.

'I'll be all right,' she told him. 'I've made plenty friends at this end of the town – boys as well as girls. She smiled shyly.

'Oh, is there somebody special?'

'I wouldn't mind if there was but he hasn't . . .'

'Well, I hope it goes well for you, Abby.'

'I hope you'll find the right girl for you and all when you're a few years older.'

'Aye. I'll have to go back to Craigdownie in the morning to return Mick's bike. If John Legge doesna keep me on, I'll look for some place else but, wherever I am, I'll come and see you as often as I can. Now, I think we need to get some sleep.' His stepmother's disgust coming back to him, he went

44

on, 'But not in the same bed. Nessie was right – we really shouldn't have.'

Unfortunately for Henry, the couch in the parlour was so uncomfortably lumpy and noisy that he couldn't sleep but the only alternative was his grandmother's bed, where her body had lain until it was transferred to the coffin, and he certainly wouldn't have been able to sleep there.

Going over what had happened three days before, he wondered if it had been his fault that his grandmother had died. He had more or less accused his mother – her daughter – of adultery. But Gramma had been tough. She had known why he said it and she hadn't seemed angry with him.

She also had a long experience of life. She knew what she spoke about and he was definitely not going to turn his wife – if he ever took a wife, which he didn't feel too sure about at the moment – into a machine for producing babies. He would ask her, just after putting the ring on her finger, how many children she wanted and he would abide by her decision. No woman would die because he couldn't control his passions.

His mind made up on that, he turned over with a lighter heart and, just before falling asleep, he made another vow. According to Gramma, it was the strong drink that fuelled lust and he would never, ever, touch liquor of any kind. It was true what the Band of Hope taught. Drink was the downfall of all men.

CHAPTER FOUR

Jim Legge was furious. 'Are you sure he knew he'd to come back last night?'

Mick Tyler shrugged. 'I didna tell him, Mr Legge. I thought he'd ken.'

The farmer looked round the breakfast table. 'Did he tell any of you where he was going?' He bared his teeth for a moment at the blank stares that were the only responses. 'He didn't definitely say he was going to see his sister so he could be anywhere?' A new thought struck him. 'Has he left any of his things?'

Mick looked at Frankie Ross who mumbled, 'We never looked, Mr Legge.'

'He'll turn up.' Mrs Legge was something of an optimist. 'He could have had a puncture.'

Her husband had spent enough time on the missing second horseman. 'Harry,' he snapped, turning to the lad at the corner table, 'you can give Davey a hand today and, if Henry doesn't turn up by tonight, you can have his job for good.'

The orra loon's eyes lit up at the prospect of this unexpected promotion. 'Right you are, Mr Legge. 'You can trust me. I'll not let you down.'

This was too much for Janet Emslie. 'The poor laddie could be lying in a ditch for all you folk care. Somebody should be out looking for him.'

It was a busy time on the farm with fields to be ploughed for the spring planting as well as seeing to the new lambs and all the other on-going jobs and Jim Legge did not relish the prospect of another of his men taking time off. His conscience, however, gave enough of a twinge to make him say, 'I suppose

I could let you take the trap, Mick, and see if he *did* go to his sister's. Is she married or is she still at home with their mother and father?'

Mick shook his head. 'He's never said nothing about a mother and father. He just said he'd a sister but he never said where she bade.'

'He once said something to me about his grandmother,' Charlie Simpson offered, 'but he didna say where she bade either.'

'That's it, then!' The farmer obviously considered that they had wasted too much time already. 'You go with Charlie, Harry, and the rest of you get on with what you were supposed to be doing. Mick, just a quick scout around, remember. I want you back here in an hour.'

When the men had left, the farmer's wife turned to the cook. 'I can see you're not happy about this, Janet, but there's nothing we can do. Henry might have had too much drink yesterday and wasn't fit to cycle back but no doubt he'll turn up today.'

'I suppose so.' Janet watched the mistress and her daughter as they went out, then she turned to her young assistant. 'What do you think, Maidie? Henry wouldna have been drinking, I'm near sure o' that.'

'He was dead against the drink,' the girl agreed.

The absentee was the main topic again the following morning, the discussion ending by Jim Legge officially giving the second horseman's job to Harry. By the next day, everyone had got back to normal and forgotten about him – except Janet Emslie. She had taken to Henry Rae the first day she saw him. He was different from all the uncouth orra loons they'd had before – quieter, more serious, innocent. A smile played at the corner of her mouth at the memory of his childlike confusion over the 'pencil' he didn't have.

This latest business wasn't funny, though, she chided herself as she pounded a great lump of dough. The lad could be ill – or his sister – or his grandmother, if that was where he'd gone. They would surely have heard by this time if he'd had an accident – so he could still turn up and there would be no job for him. Young Harry was managing fine in his place and the ploughman's laddie had now been taken on as orra loon. It was as if Jim Legge had thrown Henry on the midden.

For the rest of that day, the cook got more and more depressed worrying how he would feel when he learned what had happened and, by the time she went to bed, her heart was as sore as his would be when he did make his appearance.

She found herself drifting in and out of a troubled sleep and rose even more tired and upset than she had been the night before – even remembering that it was Sunday and her afternoon off did nothing to cheer her. Her brother had promised to take her to see their mother and she was actually dreading the confrontation there was bound to be but, once she rose, she had no time to brood on her own problem – or Henry's.

At twelve o'clock, with everything left ready for Maidie to serve at one on the dot, Janet went up to her room to make ready. She dressed in her winter dress, a black bombazine with a line of black pearl buttons marching from the high neck to just below her waist, and black satin ribbon highlighting the pin tucks. She usually felt her spirits lift when she wore it but not today. She took her best bonnet listlessly from its tin box, giving the curled feathers a blow before putting it on and studying her reflection in the tilting mirror. She supposed she would pass in a crowd but what did it matter where she was going?

She still felt guilty at having put Ma away but, as Roderick had said, they couldn't have left her on her own. She was over eighty, though she didn't like to admit it, and her mind had been going for some time now. She had nearly set the house on fire once – only her next-door neighbour's keen sense of smell had prevented it. She had broken practically all her dishes – whether by accident or on purpose was difficult to know for she had a vile temper when something upset her.

It was heart-breaking to see the once fastidious, hard-working woman in the state she'd been that last time, unwashed for weeks on end, thin as a knife blade for want of the food she believed she had eaten, yet not a morsel could have passed her lips.

Janet had had to draw Roderick's attention to that, she recalled sadly, for men never see what they don't want to see and they had talked over what they should do – talked and talked without coming to any decision. Luckily, the same neighbour had mentioned her worry about the old woman to her doctor and it was he who had solved the problem.

Hearing the sound of a light carriage crunching on the gravel, Janet put on her cape and went out at the back door, where Roderick helped her into his little gig. As manager of a drapery shop in Oldmeldrum, he was always dressed in a smart suit and dark homburg which, with his neatly trimmed moustache, made him look quite distinguished. Janet felt quite proud to be sitting beside him as they bowled along.

'I wonder how she'll be?' he asked suddenly.

Janet made a wry face. 'I hope she's settled in.'

'They would have let us know if she had not.'

'Aye, I suppose so.'

No more was said for another few minutes until Janet burst out, 'I hope they treat her all right. I'd hate to think they were ill-using her. I've heard stories about what goes on in mad-houses.'

Roderick tutted loudly. 'Nonsense! The doctor said The Sycamores is nothing like an asylum.'

'But it's for mad folk.'

'They are not mad in the sense that you mean. With some, like Ma, it is just the effect of old age but there are others who have had some sort of bad experience that has knocked them off balance for a time.'

'But it's costing such a lot o' money, Roderick. I feel terrible that I canna help.'

'I do not begrudge it. She made sure that I had a good education.'

Janet was well aware of that. Her brother's schooling had been the reason for her lack of it, for her having to go out to work at such an early age to help pay for his books, but she wasn't one to hold a grudge either. 'What'll happen if she's in there for years? Her body's good for a long time yet.'

'What a worrier you are, Janet. I would not have let her be sent there if I had not given thought to that. As long as my business keeps up and the fees are not increased too much, she can stay there for as long as she lives.' He patted her hand. 'Does that ease your mind?'

'Roderick, I don't know what I'd have done if you hadn't been able to pay . . .'

'I know that you had to make sacrifices for my sake when we were younger so look on this as me returning that kindness. Put your mind at rest now, my dear sister; there is nothing more for you to worry about.'

Janet was in a far better mood on the way back to Craigdownie – even though her mother had not recognised either her or Roderick. There was such an improvement in her – her cheeks rosier and not caved in, as they had been, her movements and speech much more decisive. She had held a sensible conversation with them about the daily routine; she had described some of the women she seemed to have made friends with; they had learned about the changing menus, the choices they had. 'And they won't let us wash any dishes,' she had beamed, proudly. 'There's women to do all that and keep the place clean and all and there's nice girls to look after us.'

They had not known what to say to her but obviously, under the impression that they were strangers, she did not expect them to say much. Even when they rose to leave, she showed no sign of recognition. 'It was nice to speak to you,' she had smiled, holding her hand out. 'Will I see you again?'

Roderick had lifted the veined hand to his lips. 'Yes, of course. We will be back, be sure of that.'

Janet had bent over to kiss her cheek. 'I'm sorry I can only manage to come once a month, Mother.'

The old lady's eyes had clouded in puzzlement. 'I don't know who you are,' she had stated, coldly, 'so don't pretend I'm your mother.'

The leave-taking had not really upset them. In fact, they were relieved that she was happier now. 'She will not miss us if we do not go every month,' Roderick smiled. 'She is living in a different world now, with people to look after her and attend to her every whim.'

Janet nodded. 'I wouldn't have believed she'd be so at home. Did you see how her face lit up when Innes Ledingham came over to speak to her?'

'I was meaning to ask about that. I didn't know that it was he who ran the place.'

'Neither did I,' Janet smiled. 'I got a right shock when I saw him.'

'You had quite a tête-à-tête with him. What was that about?'

'Nothing much. I hadn't seen him for years and years but we were just speaking about Ma. He says she's settled in fine, she's well liked and she's eating three good meals a day. So I needn't have worried.'

'I told you.'

Janet didn't want to tell him what had also transpired during her conversation with Innes, who had been a very close friend at one time. She'd even had the feeling that he was on the verge of courting her but she had met Tom Aitken and that was that. Anyway, Innes had gone away, down to England somewhere, and, the last she had heard of him, he was married. When she asked him how he came to be in charge of The Sycamores, he had just said that he loved the challenge. Then he had added, with a wry smile, that his biggest problem was getting staff.

'Cleaning women are easier to come by but finding girls willing to tend to needful patients is quite difficult. Once they have been here for even a day, however, they find that they quite enjoy making life easier for those under their care. At present, I am looking for a young man who can turn his hand to anything, repairing doors or windows, fixing loose screws, a bit of painting – maintenance work in other words.'

The upshot of this was that, on her recommendation alone, he had hired young Henry Rae without even seeing him. Janet pulled her cape closer round her as if hugging herself for being so clever. She pushed aside the thought that the boy may never return to Craigdownie – she had faith in him.

Her first words to Maidie when she went into the kitchen were, 'Is Henry back?'

'Oh, Janet, it was awfu'! You werena long away when he turned up and Mr Legge gave him a right telling aff! And when he was finished ranting, he said Henry had better leave for there was no job here for him and Henry ran oot wi' tears rolling doon his face.'

'Oh. Lordy!' Janet thumped down on the chair by the range with her hand on her chest. 'The poor laddie and I wasna here.' For a few moments, she breathed heavily, then gave her head a little shake and sat up straight. 'Where is he, Maidie? Where did he go?'

'I couldna tell you that, Cook, but I some think he went across to the bothy to collect his things.'

Forgetting, in her anxiety for the boy, that some hours had passed since he learned the brutal news, Janet went out as fast as her tired legs would carry her and burst into the bothy without even knocking.

'God a'michty, Janet!' A startled Mick looked up from cutting his toenails. 'I could've been changing my drawers.'

'I wouldna have seen nothing I hadna seen afore,' she barked. 'Where is he?'

'Where's who?' Understanding dawning, he said, 'He's nae here.'

'I can see that. He took his things?'

'Aye, afore we come in and I dinna ken where he went.'

It was young Harry who gave Janet at least some inform-ation. 'I saw him speaking to the grieve for a while.'

With no word of thanks, Janet rushed out again and made for the grieve's house, one of the four cottages built for the married workers, and, when Ina Sim answered her knock, she gasped, 'Is Henry here?'

The woman's cheery face sobered. 'He was but he wouldna bide. Davey was that sorry for him when he said what had happened, he offered him a bed for the nicht but he wouldna hear o't. Are you coming in?'

'I'll nae come in, thank you. I need to speak to him for I found him a new job. Have you nae idea where he . . . ?'

'Maybe he said something to Davey. He *did* say his Gramma had died – that was what kept him away.'

'I ken't there was something!' There was no triumph in Janet's words.

'You'll be asking aboot Henry?' The grieve himself, a tall stout man in tweeds and a flat cap, had walked up the path not far behind her. 'You'd best come in.'

She followed Ina into the cosy kitchen where a large lurcher was sprawled on the hearth. 'Shift yoursel', Davey grinned, giving the dog a nudge with the toe of his boot. 'Other folk need to get in aboot for a heat.'

Clearly accustomed to this order, the animal didn't move as much as an eyelid and the three 'folk' sat down, careful not to disturb him. 'Did Henry tell you where he was going?' Janet couldn't wait another minute.

'He was real upset, hardly ken't what he was saying, poor loon, but he let slip his grandmother had died sudden and he bade wi' his sister till the frunial was by.'

'He'll have gone back to his sister, then. Did he tell you where she bade?'

'I never thocht to ask.' The grieve looked ashamed for his lack of interest.

A brooding silence fell during which Ina got up to make a pot of tea. She busied herself further by taking three enamel mugs from the dresser and laying them on the well-scrubbed wooden table. Then she took a flagon of milk – one of the perquisites of farm employment – from the pantry where there was a marble slab to keep perishables cool and poured a little into each mug. She was in the act of swirling boiling water in the brown china teapot to heat it when her husband banged his fist on his knee. 'Dammit! I clean forgot!'

'You daft beggar!' she exclaimed. 'You near made me burn mysel'.'

Janet was more interested in what the man had said than in the wife's imagined catastrophe. 'What did you forget? Did he gi'e you a hint?'

'I tell't him to tak' oor Doddie's auld bike to save him walking and he promised to send it back wi' the carrier in the morning.'

Ina, still recovering from the fright he had given her, was none the wiser but Janet gasped, 'You think the carrier'll be able to tell you?'

'I wouldna be surprised and it's worth a try. I'll keep a look-oot for him – and you and all, Ina.'

'And me!' declared Janet.

She stayed in the cottar house for another fifteen minutes or so, then went back to her upstairs room in the farmhouse. She felt a good deal better now. At least there was a chance of learning what she wanted to know, though she'd have to wait till the morrow morning. Her mind turned to The Sycamores. Innes Ledingham was still a handsome man, just over six feet, body still as lean as it had been when he used to see her home from the kirk all those years before. His dark hair, worn brushed right back off his face, was shot with grey now and his moustache was lighter than she remembered but still as thick. There were a few lines etched on his forehead yet his brown eyes still held something that made her blood flow faster in her veins. And his mouth was still turned up at the corners in a smile. Oh, Lordy! What was she thinking about? They were both well over forty – and he had a wife.

Switching her thoughts to Henry Rae again, she hoped that the carrier who took back the bike came from the same place as Henry's sister, otherwise he wouldn't know where she lived. That would be the end of it for there was no other way she could find the boy.

It would have been natural if Janet had spent another troubled night but she was so tired – so much had happened that day and her emotions had see-sawed so dramatically – that she fell into a deep sleep the minute her head touched the pillow.

'Henry! You did lose your job, then?' Abby held out her arms and her fourteen-year-old brother ran into them with a sob.

'I didna really think Jim Legge would sack me,' he gulped.

'Dinna worry,' she soothed. 'He'd been angry but he'll likely tell you to come back once he cools down.'

'No, he'll not ask me back.' He moved over to sit down on what had been his Gramma's chair, although that didn't cross his mind, he was so depressed. 'Davey said I was doing well as second horseman,' he sighed, 'but Harry's got my job. Mr Legge said he didna ken if I had left for good or what.'

'He could surely have waited a while but, never mind, you'll be fine here wi' me till you find something else. Henry, where are you going?' she added as he got to his feet again.

'I've to tell the carrier to take a bike back to the grieve. I'll not be long.'

He returned after only ten minutes, looking a little less distraught than when he had come in before, but his face fell again when Abby said, 'You'll be sleeping in Gramma's bed. I've put a pig in to heat it for you.' Noticing his agitation, she smiled, 'I've washed all the bedding, Henry.'

'Abby, I canna . . .'

'All right, then. I'll sleep in her bed and you can have mine.'

Henry fell asleep quickly, exhausted in body and mind, but his sister lay awake for hours, thinking about Pogie Laing. She'd often wondered how he got the nickname because his real name was Clarence, according to the minister. At Gramma's funeral, he had gripped her hand for a long time and his eyes had burned into hers as if he wanted to say something other than how sorry he was.

She had turned seventeen, time for having a lad, and Pogie was the lad she wanted. She had hoped he might come to see her now that she was alone in the house but he wouldn't come if he knew Henry was back.

In spite of that side of it, though, she was glad her brother had come back to her. She had never seen him so upset as he'd been when he came in and he had comforted her twice before so it was up to her now. They would surely manage. It would be a struggle but it shouldn't be long till he found another job. Even though he was so short, he was a hard worker, with an ever-ready smile, willing to do anything.

CHAPTER FIVE

1887

The Sycamores had once been the residence of a very minor peer of the realm who had been forced by circumstances, in the middle of the century, to sell up and emigrate to South Africa. The purchaser of the estate, an Aberdeenshire man now permanently domiciled in London but mindful of his roots although he was an immensely rich businessman, had founded an institution for the mentally afflicted. This had been in the charge of Innes Ledingham for the past twelve years. He was a strict disciplinarian as far as his staff was concerned but sympathetic and understanding with his patients, male and female, who ranged from fifteen or sixteen years of age to eighty and over.

Because of steadily rising costs – wages, food, oil and coal – he had applied, about five years earlier, to the now deceased owner's sons for extra funding. He had been told, however, that they were in financial difficulties themselves and that he would have to start charging the families of the 'unfortunates' for looking after them – otherwise they would have to close the place. After discussing this with the board of governors, Innes had decided to set the fees high enough to cover the few places he meant to keep for the 'truly poor or destitute' but, sadly, there was currently only one such place available now.

The introduction of fees had certainly upgraded the type of people under his wing, effectively wiping out the slavering incontinents and other undesirables. It was rather unfortunate that those not in this range, and with no relatives left to provide money for their keep, had also had to be transferred to parish-run asylums but it was really out of his control. It was now much easier to recruit nurses and young girls to tend to the needs of the residents and just one male orderly was needed in case of any trouble.

The only problem he now had, Innes reflected one day, was in getting incidental workers. Those employed to actually come in contact with the patients were dedicated to looking after them whereas some of the gardeners, grooms and odd-job men he had taken on seemed to be afraid that they were endangering their lives by working at The Sycamores. He was quite fortunate with his present company, however, every man and woman willing to do whatever was asked of them and, more importantly, all scrupulously honest and reliable.

He had been a little unsure of young Henry Rae at first, with him never having had any experience outside farm work, but he was proving to be a veritable treasure. No work was too demanding – or too demeaning – for him and staff and patients alike adored him and sought his advice on their little problems, real or imaginary – even Gloria, his own wife. Innes felt grateful to the youth for this – it saved her pestering him.

An apprehension lurked at the back of his mind, however, a feeling that perhaps things were running too smoothly. The elderly matron and the two nurses of indeterminate age were not the cause of this – it was the four girls, employed because they needed less pay than the older women. They were all bright, nubile young things and Henry was a dashed good-looking lad. He had dark curly hair, a round tanned face, which would no doubt lose its chubbiness as he grew older, and dark green eyes that always held a smile. There was no flabbiness about him and, although he was quite small for his age, there was still time for him to grow. When he was fully grown, he would have a devastating effect on the female sex, that was a certainty.

Innes pulled his meandering thoughts together. By all appearances, he had nothing to worry about as far as the girls were concerned. Young Henry had shown not the slightest interest in any of them. He treated them in the same friendly, light-hearted manner that he treated everybody he spoke to but, strangely, he kept himself to himself after work. Lack of interest in women could, of course, mean that he was homosexual yet he showed no interest there either. Innes decided that it was as well to let life go on as usual. He was only stressing himself by worrying about something, he knew not what, that may never happen. A far more exciting concept had stirred in him recently, a concept which would require much consideration and careful handling to reach fruition.

Henry felt it his duty to keep an eye on old Mrs Emslie; after all, he owed his job to Janet. She and her brother could only visit their mother once a month and the old lady must miss them. She had made friends with a few of the other women – if you could call it friendship with each keeping to her own train of thought, content to receive no answers to or comments on what she said.

He was fully aware that Mrs Emslie had taken a fancy to him the first day he went to see her but he hadn't realised until that afternoon how she really felt about him. One of the nurses, a keen lover of nature, had been taking three of her charges for a stroll around the grounds when Janet's mother spotted him dead-heading some hydrangeas.

'That's my son, you know,' she said loudly – and proudly.

Thoroughly embarrassed, he had mumbled, 'No, I just work here. I'm helping the gardener today but I do other jobs as well. My name's Henry Rae.'

A pained uncertainty had flitted across her lined face, then she turned to her companions. 'I can't think what's making him say that. Fancy not minding his own mother.'

He had shot a look of appeal to the nurse who soothed, 'It's all right, Mrs Emslie. We should be getting on. Henry's too busy to speak to anybody just now.'

He bent his scarlet face to his work again, praying that her ploy had worked. It had because, as they moved away, one of the other women observed, 'What a lot of these wing things there are lying about here.'

And Mrs Emslie said, 'They're the seeds from the sycamore trees.' She hesitated for a moment, then, having put two and two together, added proudly, 'I suppose that's why they called this place The Sycamores?'

Their escort nodded thankfully. 'That's right and the winged bits are called samaras.'

To a chorus of 'Samaras? I didn't know that,' the little group moved out of earshot.

Henry didn't lift his head or pause in what he was doing. He had gleaned many titbits of information about the flowers while he worked with the head gardener, but he'd had no idea that the lovely old trees scattered about the grounds were sycamores, nor that their seeds were called samaras. It was a funny name – but interesting. Intriguing.

The next day was one of Janet's Sundays, as he thought of them, so he would have to make a point of seeing her to explain what had happened.

'Isn't that your friend Henry standing at the gate?' Roderick Emslie asked his sister.

'Yes, it is.' Janet felt as if a heavy weight had fallen on her. 'He looks awful worried – something must be wrong with Ma. You'd better stop. Yes, Henry,' she called as the small vehicle came to a halt, 'what is it?'

'I wanted to catch you before you went in,' he muttered. 'I want to explain about yesterday. I don't know why but your mother thinks I'm her son. I didn't do anything to . . . I did try to tell her she was wrong but . . . I'm sorry,' he added a little belatedly.

'You've nothing to be sorry for,' she soothed. 'The very first time we came to see her, she said she wasn't my mother. The doctor says it often happens. They honestly don't remember. How are you getting on? Still liking the job?'

'I love it,' he assured her, relieved that his worry had been banished so effectively. 'I'll always be grateful to you for speaking up for me, Janet.'

She grinned at him. 'It was a two-way good turn. I was helping Innes Ledingham as well as you. He's an old friend of mine.'

Her brother lifted the reins. 'It's good of you to look in on my mother occasionally,' he smiled as the gig moved away.

The sturdy pony trotted up the wide avenue, thick with the samaras the birds picked up and spread farther afield, carrying on the cycle of propagation. Mr Ledingham was also waiting for them they discovered when they came to a final stop at the imposing oaken door.

Despite being pleased to see him, Janet's heart turned over with the fear of what he might have to tell them. But he, like Henry, had a worry of his own. 'Janet, I wonder if you would mind coming through to my sitting room for a moment. There is something I would like to discuss with you . . . privately.'

She glanced at her brother who said, 'It's all right. I'll go in and talk to Mother.'

Shutting the door behind them, Innes said, 'I hope you do not think this an imposition but I have a problem you may be able to solve . . . if you will.'

'I'll do my best whatever it is,' she smiled, flattered that he was asking her help. 'Just tell me . . .'

'It is rather embarrassing. You see, my wife had an argument with our cook, over nothing at all really – she has a vile temper at times, Gloria, I mean – and it ended with Mrs Gall walking out. I told Gloria she would have to take over the duty until I found another cook and she told me . . .' he hesitated, his face flaming, his eyes held down.

'Go on,' Janet urged, softly.

'She told me she had had enough of this place and I could jolly well do it myself.'

'And?'

'And she has . . . left me.'

'When was this?'

'Last Monday. So, you see, she will not be coming back.'

Realisation of his target was dawning. 'Who has been making the meals?'

'The nurses and the maids have taken it in turn but some of the residents are beginning to complain and I do not blame them at the prices we charge.'

'Have you tried to find a replacement – for the cook?'

'I have tried but the agencies say no one is willing to come to a place like this.'

'That's terrible!' Janet exclaimed. 'The Sycamores is a very nice place.'

'To people who know no better, it is simply an asylum, a madhouse, but you . . .' He broke off but his meaning was quite clear now.

There was a pause before Janet said, 'You're offering me the job?'

'I am asking you to take pity on me, Janet.'

His pleading eyes, his look of utter defeat, were not genuine but, although she knew she was being manipulated, she could not refuse him. 'I'll have to work my notice at Craigdownie,' she said quietly.

'How long?'

'A month? I don't know.'

After thinking for a minute or so, Innes said, his voice low and caressing, 'There is a way to get round that, you know.'

Janet's eyes showed her bewilderment. 'What do you mean?'

'Your mother.'

'What has my mother got to do with this? I want to take the job, Innes. I want to be where I can see her every day but I'll have to work out my notice.'

'Not if you tell your present employer that your mother is . . . dying.'

'I knew it!' she cried, apprehension widening her eyes. 'I knew you had bad news but why didn't you tell me right away, instead of . . .'

'No, Janet, do not alarm yourself. Your mother is not dying. It was a suggestion – a way to make the farmer free you from any commitment. Do you understand?' He waited, watching her changing expressions – perplexity, angry comprehension, doubt and, finally, guilt. 'I canna,' she muttered at last, her confusion making her forget that she had been trying to speak to him, a university graduate, in a more refined manner. 'I canna tell a lie, nae a lie like that. Besides, it's asking for trouble.'

'Yes,' he agreed, 'it is a lie but it is not malicious. It will hurt no one and benefit many – you, your mother, the residents and staff here and . . . me.'

'But Mr Legge will be left without a cook.'

He could see that she was wavering. 'He, unlike me, will easily find another. Oh, Janet, please?' He took her hand and squeezed it.

The entreaty in his eyes, or maybe it was more than that, was her downfall. 'I'll try,' she whispered. 'I will try, Innes, but I can't promise anything. He sacked Henry for taking some days off, remember?'

Exultant now, sure it would work out as he hoped, Innes kept his voice on an even keel. 'You said that he did not know of the grandmother's death.' His free hand slid around her waist.

Savouring the thrill of it, it was some seconds before Janet pushed him away. 'No, Innes. Don't try to take advantage. I'm doing this for my mother's sake and to help you out but don't forget you are a married man.'

His eyes darkening, he murmured, 'I am sorry, Janet. I honestly did not mean to take advantage. I was merely expressing my joy at having my problem solved.'

'It's not definitely solved,' she reminded him.

'I have confidence in you, my dear, and, to prove it, I shall send my carriage to collect you and your belongings tomorrow afternoon, around two o'clock. That will give you time to prepare their breakfast and lunch and to do your packing.'

'But . . . what if he won't let me go?'

'Unthinkable but, should the worst happen, you will have to send my groom away and I shall welcome you with open arms when you arrive next month, all ready to take over in my kitchen the following morning.'

As Innes had foreseen, Jim Legge was sympathetic to Janet's request, her trembling voice and fearful expression (both a result of her guilt at deceiving him) lending authenticity to the fiction. 'Yes, of course you must go to be with your mother. It was providential that The Sycamores' cook left when she did. Now, you say you want to leave tomorrow. How will you get there?'

'Mr Ledingham's sending a carriage in the afternoon.' Even as she said it, she wished she hadn't. He could be angry at Innes's presumption.

The farmer, however, was amused, not angry. 'He takes things for granted, doesn't he?' he grinned. 'Though I suppose it's a compliment to me.'

Janet's conscience kept her awake that night. Not only had she told a dreadful falsehood to Jim Legge, she'd had to repeat it to Maidie, who kept wanting details of her mother's illness, so she'd had to concoct a few more untruths. It was awful. She had never sinned her soul in all her forty years, and now the lies came tripping off her tongue.

Not only that, she was having sinful thoughts. No matter what Innes had said, she knew he would make advances to her once he got her there and she didn't know if she had the strength to refuse him – or even if she wanted to refuse him. The way he had looked at her that afternoon had stirred emotions that would be better undisturbed. She was remembering how she had felt with poor Tom Aitken – how his caresses and kisses had taken her to the point where it hadn't been a case of not wanting to refuse him but of longing for him to get on with it.

The circumstances had been different with Tom, though. He had loved her and she had loved him. They had both been in their teens and he had been going off to war. There was an excuse for what she had done on that wonderful, special night but there would be no excuse if she fornicated with a married man – for that's what it would be, not an act of love. Even an act of love would be a sin for them . . . in other people's eyes.

Flooding with shame at the imagined copulation, Janet sent up a prayer for her own salvation.

Oh, dear Lord, help me to keep my mind on the proper things.

Don't let me get carried away by what Innes does to me – if he does do anything to me. Don't let me forget that my mother taught me to keep myself pure for the man I take as my husband.

She stopped, brought up short by what she was thinking. She wasn't pure. She wasn't untouched. Even if, heaven knew how, she was ever in a position to marry Innes or any other man, she couldn't pretend she was pure. In any case, would it matter all that much? Did all men expect their brides to be chaste? What would happen if they found out that the woman they had chosen was not what they thought?

She gave herself a shake. What rubbish she was thinking. There must be a lot of women and girls who had gone down the slippery slope before their marriage. Letting a man prove his love was a natural thing, wasn't it? And it couldn't be unusual for that man to die or go away or transfer his affections to somebody else. So . . . there must be a lot of men whose brides were not pure.

This did not make her feel any better, though, and the following forenoon was an ordeal, too. Saying goodbye to all the decent folk who hoped that her mother would recover and wished her well in her new job, made her feel thoroughly ashamed but, at last, it was over. The trap arrived to take her away and she climbed up beside the driver because she couldn't bear to be alone with her thoughts.

A month short of his sixteenth birthday, Henry Rae knew that he couldn't hold out for much longer. He had made it quite obvious to everybody at The Sycamores that he didn't want to get over-friendly with any of them – even Janet. Although she always took time to speak to him if they met, a rumour was going round that Mr Ledingham was smitten with her and he didn't want to spoil things for her. It was a pity that Ledingham was married, of course, but his wife had left him and why shouldn't he and Janet find some happiness together?

He, himself, had reached a stage where his evenings and night-times were becoming preoccupied with thoughts of the girls he saw during the day. He hadn't settled on a special one yet but he likely would. Which one, though? That was the question.

Gladys wasn't too bad but, as always when he met a girl he quite liked, she was far too tall for him.

Daisy was a real bonnie wee thing with a sweet, heart-shaped face, wide baby-blue eyes, soft mouth – but long, flaming-red hair with a temper to match, not that she ever lost her rag with any of the folk she was looking after. Just the same, life probably wouldn't be easy if he took her for a wife – yet maybe it would be fun?

Poll was about his own height but quite dumpy. Her hair was dead straight, usually tied back with a blue ribbon that was always in danger of sliding off. She had dull grey eyes and a mouth that was often gripped together at being teased. It was a shame the rest of them tormented her about her shape – the poor lass couldn't help it. Maybe, if he chose her, he could make her stop stuffing herself at the table and her figure would slim down? Maybe all she needed was to know that somebody cared for her?

Nora was quite nice but just a bit too old – or was three years not that big a difference? She was couthy in her manner to them all, she laughed a lot, she didn't fuss about her appearance though she was always neat and tidy – mousy hair tied back so that no strands could work loose, cheeks shining with cleanliness. Being older than the others, her bosom was more rounded, her waist more slender, her bottom trimmer, her legs more shapely.

Stopping to draw in his breath, Henry became aware of a new unaccustomed warmth inside him and he resolved to concentrate on Nora. He would court her for a good few months before he told her what was in his mind for he was sure she would make him a good wife and give him just the son he wanted. Then he wouldn't touch her in that way again for he could easily have inherited his father's . . . he couldn't find one word for it but 'ability to make babies' fitted the bill. He had no intention of making his wife have thirteen babies or even half of that – minus the half, of course, for you couldn't have half a baby.

But, even if he knew several families with five or more children, he also knew some with only one or two so what did the fathers do to stop having more? There must be a way so how could he find out? Happy at having chosen Nora on whom to lavish his attentions, Henry fell into a deep sleep.

His high hopes were shattered about an hour after breakfast while he was mending the broken posts in the fence round the vegetable garden. Seeing the girl in question coming towards him, he tried to think what to say. She smiled pleasantly as she came closer but his tongue seemed to be fixed to the roof of his mouth.

She broke the ice herself. 'Aye, Henry. You're busy, I see.'

'Aye.' He couldn't leave it at that and suddenly he found himself laying down the heavy mallet and saying, 'Not so busy I canna give you a hand.'

'I'm nae needing a hand. I just need a puckle sprigs o' parsley for the cook.'

He still couldn't let the opportunity slip. 'Would you like to meet me after supper the night? We could go for a walk.'

She let out a great roar of laughter. 'Me . . . walk wi' you?'

Stung, he demanded, 'What's wrong wi' me?'

'You're nae even the height o' tuppence and you're still a bairn.' Having cut a bunch of parsley, she drew her skirts away from him and stalked off, still chuckling.

Henry resumed his task, bedding the new posts in all the quicker because of the force behind the mallet strokes. Only his pride had been hurt, however – he'd had no deep feelings for the girl – so he didn't take long to calm down but he was soon to get a shock that put everything else out of his mind.

Mr Ledingham waited until the last straggler was seated at the supper table before saying, 'I am sure that you have all been wondering what was going to happen about George Reid. He has been off work for almost eight weeks now and I am very grateful to every one of you for helping out in the gardens when the need arose. I know that I was expecting too much of you with your own work to keep up to date as well but I was prepared to let the situation carry on until George was fit to come back to work.'

He stopped, looking round the puzzled faces. 'Unfortunately, he came this afternoon to tell me that he wants to retire. He is almost seventy, after all, and his wife has persuaded him to sell their cottage and go to Glasgow to be near their son and daughter. Thoughtful to the last, he gave me the name of a young man, his wife's nephew, who is willing to step in to the breach and save me the worry of finding someone. Lennie, you, of course, will take over as head gardener, with Bob as next in line and young Maxwell taking up the rear. That is all I have to say so you may carry on with supper.'

He sat down and there was a buzz of conversation as the others discussed this unexpected development. Henry was the only one who remained silent. He went through the motions of supping his soup and eating his skirlie and tatties but, in reality, he had no idea what he was shovelling into his stomach. He was hoping against hope that the Maxwell who was coming wasn't Maxwell Dalgarno. If Maxie came to The Sycamores, Henry Rae would stand no chance with any of the girls.

Maxie – or Max as he preferred to be called now – was seventeen. He had grown much more than Henry over the years and now towered above him. His face was leaner and his muscular body was evidence of the hard farm work he had been doing since he left school. He had let his hair grow longer, making Henry envious of the blonde curls that lay on his shoulder. His eyes held a mischievous glint and seemed a darker blue than before, with a jet-black centre, but Henry was pleased to see that Max's hands were quite large and callused. Girls wouldn't like rough hands.

Before Max had been at The Sycamores for a fortnight, however, it was quite obvious to a saddened Henry that the roughness of his hands didn't discourage the girls. Even Nora, who had spurned *him* and mocked *him*, was flirting with Max and they made a striking pair, he had to admit. The man was about six inches taller than the girl – which was as it should be, not the other way round.

Even with that faint tinge of jealousy ever present, Henry still considered Max as his friend. They'd relive their schooldays and laugh at the fight they'd had over a girl which had resulted in seven of the best each from the dominie. It wasn't long before Henry's spirits rose. Max was there with him every single evening, from suppertime till time to rise in the morning, so he wasn't walking out with any of the lassies.

Janet had been looking in to see her mother every day – quite glad, in a way, that there was no change for she had something else on her mind. Innes Ledingham had been a proper gentle- man for weeks after she started as cook, letting her join him in his sitting room in the evenings but never saying one word out of place. They would discuss the patients – residents, he pre- ferred to call them – or the weather or people they had both known in their young days or the failings of one of the staff. She had felt easy with him – she could laugh with him and it was good. But another element had crept in that made her feel quite uncomfortable – little hints here and there. Then the hints grew more specific and he made so bold as to suggest she should share his bed.

'Don't look so shocked,' he went on. 'I know you want to as much as I do.'

She was more than shocked. Her legs were shaking, her very teeth started to chatter and it took a tremendous effort to speak. 'No, Innes,' she managed to get out, 'I thought you understood there couldn't be anything like that.' Her voice strengthened. 'My mother always said a woman should never give herself to a man until he marries her. Oh!' She broke off in confusion, 'I'm sorry but I can't. Not with her being so close.'

The moisture gathering in his eyes was evidence that she had seriously wounded him and his voice was low. 'You know I would marry you if I could, my dear Janet.'

'That's just it! You're a married man.'

'In name only.' He paused, then added, 'Think about it, please.'

Sorely tempted, she had thought of nothing else but she knew that she could never overcome her horror of taking such a step – however deeply she felt about him.

Innes shook his head sorrowfully the following day when she repeated her refusal. 'Perhaps I did not make myself clear,' he murmured, gripping her hand and staring into her eyes as if trying to hypnotise her into agreeing. 'I love you, Janet, with all my heart, and I foolishly thought that you loved me.'

A strange ache started deep inside her – he had never before said that he loved her. 'I do love you,' she whispered, 'but I . . . I just can't. Don't ask me again, please.'

Dropping her hand, he said, perhaps more sharply than he meant, 'Not until the two obstacles are out of the way?'

Because she had hurt him, she could excuse him for being so blunt.

It was Henry Rae who made the discovery – just two days later. After fixing a window blind that had been sticking, he decided to nip into the next room to find out how Mrs Emslie was. He hadn't had time to visit her much lately and had heard that she had a very bad cold so he wasn't surprised that she was lying down. Then it dawned on him that she should have heard him coming in. Her door groaned and creaked annoyingly no matter how often he oiled it yet she hadn't even stirred.

Running out, he searched for a nurse and, when the death had been confirmed, he made for the kitchen and it was Janet who took him in her arms and comforted him when he sobbed out the dreadful information. 'She was old, Henry,' she whispered, 'and she hasn't had much of a life for years.'

'Don't you feel anything?' he asked. 'You've just lost your mother.'

'Oh, laddie, it's not that I don't care. When you get to my age, death doesn't have the same effect on you. She has been well cared for since she came to The Sycamores. I've no regrets about sending her here and I'm sure my brother will feel the same.'

When he turned up the following day to attend to what had to be done, Roderick Emslie expressed himself in much the same way. Of course, as Henry knew because Janet had once mentioned it, her brother would no longer have fees to pay for keeping his mother at The Sycamores so that would be a relief for him.

A few days after the funeral, Janet had to admit to herself that she, like her brother, felt a great sense of relief at her mother's death. She no longer had the feeling that the old woman was at her side every minute of the day, watching what she was doing, finding fault, making sure she stayed on the straight and narrow path, the way of the righteous. Yet, even accepting that she was free of this burden, Janet still held Innes at bay if she felt that he was about to ask her 'that' question again.

One obstacle had certainly gone but the one that remained was insurmountable. Innes already had a wife and she, Janet Emslie, would never step into the absent woman's shoes – or her bed – however much he pleaded with her and however much she wanted to.

CHAPTER SIX

Henry had been wondering who Max had been out with on the past three Wednesday evenings but, when he checked, none of the girls was missing and nobody he asked knew anything. He wouldn't really have been bothered if Max hadn't been so secretive about it. All he would say when pressed was, 'It's a lassie I met a while back.' He wouldn't say who she was or where they had met.

His mind not on what he was doing, Henry cut his thumb with the scythe – a really deep gash – one afternoon in August, when he was helping Max to cut the grass for horse fodder. The wound kept bleeding, spurting out, and Max told him he should get one of the nurses to bandage it. Janet, however, happened to be in the kitchen when he went in. She was supervising the potting of a huge panful of raspberry jam and, after a quick look at his hand, she said, 'Get Meg to bandage it but you need it seen to proper. I'll tell young Roddy to make the gig ready to take you to Drymill. I've heard the druggist there's near as good as the doctor.'

He stood silently while the nurse came and wrapped wads of cotton wool and bandaging round the injured hand. He couldn't afford the services of either a doctor or a druggist so this would have to do. 'Thank you, Meg,' he muttered as he turned away. 'I'll be fine now. I'll not need to see anybody else.'

'Just you do as you're told and tell the man to send the bill to Mr Ledingham,' Janet stated firmly, correctly assessing the reason for his refusal. 'And you'd better hurry afore you bleed to death.'

Looking down, he saw that the blood was already soaking

through the wadding and the likelihood of her dire prediction made him feel less brave.

Thirteen-year-old Roddy, the stable lad, could hardly keep his fascinated eyes off the bloody channel inching its way through the grime on Henry's arm, which he was holding upwards because it was less painful than letting his hand hang down.

'Will they need to cut aff your hand?' The urgency of the situation was making the boy tug the reins and click at the pony to make it go faster.

'Don't be daft!' In spite of his vehement denial, Henry was feeling slightly light-headed and leaned back with his eyes closed.

Terrified that he would be left transporting a corpse to the village, Roddy urged the pony on to yet greater speed and heaved a sigh of relief when his passenger murmured, eyes still closed, 'How far yet?'

'Jist aboot there. We've passed the first house.'

Seconds later, he had to help the patient down and support him till he walked into the shop and collapsed on to the chair placed conveniently at the counter.

Taking the situation in at a glance, the pharmacist hurried round to remove the sodden bandage, then raised his head to call, 'Fay! Bring me a bowl of hot water – as quickly as you can, please.'

Drifting in and out of consciousness, Henry was aware that two people were treating him – a man dishing out the orders and a girl handing him whatever he asked for. The application of iodine brought him round immediately. He screamed at the pain but the girl whispered, 'I'm sorry but we must clean out any dirt – otherwise infection could set in.'

His stomach churning, Roddy took himself outside and stood stroking the pony until, about ten minutes later, he was called back to the shop, where the girl was fixing a sling round Henry's neck. 'You must keep this on and come back here tomorrow,' she advised the chalk-white Henry, who seemed to be still in a daze.

'It is very deep,' the man observed, 'and in a very nasty place – between the thumb and forefinger. It would be best if we could keep an eye on you, young man, until we can be sure there are no after effects.' Getting no response from the patient, he turned to Roddy to ask how it had happened and where they were employed. After learning that they came from The Sycamores, he said, 'I do not know your employer but I am sure that he will understand the position.'

'It was the cook tell't me to tak' him here,' Roddy managed to get out.

The pharmacist walked round behind the counter again. 'Right, then, um . . .'

'Roddy,' supplied the boy.

'Good. You can go back to The Sycamores now, Roddy, and let the Superintendent know that we are keeping your friend here until tomorrow.'

A distant memory returned to Henry. 'Janet said to send the bill to him.'

'Fay will attend to that later.'

After making sure that Roddy had turned the gig round safely and was on his way again, the chemist said, 'We had better introduce ourselves. My name is Joseph Leslie and this is my daughter, Fay.'

'I'm Henry Rae.' The effort of talking was beginning to tell on him, however, so he sagged back, utterly drained.

'Fay, my dear, take Henry up to the sitting room and make him a bed on the couch. I think he will be quite comfortable there for one night.'

The stairs to the upper storey were steep and he was forced to lean quite heavily on the girl as they negotiated the bend on the top landing. 'I'm far too heavy for you,' he whispered. 'Sorry.'

'No, no,' she smiled, tightening her hold on his waist. 'I'm as fit as a fiddle. Father says I should have been a boy.'

It did not take long for her to settle him down with a pillow under his head and a large eiderdown to cover him and, in no time, he had fallen asleep.

When he awoke some time later, a middle-aged woman was knitting in a chair nearby and he lay without moving, studying her and deciding that she must be the pharmacist's wife. Her hair was just a shade lighter than her daughter's gold, the shape of her head and the way she was holding it were exactly the same as Fay's . . .

Something alerted her to his scrutiny and she looked up at him. 'Ah, so you have come back to the land of the living, have you?' She put her knitting into the sewing stool at the side of her chair. 'How do you feel now?'

He sat up a little. 'Better, I think. I'm ashamed of being so weak.'

'You have no need to be. Joseph said you had lost a great deal of blood. Is your hand still very painful?'

'It is a bit but I could easily have gone back with Roddy.'

'In the gig? No, no, you were certainly not fit for that. But now that you are sitting up and taking notice, will you be all right on your own while I prepare supper?'

'Yes, thank you.' He was quite glad to relax when she went out and closed his eyes to go over what had happened. He couldn't remember much about what had been done to his hand – all he could think of was the girl's beautiful face.

After some deliberation, he decided that she wasn't one of those raving beauties he'd seen in books and magazines, who wouldn't have lowered themselves to speak to anybody like him, but she had been kind and quite concerned. She had actually held his uninjured hand, clasped him against her until they climbed the stairs, had spoken to him sympathetically, had looked at him as if she actually liked him.

Her fair, golden hair was loosely curled, swinging round her shell-like ears and swan-like neck. He gave a rueful giggle. He couldn't think of anything original – every writer and poet compared girls' ears to shells and their necks to swans – but it was the only way to describe her. Her face was a sweet oval shape, with definite bones above rose-pink cheeks, one with a dimple, and a darling, darling mouth. Her father had said she should have been a boy? Thank God she wasn't!

He had drifted off again into a light doze when the rattle of dishes made him jump.

'Oh, I'm sorry.' It was Fay. 'Did I wake you? Mother asked me to take you some of her broth and there's beef stew and dumplings to follow.' She laid the tray down on the davenport and crossed over to him. 'Here, let me help you to sit up.'

He had believed that he was quite able to sit up by himself, but he did need her support, her arms under his, her face so close that her breath fanned his cheeks. If this was heaven, he wouldn't be afraid to die. Then she laid the tray across his legs, packed the pillows behind his back and made sure that he was coping before she left him.

After supper, he was joined by Mr Leslie. 'The ladies are washing up, so I hope you don't mind my company?'

'I'm glad of the chance to thank you for what you did,' Henry said earnestly if rather weakly. 'If it hadn't been for you, I could have died.'

The man's expression sobered. 'Yes, I am afraid you are quite right. You should really have been in a hospital or gone to the doctor but I did what I could and, apparently, it was enough. Now, would you like to tell me a little about yourself if you do not think I am being too inquisitive?'

'Not at all.' Recognising that a man has to be careful about the people he brings into his house, Henry gave him a brief outline of his life until the ladies came in and the conversation broadened.

'I usually have my last pipe outside so that the smoke will not bother the ladies,' Mr Leslie observed as he stood up at nine thirty. Then, taking a small hand-bell from a drawer in the beautiful mahogany davenport, he handed it to Henry, 'I will not bother you again but do not hesitate to ring this if you need me in the night.'

In another fifteen minutes, Fay and her mother had also left and he was alone with his thoughts. All his reflections led him to the same conclusion. Despite having almost sliced his thumb off with a scythe (he had hardly felt it at the time – the pain came later), the prolonged loss of blood then the agony of the iodine applications, it was the best day he had ever spent in his life. He would go through it all again if he could have more time with the girl he had met because of it.

Fay Leslie was in a class of her own. She had softness about her yet she had an air of superiority – although she hadn't made him feel in the least *in*-ferior, quite the opposite. She had been warm and friendly, sympathetic while she attended to him and worried about leaving him on his own all night. Even after he assured her that he would be fine, she had been reluctant to go. She was a girl in a million, a girl who clearly had brains as well as beauty, a girl he would be happy to have as his . . . wife?

He heaved a great sigh at this point. *He* would certainly be happy, more than happy, but would she? It was an impossible dream. Even if Fay did respond to his feelings, a man with no real trade or profession wouldn't be her father's choice of son-in-law. The chemist would want his daughter to marry some-body who came of a well-to-do family, who could keep the girl in the manner to which she was accustomed, as the saying went, or in an even better manner, so what chance would an odd-job boy have?

Henry changed position now but it was some time before he fell asleep, a deep sleep of reaction to what he had gone through. Only about an hour later, he woke up drenched in sweat, pain shooting up his whole arm. Determined not to ring for help, he gritted his teeth and braced himself to bear it, thole it, as his Gramma would have said, but the pain only intensified. Not only that, he was sweating like a stuck pig.

Of course, he reassured himself, he was bound to get some discomfort; the cut could hardly have been worse. It wasn't just discomfort, though. He tried to lift the affected left arm and found he couldn't move it. He was being slowly paralysed yet he could feel the blood pounding in his head, louder and louder until he was almost screaming.

It had been an eventful day and Fay was far too emotional to sleep. She had never before met anyone like Henry, a working-class boy who was softly spoken and well mannered. She had to admit that she didn't know many young men of any class, except the sons of her father's friends and they were either too stuck up to talk to her or they flirted outrageously if they had the chance. Most of those who came into the shop were rough in their speech as well as their dress and lacked respect when they spoke to her. The majority of them, give them their due, did pretend that they had come to purchase a cake of soap or something equally innocuous but a few asked boldly for 'ointment to cure the pox' or other even more indelicate items and it was she who was the embarrassed one.

She had been asked out a few times since she turned sixteen and had accepted one invitation because her father had been away on business. The young man, tall and handsome, had taken her for a walk and she had been somewhat disappointed, if the truth were told, that he said or did nothing out of place which was why she had agreed to meet him again – and again. By the end of that third evening, she had seen through him. His bland compliments, the 'accidental' brushing against her bosom with his large rough hands told her that he was an accomplished ladies' man. The final straw had come on the return walk to the village. She had expected him to kiss her but he tried to go much further than that and she had to fight against him fiercely to get free. It hadn't been funny at the time but she could laugh at it now.

Her thoughts returned to their guest for the night. Was he having a peaceful sleep – or was he in too much pain? He had not rung the little bell – or maybe she hadn't heard it? Feeling a tightening in her chest, her stomach turned over in apprehension, sure that all was not well with him. She had to find out but she couldn't possibly go through to him – especially not in her nightdress.

She lay for a few more minutes but the urge to go to his aid was too strong and she swung her feet out of bed and into her slippers. Then, pulling on her wrap, she stepped quietly out of her room. She had meant to go directly to the boy but decorum prevailed and she tapped on her parents' door first.

Her father did not laugh at her fears as she had been rather afraid he might but lit the cruisie lamp at his bedside, threw on his dressing-robe and led the way along to the sitting room. Even in the dim flickering light, she could see the beads of perspiration rolling down Henry's face and neck and she held up the small lamp willingly so that her father could examine him.

'Abby! Abby!' Henry moaned suddenly.

'He is raving with the fever,' Joseph whispered. 'We must get his temperature down as quickly as possible. Ask your mother to bring us a bowl of cold water and a piece of flannel and you can bathe his body while I loosen the bandaging. Infection must have set in after all and, if we do not arrest it, the poison will travel all the way up his arm and straight to his heart.'

When his wife came through with the requested articles, she took one look at their patient and whispered, 'It's touch and go, isn't it?'

Joseph nodded. 'Get the fire going in the kitchen as quickly as you can, Catherine, and, while you wait for the kettle to boil, look out an old pillowcase or something that will be stronger than these flimsy bandages. Then make a bread poultice with the boiling water and try not to let it cool. We will have to keep applying poultices until . . .' He pointed to the angry crimson line that stretched from the swollen cut almost to the youth's shoulder, 'Until we get rid of that.'

'Abby! Where's . . . Abby?' For a few seconds, Henry thrashed about but he calmed down when Fay started tenderly sponging his face and neck and a little way down his chest, drawing back when she encountered a layer of curly hair. She felt her pulses quicken at this. She had once seen her father with his shirt and linder off and he had only had a few straggly hairs on his chest. Did this thatch mean that Henry was more of a man, more virile, than her father?

The thought was swept aside when Henry opened his eyes. He looked around him, quite alarmed at seeing the man and the girl, two strangers, hovering over him and a woman looking over the girl's shoulder.

'It is all right, my boy,' Joseph soothed. 'You had an accident and the wound festered but we will soon have you as right as rain.'

Wringing out the flannel in the cold water again, Fay mopped his brow, smiling when his eyes turned to her inquisitively. 'I'm Fay, remember?'

A trace of recognition flickered but, in a moment, the eyes took on a new haunted look. 'Abby?' he muttered. 'Where's Abby?'

Hoping to soothe him, Fay murmured, 'Abby will be here shortly.'

That seemed to ease his mind and he lay still once more, although he did wince when Joseph applied another skin-blistering hot poultice.

Fay's fears lessened. The dangerous line on his arm had fallen back and what there was of it was not nearly so red. The fever was abating – he was on the road to recovery.

Instead of the extreme happiness she should have felt when her father announced that their patient was out of danger, she was dismayed to find herself wishing that he would not recover properly, that he would never have to return to The Sycamores, that he could stay with her for ever and ever. For the few hours that were left of the night, she wove dreams of them courting, marrying, having children.

A single thought drove her abruptly back to reality. Who was the Abby he had called for in his delirium? He must be really fond of her – maybe even loved her? Disconcerted, Fay made up her mind to forget Henry Rae when he left. There was no earthly reason why they should ever meet again. No reason whatsoever. Was there?

*   *   *

Henry was still quite weak when Catherine Leslie dropped him off at The Sycamores and Janet managed to persuade Innes Ledingham to let him go home for a week or so to recover properly. 'He won't be able to do much here anyway,' she went on, to stress her point.

Not altogether happy about this, the Superintendent instructed young Roddy to take Henry to Corrieben Halt, where he would get a train to take him to Ardbirtle. The 'invalid' did not argue about being given time off work. He knew perfectly well that he was no use to man or beast at the moment, as farmers might put it, and it would be good to see his sister again. He had neglected her shamefully.

With only two trains per day stopping at Ardbirtle, it was early evening before he arrived at Abby's house.

'Oh, Lordy, Henry, what a fleg you gave me,' she exclaimed, when he walked in without knocking. Then the shock in her eyes changed to concern. 'Why's your arm in a sling? What happened? Are you all right? You're awful white!'

'I cut my hand wi' a scythe,' he explained, sitting down as the weakness took a greater toll on him. He'd only had a short walk from the station but it had sapped what little strength he had. 'I havena to go back till a week on Sunday.' Noticing that his sister was looking embarrassed now, he added, ' If that's all right wi' you?'

'It's fine, Henry. It's just . . . ach, what does it matter? I'd better tell you.'

'Aye?' he urged, sensing that she was unwilling to come out with it.

She took a deep breath. 'Well, you see, me and Pogie have been . . . he's been coming here when he finishes his work every night . . .'

'You and Pogie Laing?' Henry's tone disclosed what he felt about this liaison. 'Don't say you're taking up wi' *him*, Abby? You're not . . . *sleeping* wi' him?'

'No, no!' She was as appalled by this idea as her brother was. 'He just comes for his supper, then we sometimes go for a walk if it's fine but sometimes . . . we bide in . . . just speaking.'

'Just speaking? Is that it?'

'Some kissing and hugging but nothing else. Honest, Henry, I wouldn't let him do one thing he shouldn't.'

'I would hope no'! The thing is, though, maybe he'll nae aye stop when you tell him. Once a man's body gets fired up . . .'

'Oh, Henry, what do you ken aboot it? You surely haven't . . .'

'No, I haven't, but Janet once tell't me.'

'Janet? How did she come to be telling you that kind o' thing?'

'It was when we were at Craigdownie and the other lads were tormenting me and I didna ken what they meant so I asked her.'

'Oh.' After considering this and apparently being satisfied that he was telling the truth, she said, shyly, 'I think Pogie's near ready to ask me for his wife.'

'Is that what you want?

'It is, Henry,' she whispered, face flaming. 'He's maybe not the best catch in the world but him and me get on just fine.'

Henry could hardly believe that a girl as attractive as Abby would want to tie herself to a man as unattractive as the Pogie Laing he remembered. His teeth were too big for his mouth, sticking out so his lips couldn't meet. His head was too big for his body, though it must be more than half-empty, for he hadn't much of a brain. Not only that, he had always been a smarmy king of lad, a 'creeping Jesus', Gramma used to describe him and he'd picked the right job. A funeral undertaker's assistant! Still, if he was what Abby wanted . . .

'Well, I hope things work out for you.'

'They will, Henry. I'm sure they will'

By the end of his short stay, Henry, too, was sure of it. Pogie Laing was much more presentable than he used to be, his face seemed to have grown to contain his teeth, although it remained to be seen if his brain had grown to fill his head. He had never been a great talker but it was quite evident how he felt about Abby. His eyes followed her with a dog-like devotion, he helped her to set the table, to dry the dishes after the meal and lay them away. He even brought in coal and chopped sticks – all the chores of a married man without any of the benefits, Henry mused in bed on his last night there. Abby could do an awful lot worse.

What about himself, though? His heart was set on Fay Leslie but he wasn't good enough for her. It would probably be better all round if he left things as they were. He would only make a fool of himself if he told her how he felt.

In the morning, a blushing Abby said, shyly, 'Pogie asked me last night.'

Not understanding, her brother asked something he had wondered about for years.

'Why do they cry him Pogie? What's his real name?'

'He was baptised Clarence but when he was a wee laddie and his Granda took his pipe off the mantelpiece, he used to hand him the packet of Bogie Roll and shout, "Pogie, Ga-da?" And the name just stuck.'

Henry couldn't help laughing at this. 'I suppose Pogie suits him a lot better than Clarence. Now, what were you saying about last night?'

'He asked me to marry him . . . and I said yes.'

'Oh . . . well . . . ach, I'm pleased for you, Abby. He's changed a lot since I mind on him and he thinks the world o' you.'

'I think the world o' him and all. I want to tell you something else, Henry.'

'Go on, then, for I'll need to be leaving in a wee while.'

'We're not having a big wedding but . . . I'm going to ask Father and Nessie.' His frown made her carry on before he could say anything. 'Pogie's got his father and mother and two brothers and three sisters and I've only Father and you . . . and Nessie.'

'There's Jeannie and Bella and Kitty,' he reminded her.

'They canna afford to come and, if I write and invite them, they'll think I want them to send a present. You'll come, though, Henry?'

'Have you set the date?'

'Not yet but I'll let you ken.'

'I'd like fine to come but . . . Father and Nessie . . .'

'They've mellowed. They visit me at least once a fortnight. Nessie sometimes comes on her own and asks how I'm managing. She's offered me money more than once, though I never take it. So, will you come, Henry?'

Not wanting to spoil his sister's happiness, he smiled, 'I'll do my best.'

Back at The Sycamores, Henry was excused from all heavy work for another week, but he soon grew worried by Janet's obvious unease whenever the Superintendent was around. It was a few days, however, before he got the chance to ask her what was worrying her. At first, she denied that anything was wrong, but he said, 'Do you not trust me enough to tell me? I thought we were closer than that.'

She gave in. 'It's Innes.'

'I thought it might be. Has he taken up wi' somebody else?'

'Just the opposite. You see, he's been trying for ages to get me to sleep with him and, when I kept refusing, he said he would marry me if it wasn't for the two obstacles.'

Henry nodded. 'Your mother and his wife?'

'Exactly. Well, Ma passed away just days after that . . . and now . . .'

'I suppose he's saying his wife's going to divorce him?'

'Worse than that, Henry. He says she's died and all.'

'You think it's a lie . . . to get you to . . . ?'

'I hardly like to think that.'

'If it's true, would you marry him?'

'If I was sure it was true, I would.'

'Janet, a man in his position wouldna tell lies. I'm sure you're worrying over nothing. If he does offer marriage, jump at it. You deserve to be happy.'

She patted his shoulder. 'Thank you, Henry. You've made me feel a lot better. What about you, though? Have you found yourself a lass?'

'I've found somebody I'd like to be my lass but that'll never happen.'

Intrigued, Janet persisted, 'Is she anybody I know?'

'It's Fay Leslie.'

'The druggist's lassie? Why can it never happen?'

84

'She would never look at the likes o' me.'

'That's daft, Henry, and you'll never find out unless you go and ask her.'

'You think I should?'

'Of course you should!'

Janet's encouragement being all he needed, Henry set off on foot for Drymill the following Sunday just after eleven o'clock. It wasn't much more than three miles so he didn't need to borrow the old bicycle that Max had bought at a roup a few months before. Besides, why should he tell Max where he was going? Max never told him.

Arms swinging, heart beating just that tiny bit faster at the thought of seeing Fay again, he stepped out confidently once he was on the road. The time and the distance passed quickly as he planned what to say, his thoughts interrupted every now and then by the sight of a pheasant crossing a field, with her wee chicks trailing behind her, or a rabbit scuttling to reach his burrow or a flock of starlings darkening the sky as they flew south for the winter.

The coldness of the bright October morning did not bother him – his steady pace kept him warm – and it wasn't until he came to the first house in the village that the doubts began and the impetus left him. Should he carry on? This journey was a complete waste of time. How could he expect a girl like Fay, middle class, well educated – she had likely gone to one of the academies – to consider him as a suitor? Of course, being the girl she was, she would try not to hurt his feelings. She would turn him down as gently as she could but it would still be painful.

He had slowed down and almost abandoned his mission before reaching the chemist's shop but something made him keep moving . . . straight on, past his intended target. He wasn't quite ready yet. He needed some more time to prepare himself.

Fay had been tidying up the little storeroom behind the shop, the place where her father did his dispensing; where she made up the pills the patients needed and put them in little round, labelled boxes; where the powders – sleeping, laxative and other kinds – were placed on squares of paper and folded in a special way to stop spillage. Her parents had gone to church and it was her turn to stay behind in case someone needed something – only medications prescribed by the doctor, of course. It was against the law to sell anything else on a Sunday.

Every shelf and bottle as neat as she could make it, she went into the shop itself to see the time. Quarter past twelve. It was difficult to know exactly when her parents would be home because the minister had a habit of not bringing his sermon to an end until folk were beginning to fidget in their seats. Furthermore, they usually stopped to speak to friends – being the chemist, her father was known to every family in Drymill and miles around.

Hearing footsteps, she looked up expecting to see her father and mother outside but it wasn't them. It was a young man who reminded her of . . . it *was* Henry Rae and he had walked straight past. Not taking time to wonder why he hadn't come in to see her, Fay raced out to call him back. 'Henry! Henry!'

He turned uncertainly, even reluctantly, she thought, wishing that she had just let him go wherever he was going but his slight frown disappeared into a broad beam of sheer delight as he ran towards her. 'Henry,' she murmured, her throat constricting, her cheeks on fire, her heart thumping a merry tattoo.

Caught up in emotions too strong to deny, she ran into his open arms and was swung off the ground in his exuberant hug. Little they knew, or cared, that the church had disgorged its congregation and that dozens of people, her parents included, were witness to their show of love.

Their euphoria was not to last. In just a few seconds, Joseph Leslie was hauling his daughter away and pushing her through the shop door, waiting until they were inside before he gave vent to his feelings. 'What do you think you were doing?' he roared. 'Not only were you making a fool of yourself, you were making a fool of me. What must people think of me for not teaching my daughter what is decent and what is indecent behaviour? I have never, ever, seen such a disgraceful show . . .'

'I think you have gone far enough, Joseph.' His wife had brought the shaken Henry in with her. 'They were doing nothing indecent, as well you know, and everyone was smiling, not criticising. Just the same,' she continued, addressing the two young people, 'it is not exactly seemly to hug in the street.'

'I'm sorry, Mrs Leslie.' Henry's face was burning now with embarrassment at what he had done and the disgrace of it but also with the heat of the passion which had swept through him when he was holding the girl of his dreams in his arms. 'I didn't mean any harm, it was . . . I thought Fay wouldn't want to have anything to do with an odd-job man and, when I realised that she felt the same as I did, I . . . didn't think.'

Fay, who had been reduced to tears by her father's verbal assault, now plucked up courage to say, 'It wasn't all your fault, Henry. I was just as much to blame.'

Taking note that boy and girl were holding hands, Catherine Leslie looked sternly at her husband. 'Have you forgotten how it feels to be young and in love? There were times when you couldn't wait and you kissed me wherever we were.'

'Certainly not if anyone could see us,' he retorted but his tone was less harsh.

'I didn't notice anybody there.' Henry was almost wishing that he had not been so impulsive. It should have been a private moment, not a peep show for all and sundry.

Catherine's smile was wide. 'I think we should draw a curtain over the incident, Joseph. It was certainly not planned. Now, Henry, you will stay for some dinner? Then you and Fay can go for a walk and talk things over.'

Later, alone with her still brooding husband, Catherine asked him why he was so against Henry. 'I thought you liked him. He is a decent boy, hard-working . . .'

'I did like him but liking is one thing, having him courting my daughter is an entirely different matter. Hard working, you said? An odd-job man in an asylum? What kind of work is that? How can he hope to provide for a wife and family on what he earns?'

'I should not imagine that he will be an odd-job man for ever. As a married man, he will have ambitions but, even if he does not, I am sure that Fay would not mind being an odd-job man's wife. Love is all-powerful.'

'Love is blind!' he sneered.

'Yes, Joseph, that is true, too. I have not exactly been happy to have my only daughter coming in contact with men and women who were perhaps carrying all sorts of diseases but I knew that you loved your work and I loved you so I said nothing.'

'You have not been happy here?' Joseph sounded incredulous. 'I had no idea.'

'I got over it. I have been happy with you, Joseph, though I must say it would be nice if you showed me a little more affection.'

'Ah, Catherine, I am sorry. I was never one for displaying my feelings but I do care for you. I do . . . love you.'

'I know, really, but it needs to be said occasionally, don't you see?'

'Indeed I do . . . but to get back to the present problem. You are not honestly suggesting that I accept Henry Rae as a suitable husband for Fay?'

She grinned at his serious face. 'Yes, I *am* honestly suggesting that. They love each other and that is all that matters.'

'Love conquers all?'

'Yes, it can if they work at it.'

Fay had almost as much of a problem in making Henry understand that she loved him and didn't mind what he worked at or where.

'But your father won't agree to our marrying,' he said sorrowfully, 'and I wouldn't blame him. I would want better for my daughter if I had one.'

'We will have one,' she beamed, her kiss making him ache to marry her as soon as it was possible. 'More than one and sons and . . . oh, Henry, isn't it wonderful?'

Not so sure that marriage would ever be an option, he gave

a valiant smile. 'It couldn't be more wonderful, my darling.'

When they returned to the shop, Catherine said brightly, 'I expect you have something to ask Fay's father, Henry?'

This aspect not having been discussed, the youth hesitated, but the girl's prod made him burst out, 'Yes, I have. Mr Leslie, will you give me your permission to court your daughter . . . with a view to marriage?'

Again a little hesitation, again a little prod, before Joseph muttered, 'I have been talked into this and I am still doubtful about the wisdom of it but I give my permission for you to court Fay. Just remember, if you let her down, you will have to answer to me.'

'I won't let her down, Mr Leslie, I promise.'

On his long walk back to The Sycamores, Henry went over everything that had happened that day. Fate had made Fay notice him going past because he didn't believe, even now, that he would have had the courage to go into the shop to see her. An even kinder Fate had let him know that she felt as deeply for him as he did for her but they were not out of the woods yet.

Joseph Leslie had given his permission to the courtship but had avoided any mention of marriage. He was likely hoping that Fay would tire of the relationship and bring it to an end before it got as far as marriage. If that was the case, Henry thought grimly, he was going to be sorely disappointed.

CHAPTER SEVEN

After walking out with Fay once a week for over a month, Henry still hesitated about giving her any hint of how deeply he felt about her. For one thing, he suspected that her father was anything but happy about the courtship. No doubt Joseph Leslie had anticipated having a son-in-law he'd be proud to present to his friends – tall, handsome and, most importantly, with a business of some kind at his back, a man who could provide a home even better than the one she would be leaving. A short, scruffy odd-job lad like himself could never hope to equal, never mind better, the house over the pharmacist's shop.

This feeling of uncertainty and inadequacy wasn't all that held Henry back. It wasn't that he didn't love Fay – he worshipped the very ground she walked on – but he was afraid that he could have inherited his father's outrageous needs. He was determined not to cut *his* wife's life short like his mother's had been but would he be able to withstand the temptations of the marriage bed?

On returning from Drymill one night, he relived the thrill of just being with Fay and having his arm round her slender waist. He had tried this for the first time that very evening and she hadn't objected. The thing was, he reflected sadly, he had better not go any further than that. It would be so easy to lose his head altogether, which would put a full stop to their relationship.

His workmates, of course, teased him about his lass and Max was desperate to meet her but he meant to prevent that at all costs. He wasn't going to run the risk of her falling for his friend who had much more charm than he had. None of the lassies at The Sycamores had ever turned Max down –

they even seemed content to share him for he made no secret of the fact that he didn't stick to one.

Not for the first time in his life, Henry felt a flicker of jealousy at his friend's good looks. Apart from standing six feet two in his socks, he had a slim, yet muscular, body, his skin was healthily tanned from working out of doors, his fair curly hair had been bleached by the sun and his eyes, a piercing blue, always had the glint of mischief with a hint of passion lurking within. There was no comparison between the two of them, the dejected Henry concluded. His own mousy hair was dead straight, with a bit sticking up at the back no matter how much he brushed it or dowsed it with water – a cow's lick, his Gramma had called it. His fair skin didn't tan so his face was as red as . . . a turkey cock. He was too short and, although not really fat, he was undeniably chubby. The minute Fay set eyes on Max, she would be lost.

There were other times, thankfully, when Henry laughed off his fears, when he was sure that Fay wasn't the kind to jump from one lad to another, that she at least liked him, which was a good foundation, a solid foundation, for a courtship.

The two youths were taking a stroll one frosty night in November, before going to bed, when Max said, 'I can tell you're serious about your lass but you never tell me any of the . . . you ken . . . the juicy bits.'

Annoyance at what he took as a gross indelicacy passed over Henry's face. 'There's no juicy bits to tell.'

Max's eyes widened in disbelief. 'Dinna try to tell me that! How d'you feel when you kiss her? Does she kiss you back? Does she?'

'I havena kissed her.'

Screwing up his nose now, Max gasped, 'Govey Dick, man, what d'you do when you're out wi' her?'

'I put my arm round her waist a couple o' weeks back and . . .'

'You mean it took you a' this time to put your arm round her waist?'

'I'm not like you, Max. I respect her, you see.'

'You'd best hurry up and let her see you mean business, then, or some other lad'll turn her head and you'll end up losing her.'

In bed, Henry gave this statement deep consideration and came to the conclusion that Max was right. Whatever sacrifices he had to make in the future to avoid filling her belly, he would have to court her properly and let her know that he was serious. He would have to ask her to marry him as soon as he could – next time he saw her.

During the two days he had to wait, Henry's courage ebbed and flowed several times but, fortunately for him, when Fay came out in answer to his knock, it was at its peak. He slid his arm round her waist in just a few minutes and once they were clear of the houses, he pulled her towards him. 'I've something to ask you, Fay,' he began, his wavering voice gaining strength as he went on, 'and I'd thank you not to say anything till I've finished.'

Her trusting eyes were almost his undoing but he carried on after a brief hesitation. 'We've only been going out for a few weeks, but . . . well . . .' He stopped to clear his throat. 'What I'm saying . . . what I mean . . . you'll likely think I'm too forward but . . . it's like this . . .'

She laid her finger over his lips. 'I know what you're trying to say, Henry, and I know you're scared to come out with it but I'd really like to hear it. Would it help if I told you that I love you, too?'

With a strangulated moan, he held her tightly and kissed her soft, sweet lips as he gathered the strength to utter the words she wanted to hear. Then, letting her head rest on his shoulder, for she scarcely topped five feet, he murmured, 'Aye, I love you and all, Fay Leslie, and I want to wed you but . . .'

She lifted her head to look at him. 'No buts, Henry. If you want to marry me, ask me properly. Ask me now!'

'Dearest Fay,' he whispered, his lips against her cheek, 'will you . . . do me the . . . honour of becoming my wife?'

'My darling, darling boy,' she said softly, but triumphantly, 'it was easy, wasn't it?' She gave his ear a teasing nibble. 'And the answer is yes so there *are* no buts.'

'But there *is* a but. What will your father say? I've nothing to offer you . . .'

'All I want is you,' she breathed, her kiss proving the truth of it.

'What about your father?'

'It might be better if you ask him but we are both over sixteen and we don't need parental permission – not as the law stands.'

When Henry returned to The Sycamores, Max took one look at his smug expression and burst out laughing. 'You sly dog! You've done it, haven't you? You've actually gone and done it?'

Henry couldn't help puffing out his chest. 'I have that.'

'Tell me, then! What happened? How does it feel? Is it as good as they all make out? Did she just let you do it without trying to stop you?'

Gradually realising that they were talking at cross-purposes, Henry blushed a deep crimson. 'I didn't do what you're meaning . . . I wouldn't do anything like that to her . . . I just . . . asked her to marry me . . . and she said yes.'

'Och, you!' Disappointment oozing from every pore, Max shook his head as if despairing at his friend's lack of backbone. 'Well, you've done it now, lad, and there's no going back.'

'I wouldn't want to go back,' Henry said spiritedly. 'We love each other and it won't matter what her father says or . . .' He paused, then added pensively, 'So you don't know what it's like? You that spins stories about what the lassies say and do and . . .' Throwing back his head, he roared with laughter. 'The great Max Dalgarno, lover of more than half-a-dozen . . . or so he says . . . and he's never done it once.'

Max did have the grace to look shamefaced. 'It was them tormenting me, the other lads . . . you ken. I couldna let them think I was . . . scared to touch a lassie . . .'

Henry could scarcely believe this. 'Scared? You? The things you said . . . Were you never even tempted?'

'If there had been a lass I really fancied, I suppose I'd have been tempted but . . . well, it was all just a bit o' fun, just kittlin' an' larkin about.' Max turned his powerful blue eyes on his friend in appeal. 'You'll not tell?'

Feeling that he had the upper hand for once, Henry smiled beatifically. 'I'll not tell . . . if you stop asking things you've no business asking.'

'You're right, Henry. It was none o' my business and I'll not tease you again. I'm pleased for you, honest I am, and I hope everything works out for you.'

Joseph Leslie, however, was not pleased. The apprehensive, white-faced Henry had hardly finished speaking when he burst out, 'Marry Fay? Has the madness in that place rubbed off on you or were you born an idiot? What made you think I would agree to my daughter marrying a . . . a . . . how old are you, boy?'

'Newly seventeen.' It was said through chattering teeth.

'A seventeen-year-old who does not have a decent job or a home to take her to! Or were you intending to make her share your bed at the asylum?'

'That will do, Joseph.' His wife laid a restraining hand on his sleeve. 'Nothing will be gained by ranting and raving. Listen to the boy before you say anything else. Surely you can see that he loves our Fay.'

'Yes, Mr Leslie,' Henry said quietly, faltering a little as he turned his head again and met the force of the man's venomous eyes. 'I love Fay as I could never love any other girl and she says she loves me so it's useless to try to split us up. We're both old enough to marry without your permission but I would have liked, for her sake, if you'd been more . . . amenable to the idea.'

'More amenable?' Joseph roared. 'You insolent young . . .'

Fay, having stood all she could, now butted in. 'We *do* love each other, Father, and nothing you say will make us change our minds. We shall marry with or without your blessing and even if Henry does expect me to share his bed at The Sycamores

– something we have not yet had time to discuss – I would willingly do so. In fact,' she added hastily, as the man was clearly building up to another explosion, 'I am even prepared to go with him right now and share his bed, married or not! So there!'

Clearly shocked by this, her mother endeavoured to stay calm. 'There is no need for that, Fay, dear. You are at liberty to live here for as long as . . . Your father and I need time to come to terms with this and Henry needs time to plan what he has to do.' She smiled kindly at the boy. 'I get the impression that you have given no thought to the material things in life. You will have to provide a proper home for a wife, money to buy food and clothes for yourselves . . . and for the children you will no doubt produce.'

Henry nodded wretchedly. 'Yes, you're quite right, Mrs Leslie. I haven't thought it out but, as long as I know Fay is willing to wait, I'll do my utmost to find a better job so I can give her everything she needs.'

'I was sure you would see sense so we have no objection to you carrying on seeing Fay but I must warn you . . .' Catherine halted, turning a delicate shade of pink. 'There must be no . . . intimacy, no "accidents" . . . do you understand me?'

His own face deepening to puce, Henry muttered, 'I understand and I can assure you there'll be nothing like that. I respect Fay far too much to shame her.'

'I am glad to hear it and I am quite sure that I can depend on you to keep your word. Now, I think you should go so that my husband and I can discuss the matter.'

'Yes, of course.' On his way to the door, Henry turned and said, 'I'm truly sorry to have caused you so much distress, Mr Leslie, but I do love Fay.'

The girl pulled him outside and they walked a few yards from the doorway before he moaned, 'I knew it wouldn't be any use. I knew your father didn't like me.'

'He does like you. It's the fact that you have no prospects that he doesn't like but I don't mind what you work at. I meant it when I said I'd marry you tomorrow and share your room at The

Sycamores, you know, and I will if the worst comes to the worst.'

'I couldn't let you do that. I'm sorry, Fay, my dearest, I didn't think things through but I'll find a better job, with a house along with it, I promise.'

She pulled him to a stop to kiss him and, after a few minutes, she whispered, breathlessly, 'I'd better go back now . . . before you break your promise to my mother.'

He was ashamed of the passion her kisses had aroused in him which was plainly the reason for her last remark. 'I'm sorry. I'm all . . . at sixes and sevens. Oh, I know that's not really an excuse and I won't let it happen again.'

She stroked his cheek. 'I wouldn't object if you did but it's better that we don't tempt fate, don't you think?'

Max was astonished when he heard what had happened but he relieved Henry's tension by laughing, 'I wouldna mind if you took your lass here. She could share my bed for I'd be glad to do the needful for her if you were feared.'

Despite his bitter disappointment and his chagrin at not having planned ahead, Henry was forced to smile at this . . . and boast. 'If there's any needs on her side, I'll be the one to fulfil them and be damned to her father.'

Janet Emslie had wrestled with her fears for several weeks. As Innes kept telling her, there was nothing to stop them being married now but she still held back. The deaths – first her mother's and then his wife's – bothered her. They were far too convenient to be coincidences – one, perhaps, but not two. Gradually, however, his persistence wore her down. There really were no encumbrances so why shouldn't she grab what would likely be her last chance of happiness?

Innes, naturally, was absolutely delighted, announcing their betrothal at breakfast the day after she had told him of her decision. His thoughts were concentrated now on making arrangements, asking their own chaplain to carry out the ceremony. He also insisted on accompanying her to Aberdeen to buy a wedding gown for her, although she told him it was unlucky for the groom to see it before the wedding.

'Old wives' tales,' he laughed. 'How could it be unlucky when I have waited so many years to make you mine?'

This confession that he had loved her since they were in their teens made her uneasier than ever but the die had been cast. He had invitations printed, giving one to every employee and patient at The Sycamores, with wives or lady friends welcome.

'You must take your girlfriend with you, Henry,' Janet smiled. 'We all want to meet her.'

The wedding day dawned amid grey clouds, which Janet took to be a bad omen, but, even before breakfast was over, the sky had cleared and the sun was sending out rays of comforting heat as well as light. The bride, despite being forbidden to enter the kitchen that day, had gone down to cook breakfast as usual but felt quite embarrassed by the banter round the table, although nothing truly outrageous was said.

Then her groom-to-be ordered her to go to her room and rest until it was time for her to get ready and she was quite glad of the hour she lay down on her bed. Then one of the maids brought up a kettle of hot water for her to wash, asking, rather cheekily, if she wanted a hand to get dressed.

'I've dressed myself for over forty years,' Janet smiled. 'I think I can manage today.'

She managed very well as she discovered an hour or so later. She had gone down the top flight of stairs in the Albert wing, which was mostly occupied by staff – the other wing, for the patients, was called Victoria – and had reached the main wide staircase when there was a burst of applause from the people gathered below and murmurs of, 'Oh, isn't she bonnie?' and, 'She's a perfect picture.'

This gave her flagging spirits a tremendous boost, which intensified when she caught sight of herself in the huge mirror on the middle landing as she went slowly down. She had said she just wanted a nice new dress, nothing fancy, but Innes had chosen, and paid for, a trousseau fit for a society wedding. The deep ivory of the dress, absolutely plain and shaped to make her look slimmer, was lightened by the paler, almost white lace veil, which was embroidered with tiny sprigs of pale pink rosebuds. Instead of the usual tight bun at the nape of her neck, she had fashioned her long hair into an elegant chignon, round which she had pinned a small strip of similarly embroidered lace as a headdress. She wore elbow length gloves, matching the gown, and dainty ivory satin shoes. She not only felt like a queen, she also looked like a queen.

When she was on the last step, Innes stepped forward, handed her a white bible with a small spray of rosebuds the same pink as on her veil, then tucked her arm under his. He, too, was in formal wedding attire – black tailcoat, grey striped trousers and matching top hat. He smiled at the ripple of admiration that went round the assemblage. 'We do make a lovely couple,' he whispered.

The bride and groom led the way to the quaint little chapel behind the house itself. It was the place of worship the original owner of The Sycamores had built for his family. The ceremony itself was fairly short, fairly basic, with Roderick Emslie giving his sister away and the oldest nurse as the other witness. Most of the guests had made some effort to be wedding-like, their best clothes decorated with posies or single flowers – whatever they could find.

Having been pronounced husband and wife and signed the register, Mr and Mrs Innes Ledingham led the party back to the large dining hall which, in its former glory, had once been a ballroom, although there was nothing so grand planned for this occasion. The meal had been prepared beforehand by Janet, who was not allowed to raise a finger while it was being served, and everything passed off without a hitch.

There was no dancing, no real frivolity, but no one seemed to mind. It was enough for the staff that they could circulate through each other, being idle and still being paid for it, and the patients were obviously enjoying watching what was going on – whether they understood that it was a wedding, of course, was debatable. Fay Leslie found herself shaking dozens of hands, although the smile raised by the first, 'It'll be you and

Henry's turn next,' became somewhat fixed after the umpteenth time of hearing it.

Her one big surprise, quite a shock really, had been when Henry introduced his friend. She'd had no idea that the only other boy she had ever gone out with also worked at The Sycamores and she was extremely thankful when he gave no indication that they had met before. His dark eyes had twinkled mischievously each time they met hers for the rest of the afternoon yet, when he managed to speak to her on her own at one point, all he said was, 'Henry's a lucky beggar but he deserves some happiness. He's a right decent lad.'

'I know that.' She allowed Max to envelop her hand in a crushing grip before he moved away.

The bride and groom disappeared to change into travelling clothes and it was just after six o'clock when the well-wishers waved them off in the landau that was to take them to the Crossroads Hotel, a small inn some miles away, where they were to spend a three-day honeymoon. Things fell a little flat after their departure – the maids having to clear up, the nurses having to shepherd their charges back to their rooms and settle them down after all the unaccustomed excitement. The married men went home with their wives and only the bachelors were left, some bemoaning the fact that 'Ledingham was a hungry bugger, nae laying on ony booze'.

An exhausted Fay was quite glad when her father came to collect her in his gig, although he didn't say a word to Henry, merely gave him a curt nod as they drove off.

Catherine Leslie never divulged to her daughter or to her intended son-in-law how she had succeeded in changing her husband's mind about their marriage. It was no one's business that her lord and master, as he certainly must appear in the eyes of the public, could be held to ransom by the words, 'If you do not do as I say, I will tell everyone that you are . . . impotent.'

It had taken a full eighteen months – during which she had hardly ever had one night's peace, had given birth once and had three miscarriages – before salvation came. It had happened gradually, just a sort of winding down, until she realised the truth but, once she found the flaw, she had made good use of it.

Not knowing the reason behind her father's change of heart, Fay was delighted when he told her that he had been over-hasty in his judgement. 'I am now quite *amenable* to the marriage. Furthermore,' he had continued, his chest swelling with pride at his own generosity, 'I have decided to make you a wedding gift of sufficient money to let you buy a house or . . .'

'Or do whatever you want,' Catherine butted in.

'Perhaps Henry could start some kind of business . . . doing whatever he considers himself capable of doing,' Joseph had added, resentment at being so manipulated by his own wife making him unable to keep the sarcasm out of his voice.

Luckily, his daughter was too happy to notice his last few words and, when Henry arrived and was told the good news, great was the jubilation in the house above the pharmacy that night.

It was Max who caused him some aggravation some hours later. 'You'll need to show your birth certificate to the minister, mind,' he told his friend.

'Aye,' Henry nodded. 'I know my Gramma kept all that kind of things and Abby likely still has it somewhere.'

'So you've never seen it yoursel'?'

'I've never needed to see it.'

'Aye, well.'

His euphoria ebbing, Henry wondered what Max was hinting at. Something was behind his remarks, that was certain . . . unless he was just warning him that it might be lost. Without proof of his date of birth and his legitimacy, he might not be allowed to marry Fay at all.

That Sunday, instead of going to Drymill, he asked Max if he could borrow his bicycle and went to Ardbirtle to see his sister. He hadn't seen her since her wedding to Pogie Laing, not quite five months before, and was quite unprepared for what he found. Abby was well on in pregnancy, seven or eight months at least, though he wasn't an expert in judging such matters.

'Aye,' she admitted, her face flaming at the accusation in his eyes, 'I'm in the family way but you needn't look at me like that.'

'You swore to me you hadn't done . . .'

She laughed now. 'So you think it was made before the wedding? No, I said I wouldn't let Pogie touch me and he didn't. I'm just four month gone but I'm as big as a baby elephant.'

Relieved that she hadn't blotted her copybook, Henry teased, 'Maybe you're having twins – or triplets?'

'I hope no'. It'll be bad enough having one, though Nessie says she'll come and help. She's really good to me, Henry, and you got on with her at the wedding, didn't you?'

'Aye, she seemed nice enough and Father was a lot better humoured and all. If that's what married life does for a man, I'm glad I'm joining the club.'

'You? Are you thinking on taking a wife?'

'I am that. It's the druggist's daughter. Mind, I told you how good they were to me when I hurt my thumb?'

'That's a blessing, then, for in-laws can sometimes be a real problem.'

'Her father wasn't too happy about us at first but he came round.' He did not tell her what Joseph Leslie was also doing in case she thought he was boasting. 'Um, Abby, Max says the minister'll need to see my birth certificate afore he can marry us. Would you happen to ken where Gramma kept it?'

'It'll be in the same place as mine was – that old wooden box in the bottom of the dresser. I didn't notice yours but it's bound to be there. We'll have a fly cup first, then I'll look it out for you.'

About fifteen minutes later, Henry watched his sister taking a beautifully polished mahogany box from one of the cupboards in the old pine dresser, its top shelves crammed with bric-a-brac. 'Gramma kept the birth certificates in it and marriages and deaths and any other important papers. Look, here's mine right on top in a blue envelope.'

Abby went through the contents carefully, coming eventually to an identical envelope almost at the bottom. 'This must be it,' she smiled, handing it over.

Henry drew out the old document, unfolding it and smoothing it on the table in front of him. Then he exclaimed, 'This isn't mine! It's for somebody called Tchouki.'

Puzzled, Abby took it from him again. 'Who on earth . . . ? I never heard Gramma speaking about a Tchouki. Maybe she had a baby that died . . .' She drew in a quick breath. 'Oh, no! It *is* yours. Listen to this. Tchouki Henry McIntyre Bruce Rae – Father, William, blacksmith – Mother, Isabella, maiden name McIntyre.'

He practically tore it out of her hand and scanned it in disbelief – but there it was, in black and white, in beautifully formed copperplate handwriting. 'Henry McIntyre was Gramma's man, wasn't he?' he ventured for the sake of something to say.

'That's right. I don't know when he died . . . but his death certificate will likely be in that box as well.'

'It doesn't matter.' Henry mumbled, putting his hand over hers to stop her from standing up to find it.

'I suppose no'. And Bruce was Gramma's name before she married him so that explains that. But Tchouki . . . ?' Abby sighed, her brow crinkling in puzzlement. 'I've never heard the name before but it looks foreign to me.'

Max's warning coming back to him, it dawned on Henry that his friend must know something about the strange name so he folded up the document he wished he had never seen and put it in his jacket pocket. Unfortunately, other people would have to see it if he married the girl he loved.

'Don't worry, Henry,' Abby soothed as if she knew what he was thinking. 'The minister's the only person who needs to know and he wouldn't tell.'

This did nothing to comfort her brother. Max already knew something about it and, if he knew, somebody must have told him and how many somebodies had been told before that? It could have been going on since the day he was born. The whole of Ardbirtle could have been laughing at him for years for all he knew. Too upset to discuss it further, he said, 'I'm going back now, Abby. Tell Pogie I'm sorry I missed him but . . .'

As he had hoped, Abby knew exactly what he was feeling. 'Aye, off you go, but you'll come and tell me if you find out . . .'

She, too, left her sentence unfinished and her brother gave her a quick pat on the shoulder as he went out.

Henry had originally intended making a detour to Drymill on his way back but he could not face Fay and especially not her father until he had sorted things out in his mind, until he had found out exactly who he was.

At The Sycamores, he left the bicycle in the shed where it was kept and made straight for Max's room. Most uncharacteristically, his friend asked no questions of him but he himself wanted to discuss what he had learned. 'Max,' he began, uncertainly, 'do you know the first name on my birth certificate?'

'I know it's not Henry and it's foreign. Russian, she tell't me.'

An icy clamp squeezed Henry's heart. 'She? Who told you?'

'It was a few year back and I gave Mrs Gow a hand to carry the tatties she'd bought off Jemsie Milne's cart, for the road was awful slippy. Well,' he went on quickly, noticing Henry's frown of impatience, 'she took me in for a drop tea to warm me up and we got speaking and, after a wee while, she asked if I was still friends wi' you. I said I hadna seen you for a good while and she said, "That poor laddie. I wonder if he kens." So, of course, I asked what she meant.'

'But what did she tell you?' Henry snapped. 'That's what I want to find out.'

'She said her man – he was the Session Clerk in the kirk, mind? – well, just afore he died, he'd been raving a bit, rambling, and she couldna make sense o' it until she picked up the name Bella McIntyre.'

'That was my mother's single name.' Henry whispered, wondering, with a sinking of his stomach, what she had done to make John Gow speak about her on his deathbed.

103

'Then he'd said he could hardly believe she'd been taking up wi' a Russky and her such a nice lassie. He'd nearly courted her himsel' at one time.'

Every part of him ice cold, even the tips of his toes, Henry swallowed hard. 'Go on. What else did she tell you?'

'It seems Willie Rae had had a good drink in him when he registered your birth and he gave the Russky's name first, then he came back and tried to get it changed. He hadna been wanting folk to ken you werena his, I suppose. But, as Mrs Gow said, it's a crime to change a certificate like that, so her man just added on the other names Willie wanted and naebody ever ken't you were really half Russian.'

'And now it'll all have to come out.' White faced, Henry got to his feet unsteadily.

'Are you all right?' Max enquired, his friend's dazed expression, his sagging body, making him fear for him. 'I think you'd best bide wi' me till you . . . I'm sure Mrs Gow has never said a word to onybody else.'

'I've got to think. I've a lot of thinking to do . . . by myself.'

He was relieved that Max let him go – otherwise he might have broken down in front of him. In his own room, spartan like all the others at The Sycamores, he stretched out on the bed, taking only his boots off because he knew that he wouldn't be able to sleep. As Max had pointed out, he wasn't who he thought he was. Instead of being truly Scottish, he was a crossbreed – and he'd had no idea of it. His father, of course, would never have told him – not when it meant admitting that his wife had been unfaithful to him. God, it must have been awful for him.

Brooding over what the man had gone through at that time, it dawned on Henry that his father had probably not been the cause of his mother's death. She must have been a loose woman, letting all and sundry take her, and maybe she had done away with the other bairns, his half-sisters, so her misdeeds wouldn't come to light. She could even have ended her own life for the same reason. To think he had blamed his father all those years when it was the woman he'd always thought of as an ill-treated saint who had been the villain – villainess? – of the piece.

His mind jumped now to how this news would affect him. As Abby had said, the minister who performed the wedding ceremony would definitely not pass on any information but there were others to consider. What about Joseph Leslie? It would be the perfect lever for him. He would forbid the marriage altogether – even if his wife and daughter could overlook this awful revelation.

Oh, dear God! How could he tell Fay? No, no, he could never tell her – it was too shameful. If Max was to be believed, nobody knew except Mrs Gow and him and it had better stay that way. He had better tell Fay that . . . What? That there would be no wedding? She would want to know why and what could he tell he then? It would break her heart if he said he didn't love her any more and it would tear him apart but it was the only way.

The night hours dragged on into daylight, the three cockerels started their dawn cacophony and Henry Rae rubbed his sleep-drugged eyes and peeled himself off the bed. There were jobs to be done and there were over twelve hours to go before he could drag himself to Drymill to tell Fay.

CHAPTER EIGHT

Even before she returned from her three-day honeymoon, Janet Ledingham was again having doubts about the legality of the marriage – the two barriers had been cleared far too easily. This, in turn, gave rise to renewed suspicions that Innes had been responsible for at least one of the deaths. Her mother had been old and feeble and, although it was so unexpected, it was just possible that she had died from natural causes. His first wife, on the other hand, had been much younger and he had never mentioned her having any sort of illness. Surely he would have suggested something if he had been planning to do away with her?

But how *could* he have done away with her? He had never left The Sycamores for more than a few hours at any time – long enough to go to Aberdeen to carry out whatever business he had there but not long enough to go any farther. Unless . . . ! Had he known where Gloria was all along? If she was living within twenty-five or thirty miles, he could have . . . It was too horrible and totally disloyal, Janet berated herself, to wonder how her husband had accomplished his ex-wife's demise – yet she couldn't put it out of her mind.

Innes had changed, of course, which made it a little more believable. He had been lovingly tender on their wedding night, soothing away what he obviously took to be her fear of the act itself but which was actually fear of what he would find out. He had said nothing then – for some reason, he had waited until the second night before he sneered about her not being a virgin. He clearly hadn't believed her when she swore that there had only been one other man in her life but he would come round, wouldn't he? Everything would come all right, wouldn't it? He wouldn't dare to tell anybody – he wouldn't want anyone to know.

She needed little persuasion to carry on as cook, even knowing that the other employees would think it queer, but it had slowly dawned on her that this had been Innes's plan from the start. As an ordinary employee, she could up-tail and leave at any time to go to a better-paid job or whatever but, as his wife, she was bound hand and foot to The Sycamores. If only she had somebody to confide in. All the women had been really friendly with her before but, since she married the Superintendent, they were cool towards her, probably scared that she would carry tales.

The only real friend she had was Henry Rae, a seventeen-year-old boy who was shortly to be married himself, and she would do anything rather than spoil his happiness.

When she opened the door to him, Fay had wondered why Henry looked so miserable. He had refused to go in to say hello to her parents and just waited for her to put on her coat. He had walked more quickly than usual, making her almost run to keep up, and she knew that something was far wrong.

When they came to the little path into the wood, he turned in and thumped down on the mossy bank, the spot where they did most of their talking. 'What's the matter, Henry?' she asked, taking care to sit a little apart from him for it seemed he didn't want any contact with her. 'I know there's something so you had better tell me. It surely can't be all that bad.'

A low, agonised groan came from him at that. 'Oh, God, Fay, it's worse than you could ever imagine.'

'Don't say that! Tell me now and let me judge for myself.'

He heaved a long sigh. 'I was going to tell you I'd stopped loving you . . . but I can't, I can't. I love you even more than ever – if that's possible – but I can't marry you.'

He chanced a quick glance at her then and was horrified at the pallor of her cheeks. 'I'm sorry, Fay,' he muttered, 'but I can't explain.'

'No, Henry, that's no good. You say you can't marry me

yet you can't tell me why? I'm not letting you off with that.'

He had always known that she was strong-willed and had admired her for it but, at this moment, he wished that she could just accept what he was saying and leave it. 'Fay,' he began, 'you'll hate me for what you're making me say . . . but all right. I'll tell you the truth . . .' He paused, then took the blue envelope from his pocket and laid it on the ground between them. 'Better still, read that.' He sat back and waited while she peered in the gathering gloom trying to make out what was written on the document.

After only a few moments, she whispered, her brow furrowing in perplexity, 'This is *your* birth certificate?'

'Yes, so now you see why . . .'

'I don't understand. Why this funny name? Where did it come from? Who were you named after?'

'My . . . father.' He was too ashamed to look at her.

'But . . . you said your father's name was William.'

'I thought he was my father till I saw that. It seems my mother had been . . . she had me to a Russian she met somewhere or so Max was told.'

'Max? How would Max know about it?' Her tone was accusing.

She was no happier after Henry gave her the details. 'But I still don't understand. If your mother was already dead, why did your father . . . you know who I mean. Why did he give you that name? No one would have found out what your mother had done if he had just called you Henry.'

'Abby says . . .'

'Abby?' Fay had almost forgotten about the girl he had called for in his delirium at the time of his accident.

'My sister. She says Gramma told her Father had really loved our mother so I suppose he'd wanted to carry out her dying wish.'

Relieved that Abby posed no threat to her, Fay shook her head. 'That doesn't ring true. If he loved her, he wouldn't want her name besmirched.'

'Well, I can't explain it any more than that,' Henry mumbled, wretchedly. 'That's what Mrs Gow, the Session Clerk's widow, told Max.'

After a moment's hesitation, Fay said softly, 'Are you sure Max was telling the truth?'

'Why would he tell me a lie?'

'You see, before I knew you, I walked out with him three times . . .'

'You and Max?' To Henry, the situation had grown even worse than before. It was awful to think that Max had . . .

'Why didn't you tell me?'

'I didn't know he worked at The Sycamores. I got a shock when I saw him at Mr Ledingham's wedding.'

'But he didn't say anything either. Why did you only go out with him three times? Did he try to . . . ?

'He got a bit too . . . ardent for my liking so I stopped him and I didn't want to see him again.'

'But you think he bears a grudge at you?'

'I don't know.' She took a deep breath and let it out slowly. 'It doesn't really matter, does it? You would have learned the truth as soon as you saw your birth certificate.'

'True enough.'

'And that was your only reason for saying you can't marry me?'

'Isn't it enough? Maybe you don't care what kind of woman my mother was but, if your father finds out, he'll forbid the wedding anyway.'

'He doesn't need to know, does he?'

'I can't see how to stop him. The minister will have to say my full name . . .'

'Look Henry, we haven't discussed this yet but, if we get married in the church here at Drymill, Mr Barclay's a good friend of mine and . . .'

'And a great friend of your father?'

'To be honest, no, he's not. He's only been here for five years and the minister he replaced was seventy-six when he retired so a lot of people still think Paul Barclay's too young – including my father. What I'm trying to say is, if I ask him not to mention the Russian name during the service, your full name can be entered in the register for you to sign. That means only the two of us and the best man and bridesmaid would see it.'

Fay's voice was rising in excitement. 'You'll naturally want your friend Max and I don't have any close friends so I could have Janet as bridesmaid – matron-of-honour. You wouldn't mind her knowing as well, would you?'

His spirits lifting, Henry said, 'No, I wouldn't mind Janet knowing. Do you really think that would work?'

'Have faith in me, my darling boy.'

He still did not feel altogether happy about it and, while he walked her silently back home, he kept turning it over in his mind. They had almost reached the shop when he burst out, 'No, Fay, I can't do it. It's deceitful to pretend I'm something I'm not and it's not fair to expect your minister to overlook it. I'm going to face up to it and let everybody know the truth.'

'Even my father?'

'Especially your father. How could we expect to be happy if I lived in fear of being found out?'

Fay snuggled against him. 'That's why I love you, Hen . . .' She paused and went on mischievously, 'That's why I love you, Tchouki Rae. You're so honest, I know I can depend on you for the rest of my life.'

'You mean, you'll marry me even if your father . . . ?'

'I mean I'll marry you supposing everybody in Scotland turns against us.'

He gave her a quick hug. 'That's why *I* love *you*, Fay Leslie. You've got a will of your own and you won't let anybody sway you. We'd better go in and face the music.'

As they had both known, the 'music' was loud and discordant as Catherine vainly tried to keep her husband within the realms of reason.

'You little bastard,' Joseph shouted for the umpteenth time, his face so purple that his wife took hold of his sleeve in alarm. 'Let me go, woman! There is no way on God's earth that I will allow that liar to marry my daughter.'

It was Fay who stood up to him. 'He did not tell any lies,

110

Father, and I *am* going to marry him whatever you say . . . or do! Henry, don't go. Wait until I get some things and I'll come with you.'

She took no heed of her father's manic screeching and left Henry standing helplessly as Catherine guided her husband to a seat and slackened his high collar. 'I didn't think he would take it so badly, Mrs Leslie,' he muttered. 'I've tried to tell him he has nothing to worry about. I'll look after Fay, I swear. I'll work my fingers to the bone for her . . .'

'I know you will Henry,' she soothed, 'and I will do all I can to make him see sense. He should realise that he is driving our daughter away for good with his outrageous behaviour.'

When Fay returned a few minutes later, she handed Henry a small Gladstone bag and slipped her hand under his arm. 'I'm sorry it has come to this, Mother,' she said clearly, 'but my life would be intolerable if I stayed here.'

Catherine turned to her husband. 'Are you happy now? Would you spoil Fay's chance of happiness because of your own pride? Well, my fine fellow, two can play at that game.'

'No, Catherine,' he moaned. 'You can't!'

'Yes, Joseph, I can. If you do not climb down from your high-and-mighty ridiculous principles right this minute, I will make sure that you will soon be the laughing stock of Drymill and for miles around.'

Fay's last glimpse of her parents was of them sitting, eyes locked, as if each were trying to force the other to climb down.

It was some minutes after the door closed behind the young couple before Joseph mopped his sweating brow. 'I can see by your face, Catherine,' he said, his voice little more than a whisper, 'that you mean to carry out your threat this time.'

She gave a tight smile. 'The choice is yours. Either you agree to the marriage or I will tell all Drymill the truth about you.'

He took a little time to consider it, then he roared, 'Tell and be damned, then! You'll be as much a laughing-stock as I will. Just think how your friends will talk about you behind your back.'

He had hit on the right note. Although not to the same extent as her husband, Catherine valued her standing in the community and she slumped down against the back of her chair. 'All right,' she mumbled, 'have it your own way but, if Fay invites us to the wedding, I will go and you can please yourself.'

The farther they walked, the more despondent Henry grew. 'This is no good, Fay,' he said at last, pulling her to a halt as they came to the wrought iron gate of The Sycamores. 'I can't take you away from your parents like this. That's not what I meant to happen.'

'You would have cast me off like an old clout,' she retorted, 'but I'm made of stronger stuff than that. I have made the break from my parents and it remains to be seen what will happen here. Come on.'

They walked round the side of the building and went in through the kitchen, Henry intending to smuggle her up to his room and to take her home the following morning. It was hardly nine o'clock, a time when this area was usually deserted, but Janet had come down to turn some meat she was marinating for cooking the following day.

'Oh, my!' she exclaimed. 'You gave me a fright, Henry.' Then, catching sight of the girl behind him, she frowned. 'What's this? Why have you brought Fay here?'

'It's not what it looks like, Janet,' Henry said, flustered. 'Her father won't agree to us getting wed and she . . . walked out.'

'Where did you think she would sleep?' Janet asked, sharply. 'Not with you?'

'I was going to let her have my bed and I'd have slept on the chair.'

Noticing the girl's ashen face, Janet smiled comfortingly. 'Fay, my dear, I'm not putting you out but a young lassie and laddie in the same room . . . ? No matter how good the intentions, the feelings get stirred up . . . and things happen that cast long shadows. I'll tell you what we can do, though. Young Nancy's mother broke her leg this afternoon . . . that's the kitchen maid,' she explained, 'so she'll be off for a wee while. You can get her room if you wouldn't mind. The sheets are clean for I had them changed.'

'Thank you, Janet, I'd be glad to use her room. Can I go now? I'm really tired.'

'Aye, surely, m'dear,' Janet said, her voice full of concern for her. The poor girl looked fit to drop. 'Henry, you can carry her bag and show her where to go but come right back.' She issued no further warning – she was sure she could trust them.

He was back in minutes. 'Thank you, Janet. I think she was worrying about us being in the same room. Her father was awful mad and she's real upset.'

Janet sat down on the other side of the fire. 'I can't understand what he's got against you, Henry. You're a genuine, hard working lad and she couldna find a better man anywhere.'

Henry gave a resigned shrug. 'You may as well know everything for you'll find out soon enough.' He gave her the blue envelope.

The foreign name did come as a surprise to her but she did not castigate the boy as Joseph Leslie had done. She could understand how he felt and did her utmost to cheer him. 'Ach, Henry, laddie, what does it matter if folk know? A nine days' wonder and then it'll be forgotten. In any case, you've done nothing to be ashamed of.'

'It feels like I have,' the boy said despondently. 'I'm sorry you've been roped into my troubles for I think you've got some troubles of your own – though that's none of my business,' he added apologetically.

'It's not,' she nodded, 'but, d'you know, I'd be glad of somebody to tell.'

'I'll be glad to listen,' he assured her.

So the middle-aged woman bared her soul to the youth, telling him first of her suspicions about her husband and then reminiscing about her love as a young girl for Tom Aitken – and, during it all, he said not one word. At last, she dragged her eyes from the barely glowing embers in the range and turned them on him in appeal. 'What do you think, Henry? Is Innes capable of doing what I've been thinking?'

He didn't answer straight away, obviously giving it careful consideration, and then he gave a deep sigh. 'I don't know,

Janet, honest I don't. I once heard somebody say that every one of us is capable of a criminal act, even murder, if circumstances force us into it but . . . I can't say I believe that. Besides, like you said, Mr Ledingham was never away long enough to . . . do anything to his first wife.'

'He could have paid somebody else to kill her. No, I'm being over-sensitive. Innes isn't like that, I'm sure . . . almost sure. It's likely the change that's making me imagine things.'

'What change? The change from being single to being married?'

Janet gave a wry laugh at his puzzled face. 'Oh, laddie, I'm sorry. I'm forgetting how young you are. The change is a stage in a woman's life when her whole body . . . Ach, it's difficult to explain. There comes a time when a woman stops . . .' She halted again, her face red. 'It's when she can't have bairns any more. Now that's all I can tell you but it's something all women go through and it upsets their whole systems. I've heard of women that went off their heads but thank the Lord that doesna happen very often. Now that's enough of that. I've been daft, letting things get to me that havena one grain o' truth in them and I'm ashamed at myself for burdening you with my fancies.'

'I'm pleased you told me, Janet, and maybe just speaking about it will help but you shouldn't be ashamed of . . .' his face coloured with embarrassment at what he was about to say, 'of giving in to your sailor when you were a young girl. I'm sure dozens of girls do the same – it's only natural.'

Janet regarded him keenly. 'Fay hasn't . . . has she?'

'No,' he admitted, omitting to add that he had never placed her in the position of having to give in or not. 'But then, we haven't known each other very long.'

'No.' Janet turned her attention to the fireside again and they sat in silence for a full three minutes. Then she straightened her back. 'Look, Henry, forget what I've been telling you. You can't do anything about that but I'll do my best to help you and Fay. And that reminds me – it's time we were going to bed.'

He couldn't sleep for going over and over the awful scene in

114

the house above the chemist's shop. He wished he knew what Mrs Leslie meant about telling all Drymill the truth about her husband but he hadn't liked to ask Fay and, in any case, she probably didn't know. It couldn't be anything really bad – not if it involved Mr Leslie. The man was too strict with his daughter, too strait-laced, too unbending in his opinions, but he wouldn't do anything that would make him a laughing-stock. His wife had just been making empty threats in her anger at him. Maybe this 'change' was affecting her as well? The big question was, of course, would she manage to change his mind? Fay had said she would get married however much her father was against it but would she, when it came to the point? And, if she did, would she regret her defiance at some later date? Would she be so unhappy that she would leave her new hus-band and go back home?

Finding no answers, no resolutions, to his own problem, Henry turned his mind to Janet's. He had always respected Mr Ledingham, thought of him as a fair man, a decent, honest man, so why was Janet so unsure of him? Even though her mother's death had been so sudden, there really was no reason to think it wasn't natural. Old people often died suddenly but, maybe, if the person concerned was your own mother, it wouldn't be so easy to accept it. That must be it.

The other death was a different matter altogether. What would Innes Ledingham have to gain by that? Apart from leaving him free to marry again, that was. Nothing, as far as anybody could tell. It was a bit too far-fetched to believe that he had got another person to do the needful for him and Janet had admitted that he had never been away from The Sycamores long enough to do it himself.

It struck Henry suddenly that two honourable, upstanding men were being accused by their wives of doing something entirely out of character. In one case, it was only something ridiculous that other people would laugh at but, in the other, it was a criminal act. Both women were in their forties . . . Was that significant?

CHAPTER NINE

Having expended so much anger, Joseph Leslie slept as if he had been drugged but woke up much calmer – alone because Catherine had slept in Fay's bed. It was hardly twenty past five – forty minutes before he had to get up – which gave him time to consider the situation. He had always stuck rigidly to his principles but had he been wrong in wanting the best for his daughter? He had even called his wife's bluff and got away with it but perhaps that had not been the most sensible thing to do.

She, too, could be changing her mind at this very moment, deciding to carry out her threat to shame him unless he gave in. It would make little difference to *her* if her friends knew that he had not been a proper husband to her for years – it was what *his* friends would say that bothered him. It would be wiser to give in, accept what was plainly inevitable and put a brave front on it. Fay's happiness was really all that mattered, was it not?

Throwing off the bedclothes, he went out into the narrow hallway, with the intention of going to the smaller bedroom to acquaint his wife of his decision, but the clatter of dishes told him that she was already up. When he went along to the kitchen, he discovered that she had been up for some time – the fire in the range was blazing merrily, steam was issuing from the big black kettle and two places were set on the pristine white tablecloth.

'I hope you slept well, my dear,' he said, cautiously.

Her expression was inscrutable. 'Yes, thank you.'

Her bleary, red-rimmed eyes told a different tale but he thought better of arguing and sat down to drink the tea she

116

poured out for him. This was the normal procedure first thing in the morning. It was followed by him washing and shaving in the little scullery and then returning to his bedroom to dress in his black suit. He could cope with the buttons on his snow-white shirt but the task of fastening the stud at his high, starched collar was always carried out by one or other of his women-folk and they also saw to the fashioning of his dark tie.

Back in the kitchen for these two items to be seen to, he glanced at the wall clock and did not know whether to be glad or sorry that it showed quarter to seven, fifteen minutes before he had to open the shop. He sat down at the table again and gestured to his wife to do likewise.

'You want to say something?' she prompted.

His mouth was full of tongue, a most unusual experience, and the two sides of his throat seemed to be glued together so he made several chewing movements to get some moisture in his mouth. 'I have been thinking, Catherine,' he got out at last, 'and I realise that I was totally unreasonable last evening.'

'You could say that,' she murmured dryly.

'You must understand that I have not been influenced by what you said when I tell you that I have changed my mind. Fay is quite at liberty to marry that boy . . .' His wife's slight frown made him correct himself, 'to marry the boy she loves. I still do not consider him . . . worthy of her but perhaps he will prove his mettle as he grows older. When I was under the impression that the courtship would end long before it came to marriage, I made a very rash offer but I am still prepared to honour it – fifty pounds and they may do with it what they will.'

He looked directly at his wife now, expecting her to be profuse in her thanks but she was regarding him coldly.

'So that is your decision? Half of what you originally led them to believe?'

'As I said, that offer was made when I thought . . .'

'I am quite sure that Henry is not marrying Fay in order to get your money.'

'Perhaps not but I am just as sure that he will not refuse it.'

She gave a small, lady-like snort. 'I would not be so sure of that, my man, if I were you.'

'We shall have to wait and see then. Now, I will get the pony and trap ready for you and you will go to The Sycamores to impart the good news . . . and bring Fay back with you.'

At The Sycamores, things had gone much further than either Joseph or Catherine could have imagined. When Janet told her husband the night before about 'the poor young lassie's father throwing her out', he had applied his not inconsiderable knowledge to trying to find a sensible solution and had roused her in the middle of the night to tell her what had occurred to him.

'In Scotland, there is what is called an "irregular" marriage ceremony. Both the parties concerned make a declaration of their commitment to each other in front of at least one witness and this has to be recorded in Aberdeen to make it legal.'

Janet looked somewhat sceptical. 'But doesn't the witness need to be a minister or a member of the clergy?'

'No. Anyone is acceptable – an ordinary man or even a woman – and I am quite willing to fulfil the task.'

'But Henry might want Max to do it . . . as his best friend?'

'If that's the case, Max will no doubt be pleased to step in and perhaps Fay would like you to be present too.'

Fay and Henry were given this news straight away and they lost no time in making their declaration of commitment to each other before Max and Janet, their chosen witnesses. By the time Catherine arrived at The Sycamores, bride, groom and witnesses were on their way to Aberdeen to have the declaration legalised. Catherine almost swooned when Innes Ledingham told her but, perfect gentleman that he was, he revived her with a small glass of brandy and sat with her for over an hour to make sure that she was well enough to drive the trap home.

As she drew nearer to Drymill, her heart began to churn with the fear of Joseph's reaction to this latest development.

She expected him to fly into a red-hot fury but he closed the shop and stumbled, white-faced, upstairs to sit down.

'Do not take it so badly,' she urged. 'How were you to know that they would take the law into their own hands?'

'If I had not acted in such a ridiculous, uncalled for manner . . .'

'It is too late for ifs. The deed will have been done by now and we will just have to accept it. You *will* accept it, will you not?'

'I have no choice,' he muttered, 'but I would have wished things had turned out differently.'

'At least, as Mr Ledingham assured me, they were in separate rooms last night so that is a blessing. Fay has committed no sin.'

At that moment, the irregular marriage was being recorded and thus made legal and, although the room was small, dim and not particularly clean, Fay scarcely noticed it. The wedding ring had been bought from a jeweller on their walk from the railway station and, when Henry slipped it on to her finger, she considered herself the happiest girl alive. The registrar was a tall, lanky man with grizzled hair and a bushy moustache, abrupt in his manner, even accusing – as if they were too young to be married. He had some difficulty in pronouncing Henry's real first name and got it out eventually with a deep scowl. But what did any of that matter? In no time, the ceremony, as such, was over. Max and Janet signed their names in the large book on the table first, then Fay, then Henry who had been told that he must sign the foreign name to make it legal.

Out in the street again, Janet said that Innes had given her money to treat them to a meal before they went back, so they all trooped into the Royal Oak Hotel in the Castlegate where, for the first time, Fay wished that she could have been wed with all the people she knew and loved – even her father – around her. Noticing her sadness, Max did his best to amuse them by telling them anecdotes about his time on the farms. Janet took this up and had them smiling about some of the awful kitchen maids she had had to put up with. Determinedly shaking off his despair at giving Fay such a drab wedding day, Henry told them something of his time as orra loon at Craig-downie and the bride surprised them all with quite humorous descriptions of awkward customers she had served in the pharmacy and some of the daft things they asked for.

'Old Mrs Robbie used to come in for a "sleepin' poother" for her cat because it kept her awake all night with its yowling. And wee Billy Fraser once asked me to make up a black-sugar-ellie bottle to look like the awful cough mixture his mother bought for him. I didn't know that black-sugar-ellie was liquor-ice and water shaken together and left standing for days so I just gave him his usual mixture and told him it would do him more good than black-sugar-ellie – whatever that was.'

The whole party was in a more festive frame of mind when the meal was over so Max suggested that they had a look round the city for an hour or so before they got the train back to Corrieben. Having once spent a week's holiday in Aberdeen with an old aunt, Fay guided them down Constitution Street to the beach. The sun was at its height now and it seemed the right thing to do to take off their footwear and skip along the sands at the edge of the sea, the ladies draping their long skirts over their arms in case they got wet. They were all laughing breathlessly when they reached the estuary of the River Don and sat down on the grass to make themselves presentable for the next part of their expedition – up King Street, long and straight, lined with tall tenements of glistening silver granite. Janet was fascinated by the bustle in the shops on the ground level and would have tarried a while out of curiosity if Max had not hustled her on.

King Street came to an end at the Castlegate, their starting point, but the Town House clock told them that there was still almost an hour before they had to catch the train back – time to have a quick look at the big stores in Union Street.

When Janet noticed that Fay was looking wistfully at a lovely display of wedding gowns in one impressive window, she whispered, 'Your wedding was just as legal and binding in a plain navy skirt and jacket as it would have been in one of them.'

'I know but it would have been nice.' Fay didn't linger on the subject, however, she was too happy.

All four dozed off on the train – even Max, usually full of energy, had difficulty in keeping his eyes open while he was driving the trap from Corrieben back to The Sycamores.

Innes Ledingham welcomed them home, shaking hands with 'Mr and Mrs Rae' amid much laughter and wishing them good fortune. 'I have had everything made ready for you,' he murmured to Henry when he had a chance. 'I have put in a small chest for Fay to keep her underclothes and that sort of thing but there should be room in the closet for her skirts et cetera. It will be a tight squeeze for two of you in that room but I am sure you will not object to that? Heh, heh.'

The small chuckle greatly embarrassed Henry. If only he could have taken Fay off somewhere, even for this one night, their wedding night, it wouldn't be so bad but how could they be comfortable with each other when everybody would know what they were doing?

He need not have worried. He and Fay were so exhausted by the time they got to bed that the marriage was not consummated that first night.

The newlyweds went to Drymill the next forenoon and, when they related the events of the previous day, Catherine felt angry that her husband had deprived his daughter of a decent wedding. She was glad to see, when she looked at him, that he knew what she was thinking and that his eyes were pleading for her forgiveness.

As she had known, Henry was not happy about Joseph's offer of money but, with Fay's help, she managed to persuade the young man that it was purely a wedding gift – there were no obligations and there was no shame in accepting it.

The two men shook hands then and Catherine took her daughter in her arms as she had longed to do since they came in. 'I never got the chance to tell you . . . what to expect,' she whispered, 'but you'll have found out for yourself.'

121

'Oh, Mother, don't be so indelicate!'

Catherine thought nothing of this. It was natural that the girl did not want to talk about what had no doubt come as quite a shock.

'Mr Ledingham has given Henry the whole day off,' Fay went on, 'so we are going to Ardbirtle in the afternoon to let his sister know we're married.'

* * *

A flustered Abby didn't know what to do. She hadn't been expecting visitors and her washing from the day before was still lying all over the place. Pogie kept telling her she was getting to be something of a slut – he was always teasing her so she never paid any heed – but seeing her kitchen through the eyes of this dainty, elegant girl made her vow inwardly to change her ways.

'Don't bother doing that for us,' Fay laughed as her new sister-in-law scuttled about folding up napkins, baby clothes and even her husband's drawers. 'It must be difficult to keep a house tidy when you have a baby to look after.'

'That's what I keep telling Pogie,' Abby gasped, breathless with the idea of having to entertain a person like this as much as from her own activity.

Fay's eyes had widened. 'Pogie?'

Henry made the explanation, adding, 'He's a funeral undertaker and I hope none of the families he undertakes for knows what his own family call him. It's not really dignified, is it?'

Fay laughed in delight. 'It's not but maybe it suits him.'

When the man in question came in, however, she revised her opinion. Judging by Abby, she had pictured her husband as a short, tubby man, rather like Henry in a way, but he was over six feet and straight-backed, wearing a perfectly fitting tailcoat and a tall bowler hat. His boots were highly polished and the creases in his trousers were like knife-edges.

Abby was making the introduction so Fay held out her hand and had it grabbed and pumped up and down enthusiastically.

122

'My goodness, I'm really pleased to meet you,' Pogie told her, his voice another shock – perhaps higher than usual in his excitement at discovering that he had a new sister-in-law.

'And I'm very pleased to meet *you*,' she smiled, looking into his keen grey eyes but noticing his bushy head of hair and equally bushy moustache, both mousy brown. 'Apart from your clothes, you're not what I imagined an undertaker to look like.'

His exuberance disappeared like magic, his face seemed to lengthen and sober, his mouth was drawn in. His expression was entirely different from that of a minute before and, when he spoke, his tone was low and mellow. 'I do my best to be a credit to my profession,' he intoned softly, then burst out laughing at her amazement. 'I am something of a chameleon,' he giggled. 'I can change my mood to suit the occasion.'

'All right, then,' Abby said sharply. 'We'll have no more of the seriousness.' She turned to Fay. 'He doesn't often take his serious manners inside the house.'

Pogie beamed at her fondly. 'How can I be serious when I have a lovely wife, a lovely son and a lovely home, even it if can be like Paddy's Market at times.'

Fay couldn't help liking him. An undertaker he may be, and probably one of the best, but he was full of fun and he obviously doted on his wife and child.

At that moment, the baby, who had been sleeping peacefully in the cradle, gave a loud roar, at which Pogie hurried across and lifted him up. 'A sore gut, is it?' he asked, as the infant curled up as if in pain. 'Let Father rub it.' He held the child over his shoulder and rubbed his back gently until he gave a loud burp. 'That's the way, my fine fellow.' He looked at his wife now. 'Is it feeding time? See, I'll turn your chair round for you, so the visitors can't see you.'

Abby stood up to take the baby and Pogie heaved the solid armchair up and swung it round to face the other way. 'That's it, then. Off you go.'

Fay glanced at Henry, who had turned red at the thought of what his sister was doing, and realised with a shock that she, herself, wasn't in the least embarrassed. In fact, she wished

123

that she could watch how the infant suckled and even felt a tingling in her own breasts.

Pogie kept the conversation going while his wife was thus occupied, asking Fay about herself, how had she met Henry, what her parents thought about the hasty wedding. This had Abby, listening to his every word, exclaim, 'Oh, Pogie, you don't ask things like that.'

'I don't mind,' Fay assured her. 'I left home because Father was against us getting wed and I went back to The Sycamores with Henry. It was Mr Ledingham who arranged for us to go to Aberdeen the next morning to be married and, as it turned out, we needn't have gone. Mother got my father to change his mind, so we could have had a proper wedding after all . . . if we'd waited.'

Pogie nodded. 'But won't it be fun telling your children and grandchildren that you had to run away to be wed? That's much more romantic than having arranged it weeks, even months, ahead, don't you think?'

'I suppose so.' After giving it some thought, she laughed, 'Of course it is and it was still as legal as being in a church.'

'You don't regret it, then?' Henry asked, having worried about this.

'Not for one second. Pogie's right. It was far more romantic than being in a church.' She turned to her new brother-in-law again. 'That clerk was not very welcoming and the room was not at all inspiring but, yes, all in all, it was romantic and I'll never forget it.'

When the infant had finished feeding, Pogie took on the task of changing him, to let his wife talk to the callers. Not a natural conversationalist, Abby felt inadequate at first, merely answering their questions, but she was soon talking to Fay as if they were old friends. In fact, she felt so easy in her company that she turned to Henry and said, 'You'll be going to tell Father and Nessie, as well?'

'No,' he said at once. 'I told you before, I'll never go inside that house again.'

To cover her gaffe, Abby jumped up. 'You'll take some

dinner before you go back to The Sycamores?'

While she got out the plates, Pogie offered his son to Fay who accepted him timidly. 'I don't know how to hold a baby,' she mewed.

'You're doing fine,' Pogie grinned. 'He'll let you know if you're hurting him.'

'What's his name?'

'We called him Clarence – that's Pogie's real name,' Abby said over her shoulder as she stirred the pot of soup on the hob.

As Henry watched his bride cooing over the little bundle, he was assailed by a strange new emotion. He had thought that Fay was all he would ever need but he really needed a proper family. They needed a son but he would let the suggestion come from her. She was hardly seventeen, a sheltered seventeen, and motherhood would be too much for her to cope with for years yet.

The dishes had just been washed and laid away when someone else knocked at the door and walked in, halting when she saw that Abby and Pogie were not alone. 'Oh, I'm sorry, I didn't know you had visitors.'

'It's all right, Nessie.' On his feet now, Pogie shepherded her in. 'You know Henry, of course, and this is his bride, Fay. They were wed yesterday.'

Her surprise quickly hidden, the woman walked across to Fay and shook her hand. 'I'm very pleased to meet you, and congratulations, to the both of you.'

'Nessie's my father's wife,' Henry murmured, wishing that he was somewhere else.

She smiled broadly. 'You'll have to come home wi' me and tell him the good news yourself.'

Fay jumped in before Henry could refuse. 'That's very kind of you, Nessie. We'll be glad to, will we not, Henry?'

It wasn't actually anger at his wife that he felt at that moment. He just wondered if she was always going to take her own way. 'Yes, thank you,' he mumbled. 'But we've got to get back so we can't stay long.'

On the way to Oak Cottage, Henry prayed that his wife would not ask his father about the name Tchouki. The man wouldn't like to be reminded about his first wife's infidelity.

Thankfully, Fay did not touch on the subject. She was her natural amiable self and he could see that his father was bowled over by her.

Eventually, Willie turned to him. 'And how do you like working at The Sycamores?'

'I like it fine,' Henry said honestly, 'but I'll need to look for a better paid job if I'm to keep a wife.'

'We've plenty room here for you and your wife and as many bairns as you want to have,' Willie said without consulting his own wife. 'My hands are getting stiff wi' the rheumatics so you could move in here and help me in the smiddy.'

Henry had trouble believing this. Just a few years ago, his father had practically thrown him and his sister out yet now he was being invited back. 'No, Father,' he said, firmly. 'I am not built to be a blacksmith and, in any case, I want to find a house for myself. It's my responsibility to look after my wife and any family we have – not my father's.'

Nessie defused the delicate situation by putting her arm round his shoulder. 'Of course he doesn't want to move in wi' us, Willie, for the same reason we sent him and Abby to their Gramma. They want to be on their own – just like we did.'

His father's knowing expression annoyed Henry but Fay said shyly, 'It will be best for us. I have little experience of cooking or actual housework so I am bound to make mistakes and I would hate anyone to know. It's very kind of you to offer, Mr Rae, but we cannot accept.'

Her gracious manner was all that was needed and Willie put *his* arm round *her*. 'Aye, I can see what you mean but you'll be welcome here any time, mind that. And if you ever need anything . . .'

'We'll manage,' Henry said brusquely, then, at Fay's slight frown, he qualified it. 'If we do need anything, I'll know where to come. Thank you, Father. Well, we'd better be going. We've left the pony and trap at Abby's.'

Willie and Nessie both saw them out and they were aware of being watched as they walked smartly along the road. Less than five minutes later, Abby was telling Fay to come back any time and Pogie was asking Henry how the visit to Oak Cottage had gone. 'Willie's been a good father-in-law to me,' he said earnestly. 'I know Abby and you had a pretty rough time with him and Nessie for a while, but they have both mellowed. It is far better to be friends than to harbour grudges from years back.' He bit his bottom lip and went on, 'That goes for Fay's father as well. He was thinking of his daughter's welfare without considering her happiness. But that is also in the past, don't forget.'

'Aye, you're right. It takes two to keep up a quarrel.'

In Oak Cottage, Nessie could see that her husband was brooding over something. 'What's troubling you, Willie? Henry's got himself a real nice wife.'

'That's nae what's worrying me. Tell me, did he say anything to you about . . . his birth certificate?'

'Not a word but he must have got it or he couldn't have got wed.'

'So he kens.'

'Kens what? Is there something queer on his birth certificate? Was your first wife not his mother? Was it some other woman?'

'Nothing like that. Bella was his mother. She died giving birth to him.'

'Well, what . . . ? Are you not his father, then?'

'Of course I'm his father but . . .' Willie shook his head hopelessly. 'I'd best tell you but it's a long story.'

'I've got plenty of time.'

Nessie had been apprehensive, wondering what on earth could have been wrong with a birth certificate but, as the tale unfolded, she couldn't help smiling. 'You believed the Session Clerk when he said it was a Russian name? Oh, Willie Rae, that's the funniest thing I ever heard and I'm not surprised Isie sent you back to get it changed.'

The final touches, the whisky drinking, John Gow's refusal

to alter the name, made her double up with laughter. 'I had the feeling you'd been a boozer before we wed,' she gurgled after a while. 'That's why I wouldn't let you out on your own if I could help it but I know you used to sneak out to The Doocot when you got the chance.'

Deeply put out by his wife's reception of what he considered a big problem, it did not occur to Willie to warn her to keep it to herself so Nessie, quite innocently, passed the hilarious story around her small circle of friends who, in turn, circulated it to a much wider audience. In just a matter of days, therefore, word had gone round most of the inhabitants of Ardbirtle, backed up, if proof were needed, by Mrs John Gow, who had been the first to know – after her husband. Unfortunately, like all gossip, the basic facts were inevitably embroidered upon and grew to be a story of Bella's adultery with a Russian sailor – although where the poor soul could have met a Russian sailor was never explained.

There were, happily for Willie, still some stalwarts who did not believe a word of it. Geordie Mavor fell out with his wife over it and his brother Tam threatened to punch his next-door neighbour for slandering the dead woman, 'innocent as the day she was born'.

It was some weeks before Ben Roberts, during a visit to the smiddy, told Willie what was being said. 'It might be a good thing if you came to The Doocot and put an end to the rumour,' the Londoner advised. 'I hardly knew your first wife but I do know that she would never have done what they think.'

Willie's first feeling was anger at Nessie for 'clyping' so, as soon as Ben had taken his newly shod horse away, he stamped into the house to have it out with her. 'I thought you would've had more sense than tell outsiders what's on my son's birth certificate!' he roared. 'Ben Roberts says everybody thinks my poor Bella had been taking up wi' a Russky.'

Nessie had turned pale. 'Oh, Willie, I'm sorry. I didn't say anything like that. I only told some of my friends about the mix-up over the name to give them a laugh. I never thought they'd twist things round to suit themselves.'

'You should've ken't . . .'

She nodded sadly. 'Aye, I should.'

'Ben Roberts says I should go to The Doocot and put an end to the rumour so I'll go there after supper – no matter what you say.'

Nessie had congratulated herself on stopping his drinking but this was different. This was a necessity – to undo trouble she had unwittingly caused. 'You'd best go, Willie, if that's what Ben Roberts says.' She issued not one word of caution as to the amount he could consume and prepared to turn a blind eye if he came home drunk.

Geordie Mavor gave his brother a kick on the shin. 'Look who's just walked in.'

Tam looked round and smiled. 'Aye, aye, Willie. We havena seen you for a good while. Sit doon and gi'e's your . . .'

'I'll keep standing if you dinna mind.' Willie's eyes went round the small room and he smiled with satisfaction at the number of men already there. 'I've something to say,' he announced loudly, making every head turn in his direction. 'I've been hearing what folks is saying about my Bella and I'm here to tell you the true story of the name on Henry's birth certificate.'

Desperate to hear this, every man in the room cocked his ears – most were so interested that they forgot about the glass in front of them. 'Some o' you can maybe mind,' Willie began, 'I was celebrating here the day my son was born but I went hame to find by wife had died. Isie McIntyre, my mother-in-law, sent me to register the birth and the death and I came back here for I'd been drinking wi' John Gow and I ken't he'd still be here.'

Geordie clapped his hands with glee. 'That's right, Willie, I can mind that. And you and him was stottin' fu' when you went oot.' A chorus of 'Wheesht, man,' wiped the grin from his face.

Willie told them everything that he could remember about his first visit to the vestry and his glare, circling the entire room, dared anyone to say a word. Then he said, 'Now I'll tell you the bit that naebody seems to ken.'

By the time he was halfway through this account, most of his listeners' faces bore some degree of smile and, when he came to the end, they, like Nessie had been, were doubled up with mirth.

'Oh, man, Willie,' Tam sniggered, 'what a idiot you was. You minded hearing Isie say Chookie to the bairn, and you thocht . . .'

'My brain was pickled wi' whisky,' Willie reminded him, humbly now.

'That's the best laugh I've had in years,' Ben Roberts told him. 'Sit down, Willie, and I'll give you a dram on the house.'

Needing no further persuasion, Willie sat down beside his two old cronies but Geordie said, nose wrinkled in puzzlement, 'But you've never tell't us where Bella met this Russian lad.'

Outraged, his brother picked up his cloth cap and gave him a wallop on the ear. 'Geordie, you never had much o' a brain fae the time you was born and what you had was pickled afore you was twenty. Did you nae listen to what Willie said? Chookie was what Isie McIntyre cried to her hens when she went oot to feed them . . .'

'Aye but where did the Russky come in?'

'Godalmichty, Geordie! There never *was* a Russky. Willie got a bit mixed-up . . . Ach, what's the use? Get back to sleep, man, it's the only thing you're good at.'

There was quite a buzz of conversation going on around them, as Willie had expected, but what he had not expected was the numerous tots of whisky laid down in front of him with comments such as, 'My God, Willie, I dinna ken if I could've stood up and tell't the truth like that.'

And, 'It takes courage to own up to a mistake like you made.'

Or, 'I admire a man that can say something like that.'

At closing time, Willie discovered that, in spite of his intention not to take any liquor, he had drunk as much as he used to take when he was a regular at The Doocot and it was having an even worse effect on him. Ben Roberts, fully aware that

Willie's condition was actually his fault, left his wife to lock up the bar while he helped the incapable man home.

Nessie accepted his help to get her husband to bed, an almost impossible task, which ended in him being practically thrown on top of the bedclothes with all his clothes on, a bulky, floppy bundle.

'I'm sorry, Mrs Rae,' Ben said as she saw him out. 'You'd be quite right to blame me for the state he is in but I do think every man there got the message he gave out. None of them thinks ill of his first wife now.'

'I'm glad of that, then, and I'm grateful to you for making him do it but now they'll be laughing at him.'

Ben shrugged his broad shoulders. 'They had a good laugh about it but they all admired him and wanted to treat him for having the nerve to make it public. That's why he is in his present condition. Don't hold it against him, Mrs Rae. He is a hero.'

'I understand, Mr Roberts, and thank you for making sure he got home.'

The men who had been present that night were all convinced that Willie's story was true – he would never have set himself up for ridicule if it were not – but there were others, the teetotallers who had never let a drop of liquor pass their lips, the prim 'Holy Willies' who condemned any kind of alcohol, who murmured to each other that it was a ruse to put people off the scent. Willie Rae had been cuckolded by his wife and he had tried to pull the wool over folk's eyes.

CHAPTER TEN

1890

It was the second night of their marriage before something occurred to Henry and he wondered why he had not realised it before. As his wife now, Fay was legally known as Mrs Henry Rae so, if she had to sign her name, she would have to write Fay Rae. Fairy! She was so small and dainty, her face, figure and temperament perfect in every way; it was an ideal pet name for her.

'Fairy,' he murmured, turning to her yet again. 'My own darling Fairy.'

She kissed the tip of his nose. 'Have you just newly noticed? I worked it out even before you asked me to marry you.'

Her quiet giggle sent delicious tingles all through him but he tried not to notice them. 'You knew I was going to ask?'

'I *hoped* you were going to ask.'

Another giggle made him move back from her so that she wouldn't feel how much they affected him.

'Do you think less of me for that?' she asked, sounding slightly hurt.

'No, no! It's not that. I could never think badly of you.'

'You are afraid I'll know that you want us to make love again?'

'Yes . . . oh, you must think I've nothing else in my mind.'

The giggle became a hearty chuckle. 'To be quite honest, Tchouki darling, neither have I. Does that disgust you?'

'It makes me want you even more but we can't – not again. We might have made a child already.'

'I hope we have.'

'We can't start a family yet, my Fairy. Living in one room like this? I'll have to find a better job and a house and . . .' He broke off as she snuggled closer.

'Other people have to bring up a family in one room,' she whispered. 'If they can manage, so can we.'

'I don't want you to have to scrimp and save to put food in our children's mouths, to give them decent clothes.'

'I wouldn't mind, my darling. As long as I have you, I would scrub floors, take in washings, do whatever I could to earn some money. I'm much stronger than I look.'

The thought of such a future drained every iota of his reviving passion and he lay round on to his back. 'We shouldn't have got wed. Like your father said, we were too young, we hadn't thought things out . . . I can't provide for you as I would like.'

'Oh, Tchouki, my darling Tchouki, forget about ordinary things. We are man and wife now, we love each other more than any other man and wife ever did or ever will and we are young enough to enjoy it – so we must make the most of it.'

With her warm body pressed against his, he groaned, 'My own, dearest Fairy.' Flinging caution – reserve, fear, everything that had held him back – to the winds he made the most of it.

Nessie could tell that her husband was having a hard time of it. He had been in this dark mood ever since he had made his confession in The Doocot. 'They'll forget about it, Willie,' she comforted. 'Another week or two and they'll stop tormenting you. You did the right thing.'

Willie looked at her sadly. 'I'm nae so sure o' that. If I'd never admitted what I did when I was as drunk as a lord, naebody would've ever found oot.'

Nessie shook her head. 'John Gow told his wife before he died and Nora Jane wouldn't have held her tongue for much longer. In fact, I don't think she did keep it to herself. Some of the women have been hinting at something queer about the Raes for months now but I had no idea what they were getting at – not till you said. To be fair, Willie, you've only yourself to blame – making such a muck-up of registering your only son.'

He regarded her piteously. 'That's the worst o' it, Ness.'

That afternoon, Willie was so engrossed in moulding a new iron rim round the mangled wheel of a cart, that had come to grief when its drunken driver had made his horse go too fast, that he wasn't conscious of another presence in the smiddy until a voice said, 'Aye, aye, then, Willie.'

Startled, he looked up into the face of the town's Provost, whom he had known since they were boys, though Augustus Fleming never usually did his own errands. It was always one of the hired hands who came to have a horse shod or whatever needed to be done. 'Good afternoon to you, Mester Provost,' he said, wiping his hands on his canvas apron and then running them across his brow to remove the sweat. 'What can I do for you?'

Never one to shirk a duty – the reason for him being voted in as Provost – Gus Fleming came straight out with it. 'There's talk in the town about your boy, Willie.'

'Ach, that!' Willie said sharply, indignant that the top man in Ardbirtle was poking his long nose into something that didn't concern him, something that had happened near eighteen years ago.

'Now, don't fly off the handle, I'm not criticising you or your son. I suppose you have heard about Phil Geddes?'

More puzzled than ever, Willie nodded. 'He's laid up wi' some kind o' disease?'

'An incurable disease, I am afraid. He has been told he will never be fit enough to return to work, which means we are without a Town Officer. We prefer this post to go to an Ardbirtle man who comes of good stock, someone old enough to take on the responsibilities the job carries and young enough to have many years of service ahead of him. Do you understand what I am getting at, Willie?'

'Are you saying . . . you think my Henry . . . ?'

'I can think of no one else as well qualified. You have a good reputation as a blacksmith and, although you were quite a heavy drinker at one time, as I recall, you have conquered the demon and become a model citizen. I admire that in a man and I admire you even more for what I hear you did recently in The Doocot. You must have known that you were holding yourself up for ridicule yet you did not hesitate to clear your late wife's name. Your son should be proud of you.'

'I . . . dinna th . . . think he would look on it like th . . . that, though,' Willie stammered, overcome by embarrassment.

'He will when he thinks about it objectively. But I diverge. From what I hear of him, he would be perfect for the post. I am told he has married recently and he will, no doubt, be anxious to settle down and provide a decent home for his wife. I believe she is Joseph Leslie's daughter? The Drymill pharmacist?'

Rather more composed now that he knew the score, Willie said, 'Aye, Gus, and my lad couldna have found a better wife.'

'I am glad to hear that. What I require of you now, William, is the address of the farm where he works so that I can write to offer him the position.'

This subtle use of his full Christian name reminding him of his lower status, Willie answered respectfully. 'He left Craigdownie a few year ago, Mester Provost. He's odd-job man at The Sycamores. You'll ken it?'

'The Sycamores? Yes, of course, I know the place you mean. Odd-job man, is it? So much the better. He will be used to turning his hand to anything.'

'He'll not be scared to tackle anything you ask o' him.'

'Excellent. Well, it was good speaking to you, Willie, and keep up the fine work here in the smiddy.'

Too excited to work now, Willie said, 'You'll come into the house for something to warm you up afore you go out into the cauld again?'

'Well, thank you, Willie, a cup of tea would be very acceptable.'

Willie closed the corrugated iron doors behind them, to save heat being lost, and ushered the Provost through the back door of his cottage proudly. Nessie was a perfect housewife, keeping every stick of furniture polished and every inch of the place sparkling clean so there was nothing to be ashamed of. 'This is Nessie, my wife,' he said unnecessarily. 'Ness, this is the Provost come in for a cup o' tea.'

She had seen the man several times, going about the town, but had never been introduced to him before and she was surprised by the strength of pressure in his handshake. 'Sit yourself down, Provost,' she said, turning to the range and glad of the excuse to hide her burning face. Watching her as she set the kettle on the fire, swilled out the large brown teapot then spooned in tea from the caddy on the mantelshelf, Augustus Fleming told her his reason for coming to see her husband.

Thirsty from working in such a hot atmosphere, Willie swiftly emptied his cup and stood up. 'Tak' your time, Mester Provost,' he smiled, 'I've a good few jobs to get through afore I lock up for the day, but Nessie'll look after you.'

He strode out without waiting for any reply, leaving them looking at each other in some dismay – the woman because she didn't know how to deal with anyone holding such high office and the man because he had been attracted to her from the moment he walked into her kitchen.

Nessie pushed a plate across to him. 'You'll have another scone, Mister Provost?'

He helped himself with a smile. 'Your own baking, obviously. They're absolutely delicious. And the strawberry jam, you made that, as well?'

Flattered, she felt more at ease. 'Does your wife not bake, Mister Provost.'

'My wife died almost twenty years ago.'

'Oh, I'm sorry.' Nessie couldn't think what else to say.

'I have a woman who comes in to clean for me but she never has time to do any baking. Willie is a lucky man.' His gaze deepened in intensity. 'A *very* lucky man.'

As had happened when she first met Willie, Nessie recalled, with a strong flicker of guilt, their eyes locked and she no longer felt awkward with him. She could see a different, far better, future stretching ahead for her.

Willie returned to the house at his usual time of six o'clock. 'How did you and the Provost get on,' he asked his wife. 'You made a good impression there.'

Having had fully half an hour to prepare for the question, Nessie answered without a blush. 'You think so? He's a nice enough man, I suppose, but not my type.'

Willie found this extremely funny, throwing back his head and roaring with laughter. 'I wouldna think so. He's been a widower for . . . losh, it must be wearing on for twenty year. He'll ha'e forgot how to handle a woman.'

She made no reply. Willie himself had lost much of his drive, a case of over-indulgence when he was younger, she supposed, but Gus Fleming's passions had obviously lain dormant since his wife died. It was obvious that their rebirth would be quick and total.

'I hope he mak's it clear to Henry it wasna me that asked for him to get the job,' Willie said, changing the subject. 'He'll turn it down if he thinks I'd anything to do wi' it.'

'No, he'll jump at the chance – a decent job and a house to go with it. What more could he want?'

Willie chewed over this for a moment or two. 'I dinna ken about the house, though. They can hardly put Phil Geddes oot when there's nae hope for him, can they? And what aboot his wife? She'll still be there when he's gone.'

'It's a tied house so the council could throw them out if they wanted.'

'Well, maybe they'd be within their rights but they wouldna . . . surely?'

* * *

It was after six on Monday night before Henry received the letter, handed to him by Innes Ledingham at the supper table, with the loud comment, 'I did not know that your first name was Tchouki. Is that how you pronounce it?'

Janet stepped in to cover the youth's confusion. 'It was all a big mistake. I'll tell you about it later.'

With every head turned towards him, the scarlet-faced Henry knew that he had to face up to the inevitable. 'It's all right, Janet. I may as well tell them.' He told the facts as he now

137

knew them with no intention of making them sound humorous but, no matter how often and by whom it was told, the tale would always get the same reaction – paroxysms of laughter.

'I am really sorry,' the Superintendent murmured to Henry. 'I did not realise . . . I would not have said anything . . .'

'It's all right. It's not long since I learned the truth myself and I suppose it's better to get it off my chest now and get it over with.'

Janet leaned across to him. 'If you and Fay want to go upstairs now, I'll take up a pot of tea for you in half an hour or so.'

Henry smiled his thanks. 'It's all right – we'll stick it out.'

When he and Fay eventually got to the sanctuary of their room, he thumped down on the big double bed that took up most of the space, tore open the envelope and drew out the slim sheet of headed notepaper.

Fay watched him scan the typed words. 'What does it say?' she asked, looking at the envelope and wanting to know what Artbirtle Town Council wanted of him.

Plainly shaken, he handed it to her. 'Read it for yourself.'

She didn't take long, looking up in great excitement when she came to the end. 'It's wonderful, Henry, just what you were looking for. You had better write as soon as you can to say you can attend the interview. Do you have a writing pad and envelopes?'

He shook his head. 'I've never had to write to anybody. Besides, I don't know if I want the job. I bet my father's had something to do with it.'

'Oh, Henry, don't be so childish. It doesn't matter who recommended you, if anyone did – it's much better than having to stay here.'

It dawned on him then, although he should have recognised it before, that life at The Sycamores must be a dreadful comedown for her. She had no role to play except being the wife of the odd-job man, when she had been used to serving in her father's shop, making up mixtures and pills, speaking to dozens of people every day. She must hate being on her own all the time, taking walks if it wasn't raining or sitting in their room reading if it was. She must be nearly out of her mind with boredom.

His wife could sense his indecision. 'It is up to you, dear, but I think you should at least make an effort to find out what the job entails. If you do not like what you hear, then by all means turn it down.'

He nodded, not wanting to tell her that he did not like the idea of living so near to his father.

'Shall I go and ask Janet for a sheet of paper and an envelope?'

'All right, if you think that's best.'

'Do you want her to know why?'

'You'd better tell her. They knew I'd have to look for another job.'

As Fay had suspected, the lure of being the Town Officer was too great a challenge for Henry to ignore. His excitement was high when he returned from his interview with the Provost. 'It's a mixture of jobs, really. I'll be the Court Usher whenever the courtroom is in use. I'll be the Town Crier, to announce all the important messages. I get to wear a special uniform for that too and when I attend any public meetings to make sure there is no trouble. Then we come down the scale a bit. I'll be the lamplighter and the street cleaner. So it won't be all moonlight and roses.'

'Did you accept the job?' Fay asked, impatiently. 'That's what I want to know.'

Henry hesitated. 'I said I'd have to think about it.'

'What is there to think about? I can see you would like to do it.'

'Aye, but there's one big drawback.'

Her smile faded. 'Isn't there a house to go with the job?'

'There is but it's occupied at the moment – the old Town Officer.'

'But he would have to move, wouldn't he?'

'He's very ill, not expected to live long, but . . .' Henry had to stop the hope that was returning to her eyes, ' . . . but his wife's not in the best of health, either. The Provost said they can't put her out, or expect her to move, if they could find her a place, which he said would be impossible anyway.'

'Didn't he offer you any alternative accommodation?'

'He did, and that's what's keeping me from taking the job. He had asked my father if he'd be willing for us to stay there till the other house is available.'

Fay lost patience with her husband now. 'Don't tell me you would give up a job I know you want, just because you don't want to live in the same house as your father?'

He took hold of her hand and looked at her earnestly, knowing the answer to the question he was about to ask her. 'Do *you* want me to take it? Would you be happy living at Oak Cottage?'

She placed her other hand on top of his. 'I am not exactly ecstatic about it but I am willing to give it a try if you are. It would only be for a short time, remember.'

Henry, therefore, wrote two more letters – one to Ardbirtle Town Council accepting the position as Town Officer and the other to Mr William Rae to say that he and his wife would take up the offer of a temporary home.

'We have to say that,' he pointed out, 'so they'll know it's not permanent.'

Two replies arrived two days later. The Clerk of the Council of Ardbirtle was pleased to confirm Mr Tchouki Rae's appointment to the position of Town Officer 'as from the first day of October, eighteen hundred and ninety'. Willie's answer (written by Nessie) just said, 'We will be pleased to see you. Come the day before you start your new job. Your father.'

At first, Nessie Rae was not at all happy that her stepson and his wife would be living with them. She had been looking forward to many pleasurable afternoons with the Provost, hopefully culminating in them running off together. Not that there had been the slightest indication that Gus Fleming wanted anything more than the innocuous half hour they'd had together

– he hadn't been near the place since – but you never knew, did you? Of course, he had his position to think of so he'd be scared to step out of line. No matter how careful he was, there would always be the chance that he could be seen if he came to Oak Cottage and, with Willie busy in the smiddy, tongues would start rolling. That would finish his career.

After several more days had passed, Nessie came to the conclusion that the passion she thought she had aroused in the man had only been in her imagination, in which case, she was better off without him.

The closer it came to the day of Henry's departure, the more Janet Ledingham wondered if she should confide in him. She had made a special journey to see her brother and attempted to let him know her fears, but he had only laughed at her.

'It's your age, woman,' he had scolded.

'It's nothing to do with my age', she had said, almost on the point of tears.

Roderick had sighed then – as if he wanted to be rid of her. 'You are imagining things that have no concrete foundation. For goodness sake, put it out of your mind.'

The trouble was she couldn't put it out of her mind. It was like a running sore, getting worse as time went on, and she could sense Innes's growing irritation at her for asking questions and bringing up facts he didn't want to remember but she could not forget. She still considered her mother's death unnatural. She couldn't make up her mind whether his first wife had actually died somewhere else or if she had never left The Sycamores at all. By all accounts, he and Gloria had not been getting along and, with his short temper, a quarrel could easily have escalated into something far worse. He could have picked up whatever was handy and let fly!

On the other hand, with the cook having walked out, and knowing that she, Janet, was an expert in the kitchen, it could have been deliberate. He could have planned it and killed Gloria in cold blood. It was this thought that made her fear for her own life and she couldn't possibly shift that fear on to anybody else's shoulders – she couldn't even share it.

In contrast to his wife, who was glad to be leaving, Henry felt quite downhearted. He had enjoyed his time at The Sycamores, chatting to the elderly inmates, attending to all the little jobs that had to be done. He had got on very well with all the staff, including Innes Ledingham himself, and would miss them all, especially Max, his old school friend. Most of all, he would miss Janet. He was really fond of her, loved her like a mother and it was going to be hard to say goodbye.

They were all up early on the morning of the thirtieth of September. The carrier was coming at nine o'clock to collect their box – only one because they only had their clothes to move as nothing else belonged to them. Nearly everyone came to see them off. The Superintendent shook hands and wished Henry good luck in his new venture and Max slapped his back and gave Fay a resounding kiss on the cheek. Then, as if it had been planned, they all stepped aside to let Janet in.

Trying to hold back her tears, she clasped Fay's hand for a few moments and then turned to Henry, meaning to give him just a little hug but emotion overcame them both and their long, tearful embrace brought moisture to several other eyes. 'You'll let me know how you get on?' she pleaded.

At last, they were on their way, both perched up beside Geordie Mavor who, understanding that Henry in particular wouldn't want to make conversation, did what his brother often told him to do and kept his mouth shut.

They were some distance on their way before Fay murmured, 'Are you all right, Henry? You're very quiet.'

'I'm fine.' He hesitated and then whispered, 'I'm worried about Janet. I'm sure something's troubling her.'

'She's very fond of you, dear, that's why she was so upset.'

'Aye, I suppose so.' But he knew, deep down, that it wasn't just that.

PART TWO

1891-1897

CHAPTER ELEVEN

Henry Rae – or T H as he was entered in the Council's list of employees, which he preferred to the Tchouki some of the wags shouted after him – was happy with his life. His lovely wife had made a wonderful home for him and given him two beautiful children: Andrew, a mischievous two-year-old, and Samara – after the seeds of the sycamore trees – just seven months. What more could he want? That was his family complete – there would be no more.

Of course, it hadn't always been plain sailing. When he first took on the role of Ardbirtle's Town Officer, he'd had more than a new job to contend with. His stepmother had made life a little uncomfortable during the three months that he and his wife had lived at Oak Cottage. It was obvious that she had resented them being there yet she had never come right out and said so. She relied on snide remarks, casting up that he should never have got married if he couldn't provide for a wife properly or heaving drawn-out sighs and saying they had invaded her privacy – although never in front of her husband.

Going over it in his mind one evening, Henry recalled how his relationship with his father had actually improved in the course of their stay in his house. Perhaps the man was ashamed of his wife's treatment of them, perhaps he had always wanted to be friends with his son, but, whatever it was, they were closer now than they had ever been.

Fay had been a saint during those twelve-and-a-half uneasy weeks. She never lost her temper with Nessie. In fact, it was her tactful handling of the woman that had eventually brought her round. What had kept him sane was knowing that they wouldn't have to put up with her for long. He had often found himself wishing for his predecessor's instant demise but, when he voiced this sentiment to Fay, she turned on him angrily. It had been the closest they had ever come to quarrelling.

Thankfully, he'd been given the keys to the large two-storeyed house in Mid Street before his dear Fairy fell with their first child – or at least before she had to tell Nessie about her condition. His worry about how they would furnish the house they were waiting for was solved for him. Mrs Geddes died just a week after her man and, because they had no family, the council had cleaned the whole place from top to bottom before they handed it over. He was told that he'd be responsible for clearing out all the Geddeses' personal belongings but that everything else was theirs to use – in other words, they got a furnished home.

As was only to be expected, the furniture was old but of good quality and whoever had done the cleaning had made a thorough job of it. The kitchen range was immaculate, the big black kettle on the hob had no traces of soot, the brass candle-sticks on the mantelshelf were gleaming and all the ornaments and using dishes had been washed and set back in place on the wide oak dresser. The two high-backed horsehair armchairs by the fireside were well worn but still comfortable and the hearthrug had obviously been hooked by Mrs Geddes herself or maybe by her man in any spare time he had.

A fender stool, covered in brown leather – possibly re-covered, for it looked somewhat amateurish – took up the whole width of the fireplace, ideal to rest the feet on when sitting on one or other of the armchairs. A heavy steel poker lay at the front of the fire at one side and a big wooden coal scuttle complete with black shovel at the other. A plain, unpad-ded chair was pushed under each side of the oblong oak table that stood in the middle of the floor. The finishing touch, a most necessary item they had found, was the set of bellows hanging on a nail at the side of the mantelpiece.

The other downstairs room, the parlour, was more 'perjink', a favourite word of his Gramma. The table here was a highly polished mahogany drop leaf, its four straight-backed chairs –

seats covered in the same deep crimson velour as the two wide armchairs at the fire – in various positions round the room. Opposite the fireplace stood a mahogany sideboard, the two shelves of its left-hand cupboard filled by a delicate porcelain dinner service, rose-decorated and gold-edged, boasting six each of side plates, dessert plates, soup bowls, steak plates, two large and two small ashets, two large tureens with lids and a gravy boat.

'That must have been a wedding present,' Fay had observed, the first time she saw them, 'and by the look of them, I don't think they've ever been used.'

The top shelf of the left side of the sideboard held crystal wineglasses and tumblers – perhaps cut glass, not crystal – and the bottom shelf had an assortment of knick-knacks, mostly of little value.

Inside the fender at this fireside was a brass companion set, with a poker, a pair of tongs, a fireside brush and a dainty shovel. The fender was also brass, with a padded stool at each end, and was clearly not to be used for feet. The hearthrug, if not actually Persian, was of Persian design, bringing some colour to the brown linoleum on the floor. There were small ornaments dotted about the room, on occasional tables, on the sideboard itself, along the shelf above the tiled fireplace. There were also three gold-framed pictures on the wall – 'Beatrice and Dante', 'When Did You Last See Your Father?' and 'Stag At Bay'.

The only thing missing in these two rooms, according to Fay, had been pot-plants but she had since taken or been given, even purchased, dozens of cuttings and she now had the place looking as lived-in as she wanted. She had worked hard at getting rid of all the useless items that Mrs Geddes had collected during their tenancy of the house. The old cuttings from newspapers with yellowing recipes and household hints, old cardboard boxes, probably kept because they were prettily decorated, old receipts and old letters were all burned in the backyard. The clothes that were presentable were packed in boxes from the grocer and given to the church for the needy in India and Africa.

'Not that they need heavy coats and trousers and skirts over there,' Fay had remarked to her husband.

'You never know,' he had told her. 'A lot of the Indians live up in the hills so they would likely be glad of warm things.'

The privy was at the far end of the backyard, not far from the midden, which was not so handy in bad weather, but, as Fay, always the optimist, said, 'It's better than nothing.'

There were two fairly large rooms upstairs, only one properly furnished with a double bed, a tall chest of drawers, a closet for hanging clothes, a small table by the window and one chair. The other had only a double bed and a chair. There were also two much smaller bedrooms, completely empty, and a tiny attic.

It had taken Fay some months to get everything to her satisfaction and Henry had to keep telling her to stop working so hard. She was well into her ninth month, however, before she gave in.

That was when Nessie had surprised them. She had called every day to see how Fay was and had given Henry strict instructions to let her know the minute the labour pains started – even if it was the middle of the night. As it turned out, she was actually with Fay when the first pain struck and she refused to leave even when Henry came home from work – even when the doctor was called and things were getting serious.

Andrew's birth, Henry recalled thankfully, had been fairly straightforward and surprisingly quick, as if he couldn't wait to make his entry into the world, and Nessie the nurse became Nessie the grandmother, who doted on the infant, still did, although he was a wee nickum nowadays, fingers into everything.

Samara's birth had taken much longer, a full thirteen hours, but Fay took it all in her stride, making her husband go to work as usual after seven hours. 'I'll be fine,' she had assured him, her darling face white, her eyes pain-filled. 'Nessie will look after me.'

That was when he had revived his old vow not to put any woman through the agonies of numerous pregnancies. This one would be the last – definitely the last.

'Are you sleeping?'

Fay's voice startled him. 'Just thinking,' he said, trying to sound alert.

'I've been thinking, too. It's more than a month since we heard from Janet, do you know that? I hope nothing's wrong.'

He turned stricken eyes to her. 'I didn't realise it was so long. I thought . . .' he paused, wondering if he should tell her of the fears he'd had when they left The Sycamores and deciding that it would be all right. As the saying went, no news was good news. If anything bad had happened to Janet, they would have heard. 'She used to tell me she was worried about the way her mother died. She half-suspected Innes of doing something to get Mrs Emslie out of the way.'

'Why would he want to do that?' Fay couldn't understand.

'As far as I gathered, he wanted Janet to marry him but she said she couldn't as long as her mother was alive.'

'But I thought you once told me he was married already.'

'He was. Then he said he'd had a letter from a friend saying his wife had died.'

Fay's eyebrows rose. 'Did these deaths happen soon after each other?'

'Not all that long.'

'Well, that's it, then.' She looked at her husband triumphantly. 'Janet must have been afraid that he'd got rid of them both.' Her face fell again. 'She still married him, though, so she couldn't have been afraid of him . . . not at first.'

'What are you getting at?'

'It could have taken a while for her to come to that conclusion and, once a person starts to imagine things, it grows and grows in the mind until . . .'

'Yes, but on the other hand, she could have realised she was being stupid.'

'Do you think she was being stupid? I never really took to Innes Ledingham, you know. There was something about him . . .'

'He wasn't so bad. He thought a lot of himself and was a bit . . . what's the word?'

149

'Bumptious,' his wife supplied.

'Aye, but he wasn't a villain. He wouldn't have . . .'

'You can't be sure.'

Henry thought for a moment. 'I'll write and ask him if Janet's ill or . . .'

'Don't write to *him*! If he thinks we know about him, he might do away with her . . . if he hasn't done it already.'

'Oh, Fay!' He looked most distressed now. 'Don't say that.'

'I'm just being realistic, dear. If we can suspect him of two murders, it follows that he could quite easily do a third. What you must do is write to Max. Just say we want to know how Janet is since she hasn't written for a while and we didn't want to bother Mr Ledingham. Don't say anything else . . . please, Tchouki, don't.'

He never objected to his wife's use of his true Christian name. It was her way of showing him her affection.

When he passed along the letter to Max Dalgarno, the Superintendent commented, accusingly, 'It's postmarked Ardbirtle. From Henry . . . I mean Tchouki Rae, I suppose?'

Max, however, was fit for him. 'It'll be from my mother,' he said brightly, knowing full well that it wasn't her handwriting and wondering why Henry was writing to him. 'I'll read it later on.'

To make sure that no one could see him, he opened it in the potting shed behind the stable and was surprised to find that his friend had just written two lines. What they said, however, did not surprise him. He had been worrying about Janet himself for the past few weeks. According to her husband, she had taken to bed with a very bad form of influenza and he had later described her condition as 'an illness Doctor Harris cannot identify'. That was when he had employed a temporary cook, as he called her, but she was still there.

Knowing that he couldn't ask if he could see Janet – that would put her husband on his guard – Max tackled one of the maids that very afternoon. 'Nora, I want to ask you something but I don't want Ledingham to see me speaking to you. Come in here.'

He realised, from the way her face lit up when he closed the shed door, that she thought he wanted to ask her out – or to kiss her even – so he said hastily, 'Have you seen Janet lately?'

Obviously disappointed by his question, the girl nodded. 'Aye, I took up her breakfast this morning, Max. She looks real bad.'

'How d'you mean?'

'It's difficult to say but her face is clapped in, she's got black rings round her eyes, her lips are near white and her hands are shaking. She'll not be fit to work for ages yet . . . if she's ever fit again,' she ended, gloomily.

'What d'you think o' Mrs Rattray?' Max persisted.

'She's nae near as good a cook as Janet.'

Max rubbed his chin reflectively. 'No. In fact, she's bloody awful.'

'Ooh, Max,' Nora giggled, looking at him coyly, 'the things you say.'

He opened the door and, to keep her from being too disappointed, he gave her a quick squeeze as he let her out.

For the rest of the afternoon, he couldn't stop thinking about the letter and what it conjured up. Henry had obviously been worried at not hearing from Janet and the more he, himself, was learning about her illness, the more he was worrying too. Something was damned queer about it.

It was not until Max realised that Ledingham usually had some business to attend to in Aberdeen on the cook's day off that an answer occurred to him and he could have kicked himself for not noticing before. The Superintendent was taking up with Mrs Rattray! He must be doing something to Janet, giving her something to keep her out of the way.

Max felt his hackles rising at the thought of it but he couldn't tell anybody. He had no proof – it was just supposition on his part. In any case, what could he say? That the man was making sure his wife couldn't catch him out in his love affair – or was it more sinister than that? Was he trying to get rid of Janet for good? Bitter bile burned the young man's throat now and, in his torment, he yanked out a whole row of turnip seedlings

151

before he came to his senses. What could he do? Even if he did get to see Janet, by hook or by crook, and told her what he suspected, she wouldn't believe him.

An hour before stopping-time, he saw Nora coming hell-for-leather round the side of the stable and making straight for him, her urgency making him take a few steps forward to meet her. 'Is something wrong?' he asked, in some concern.

'Not with me,' she assured him. 'You'll not believe this but I wanted to ask Mrs Rattray about something earlier on and, when I went to speak to her, she wasn't in the kitchen. So I went along to her wee sitting room and . . . I heard a man's voice saying lovey-dovey things. Well, I mean, I wondered who it could be . . . so I put my ear to the keyhole and . . . guess who it was?'

'Ledingham!' Max almost shouted it in his triumph.

She seemed disappointed that he had guessed correctly but carried on, 'Aye and he says, "Oh, Glo . . . this is awful and I nearly called you by the wrong name at breakfast. I can't think of you as Kate, you see. You'll always be my Glo . . . " I think she must have put her hand over his mouth to stop him saying her real name and then he kissed her. I heard it as plain as day so I wouldn't wait any longer. I would see her right there and then and it's their ain fault if I catch them doing what they shouldna be doing – and him wi' a wife that's at death's door in her bed up the stair. So I gives a wee tap and in I goes.'

'Good for you!'

'They'd sprung awa' from each other, of course, but they was flustered and red in the face and he stamped out. Did you ken about them, Max?'

'I suspected he was up to something but I'd no proof.'

After a few moments' silence, Nora whispered, 'D'you think he's giving Janet something so she'll nae ken what's going on?'

'Either that or he's trying to do away wi' her for good.'

Nora's eyes widened, 'To murder her, you mean?'

'That's exactly what I mean.'

'Oh, God, Max, we'll need to do something – but what?'

'I havena managed to think what to do but it'll come to me and it would be good to have somebody to back me up if things go wrong.'

'You can depend on me, Max. I'll back you up. I'll tell folk exactly what he's getting up to.'

At supper, two of his workmates commented on how quiet Max was – one even asked him if he was feeling ill because he looked so flushed. But he shrugged his shoulders and, as soon as the meal was over, he made for his room. Stretched out on his bed, he racked his brain for inspiration, for a way to see Janet without fear of being seen, but nothing would come to him. The night passed slowly, one thread of hope after another being discarded as being too open to discovery, and he rose in the morning still in his work clothes. Shaving in the cold water usually banished any sleepiness but not this morning. He felt as though he had been drugged.

A comment by the grieve at breakfast time on how ill he looked made light dawn. Why shouldn't he say he *was* ill? He would be sent back upstairs to bed . . . at the other end of the same corridor as the Ledinghams' bedroom. Nora would likely be told to take some dinner to him and he could ask her to keep watch till he went in to speak to Janet. He could plan no further than that. It was up to the poor woman herself after that – if she believed him or not.

Pushing his chair back, Max pretended to stagger and the Superintendent said, sharply, 'You may as well admit that you are ill, Maxwell. There is no point in trying to work in that state so go back to bed till you shake it off – whatever it is.'

'If it's what Janet's got,' Max mumbled, unable to resist the chance, 'I'll not be able to shake it off.' He walked unsteadily to the door and went out but, once on the stairs, his step was more purposeful, his eyes had a glint of steel in them.

Again, he lay down fully clothed but, this time, he had a plan in mind. It should be easy enough to get from his side of the house to the Ledinghams' room. He knew that what had originally been two different wings of the building had been separated by locked doors when The Sycamores became a 'refuge for the infirm' but would they still be kept locked after all this time? Ledingham had once told them that the severe increase in fees some years earlier had effectively banished the truly insane so there was no danger nowadays of an inmate going berserk and attacking somebody.

After mulling over the chances of finding the communicating door still locked, Max felt reasonably satisfied that it was most unlikely. So . . . what would he do when he came face to face with Janet? Should he just jump in with both feet and tell her the truth right off or should he work round to it? Working round to it would take time, though, and that was something he didn't have. In any case, was she in a fit enough state to understand what he was saying?

Despite his feverish excitement at the thought of outwitting a devilish fiend, Max's lack of sleep the previous night got the better of him and he sat up, startled, when someone knocked on his door. 'Come in,' he yawned, thinking that it was Nora.

'I have brought something for you to eat.' It was the Superintendent himself.

Positive that the man had guessed he was up to something, Max's heart plummeted. His dazed expression, however, had he but known it, evidence of his having been asleep, was enough to clear the faint doubt from his employer's mind.

'I am sorry to disturb you,' he said solicitously, 'but I thought you would be glad of a little soup.'

'Thank you, Mr Ledingham,' Max muttered, wishing that he had at least gone under the blankets but the Superintendent didn't seem to think it odd that he was still fully clothed.

Left alone again, Max supped the soup and ate the crusty bread the new cook had baked. It wasn't really so bad and he used the last piece to wipe up the drops of moisture from the bowl, while he engaged in concentrated thought. He had planned on having Nora to keep watch, and maybe to help him to get Janet downstairs if she wasn't able to walk. Without Nora, he would be facing more than a challenge – it would be an outright impossibility.

He lay back to consider it, hearing, without being aware of

it, the usual kitchen sounds, the banging of heavy doors as the other employees returned to their tasks. It was only when absolute silence reigned that he became conscious that it was so and wondered, warily, if he dared to make a move.

He slid off the bed and opened his door, listening intently for any sound. Hearing nothing, he crept back to the bed, picked up his boots and tied them round his neck. He was about to set off on his mission when another knock froze him to the spot in panic but his fears disappeared when Nora poked her head in.

'It's just me, Max. That's himself gone off to Aberdeen to attend to some business and he says he'll not be back till some time tomorrow. It's kinda funny though, for Mrs Rattray's off and all. It looks to me like they'll be meeting some place for I'm sure they're having a romance or whatever you like to call it.' She giggled delightedly. 'You wouldna think folks their age would still be at it, would you?' Her manner sobered. 'What was you wanting me to do?'

Barely able to believe that fortune was smiling on him, Max gave her a brief outline of his plan, then led the way along the top corridor. When he placed his hand round the knob of the connecting door to the other wing, he looked at her with raised eyebrows but, before the disappointment of finding it locked had fully registered, Nora drew a large key from her apron pocket. 'I ken't it was locked so I took this aff the board in the kitchen.'

Relief caused such a rush of emotion that he grabbed her round her waist and kissed her squarely on the lips. 'Oh, Nora, you're a darling!'

Scarlet with delighted embarrassment, she put the key in her pocket when it had served its purpose and, leaving the door unlocked in case they needed a quick exit, they carried on to what she said was Janet's room and where, again, she produced the necessary key.

'I'd have been up a spout without you,' Max whispered. 'I'd no idea which room it was. Now, I just want you to stand guard at the top o' the stairs and, if you hear somebody coming, tap on this door and run like hell.'

155

'I canna leave you . . . Ledingham might come back for something.'

'I'll hide – under the bed or behind a curtain – I'll be fine.' In fact, all panic gone, all fears and doubts subsided, he felt exhilarated. He was pitting his wits against a master of deception . . . and may the best man win. As long as it was himself.

The door opened without a creak – Vic, Henry's replacement as odd-job man, was obviously a conscientious worker – and Max tiptoed across the darkened room to the bed. 'It's only, me, Janet,' he murmured.

The inert hump shifted slightly. 'Henry? What are you doing here? Go away, before Innes catches you.'

'It's Max, Janet. I've come to take you away from here.'

'You knew?' she whispered. 'You knew Innes is trying to . . . ?'

'I havena known for long but he'll not get away with it if I can help it.'

The hand that inched over to touch his arm was wasting away and this made a fierce anger bubble up inside him.

'There's nothing you can do, laddie. I'm just a rickle o' bones and I havena even the strength to stand up.'

'Ah, but I've made an allowance for that.' Max's voice was triumphant. 'Just a minute.' He darted off and brought Nora back with him.

'Me and Max'll easy manage to get you doon the stair, Janet,' the girl boasted. 'I'm as strong as an ox.'

'I wouldna be surprised.' Janet gave a weak laugh.

Before they did anything else, Nora issued an order. 'Open the curtains a wee bit, Max, so I can see to get her coat out o' the closet – else she'll get a chill.'

The skeletal woman covered in a fashion, Max slid his arms underneath hers and got her manoeuvred to the edge of the bed, allowing her to sit for a moment to get her breath back. Then he hoisted her to the floor, gesturing to Nora to bolster her at the other side when he turned her round. It was awkward and difficult, for Janet had no power over her legs or feet

156

and kept slipping downwards, but they persisted. Getting her through the door almost beat them but, going sideways, Max first, then Janet, then Nora, they finally managed.

Now came the worst part – if she slipped through their grip here, Max thought, she would tumble right to the bottom of the three flights of stairs, making enough noise, no doubt, to alert the whole building. Not only that, such a fall would probably be the finish of her.

The first flight laboriously, but safely, negotiated, the landing was easier but they still had the middle flight, another landing and another flight to go before they reached ground level. After many hair-raising near-calamities, they were on the second last step when Beenie, the scullery maid, came out of the kitchen, halting in amazement when she saw what was going on. Afraid that Janet would sink down if he removed the support of his left arm, Max scowled a warning to the girl and shook his head to let her know to keep quiet. She kept looking at them till they reached her, her mouth as well as her eyes wide open. Then understanding seemed to strike her and she ran to hold the kitchen door open for them.

With three of them working together, it was much easier to get Janet to the stable, where she was able to sit down on the chair Beenie had taken with her from the kitchen. Max now hitched one of the horses to the only completely covered carriage. At least the poor woman would be shielded from the wind.

Having completed the part of his plan that had given him most cause for concern, Max turned to the two girls when his patient was sitting inside the conveyance. 'You had better go back and lock that door again, Nora,' he said firmly, 'and then I want you both to carry on as usual. I don't want anybody else to know about this.'

'What about you?' Nora wanted to know.

He took a moment or two to answer. He hadn't thought of what would happen after this. 'I think I'll manage to get back tonight but it'll likely . . .'

'You're coming back?' gasped Beenie.

'If I dinna, Ledingham'll get the police on me for stealing the horse and carriage and God kens what else. Will you two manage to find some excuse if onybody wonders why I'm not in for my supper?'

It was young Beenie who supplied an answer. 'You could say you went to meet your lass seeing Ledingham and the cook was baith awa'.'

'You'd get a richt row for that if he found oot,' Nora warned. 'You're supposed to be ill.'

'I'm going to get a bloody awful row in any case,' Max muttered, wryly. 'Well, I'd best get going. Mind what I said, now.'

'How're you feeling, Janet?' he asked when he swung himself up on the seat.

Under cover, Janet was still recovering from the not-altogether-gentle handling she'd had to suffer but she would have borne worse pain than that to be free of her husband. Max Dalgarno had only doubled her fears. 'Don't worry about me, laddie. I'll be fine now – wherever you're taking me.'

'I'm taking you to Henry,' he told her, somewhat tentatively.

'Oh, thank God for that. Henry and Fay'll look after me. They'll get me back on my feet in no time.'

The two young Raes, despite their shock at seeing her in such a poor condition, welcomed Janet warmly into their house, asking no questions but letting her know that she had a home with them for as long as she wanted. Then, after making her sup a small amount of strained and diluted lentil soup, Max wolfed down two platefuls of the thick original while Fay went to make a bed for Janet on the couch in the parlour. Climbing the stairs would be too much for her for a few weeks yet. The two men practically carried the exhausted woman through and Fay insisted on staying with her to make sure she fell asleep.

Alone with his old school friend, Max related what had been happening. 'It's a damned good thing you wrote me that letter,' he ended. 'I'd say we just got her away from that bugger Ledingham in time.'

'I wish I'd written sooner,' Henry moaned. 'No, I should have gone to find out why we hadn't heard from her.'

'He wouldn't have let you see her.' Max lapsed into a brief, pensive silence, then said, 'Ledingham's been taking up with the new cook he got in.'

This surprised Henry even more. 'I'd never have put him down as a ladies' man. By what Janet said, he'd loved her since they were at school. Then, when he learned she'd been seeing a sailor, he got wed to somebody else. Gloria, Janet said her name was.'

Max snapped his fingers. 'Gloria! That's it. Nora heard him saying "Glo . . ." and he said he could never remember to call her Kate. Well, well, then! Mrs Rattray's his first wife?'

A bewildered Henry muttered, 'But . . . she's supposed to have died. Janet was sure he'd murdered her. That was why she was so scared of him.'

'She's right to be scared of him,' Max declared. 'I'm near sure he's been trying to do away wi' her. He'll want to get back to his Gloria, now she's turned up again.'

'We'd better not tell Janet she's back from the dead. She's not up to the shock.'

Max gave a dry laugh. 'I'm not sure I'm up to the shock I'll get when I go back.'

For all his seeming light-heartedness, however, the immensity of what he had done was festering in his mind as the carriage bowled along the road to The Sycamores. He had got away with it so far but, once Ledingham came back and found Janet gone, there would be a God-awful row. He would know right away that somebody had helped Janet – she wasn't capable of walking out by herself. Then the questions would start and he wouldn't be happy till he'd got at the truth. The trouble was, he, Max, was the only one who had been away from the place, so he would be the obvious suspect. There was no getting round that.

CHAPTER TWELVE

'I've been thinking.'

Her husband's loud whisper told Fay that he had not been asleep either. Despite talking about it for hours the night before, what had happened was too momentous to be pushed to the back of their minds. 'What?'

'What'll Innes Ledingham do when he finds out Janet's not there?'

'I suppose he'll start looking for her.'

'And he knows how close she was to me so he's bound to come here first.'

'Oh,' Fay gasped, 'that's right. What'll we do?'

'We can't ask anybody else to take her; we don't want other people knowing. In any case, it's up to us to look after her, seeing Max brought her here.'

'I hope he doesn't lose his job because of it.'

'Losing his job would be the least of it, my Fairy. Ledingham could report him to the police for abducting her.'

'He surely wouldn't do that?'

'I wouldn't put it past him – he's devious enough for anything.'

They looked at each, realising that they might be in just as much trouble as Max Dalgarno. 'I'd better go down to see how she is,' Fay said at last, 'and you should try to think of something we can do.'

Henry could think of nothing else. If it were not for his wife and his two little children, he would face anything, any punishment, for Janet's sake, but, if he lost his job, it would be his family who would suffer. He might have asked Abby to take the poor woman in but her new baby had not been well since his birth, five weeks ago, so she had enough to contend with. Besides, everyone at The Sycamores knew he had a sister and Ledingham would go to her if he didn't find his wife here.

If only Janet was well enough to go upstairs. There was a little bolthole in the closet in the attic – possibly put in originally to hide a priest during the troubled times of the Jacobite rebellions. He had only come across it by accident when they were clearing out some of the previous tenants' rubbish. He had taken out the well-worn leather couch and the small table with the intention of throwing them out but Fay had stopped him.

'This would be a good place for our children to play,' she had smiled. 'That will be a few years yet, of course, so give these things a good scrub, and cover them when you put them back, to prevent the dust and cobwebs clinging to them again.'

That had been before Andrew was born, Henry recalled, but even then, Fay had been determined to have more than one child. His mind turned to Janet again. It would be a long time yet before she was fit to run up there and hide if anyone came looking for her.

Noticing the time, he jumped out of bed – he had never once been late for work since he became the Town Officer and he didn't mean to start now. He could hardly go downstairs today in just his flannel linder and long drawers like he usually did so he pulled on the moleskin trousers that he wore to sweep the streets. His jacket and dark cloth cap were hanging in the porch. The uniform he had been given – a smart snouted cap like naval officers wore, a neat dark blue broadcloth jacket with brass buttons and trousers to match – was only to be worn on official occasions – if the court was sitting and he was acting as usher, for instance, or if he had a proclamation to make in his other capacity as bell ringer/town crier.

His first sight of Janet in the pale light of morning gave him quite a shock. Her eyes were so deeply sunk that it looked as if she were wearing heavy black-rimmed glasses. The rosy cheeks he remembered were ashen and clapped against her cheekbones so as to make them stand out like coat pegs. And her neck was pathetically scrawny.

161

Her lips quivered as soon as she saw him. 'Oh, Henry,' she moaned, holding out her stick-thin arms, and he ran to hold her, his heart almost breaking at the thought of what she must have gone through.

'You're safe here,' he managed to get out, 'We'll take care of you.'

Then he went out to the small lean-to at the back door, where Fay had a basin of hot water ready for him to wash. He had stopped shaving his upper lip almost a year ago and now had an abundant moustache which, he felt, was more in keeping with his position as Town Officer, a job that, although not very far up the ladder of success, still held some degree of responsibility. Unfortunately, he had become so well known since he took over the job that he would have no time to think. Every person who passed him would call out, 'Aye, aye, fine day, T H,' or, from the more refined, 'It is cold enough for snow, Mr Rae,' or, from the older men, with a twinkle in their eyes, 'You're aye kept busy, then, Tchouki?' Sometimes, he even got the name he preferred – Henry – but he answered to anything. What did it matter? He had nothing to hide now.

This thought pulled him up sharply, making him stop towelling his neck. He had worse to hide now. He was harbouring a woman who had been removed from her husband's home without his knowledge. Shaking his head at the predicament in which he had been landed, Henry finished drying himself and went through to get his breakfast.

The morning had passed normally for Max, whose mind was a little easier. Not one soul had thought anything of him not being there for supper the night before – a blessing he owed entirely to Nora. As she told him when he was on his way to the kitchen for his breakfast, 'The grieve did ask where you was last night and I said you was still feeling sick. They all heard Ledingham telling you to go back to your bed yesterday so you've nothing to worry about.'

He *had* something to worry about, though. As soon as Ledingham came back, he'd go up to speak to his wife and find out she wasn't there. Then the rumpus would start. He wasn't an obvious suspect now, of course. He had been in bed ill, so how could he have spirited the woman away?

'Are you feeling better, Max? You're still a bit white round the gills.'

He looked up from thinning out the winter cabbages to find the head gardener eyeing him in some concern. 'I'm nae just right yet, Mr Lumsden, but I am a bit better.'

'Well, if you start feeling bad again, just go back to your bed. Better another one day off than a week or more.'

'Aye, you're right. Thanks.'

He kept on working, hoeing the vegetable garden as if afraid that any weeds he left would engulf the whole place, including him. He barely stopped to take a few bites of the oatcakes and cheese Nora had made up for the men's dinner pieces and, when the clock on the bell tower struck six, it was with reluctance that he laid past his tools and made his slow way inside.

There was absolute silence in the kitchen, an eerie foreboding silence, warning him that the discovery had been made. With stomach churning, he took a lingering look at the Superintendent. The man was gripping his mouth and his knuckles showed white as he clutched his soupspoon. Not only that, but he never lifted his eyes from his plate – an indication that he had deep, deep thoughts to ponder over. Aye, the man had much to ponder over, Max thought with some satisfaction, moving his gaze to the cook. Mrs Rattray was even more agitated. Her face was scarlet, as if she had taken part in a terrible row – which she probably had. She was likely the only one Ledingham had told. At the moment, he was most likely trying to work out how to go about solving the mystery of his missing wife but his first reaction would have been to let fly at his paramour.

Despite the situation holding the possibility of dire consequences for him, Max felt exhilarated – he had a sense of living on the edge of danger with the challenge of trying to outwit this fiend of a man. Ledingham only toyed with his food and was first to leave the table, shoving back his chair abruptly and stalking out without a word. Next to go were the nursing staff, who had their charges to get washed and settled for the night, and then, in twos and threes the other men gradually went out. They were obviously bursting with curiosity over what could be going on but were unable to discuss it in front of the cook, who, as they were all well aware, had some hold over the Superintendent and would tell tales to him at the drop of a hat.

Because of their own preoccupations, not one of the others noticed that Max held back – not even Mrs Rattray who darted out abruptly, leaving Nora and Beenie to clear the table and do the dishes.

Max gave a loud, relieved sigh. 'What's been happening, Nora?'

She gestured to the scullery maid to close the door and they sat down at the table again. 'He's raving mad,' she reported in triumph. 'He didna go up right away for he took Mrs Rattray into his sitting room first.'

'And?' prompted the young man impatiently.

Little Beenie stepped in now. 'I took ben a tea tray to them to see if I could hear what they were saying,' she chuckled. 'I thought I might catch them having a last canoodle so I just gave a wee tap and opened the door. What a shock I got! He was on top o' her . . .'

'That's enough, Beenie!' Nora scowled. 'You was just being nosy and, any road, you shouldna ken aboot things like that at your age.'

The fourteen-year-old grinned mischievously. 'I didna ken . . . but I ken now. He'd her bloomers doon and . . .'

Having heard enough, Max interrupted her. 'Well, that's it. If he ever finds out it was me that got Janet away and reports me to the bobbies, I'll tell them he married Janet when he was still married to his first wife.'

Nora could see the flaws in this statement, however. 'They wouldna believe you.'

'They would if you and Beenie back me up.'

'No, Max. He's a Superintendent, she's supposed to be a respected cook and we're just skivvies. The police are bound to believe whatever he tells them and it'll be the worse for us. He can have us arrested and put in the jail.'

'But they could check up and see . . .' Max broke off at a sudden memory. 'There must be a record of his marriage to Janet in the register here.'

Nora shook her head at his naivety. 'He could tear that page out, you ken how he is. If he's desperate, he'll do anything to save his skin.'

Beenie piped up again. 'But I'm a witness to what he was doing . . .' Looking at both the scowling faces, she offered her last trick. 'He was . . . um . . . fornicating wi' a wumman that's nae his wife.'

'Beenie,' Max sighed, 'that's just the point. Mrs Rattray, as she calls herself, *is* his wife; it's Janet that's not legally married to him.'

The girl digested this information, then she, too, sighed. 'Aye, so she's nae. It's her that's been forn . . .'

'Beenie Dickie! Just shut up, would you?' Nora could stand no more of the scullery maid's twitterings and turned to the young gardener again. 'We'll have to wait and see what happens, Max. We can't do nothing else.'

'Aye, you're right.' He strode out, shaking his head at their helplessness.

Fay was in a fine state of nerves. Terrified that Innes Ledingham or the police or both would turn up and find Janet in the parlour, she had locked the door the minute Henry left for work. She had also been trying to keep her small son quiet so that their guest could get some much needed rest and the knock on her door at half past ten made her heart jump into her mouth. If she'd had the chance, she would have ignored the summons but little Andrew had already bounded into the tiny porch and was trying to turn the knob so whoever was there would know they weren't out.

Her hands trembling, she turned the big key in the lock and

edged the door open just enough to find out who was there.

'What's wrong, lass?' Nessie pushed past her. 'The door still locked at this time o' the day?'

Trying to prevent her stepmother-in-law from seeing what she wasn't meant to see, Fay made it all the more evident that she wanted to hide something and Nessie asked again, 'What's wrong? What's going on?'

The ever-helpful Andrew supplied the answer his mother was determined not to give. 'It's Auntie Janet!' he smiled, pointing to the parlour door. 'She's in there and she's not well.'

Nessie turned the familiar name over in her mind. '*Auntie* Janet? The cook from The Sycamores?' She moved swiftly to the other door, opened it a fraction and took a quick glance inside. 'Aye, Fay,' she murmured, as she closed the door as silently as she had opened it, 'I can see she's ill but why's she here?'

Having no experience of dealing with a situation of such delicacy, the young woman was at a loss for a moment or so, then, deciding that she may as well tell the truth, she said, 'Stay here like a good boy, Andrew, till I speak to Grandma.'

She drew Nessie back into the porch and gave the tale as she knew it, answering the woman's questions with a shrugged, 'I don't know anything more.'

With her innate perspicacity, Nessie did manage to fit most of the puzzle together and stood for a moment pondering over it. Then she looked keenly at the younger woman. 'You're scared her man'll come looking for her?'

Fay nodded tearfully. 'We don't know what to do and that's the truth. We can't let anyone know she's here and she's not fit to go up to the Covenanters' hidey-hole.'

Nessie took over now. 'Never mind. You make a pot o' tea and I'll think and think till I come up with something.'

It was not long until 'something' did come up in her mind. 'If I mind right, Fay,' she began, 'you once told me everybody at Craigdownie and The Sycamores knew Henry had a sister here in Ardbirtle.'

'Yes,' Fay faltered, wondering what was coming.

'But nobody knows he has a father here and all?'

'No, I don't think so.'

Andrew interrupted them now, running through and saying loudly, 'Auntie Janet's woke up.'

'Good!' Nessie was in the parlour before the other two realised what was happening. 'I'm sorry to come in on you like this, Janet,' she said, softly, 'but did you know Henry's father bade here in Ardbirtle?'

Janet shook her head weakly, not understanding the reason behind the question. 'No, Henry never spoke about his father.'

Nessie beamed happily. 'Well, that's the answer! Willie's got a four-wheeler in just now, something wrong wi' the axle, so I'll go and tell him to get it ready as quick as he can and come and collect Janet.'

'But she's not fit to . . .' Fay pointed out.

'Ach, Willie'll easy lift her. She's nothing but skin and bone.' Nessie sailed out, a ship on the high seas ready for anything the elements would throw at her.

Fay looked at Janet now. 'I'm sorry. That was Henry's stepmother and she's one of those people who won't take no for an answer.'

'She's a good woman, though, that's clear.'

Fortunately for Fay, her baby daughter woke up at that point, late for her ten o'clock feed and letting them know, loudly and clearly, that she was ready for it. The waiting time was, therefore, taken up by the changing, the feeding and a little cuddling.

Andrew, tearing himself away from this fascinating sight, suddenly rushed over to the window. 'A cart, a cart!' he cried and in the next breath, 'Granda, Granda!'

Willie strode in, followed by Nessie who demanded, 'Have you got all her things ready?'

'She didn't have any things,' Fay murmured.

'Just my coat,' Janet reminded her.

'We don't want anybody to see her,' Fay pointed out so Nessie went to the door to watch for the right moment.

'Excuse me, Janet,' Willie said softly and he rolled her inside the blankets, making sure that every inch of her was covered, then scooped her up in his brawny arms as if she were a bag of feathers.

'Now,' ordered Nessie and out he went with his precious cargo and swung her up to Nessie who had already jumped on board. In little more than a couple of seconds, Janet was settled into the compartment and, in another five minutes, she was inside Oak Cottage.

Fay's heart had barely settled back to its normal rhythm when someone else knocked on her door – three loud, imperative raps that told her this was trouble.

'Ah, Mrs Rae,' Innes Ledingham said, with a fawning smile, 'I am sorry to come bothering you but can tell me anything about the whereabouts of my wife?'

Fay held on to the doorpost in case her knees gave way with the lie she was about to tell. 'No, Mr Ledingham. Is she not at The Sycamores?'

He looked askance at her, then said, 'I am sorry to have to ask you this but may I take a look round your house?'

'So you do not believe me?' She dredged the strength up from somewhere deep inside her. 'Well, look all you want to. There is no one here.'

'Me, Mother!' Andrew grabbed her hand and looked at the man doubtfully.

Ledingham bent down to him. 'What is your name, little boy?'

'Andrew and . . .' pointing to the cradle, 'she's Mara.'

'Samara,' his mother corrected.

'Tell me, Andrew, has a lady been here today?'

Fay's stomach went into a spasm of fear as her son thought for a moment, then he smiled broadly. 'Grandma.'

Knowing that the man would realise that where there was a grandmother there would likely be a grandfather, Fay said, 'Yes, my mother was here.' At least he already knew about *her* mother and father.

'I see. Well, if you do not mind, I will get Andrew to show me around.'

She managed to keep her voice steady. 'I do not mind. Show Mr Ledingham the parlour, Andrew, and take him up to see the bedrooms.'

When they went upstairs, Fay stood at the bottom, listening to everything that was said. 'That's Mother and Father's bed,' Andrew was saying.

Hearing the two sets of feet crossing the landing to the other bedroom, Fay thought that would be the end of it but Andrew was taking his duty as guide very seriously. 'More,' he stated and Fay listened to him leading the Superintendent up the narrow wooden steps to the attics. She heard the first door creaking open and then the second, which always gave a peculiar little squeak.

'Well, that's it, I suppose,' came the deep voice but Andrew's treble followed, 'Nother door.'

Fay couldn't help smiling. Ledingham would find nothing in the closet, either, thank goodness. When man and boy came down, she said rather tartly, 'Are you satisfied now?'

Ledingham's face was livid with frustration. 'She is not here.'

'I told you.'

She sat down with her hand on her heart when the little trap drew away and her son came to stand beside her. 'Me a good boy?'

She lifted him on to her knee. 'Yes, a very good boy.' She had resented Nessie for taking over, had felt that she was being manipulated, but thank God it had been so. If Janet had been left here, Ledingham would have found her and goodness knows what would have transpired.

CHAPTER THIRTEEN

'I am absolutely sure that Henry Rae had something to do with it.' Innes Ledingham was pacing the floor of his sitting room like a lion padding round his cage.

Gloria, still known to everyone in The Sycamores as Mrs Rattray, looked somewhat irritated. 'You told me you had searched his house and there was no sign of Janet.'

'That does not mean a thing. He could have hidden her away somewhere else.'

'I thought you had contacted all the people he might have gone to?'

'I asked Roderick Emslie, Janet's brother, if he knew anything but he seemed as shocked as I was to learn that she had disappeared. They have not been close for some time – not since their mother died. Then I remembered that Rae had a sister who also lives in Ardbirtle so I asked at the Post Office and got her address. It took some time because she is married and has a different surname now and she, too, looked genuinely surprised by my question.'

Gloria regarded him through narrowed eyes. 'Couldn't the woman just have wandered off by herself? You said that she wasn't quite . . .'

'For God's sake! Have some sense, Gloria. Janet would not have been capable of getting to the bedroom door, never mind going down the stairs and walking away. I tell you, someone must have helped her.'

'Who, then?'

'That is what I am trying to find out! No one outside these walls could have known of her condition. She has not been able to hold a pen for weeks now, so she could not have

170

communicated with anyone.'

'You think it was someone here?'

'It must have been. The problem is, which of the staff was it?' He sat down now, but the drumming of his fingers on the arm of his chair told of his continuing, even increasing, agitation.

After a moment's silence, Gloria murmured, 'Are you sure it was one of the staff?'

Her husband looked at her incredulously. 'You cannot possibly think that it was one of the guests?'

'Why not? You said that Janet was quite friendly with all of them but perhaps there was one, or more than one, that she was very close to. Would two able-bodied women have managed to carry her out?'

'Do you know, Gloria,' he said, icily, 'I sometimes fear for *your* sanity. None of these ancient relics would have had the strength to carry her anywhere.'

'They're not all ancient,' she protested. ' There are a few in middle age and slightly younger who would have managed.'

He considered this carefully, obviously trying to pinpoint those with the physical ability, and then he shook his head. 'No, those whose bodies are still in prime condition do not have the mental ability . . . and vice versa.'

'Innes, forget about her. She has gone and that's what we wanted, isn't it?'

'Yes, that is what we wanted but I would like to know where she has gone and how. Until I learn that, I will be constantly looking over my shoulder in case she turns up again . . . as you did.'

This last dig did not please Gloria. 'You knew I was still alive so don't try to pretend otherwise. You got round that woman by telling her I was dead so you can't make out you're an angel. I know you, Innes Ledingham, and, to be honest, it wouldn't surprise me if you had something to do with her illness – if illness is what it was.'

'And what do you mean by that?'

His tone was so nasty that she raised her voice now. 'You

know perfectly well what I mean. She had served her purpose, I had come back into your life and you wanted rid of her. I know you acted the worried husband, taking up her meals yourself. So what did you put in them? Arsenic? There is plenty of that in the gardener's shed, I've seen it.'

The man's face had gone from angry red to pure white and he had difficulty now in forming his words in his temper. 'So you knew? And you held your tongue? In the eyes of the police you would be considered as having aided and abetted.'

'Who said anything about the police? I am not vindictive, Innes. I do not begrudge you your few years of passion with your mistress. I had some very close male acquaintances myself . . . very close. Just hear me out,' she added as he jumped up furiously. 'However Janet got away – and I am practically sure that nobody helped her, that she had been feigning much of her illness because she knew what you were trying to do – I believe that she will stay away. She will try to get as far away as she can and it would not surprise me if we hear in quite a short time that her body has been found somewhere.'

Innes sat down again, biting his bottom lip. 'Is that what you really think or are you trying to pacify me? Mind you, I suppose it is a possibility. I have done all I can, in any case, so perhaps I should leave it for the time being . . . until we see if anything turns up.'

Getting to her feet, Gloria said, 'I had better get back to the kitchen or else the tongues will be wagging.'

Her husband watched her go out. She was still a damned good-looking woman and she had calmed down a lot since she had been away. There had been no repeat of the blazing rows they used to have – she was always willing to do whatever he told her. Or was she trying to convince him that she was a better wife than Janet? She certainly was more exciting in bed.

Was it possible, though, that she was right about how Janet had disappeared? Not the doing it alone bit but with the help of two of the guests? It was more likely to have been one of the staff . . . or more than one. Had there been a conspiracy? If Gloria had suspected that he was dosing Janet with arsenic,

172

some of the brighter nurses or servants could also have had doubts. Men, especially men of the working class, were not so quick at noticing things.

'I still can't understand why that man came here.' Abby Laing looked at her husband as if she were expecting an explanation. 'I've never met his wife . . . and why would she have run away? And how did he know I was Henry's sister?'

Pogie, who was stouter now, made an even more impressive figure to lead the funeral corteges. He held out his hands, palms up. 'I am as much at a loss as you, my dear, but I will do my best to figure out some answers. You say he had already searched Henry's house? That means Henry must have been his prime suspect. It follows, quite logically, that Ledingham would then think of the person nearest to Henry. You, his sister.'

'But how did he know where I lived?'

'Ardbirtle is quite a small town. It would be easy to ask around until he found someone who knew you. Henry, or Janet, must have mentioned that he had a sister. As to why the woman ran away, I can only think that they must have had a bad quarrel or he had been abusing her for some time and she could stand it no longer.'

'He didn't look the kind of man to abuse his wife,' Abby protested. 'He was wearing an expensive suit and a beaver hat with a turned up brim.'

'How little you know of men, my dear Abby.' Pogie rose to lift their tiny son who had awakened from a rather restless sleep and was mewing like a kitten in pain.

'Is it too early for his next feed?'

'It's not due for another hour and a bit.'

'Can't you just let him have a little drop to settle him?'

'It's not supposed to be good for them . . . but, ach, it's the only way.'

'You know, Abby, I think we should call the doctor in again. He never seems to get any better.'

173

* * *

'Oh, my God!' Nessie Rae adjusted her spectacles and read the note again.

'What's wrong, Nessie?'

'It's from Pogie. They've lost their baby. I thought it must be bad news when their neighbour handed it in. I'll have to go to Abby but . . . will you be all right on your own, Janet?'

'I'll be fine. Off you go.'

Giving her face a quick swill but not bothering to take off her overall, Nessie was on her way within five minutes, issuing one last instruction. 'Don't go trying to let anybody in if you hear a knock, mind.'

Janet just nodded. It was almost a week since she had been taken to Oak Cottage and she felt a bit better. Not in the best of conditions but certainly much improved. She had been put straight into the downstairs bedroom when she arrived, in a bed far more comfortable than Henry's couch. Nessie, of course, watched her like a hawk but there was no reason why she couldn't test herself out a wee bit. Turning down the blankets, she swivelled round, letting her legs slide over the edge of the bed. Even that little movement was an effort so she sat there for a while to recover. It crossed her mind that it would take all her remaining strength just to swivel back again but not yet. She wanted to prove herself.

It took fully ten minutes for her to feel able to move again, this time sliding her bottom right to the edge and feeling her toes touch the floor. That was something achieved at any rate. In another ten minutes or so, she took hold of the bed knob with her right hand, steadied herself with her left hand pressing against the mattress, then tried to take her weight on her feet. She should have known. Neither her arms nor her legs were strong enough for this and, with a low moan, she slid down to the floor, the brass ball in her hand instead of on the bed-head.

Her heart chugging like a railway engine breasting a long hill, she took stock of her position. There was no pain so she hadn't broken anything – that was a blessing. She had landed on her rear end, which was well enough padded to absorb any shock. Her legs were out in front of her . . . and she could wiggle her toes. No damage there, then. Her arms seemed to move in the normal way, though it remained to be seen if she could coax her legs to get her on to her feet.

After several attempts, interspersed with short periods of rest, she had to concede to failure. She would have to sit here like a sack of tatties, on the floor, until Nessie came back or Willie came in for his supper. She glanced at the clock. Only five to two. Willie didn't usually appear until round about six. Four whole hours to sit like this?

Apart from not being very comfortable, she was beginning to feel a chill – her back was cold and her legs and feet, in contact with the linoleum, were even worse. She had to do something otherwise Nessie or Willie would find a body frozen to the floor when they came in.

Then she remembered that her back could not be far from the bed, from a lovely quilt, but could she manage to pull it down to her? Gradually, by little tugs every now and then and by dint of intense determination, she inched the eiderdown to the edge and then one last pull had it dropping on to the rug she had not been lucky enough to land on when she tumbled. Taking some moments to recharge her meagre energy, she eventually got herself covered and had managed to slide over until she was leaning against the bed.

Oh, dear God! It was Heaven! But for how long?

Sad at heart after Nessie popped in to tell her about Abby's baby, Fay decided that her best plan would be to make sure that Janet was all right. Henry would not be pleased to think she had been left alone.

She washed her son first, changed his little suit and set him down on the couch. 'Don't move, Andrew. Mother has to wash and dress Samara before we go out.'

These two tasks took some time but, at last, without bothering to check on her own appearance, she put both children in

175

the big, carriage-hung perambulator, a gift from her mother when Andrew was born. She could walk more quickly when he wasn't padding along beside her on his chubby little legs. It wasn't far to Oak Cottage but it was almost an hour since Nessie had gone.

Intent on being there in case Janet needed something, Fay did not notice the man looking into the grocer's window at the other side of the street. Nor did she sense him following her at a discreet distance and turning into Kirk Brae after her. Arriving at her destination, she gave a light tap on the door and went in.

'Oh, Janet!' she cried, seeing the poor woman on the floor when she looked into the bedroom. 'What happened? Are you all right.'

'I'm fine.' But Janet's weak voice was quivering.

'You are not fine!' Fay had left the pram in the porch and she quickly crossed the room to help her. However, she soon found that the patient was heavier than she looked. 'I'll have to get Willie,' she puffed.

In just a minute or two, Willie Rae strode in, his canvas apron flapping, his white hair wet with sweat from standing in the intense heat in the smiddy. 'So?' he demanded. 'What have you been up to, my lady?' Without waiting for her answer, he bent down to scoop her up and deposited her gently on the bed.

She lay still for a few moments, then said, 'I'm sorry for being a nuisance. I was wanting to try myself but my legs wouldn't take my weight.'

'Aye, you've put on a wee bit o' weight since you came here,' he laughed, ' but don't do anything like this again. Get somebody to help you. Now, I'd better get back or the shoe I was shaping'll be hardening already.'

When he went out, Fay took a quick look in the pram, found both her children asleep and then returned to the bedroom. 'Would you like a cup of tea?'

'There's nothing I'd like better.'

Fay stayed with her charge until Nessie came back, letting

176

little Andrew amuse Janet while she cooked the piece of lamb that had obviously been intended for the supper and preparing some vegetables to accompany it. Once relieved of her duty, she hurried home to make something for her own family, hoping that Henry would not be too upset about Abby's tragedy to eat.

Innes Ledingham practically danced back to the carriage he had left on the edge of the town. His journey to Ardbirtle had not been in vain – he had learned something that he felt was central to his quest.

'Where were you all afternoon?' Gloria demanded after supper. 'Am I supposed to manage this place as well as do all the cooking?'

He slid his arm round her waist. 'I was in Ardbirtle, my dearest, and I think I have discovered where Henry Rae has hidden Janet.'

'You think? So you do not know for sure?'

'I am almost sure,' he smiled. I saw an older woman running in to talk to Fay for a few minutes and come rushing out again.'

'If she was running and rushing, it could not have been Janet.'

He heaved an exaggerated sigh. 'I am well aware of that. No, that was not Janet but, after some time, Fay came hurrying out with her children in the perambulator and I followed her.'

'Oh, for goodness sake, Innes! What did you think you . . .'

'I believe that Janet is in the house she visited – Oak Cottage it is called.'

'What gave you the idea she was there?' Gloria sneered. 'Whose house is it?'

'I do not know yet but it is obviously one of Fay's friends or Henry's.'

Gloria mulled over this for some time, then she muttered, 'Maybe she is there, then, but I still think we should leave it alone. Janet will never come back here to bother us.'

'You never know,' he said, darkly. 'Once she regains her health, she could quite easily realise that she could . . .'

'She can do nothing. You know that.'

'She could report me to the police for trying to poison her.'

'They would not believe her. You are the highly respected Superintendent of The Sycamores, while she was just a cook.'

'Stranger things have happened and, besides that, she could blackmail me. I married her bigamously . . .'

'You told me you had removed that page from the register so there is no proof that you married her, is there?'

'I am afraid there is, Gloria. Every person here attended the wedding.'

'The police would not believe a bunch of lunatics.'

'There were the nurses, the servants and the male workers. They were all present.'

'Ah, yes. Well, what were you intending to do?'

'I have not formed a plan yet.'

Innes spent a sleepless night, thinking of several ways to get Janet away from Oak Cottage and discarding them as unfeasible but, just as daybreak filtered through a tiny crack in the curtains, his heart gave a leap. Why did he not just get hold of Henry on his own and threaten to expose him to the police for his hand in her abduction if he did not give her up? He did not actually commit the crime, of course, but he was the 'receiver of the stolen goods'.

If that failed, he could threaten to do some harm to Henry's wife and children if he did not do as he was told. The poor fool was only a street sweeper, when all was said and done, although he boasted the title of Town Officer. He was not a well-educated man and would be easily intimidated. Yes, Innes reflected, it should be easy enough but it might be better to wait a little longer until Janet was fit to walk.

Henry was still very upset when he went to bed. He had paid Abby a visit during the evening and it had wrenched at his heart seeing her grief over her infant. He was glad that Nessie had been there for her earlier on. Maybe he should suggest that Fay take Abby's little boy to stay here for a few days out of the way, until after the funeral, anyway.

Worrying over this, Henry remembered that Pogie had said he was doing his little son's funeral himself and he had closed his business to the public for the next week. Would he be able to comfort his wife properly, though, or would she feel the need to have a woman-body with her? She wasn't as strong as she would have everybody believe. He could vouch for that.

Nessie would likely offer to stay with her which would mean there would be no one to keep an eye on Janet – and look what had happened to her when she was on her own for the afternoon.

CHAPTER FOURTEEN

It took Innes Ledingham quite some effort to hide his excitement as he left Ardbirtle Post Office. His heart rate had doubled when he asked his question, wondering if his explanation for asking it sounded feasible but the postmaster had accepted it with a smile. 'Oak Cottage? That's Willie Rae's house. He's the blacksmith but the smiddy's at the back of the house, entrance in Hillview Road.'

His heartbeats had almost suffocated him then, Innes mused on his way back to The Sycamores, and the band constricting his chest was only loosening now. Willie Rae! It would be too great a coincidence for the resident of Oak Cottage to be anything other than one of Henry's relatives. A brother, perhaps? Or father? He had never mentioned either, only his sister, but that did not preclude their existence.

Allowing the mare to proceed at her own pace, he decided not to tell Gloria where he had been, nor what he had learned. She had been getting on his nerves recently, always questioning him about where he had been. He had forgotten, in her absence, how manipulative she was, which was why he had been glad to see the back of her before. That was when his mind had turned to Janet, the girl he had loved as a youth. He had thanked God for bringing her back into his life but she had proved to be less interesting and exciting than he had thought.

He had contacted Gloria then, asking her to come back to him and making no secret of his 'marriage'. He wished now that he had not bothered. He was better off without her – at least his life had run smoothly while Janet was at the helm. But he had destroyed any chance he may have had of making it up with her. She would want nothing more to do with him and it would be wisest to let her go.

A coldness came over him now. He could not afford to let her go. She must have run away because she guessed that he was slowly trying to poison her and, when she recovered properly, she would set the law on him. She had, apparently, not yet told Henry Rae anything but the time would come – no doubt about that.

His mind in a complete turmoil since Janet disappeared, Ledingham had forgotten that she could not possibly have got away by herself and was now actually believing that she had risen from her sickbed and run off. Naturally, she would have gone to Henry first – they had been friends even before they came to The Sycamores – but Rae had realised that he would be first to be suspected of harbouring her and had passed her to his brother or father. Willie!

Innes smiled in satisfaction. All that remained to be done was to find a way to outwit Mr and Mrs William Rae, to somehow manoeuvre things so that Janet was left alone in the house or to make her come outside on her own. He had not actually planned how to get her into the carriage but his ingenious mind would not fail him when the time came.

The mare stopped of her own accord at the stable door. He dismounted and entered the kitchen, where Gloria turned a venomous eye on him but said nothing in front of Beenie, who was gleefully waiting for the explosion that did not materialise. He had hardly got seated in his office-cum-sitting room when Gloria barged in. 'Where did you sneak off to this time?' she demanded.

'I did not sneak anywhere,' he answered with what he hoped was quiet dignity. 'I went to Letherton Farm to see if Jack Duthie would give me a better deal for the milk.'

This clearly took the wind out of her sails but she snapped, 'And did he?'

'He did – so my journey was not wasted.'

'You should have been doing something to get you precious 'wife' back,' she snarled. 'With her still on the loose, my nerves are in shreds waiting for the police to come and arrest you for bigamy.'

Innes almost told her that *she* was shredding *his* nerves, carrying on the way she did. Besides, when – if – he was arrested, it might not be for bigamy. The longer it went on, the more likely that he could be charged with murder, yet he was determined not to be rushed into anything. He had to be sure that there would be no slips, nothing to trip him up and alert the police. That was why he had told Gloria nothing of what he was doing. In fact, it had occurred to him several times lately that it might be a good plan to dispose of *her*, too. There was still plenty arsenic in the potting shed.

'I'm as fit as a fiddle, Nessie.' Janet had been saying this for a week now and still the other woman wouldn't let her go out. 'I could easily do some shopping to save you or take a dander along to see Fay and the bairns.'

'And give Ledingham a chance to snatch you back?'

'I don't think he's bothered. He didn't find me at Henry's house and Fay didn't tell him about you and Willie so I think he must have given up.'

'From what you've told me about him, I wouldn't say he was the kind to give up but maybe you're right. Well, well, then, I'll let you go along to see Fay but we'd better set a time limit so I'll know you're not in any trouble. One hour there and straight back, agreed?'

'Agreed,' Janet smiled.

The visit, joyfully received by Fay, went off without a hitch and Nessie was forced to admit that she had been wrong. There was still a glimmer of doubt in her mind but she kept it to herself. Janet had little enough pleasure in her life these days and she wasn't going to spoil things for the poor woman . . . unless, of course, needs warranted it.

Nessie, however, was astonished at how soon things were to be spoiled for her poor lodger.

Henry had risen with the peculiar feeling that misfortune of some kind was about to overtake him but he said nothing to Fay. With two young children to look after, she didn't need anything else to worry her.

Because of his own dread of what might happen, he changed his normal figure-of-eight route, giving himself farther to push his little handcart, which was no real hardship. He kept the horse dung separate from the other refuse, as was his custom, at the end farthest from his nose, to be given out to those who needed it for their gardens. A small smile flitted across his face as he recalled one of Geordie Mavor's favourite observations when they met in the street.

'I canna understand some folk putting horse shite on their rhubarb,' the carrier would joke. 'I like custard on mine.'

Of course, there wasn't much of anything else to pick up – the people of Ardbirtle mostly burned their rubbish or let it rot in their middens. But there were the odd bits of paper blown about by the wind or torn cardboard boxes and things like that so they were all placed at the end nearest to him.

Today, his mind was not really on what he was doing yet his sense of foreboding made him look about him as he went along Mid Street, down Beggar's Brae and into Mill Street, which took him to the other end of Mid Street. It was when he was halfway to his starting point that he caught a quick movement out of the corner of his eye. He was almost sure that it had been a man but there was no one to be seen.

Positive that someone had dodged out of sight, he left the cart and hurried to look along the alleyway that ran along the rear of the houses and did get a glimpse of a tall figure disappearing round a corner. To his frustration, it had vanished into thin air by the time he reached the spot but he would swear that it had been Innes Ledingham.

His vague unease now condensing into solid fear for Janet, he rushed to his father's house to warn her, startling the two women when he burst in breathlessly. 'I've just seen Ledingham!' he cried. 'He knows I saw him for he jinked into the back lane and I don't know where he went after that. He just disappeared.'

183

Janet said nothing but Nessie said, 'Are you sure it was him, Henry? Did you see his face?'

'I only saw his back but I'm near certain it was him. Who else would take to his heels when he saw me? Besides, he was wearing yon long black coat and the high bowler. Not many men round here dress like that.'

Having recovered from her initial shock, Janet muttered, 'Is he looking for me?'

The other two glanced at each other, not knowing what to do, then Henry said, 'I wouldn't be surprised, Janet. There's been a lot going on you don't know about but I'll have to go. I left my cart sitting in the middle of the road. You tell her, Nessie.'

She followed him into the little porch. 'What should I tell her?'

'Everything.'

'Henry, she maybe looks fit physically but I'm not so sure about her mind. That devil must have put her through hell and damnation.'

'Just tell her everything, Nessie. It's time she knew.'

'D'you think he's found out where she is?'

'If he had, he'd have been at your door, not skulking about on Mid Street.'

Innes sat for some time before he picked up the reins. That had been a narrow shave but he was almost sure that Henry Rae had not got a proper look at him.

It was a good thing that he had made himself so familiar with the layout of the town. His previous visits had necessitated some dodging out of the scavenger's sight in various areas but never had he been so nearly caught. He gave a nervous giggle. Little did young Rae think that he had taken refuge in one of the houses. The back porch door had been ajar and he had crept in and closed it behind him. He had waited there for . . . oh, it must have been a good twenty minutes before he could be sure that the coast was clear and he could make good his escape.

By Jove, he had been lucky, now he came to think about it. Not only had there been the risk of Rae finding him, he had been sweating like a common labourer in case the occupant of the house would come through but nothing had happened. He had let himself out eventually and then walked, as nonchalantly as he could, to where he had left his carriage, well out of the town.

He halted as he reached down for the reins to drive home. He could not cope with many more of these heart-stopping experiences, although he was feeling more composed now. The best thing to do at this point would be to turn round, go straight to Oak Cottage, gain entry to the house by some means and . . .

He could plan no further than that. What would happen next would depend on what had gone before.

Janet was waiting expectantly when Nessie returned to the kitchen. 'You'd better tell me – whatever it is.'

'How much do you remember about coming here?'

Janet's face paled. 'Not much, to be honest. I know I was very ill but I don't know how I got here. Was it Henry that took me away?'

'No, it was Max Dalgarno.'

'Max? But . . .'

'Look, Janet, I think I had better start at the very beginning.'

And so Innes Ledingham's treachery was unveiled, from the falsehood about his wife's death, possibly also about Mrs Emslie's death, to his decision to ask Gloria to come back to him. Nessie had to explain here that Mrs Rattray, the cook supposedly hired temporarily, was in fact his first wife and that he had actually been poisoning Janet with a view to finishing her off altogether.

Janet listened to it all, saying little but obviously becoming more and more shocked, and, when at last the quiet voice stopped, she said, 'Would you leave me on my own for a wee while, Nessie, please? I need to go over it all in my mind.'

'Aye, lass, I can understand that. I'll let Willie know what's been happening and then I'll go along and tell Fay. I'll go to the butcher as well and get a bit of ham for the tea but I'll not be very long.'

'Don't hurry back – I'll be fine.'

She wasn't fine, though, she admitted to herself when the other woman went out. So much had happened that she had no memory of and hearing about it had left her feeling utterly helpless – as if she had no control over her own life. After some deeply concentrated thought, little flashes of the past came to her – the onset of that queer illness, the sickness that always grew worse no matter what Innes gave her to stop it. But of course he hadn't been trying to help her at all. The temporary cook had turned up just the day after the first attack of what she had believed to be a stomach upset. The temporary cook! His first wife! Gloria!

Lingering on this horrible revelation, Janet was beset by an even more horrible thought – a thought so horrifying that she had to close her eyes for a few minutes to stop the walls closing in on her. She had married Innes Ledingham in all good faith but his first wife had still been alive! He had committed bigamy but what she had done was much, much worse. She had slept with a married man and done everything that sleeping with a man entailed! They had not been making love during those years of what she had thought of as marriage – they had been fornicating illegally!

Fornicating! She had never considered what she had done with Tom Aitken as fornicating. They had been young, desperately in love, he was going away and they had pledged their love in the only way they knew. He had sworn on his honour that he would marry her when he came home . . . but he hadn't come home.

She had sinned all those years ago – knowingly, willingly – and she had sinned again with Innes Ledingham – willingly but unknowingly. Was there any real difference? She had thought she loved Innes – though not in the same way as she'd loved Tom – but would that stand in her favour when she stood at the Pearly Gates?

186

She would also be held responsible, she realised, for the trouble she had caused to so many other people besides herself. Max and Nora had smuggled her out of The Sycamores – with some help from little Beenie, so Nessie had said – when they knew their jobs were at stake if they were found out. Henry and Fay had been prepared to take care of her before Nessie had taken over the job. Then there were all the folk Innes had gone to in his search for her, Henry's sister, Fay's parents, her own brother.

Janet's stomach had been churning madly yet, in spite of what she had been thinking, she suddenly felt much calmer. It was quite clear what she had to do. There was no other way out. Going through to the bedroom she had been occupying, she put on her coat and tied Nessie's old shawl round her head. It was a frosty day.

Hearing a carriage of some kind make its steady way into the smiddy, Janet left the house by the front door, glad that Willie had something to occupy him and would be too busy to see her. She walked slowly but purposefully down the hill and turned into the narrow path that ran along the rear of the houses of Mid Street. She did not care if anyone else saw her – she only wanted to avoid Henry, who was only paid to keep the streets clean, not the alleyways. If he saw her, he would turn her round and take her straight back to Oak Cottage.

She had originally intended to walk on and on until she dropped but now she was hoping in a way that she would run into Innes – somebody else who, no doubt, was keeping out of Henry's sight. That would be the only alternative open to her. Let him end her life – it might be more painful but it would be much quicker than leaving it to the elements.

Desperate as he was to get the matter over, Innes had let the mare go at an easy pace along the main street but, as they went up Hillview Road, his excited heart reached a crescendo and he had to take several deep breaths before he was fit to jump down to speak to the blacksmith. Willie Rae!

The heat from the furnace was stifling when he went in and,

although there was a wheel lying on the ground waiting for its rim to be fixed, there was no sign of the man who should be working on it. For a few seconds, Innes felt his courage drain away before it dawned on him that this was an excellent opportunity to get Janet away. He would easily overpower Mrs Willie Rae, if she were in the house, and his task would be even simpler if Janet were alone.

He walked through the small wooden gate to Oak Cottage, gave a peremptory knock on the back door and went straight in. There was no one in the kitchen or in the front parlour but there were two other doors. The first led into a large cupboard so he darted to the other and turned the knob cautiously. There was not the slightest squeak of the hinges – Rae must keep them well oiled – and the large double bed looked as though it had not been slept in but most women could make a bed look immaculate no matter who had slept in it.

Assuming that this room was used by Willie and his wife, Innes mounted the stairs to find another double bed in one front room and two single beds in each of the other two smaller rooms. There was, of course, a huge linen cupboard on the landing, stacked with sheets, towels, tablecloths and God knew what else but he wasted no time on them. Unfortunately, none of the five beds provided any clue as to whether they were in current use or not. The beds in the two bedrooms at the back were not even made up so they were definitely not used.

His legs complained as he practically crawled down the stairs. His high hopes had dwindled to nothing and he knew that he should make himself scarce before someone came in and discovered him. Luckily, there was ample room for him to turn his small carriage in the smiddy's yard but he set off on his homeward journey totally disheartened. It was said that Fortune favoured the brave but no one could have been braver, nor had so much initiative, than he had today and it had got him absolutely nowhere.

Willie Rae had searched everywhere but he had seen no one looking remotely like the man Nessie had described to him.

188

'Find the bugger,' she had ordered, 'before he finds Janet.'

He had gone along every street, every lane, every path – he had even looked behind garden walls. He had asked everybody he met and had carried on doggedly in spite of a growing sense of utter defeat. Then, just as he was wondering if Henry had imagined seeing the man, he struck lucky. Tom Mavor's wife was unpegging her washing from the thick wire they had been hanging on, her husband's drawer's and linder 'so rock hard with the frost, they could stand up by themselves', as she laughingly told him. 'There's nae drouth the day so I'll need to thaw them oot at the fire.'

'Eh . . . Jean,' Willie said, cautiously, 'Have you seen a man going past wi' a long black coat and a high bowler hat? A real tall man? Skulking about?'

Unable to make the linder bend, she linked arms with it, and neither she nor Willie saw anything comical about the incongruous figure she made. 'A tall man?' she mused. 'I wouldna ken if he was tall or short but I did see a man wi' a high bowler in a carriage going down the street. I was trying to open my parlour window but the wind was blowing in.'

'How long ago was that? Which way was he going?'

'He was going out o' the town and it would've been . . . maybe ten minutes ago, maybe mair.'

'Had he a woman wi' him?' Willie voiced his fearful suspicion.

'No, he was his sel'. I wouldna have paid him ony attention but he'd a face on him like he wasna pleased. Scowling, like he wanted to wring somebody's neck.'

Willie breathed freely again. Whatever he'd been doing, he hadn't managed to get Janet, thank God – if it was Ledingham, of course.

'Would he've been the man you're looking for?'

'Aye, I think he was. Thank you, Jean, and I hope you get your washing dry.'

He could see that she had hoped for some explanation but he could tell her nothing. The police would believe Ledingham before anything a common smith said. He could be sued for defamation of character if he as much as hinted at what had happened.

189

Reaching Oak Cottage, Willie burst in to tell Janet that the man had left Ardbirtle but his blood ran cold when he found no one at all in the house. Either Jean Mavor was short-sighted or the fiend had made Janet crouch down out of sight.

Nessie came in at that moment, stopping in dismay when she saw him. 'You didn't find him?' she asked, her voice holding little hope.

'He's got Janet.'

'No! Are you sure?'

'I'm near sure.

Husband and wife regarded each other hopelessly for some moments, then Nessie said, 'I think it's time we let the bobbies know what's been going on.'

'Maybe you're right, though he'll deny everything. Still, it's worth a try. Other folk can back us up – Max Dalgarno and the Nora that helped him, Henry and Fay. I tell you what! You go and bide wi' Fay; I'll get hold of Henry and him and me can go to the police station. We'll have to set things going as quick as we can, before he . . . for Janet's sake.'

CHAPTER FIFTEEN

It took several long weeks of making statements, of interviewing every single person who was involved, before Innes Ledingham was charged with attempted murder. During this time, Nessie Rae patiently nursed Janet's mind and body back to something resembling normal.

The poor woman had been found, exhausted and incoherent, on the edge of the moors where she had apparently been wandering for many hours. The man who came across her – a gamekeeper on the lookout for poachers – helped her to the nearest house, where he left her until he went to the police station. By this time, Willie and Henry had reported her missing (which statement was duly noted and eventually acted upon) and made the complaint against the Superintendent of The Sycamores (which was received with incredulity, even hostility).

A search had been instigated by the Police Sergeant, but was called off when the missing woman was located. When she was brought to the Station, she looked at Willie with no recognition but her eyes lit up when she saw Henry. After holding her in his arms for some time, murmuring soothing words, assuring her that she was safe now, he insisted that she be taken to Oak Cottage. Sergeant MacIver, aware that she was in no state to be questioned, ordered one of his two young constables to take her there in the Black Maria and to check at Mr Henry Rae's house on the way to see if Mrs William Rae was there. 'If she is,' he went on, 'take her to Oak Cottage with you.'

The net spread wider. Abby and Pogie were approached, Joseph and Catherine Leslie, Roderick Emslie, each employee at The Sycamores – except the cook. All this was done before

Gloria Ledingham, otherwise Mrs Rattray, was interrogated. She spoke frankly, saying that she'd had no idea that Innes was trying to poison Janet but that she *had* wondered about the woman's unexplained, prolonged illness. She also admitted to knowing that Innes had committed bigamy by marrying Janet but maintained that she had believed he would tell the other woman the truth and ask her to leave.

'I never dreamt he was trying to kill her,' she wailed.

Whilst all this was going on, Innes himself had been sinking lower and lower into a state of almost limbo, where he was not sure of anything that was happening. Gloria was very sharp with him and he could not understand what he had done to annoy her. He could not find Janet anywhere and his entire staff seemed to regard him with suspicion. He had even caught some of the guests eyeing him in a peculiar manner.

When at last the spotlight was turned on him, he clearly was striving to keep his reason. During the questioning, his answers revealed more than he actually admitted to. The arsenic was mentioned but not his purpose in using it; his seeing to Janet's meals, but not his doctoring of them; his anger and astonishment that she had walked out; his search for her but only to bring her back because he missed her.

Even MacIver, who needed everything properly cut and dried before acting on it, could see that the man was telling them what he wanted to believe himself – possibly his mind was in such a state that he *did* believe it.

Ledingham was then charged and taken away – not to prison but to a criminal asylum to await trial or, more likely, to be declared unfit to be tried and incarcerated there for life. All those who had been involved in the case now relaxed, especially Max, Nora and Beenie, whose connection with it had gone undiscovered. It was generally assumed that Janet must have rallied from her 'illness' long enough to escape on her own. The only person who had any doubts about this was Gloria who couldn't rid herself of the idea that someone else had had a hand in the poor woman's bid for freedom.

The first and legal Mrs Innes Ledingham, however, had cause

to be grateful to whoever was responsible – probably more than one – because, with her husband locked up, she now gained access to his quite considerable bank account. She had initially considered applying for the post of Superintendent, but that would entail much hard work and worry, which she could well do without at her age. With the amount of money at her disposal, she could start a new life in another part of the country, even abroad somewhere, perhaps not exactly in the lap of luxury, but certainly better than her present existence.

Having thus decided, she contacted the Board of Governors first. All fuddy-duddy old men, they had been utterly shocked by the events revealed to the public at large and their own neighbours in particular. They were, therefore, delighted to learn that the slate would be wiped clean and a new Superintendent – a man who was definitely legally married – and a new cook were to be appointed. To safeguard the well-being of the residents of The Sycamores, however, they invited 'Mrs Rattray' to stay on until all the arrangements had been made.

Gloria made her announcement at breakfast on the day of her departure, scanning the faces round the table as she spoke. Most showed no surprise at her news – they had probably been expecting it – but two pairs of eyes exchanged a glance of deep relief that she was leaving. The culprits had given themselves away, she gloated, though she should have guessed. Max Dalgarno was the only one it could have been. He was the only man with the nerve and she had heard that he was a great friend of Henry Rae, who had also been very close to Janet. And Nora? Perhaps she had known or suspected what Innes had been doing but it would have been Max's idea – that was certain.

The new cook, a Mrs Allardyce from Oldmeldrum, arrived around ten o'clock and, after telling her what was planned for supper and leaving young Beenie to show her where things were, Gloria went to look for Max.

His mind much easier now that he knew 'Mrs Rattrray' was leaving, Max was whistling blithely as he trimmed the grass verge of the path. Since their dangerous escapade, he had been thinking more and more of Nora. She was a girl with spirit and bonnie with it. She was everything he needed in a . . . wife? Yet he had held back, not daring to ask her out, not even daring to speak to her except for a few words in passing, in case Ledingham or his wife saw them and put two and two together. But the man was locked up now and, when the cook finally left, he could court Nora openly.

His whistled lilt faded away when he saw Gloria striding towards him, a glint in her eye that did not bode well. God Almighty! Not now! Not when he imagined he was in the clear at long last. 'Aye?' he said, respectfully tipping the snout of the cap he wore to keep insects out of his thick hair.

She regarded him speculatively for a second, then echoed the greeting. 'Aye.'

His smile was somewhat bleak. 'You haven't come just to bid me goodbye.'

'No,' she agreed, inclining her head. 'I came to tell you I know what you and Nora did. Well, I know you did it but I want to know how you did it.'

This is what a condemned man must feel, he thought, his mouth bone dry, but he did not try to deny it. 'How did you find out?'

'You were the only two that looked as if I'd taken a load off your shoulders when I said I was going away.'

'Oh!' He shrugged helplessly, then pleaded, 'Look, tell the bobbies about me if you like but please don't say anything about Nora. It was my idea.'

'I take it you have a soft spot for her . . . or perhaps more than that? All right, Max, I will say nothing about Nora if you tell me how it was done.'

She listened carefully, her expression telling him nothing as he explained what he had planned and how Nora had made it that much easier. 'And now I suppose you'll want me to accompany you to Ardbirtle Police Station,' he ended, with a grim smile.

'I want you to accompany me to . . .' she began, then gave a low chuckle, 'to the kitchen to carry my boxes outside.'

194

Bewildered, he asked, 'You mean . . . you're not going to report me?'

'Certainly not. In fact, Max, I want to thank you. You made it possible for me to make this move and I will be forever indebted to you.'

'Well, I'll be damned!'

He did as she asked, shaking his head in wondering disbelief several times, then stood with Beenie and Nora to wave to the departing cook as she went off in the trap to the railway station, on her way to wherever she was going.

As Beenie ran back inside to show off her knowledge to the new cook, Max whispered to Nora, 'Will you meet me at seven behind the tool shed?'

Her clear blue eyes widened as she turned a becoming pink. 'Aye, I will.'

He went back to work now, his conscience clearer than it had been for many months, his heart accelerating as he looked forward to seven o'clock.

Henry had just arrived home for his usual midday bowl of soup and chunk of home-made bread when someone knocked at the door. Tutting, he rose to find out who it was and what they wanted but his impatience turned to delight when he saw his old friend. 'Max! What on earth . . . ? I hope there's nothing wrong with your mother. I saw her yesterday and she looked the picture of health – like she always does.'

'Ma's just fine,' Max grinned. 'I came to give her my news and I couldn't go back without telling you and all.'

'What news?'

With both Henry and his wife looking at him expectantly, Max sat down. 'Any soup going, Fay? It's damned cold outside.'

'News first, then soup,' she smiled, giving a reprimanding pat to the little hand that was stretching out for a biscuit. 'Empty your bowl first, m'lad.'

Pulling an exaggerated grimace, Max said, 'So that's the kind of thing I've got to expect, is it?'

Henry's hand halted midway to his mouth. 'Are you telling us what I think you're telling us? You're getting wed?'

'You thought correct, Tchouki,' Max teased. 'I've been keeping company wi' Nora Petty for months now and I asked her last night and she said yes.'

'Oh, Max!' Fay bent down to kiss his cheek. 'I'm so happy for you both. Nora is a really nice girl and you . . . well, what can I say about you?'

'You could say I was a really nice man?' he suggested, cocking an eyebrow.

'I would say you've met the right one at last,' Henry said, quietly.

Fay sat down now. 'I wasn't the right one for you, Max, any more than you were the right one for me. Yes, Henry knows all about our little romance,' she assured him as he shot an apprehensive glance at her husband.

'I know it wasn't really a romance,' Henry grinned. 'And I know it happened before she met me – so I don't mind.'

Max was guiltily silent for a moment but then he gave a relaxed smile. 'Ach, you two. You're making fun of me. I was just testing my wings at that time but Nora . . . well Nora is Nora and I wouldna want any other girl. I'd better go, though. I told Ma I'd just be a few minutes.'

Both Raes saw him out, Henry shaking his hand and wishing him all the best and Fay, with a demon egging her on, kissed him full on the mouth. 'Congratulations, Max,' she murmured, 'and tell Nora from me she's a very lucky girl.'

She closed the door softly and turned to her husband. 'You weren't jealous, were you, Henry?'

'No, of course not.'

But he *was* jealous. Why would Fay kiss Max like that if there had been nothing between them? With her own husband standing watching? Had she not been able to help herself, was that it? Had they been seeing each other in secret after she was married? Even in the short time she was living at The Sycamores?

Taking his cap off the hook on the back of the door, he

slapped it on his head and turned to go out. He then flung his arms round his wife and kissed her in a way he hadn't done for months. 'I love you, my Fairy, don't ever forget that.'

Going back to her children, Fay became occupied in cleaning the mess her little son had made by trying to pour his soup into the bowl Max had used. Then she had to wash the tablecloth before she changed and fed little Samara. Only after putting them both down for their afternoon nap did she have time to think. She had kissed Max at the door on the spur of the moment. It hadn't crossed her mind that it could make Henry jealous but maybe it had been a good thing. For a long time now, he had not been nearly as loving as he been in the first years of their marriage. Any time she suggested having another child, he made the excuse that bringing up two was a hard enough struggle, without making it three.

There was no disputing that his last kiss had been the kiss of a lover, though – a man reawakened. But would that feeling last? Would it dwindle away to nothing by the time he finished work? She would have to wait until bedtime to find out – worse luck.

'Will I have to go to court if Innes is sent to trial?' Janet looked imploringly at Nessie. 'I couldn't face up to it if he's standing there looking at me.'

'If he is tried, I'd think you'd definitely have to give evidence but I've the feeling it will never come to that. According to all reports, he was raving mad when they took him away – that's why he was sent to that criminal asylum. The papers say he'll be judged insane, unfit to plead, and he'll be locked up there for life. In a straitjacket, I hope.'

'And there would never be any chance of him escaping?'

'Not a chance in a million.'

Janet's fear of having to testify against Ledingham was ended less than a week later, when it was announced that he had been certified and would remain in Carstairs, an asylum for the criminally insane, for the rest of his days.

'What did I tell you?' was Nessie's first comment, then she

giggled, 'Innes *Wellington* Ledingham? Was that what made him think he could do what he liked, gave him ideas of grandeur? God forgive him.'

'God might be able to forgive him,' Janet muttered, 'but I never will.'

The mood in Oak Cottage was anything but cheery until Fay came to visit in the afternoon with her little son and daughter, a trio who always lifted the hearts of the two older ladies.

'I had a letter from Nora this morning,' the young mother smiled. 'She and Max were married last Saturday in the chapel. She seems really happy and I'm so pleased for them.'

Janet nodded. 'She'll make him a good wife. He was a bit of a lad among the girls for a while, you know, so I hope he's settled down now.'

'I'm sure he has.' Fay hoped that the faint pinprick of embarrassment she felt was not showing in her face. 'He really thinks the world of Nora.'

The conversation was interrupted by little Andrew who, although a handful, was a most engaging child. 'Story!' he demanded, handing Janet the cloth book he had brought with him.

While she was thus occupied, Nessie turned to Fay. 'Have you seen the paper today?' Fay's nod needed no further explanation or discussion and they turned their attention to the baby, now cooing and gurgling in Nessie's arms.

The small item in the newspaper was the talk of the week for miles around. To those who had not known him, Innes Ledingham was a bad egg who deserved all he got. To those who had been his friends, his brain had been turned by an unscrupulous woman. To Roderick Emslie, he was a brother-in-law who had gone off the rails. And, to Joseph Leslie, he was the devil incarnate. 'To think my daughter could have fallen into his clutches,' he moaned. 'I knew Henry Rae was not a suitable match for her.'

'Henry had nothing to do with it,' Catherine reminded him. 'He only helped the woman after Max got her away from The Sycamores.'

'He did not do very much for her. He passed her on to his father and his wife.'

Catherine shook her head angrily. 'Only because he knew his house would be the first place Ledingham would look. You know, Joseph, I do not know what gets into you, sometimes. You always think the worst of everybody. We could not have a better son-in-law than Henry. He worships our Fay and their two children.'

'Humph.'

She let it go at that. He could be so aggravating that she had, once or twice, wondered why she stayed with him.

Fay was much happier now that the worry of Janet's safety had been taken off Henry's mind. He was more loving towards her but, even so, he still maintained that they could not afford to have another child. She could see his point – she had to watch every ha'penny – but she still longed for another little boy. Andrew was being spoiled – Henry always let him have his own way and so did Willie, Nessie and Janet. It wasn't good for him – he took advantage of it. He was still an adorable wee nickum, though.

Better not say anything to any of them, she reflected. She should just enjoy life, now that it was flowing on peacefully.

Her mind free of fear, Janet had something else to occupy it. The advent of the combustion engine was affecting Willie's trade and she could see that Nessie was hard pushed to feed the three of them and pay for coal for the fire and paraffin for the lamps, as well as all the other expenses. She, herself, had worried since she had been brought there that she made no contribution to the household, even though Willie and Nessie had both told her that she wasn't fit to take a job and it didn't cost much more to feed three than feed two.

'Anyway, you hardly eat enough to keep a spurdie going,' Nessie had added.

Smiling at being compared to a sparrow when her bulk was always increasing, Janet had concentrated her thoughts on the problem but it was some time before she came up with a solution.

She waited, however, until she had it all worked out before tackling Nessie one afternoon. 'You're aye saying I'm a great cook so what would you say to us starting a wee shop? A home bakery?'

Somewhat taken aback, Nessie laid down the sock she was darning and gave the matter her full consideration. By the time Willie came in from his walk, the two women were eagerly discussing how it should be done and, although he was not exactly enamoured of their plan to change the parlour into a shop, their excitement started to rub off on him.

It did not take long to put into practice. The sash window in the parlour only needed a shelf put up below it and a glass shelf, level with the window-sill, would double as protection for the goods and a counter. Then Nessie painstakingly made a placard on a firm piece of cardboard to let the public know of the venture and that 'Oak Cottage Home Bakery' would be opening on the following Monday, hours 8 a.m. to 4 p.m. daily, except Sundays.

The two women occupied their hands furiously over the weekend. Janet baked as many scones and biscuits as the two ovens at the side of the kitchen range would hold and as many girdle scones and pancakes as the big cast-iron girdle could turn out. Meanwhile, Nessie washed and made ready all the plates, dishes and containers she could find and then washed and starched all her good linen doilies and table napkins to line them.

It wasn't until late on the Sunday evening that Willie spotted the big flaw in their arrangements. 'Will you not need paper bags for the customers to take away what they buy?' he asked.

Janet looked crestfallen but Nessie was not so easily knocked back. 'I'll just need to put it on our notice,' she laughed and, in another five minutes, she had added the instruction, 'Please bring your own bags meantime.'

'Once we see if it's going to be a success,' she explained, 'we can order bags from wherever the real shops get their bags from.'

The enterprise paid off to such an extent that oatcakes and

loaves of bread were soon added to the list and, before long, by popular request, pies and fruit tarts. Nessie discovered that she had a flair for making pastry so she, too, was kept fully occupied in the evenings.

Willie pretended not to be interested in the fortune or misfortune of what was going on in his own front room but it quickly became obvious, even to him, that the home bakery was a galloping success. Even taking their expenses into account – the ingredients they needed, the paper bags, the tissue paper for the loaves, the folding cardboard boxes for the cakes, the extra rates they had to pay the council – the profits rose substantially each week.

Better still, as far as he was concerned, his wife was too busy, and too tired, to find fault with every little thing he did, as she'd been wont to do before. He could spit into the fire if he wanted to clear his throat, sit in his chair with his boots off and let the heat dry his sweaty socks, scratch his crotch when it was itchy and fart when he felt the need. Not that he felt comfortable about doing things like that. He'd been brought up to have manners, to think of other people first, and he'd had to toe the line for so long that he soon reverted to what was second nature to him. He felt easier in himself when he was behaving like a normal human being.

It was good having two women attending to his needs after the baking was done in the evenings. Nessie saw to the physical side, when she felt up to it, and Janet looked to his comforts, plumping up his cushion, handing him his pipe and tobacco tin or his glasses when he wanted to read the paper. Govey Dick! This was the life, right enough, and long may it continue.

CHAPTER SIXTEEN

1897

As usual, seven-year-old Andrew was late in coming home from school and Samara, hardly two years younger and now answering to Mara, would only say that she had seen him playing tag with some other boys. Fay could never depend on her son – he was so full of boyish mischief. She had heard from outsiders before now that he'd been seen here, there and everywhere – parts of the town where he should never have set foot. He never admitted to any wrongdoing, of course, but she couldn't help being anxious. She had warned him to keep away from the Esslemont's place, in case he fell in the mill race; she had told him not to go into Charlie Reid's field where the bull was; she had forbidden him to go anywhere near the quarry, but there was always this doubt of him in her heart.

Henry laughed at her for being overprotective but she was always ill at ease until Andrew came home – usually with his breeches torn and his knees scraped or a hole in his jacket. The thing was, as Henry should know, she didn't have the money to replace the damaged articles of clothing. Or, rather, she did have the money – the fifty pounds her father had given them as a wedding gift was still lying in the bank but her husband wouldn't let her touch it.

'There might come a time when we really do need it,' he would say and she had to do the best she could with a needle and thread, plus a bit cut from an old pair of his father's trousers as a patch.

When Henry arrived home for supper, Andrew had still not turned up and Fay was pale with worry. 'Don't fret, my dearest Fairy,' he assured her, 'He'll just be playing with the rest of the lads.'

'But it's hours now,' she wailed. 'He's never been as late as this before.'

'Dish up my supper, then, and, when I'm finished, I'll go and look for him.'

She had to be content with that and hastened to the range to do as he had bidden. She would never forget what happened next, every little detail would be etched deep in her heart. The first thing was the rush of feet outside and, as she turned round with the potato pot in her hand, the door was flung open and her father-in-law carried in Andrew's limp little body.

The pot went one way, the tatties the other, as she dashed to look at her son, almost colliding with Henry doing the same. Several people had followed Willie in but Fay and Henry could see nothing except the blood dripping from their beloved little boy on to the floor.

'I've sent one o' the laddies' fathers for the doctor,' Willie murmured grimly. 'I'll lay him on the couch. He's pretty bad.'

The devastated parents did not need to be told that – they could see for themselves that the unconscious boy was having difficulty breathing. Fortunately, the man who had run for the doctor caught him on his way home and so he was there in five minutes – the longest five minutes the parents and grandfather had lived through.

After clearing the room of spectators, Doctor Burr gave the patient a very brief examination then raised a grave face. 'I'm afraid he's too far gone for me to do anything,' he murmured to Henry. 'If he had been taken straight to a hospital, perhaps he could have stood a chance but . . .' He left the sentence unfinished, turning away to adjust the towels Fay had already packed round her son's extensive injuries.

Henry put his arm round his wife now. The nearest hospital was almost twenty miles away and it was quite plain to both of them that, even if Andrew had been whisked away in a carriage as soon as it happened – whatever *had* happened – he would probably have died before he reached it.

Another excruciatingly long ten minutes passed before the laboured, shallow breathing stopped and Burr took Fay's hand.

'It's best this way, my dear. If he had lived, he would have needed round-the-clock nursing.'

She wanted to shout, 'I would willingly have given him that!' but she knew it would have been impossible. She had Mara to think of, too. She was only five and still needed a lot of her mother's attention.

While Burr was writing out the death certificate, Willie said, 'I'd better go and tell Pogie. He'll attend to . . . things.'

The two men went out together, leaving the devastated mother and father seeking comfort from each other.

The story emerged gradually, of how young Andrew had been dared by some older boys to go into the field with the bull; of how other boys had pleaded with him not to go because it was too dangerous; how he shaken his head and said he had to do it to prove he wasn't a baby like Donal Coull had said. Once through the gate, he had been goaded into walking well away from the paling – so far away, indeed, that, when the bull turned and charged at him, his little legs were not capable of running fast enough for him to escape.

Willie, intent on getting at the whole truth, threatened to punch the ten-year-old Donal if he didn't tell him exactly what had happened but, when the words came pouring out of the terrified boy's mouth, he wished that he had let it be. The graphic, bloody details – of the bull catching Andrew on its horns, tossing him into the air, only to gore him when he came down, and then trampling on him over and over again – were too much to bear. Letting go of the boy, the bereaved grandfather sat down at the side of the road with his head in his hands, rocking back and forth with the waves of nauseous sorrow that swept through him.

For a full ten minutes, he remained there, until his grief receded a little and he was fit to stand up. He made his way home slowly, trying to put the horrifying story out of his mind, although he knew quite well that he would never forget. Strangely, he felt no anger at the boy Coull. Down through the centuries, boys had always been boys and would continue to be so until the end of time. As a boy himself, he had done things he should not have done, had played tricks which could have ended in tragedy but hadn't. He had been lucky but Donal Coull had not. He was only ten, so what did he know of danger?

Willie halted for a moment, wondering how much he should disclose to his family, and decided that he should keep the information to himself. It would be cruel to put Fay, Henry, Nessie and Janet through the agony of picturing what had happened in that field. Donal Coull wouldn't tell anybody else, he was almost sure of that, nor would any of the other boys who had been there and they wouldn't get off scot-free. They would get their punishment from the guilt they would feel for the rest of their lives. More composed now, Willie continued on his way.

On the morning after her nephew's funeral, Abby Laing got a letter from her sister Kitty, who had not been in touch for some time. Pogie watched for a moment and then stood up. He had another two funerals to arrange. 'What does Kitty say?' he asked as he fastened up his black jacket.

'She wants to come home.' Abby looked up at him. 'She doesn't want to go to Father's, though, and she doesn't like to ask Fay so she wants to come here. What do you think?'

'I have no objections, my dear, but it is up to you. She could be a help to you.'

'We don't have room. She wouldn't want to sleep with Gail and we can't put Gail in the same bed as Clarence. There's just the couch and it's too lumpy.'

'I will leave you to think it over, then.' Pogie put on his everyday hat, a dark grey homburg, and went out.

While Abby supervised her thirteen-year-old son and eleven-year-old daughter making ready for school, she pondered over Kitty's request but, even after pegging a large washing out on the line, she was still undecided. They *could* buy another bed, she supposed, but it still meant her son and daughter being in the same room and, if Kitty meant to stay for good, that just wouldn't work out. Even now, Clarence teased his sister by lifting her skirts so God knows what he would do when he was a year or two older.

She had better go to show her sister-in-law the letter and ask what she should do. Fay was usually so calm about everything, though she hadn't been so calm about Andrew – which wasn't really surprising. She, herself, had been anything but calm when her third baby died and then her fourth, though losing them in infancy might not be as bad as if they'd been Andrew's age.

Abby's heart sank when she found Fay's house full of people but Nessie, with her usual perspicacity, saw that she was worried about something. 'Janet,' she said brightly, 'what about us taking ourselves out for a while to let Fay and Abby have a wee blether? Are you coming with us, Willie, or would you rather go and have a news with the other old men in the square?'

In a couple of minutes, the two younger women were on their own and Abby took the letter from her bag. 'It's from Kitty.'

After reading it, Fay said, 'You don't have room for her, do you?'

'I suppose I could make room for a wee while but not for good. And, of course, she won't go to Father's because of Nessie – though I've told her time and again in my letters that she's a changed woman nowadays.'

'I've never met Kitty,' Fay said thoughtfully. 'What sort of person is she?'

Abby sighed. 'I haven't seen her myself since not long after Father married again. She was only about thirteen at the time and I don't remember that much about her, to tell the truth.'

'You don't know why she wants to come back here?'

'She hasn't said but there must be something wrong before she's giving up her grand job in Glasgow.'

Just then, someone knocked at the door and Fay went to answer it.

The well-dressed stranger looked at her for a moment. 'Are you Fay?'

Light suddenly dawning, Fay said, 'Yes, and you must be Kitty? Come in.'

'Ah, you are here, Abby,' Kitty said, when they went into the kitchen. 'Your neighbour said this was where you'd be.'

Abby was not to be fobbed off with empty chit-chat. 'What's wrong, Kitty? You can't be short of money with those lovely clothes to wear.'

Kitty took off her close-fitting hat and touched her beautifully coifed chignon to make sure it had not come loose. 'Yes, I have some good clothes but that's about all I do have. I had quite a bit of savings – I was intending to come home for a little holiday . . . for my honeymoon, actually – but . . . *he* stole the lot and ran off.' Her eyes clouded. 'The night before the wedding.'

'Oh, Kit, I'm so sorry,' Abby murmured and Fay echoed the sentiment.

'I can't say I'm over it yet – but it's not so bad as it was.'

Her story did not take long to tell and she had since found out that it was just a repetition of what the same man had done to several women. He had promised her the earth, given her a fictitious account of his thriving business in London, 'borrowed' all her money to 'finalise a big deal that would make millions' and that was the last she had seen or heard of him.

'How long ago was that?' Abby wanted to know.

'It's three months come Friday.' Kitty took a handkerchief from the sleeve of her cashmere jacket and wiped her eyes. 'I had given up my job the week before, to prepare for the wedding, and I couldn't go and ask for it back. I didn't want them to know how gullible I'd been.'

'But it wasn't your fault,' put in Fay. 'You trusted him.'

'More fool me.'

Something had occurred to Abby now. 'How have you been managing to live if you haven't had a job for three months?'

'I haven't managed very well, to be honest. I sometimes got a relief job as a waitress or a shop assistant or a cleaner but, in between those times, I went hungry. By good luck, I'd paid a year's rent when I moved into my wee house so I did have a roof over my head till yesterday.'

Frowning a little, Abby asked, 'Where did you sleep last night?'

'I suppose I'd better tell you,' Kitty sighed, 'but you'll just think I was mad. You see, I got to know this really nice man when I was receptionist at the hotel – a manager of a string of shops all over Scotland – and I met him yesterday in the street. Well, when he heard what had happened, he took me into a restaurant for a slap-up meal and then said I could . . . have a bed at his house for the one night.'

Two separate, horrified intakes of breath made her hurry on. 'It was freezing cold, Abby, and I'd nowhere else to go and I knew he was a decent man . . .'

'You thought the man you were going to marry was decent,' Abby reminded her, a touch sarcastically.

'Yes, I know, but Archie really *is* decent. He told his wife the truth . . .'

'He was married?' Abby gasped. 'What did his wife say about him taking a woman home with him?'

'She was so nice, made up the bed in their spare room and gave me a lovely breakfast. And she wasn't a bit annoyed when Archie said he would run me up here. He was going to Inverness, so it wasn't much out of his way. When we stopped at your house, Abby, I was going to ask him in for a cup of tea but you weren't there so he just dropped me off and went on his way.'

'What a risk you took, Kitty,' Abby said, sharply. 'He could have killed you in that car or . . . or even worse.'

Unrepentant, Kitty gave a low chuckle. 'And what would have been worse than killing me, may I ask?'

'You know! A fate worse than death, isn't that what they say?'

'Ah, yes. Well, it's not all that bad, really. No,' she added, 'Archie didn't touch me, though I wouldn't have minded if he had, but there were a few nights . . . when I was absolutely desperate for something to eat and so I had to . . . do something to save myself from starving.'

Neither knowing what to say to this, Abby and Fay exchanged shocked glances, then Kitty said, 'I'm bursting for a pee, Fay. Where's your . . . ?'

'Just outside the back door.'

'Well,' said Abby, when her sister went out, 'what a carry on.'

Fay pulled a face. 'I feel kind of sorry for her. She is gullible but that isn't a crime, is it? It's only herself she's hurting, silly woman.'

'Who's going to take her in, though?'

It was Henry who made the decision, after meeting his brother-in-law in the street.

'Abby got a letter from your sister Kitty,' Pogie began, 'and she wants to come back here for good. She doesn't want to go to your father's, though.'

Henry took off his cap and scratched his head. He wished that he didn't have to wear it because he was almost sure that it was making him lose his hair. It was much thinner than it used to be. 'I wonder what she wants,' he murmured,

'Goodness knows.'

With Pogie hurrying on to do whatever he had to do, Henry had peace to go over the possibilities as he carefully swept the leaves into heaps and then shovelled them into his handcart. As far as he knew, Kitty had never married, though she must be . . . He was twenty-six and she was at least six years older, so that would make her thirty-two – a fair age to still be a spinster. He couldn't remember her very well for he had only been about seven when she left with their two oldest sisters but Abby said she always wrote cheery letters.

It was easy enough to be cheery in a letter, of course, though her heart could be breaking over a love affair gone wrong. Her unheralded appearance suggested something of the sort, something that had made her leave Glasgow. There would be quite a problem if she wanted to move back to Ardbirtle for good, however. All the houses where she may have hoped to find refuge were full up – Father had Nessie and Janet, Abby had only three bedrooms and he had . . . an empty room now. Oh,

God, came the agonising thought, would he and Fay ever get over losing their firstborn?

But he had better get on and not waste time. There was going to be a Diamond Jubilee party on Saturday to mark the Queen's sixty years on the throne and he had to have at least the main streets free of any kind of refuse for several important personages had been invited to attend.

Despite knowing that Kitty had come back, he was still surprised to see her when he went home in the middle of the day. She had filled out a bit from how he remembered her – which was all to the good for she had been as skinny as a string bean when she went away – but the biggest change was in her clothing. Instead of the hand-me-downs she'd had to wear ever since she was born, she now looked very elegant in a light navy gabardine costume, with just the suggestion of a bustle, and the pale pink frills of her blouse showing at the neck. Her hair, not quite as dark as it once had been, was pinned up into a sausage shape at the back of her head, in the style of the ladies of the nobility whose photographs sometimes graced the newspapers. She would make a good picture herself, he thought, as he went across to shake her hand.

The pleasantries over, Fay said, brightly, 'Kitty is home for good, Henry.'

He could hear a note of appeal in her voice. She was making a great effort to appear normal but she really needed somebody to help her get over Andrew. Nessie and Janet had been doing their best but they could not possibly understand how much she was suffering – the feeling of utter helplessness, the anger, the craving to see her son again, the terrible heartache that ate away at her . . . and at him . . . during the nights.

Neither of them had ever borne a child and they were too old now to give her the amount of compassion she deserved. His heart skipped a beat. Here was Fay desperate for someone nearer her own age to whom she could talk, open her innermost soul to, and there was Kitty, having clearly survived a dreadful trauma herself. They were made for each other.

He cleared his throat, giving his wife notice that he was

about to say something of vital importance. 'We'll be glad to have you live with us, Kitty. We have an empty bed if you don't mind being in Andrew's old room.'

She shot a glance at Fay first, then said, 'If you're sure, I would be very grateful.'

Fay's lips were trembling but she held her head up. 'Yes, you are very welcome.'

Clearly relieved that the problem was solved, Abby left first and the two older women just a few minutes later.

Giving Henry a chance to speak to his sister in private, Fay said she would make the bed ready.

'Henry,' Kitty murmured, 'I was at my wit's end, contemplating ending it all, and now you're giving me a new chance to pull myself together. I don't know how I'll ever be able to thank you.'

'All I ask is for you to make friends with my Fairy Fay; to help her through this awful time.'

'Yes, Abby told me about your little boy. I'm truly sorry, Henry, and I swear I'll do my very best not to let her go into a decline.' She paused and then smiled. 'We'll be good for each other and I can help with the housework . . .'

He looked rather shamefaced now. 'That was something I meant to speak to you about. I'm sure Fay would be glad of your help but we can't afford to pay you anything. Maybe it would be best if you could find a wee job . . .'

'But that's what I meant to do! I don't expect you to keep me for nothing.'

And so it was settled, amicably and with no fuss.

* * *

On Saturday, T H, as he was known officially, had duties to perform as Town Officer. He had to meet the visiting dignitaries and escort them to their places for the banquet. He had to see that no members of the ordinary public entered this holy-of-holies. He had to organise the presentation of bouquets to the wives of the important guests. He had to make sure that each carriage was ready and waiting for its specific passengers when they wanted to leave.

The meal over, he had to make sure that the tables were cleared quickly, that the dishwashers had everything they needed and that the band was in place on the platform for the dancing. Fortunately, for he was in no mood to take on the job, the band had provided a master of ceremonies. For the rest of the evening, all he had to do was to prevent any of the men from causing a disturbance by drinking too much and he was relieved that only two had to be shown the door.

On their own, Kitty told Fay much more about her life in Glasgow and the other two men who had let her down, which was why she was still unmarried. Fay then gave her an account of how she had met Henry but neither touched on her most recent misfortune. At last, after a couple of hours, Fay, feeling an affinity with this sister-in-law she had known for such a short time, said, 'You know, Kitty, I still haven't got over . . . Andrew.'

'I'm not surprised. I haven't got over what George Laird did to me and that was a few months ago. I can only say it takes time but the pain does get less as time goes by.' She regarded the other woman cautiously. 'It maybe sounds callous but you will have other children come time – another son to . . .' She broke off in confusion.

Fay bit her bottom lip reflectively, then murmured, 'If you mean another boy would replace Andrew, you don't really know how I feel. Nobody could ever replace Andrew in my heart.'

'No, I'm sorry. That was insensitive of me but having another child would help, I'm sure it would.'

'Well, it's out of the question, anyway. I did want more but Henry always said we couldn't afford it.'

'He might change his mind now.'

'He won't – he'll be feeling the same as I do.'

'It would be worth a try. Ask him again.'

Fay did not ask her husband again. She wasn't sure herself

that she wanted another child. There would always be a risk that a new baby, especially a boy, would worm his way into Andrew's special place in the cold chambers of her heart.

As it turned out, she had no choice in the matter. Henry's actions on the night of their son's tragic death – when the passion of his grief changed unbidden to the desperate passion of love and need as he tried to comfort himself as much as his wife – resulted in a pregnancy that neither of them particularly wanted.

PART THREE

1910-1920

CHAPTER SEVENTEEN

Fay and Kitty Rae were sitting one Saturday afternoon, as they often did, talking of this and that – how things were much better during Victoria's reign; how her son's spell as Edward VII had turned people's morals topsy-turvy; and how they hoped that the new king, George V, would be a better influence on his subjects.

'He's more serious-minded than his father, anyway,' Kitty observed, tucking two of her four knitting needles into her mass of light brown hair until she turned the heel of the sock.

'I sincerely hope so,' muttered Fay. 'I've been dreading Jerry taking an interest in girls, in case he carries on like Edward when he was Prince of Wales. It was scandalous. He even had several lady-loves while he was king.'

'Jerry's got more sense than that.' Kitty was sure of this but even sensible boys could be led astray. Girls would be after him in a year or so – he was so handsome. Apart from his dark wavy hair and strong jawline, he was blessed with gorgeously green eyes that made even a hardened old bird like herself feel special when he looked at her.

Fay bit off her thread with a weary sigh. 'He hadn't much sense while he was at school but, now he's left, maybe he won't knock so many holes in his breeches and I'll have less mending to do.'

Nevertheless, as Kitty knew, Fay doted on this son just as much as she had on the one she had lost. Possibly he hadn't totally replaced Andrew in his mother's affections but it seemed as if her heart had grown to make room for both her sons. Kitty's thoughts halted until she checked the number of rows she had done – both heels had to be the same length – before letting her thoughts run on. She would have loved a son, a whole battery of sons, but, at her age, there was no chance of that. The only option open to her now would be to marry a widower who already had a young family.

She was touching on a dream that had been intensifying of late. It wasn't the old dream of finding *a* man, it was a new, delicious dream of *the* man for her – the man she had been attracted to since she returned to Ardbirtle. She had, naturally, stifled her feelings for Pogie Laing, had told herself that it was far too dangerous to even think of him as anything other than her brother-in-law. It was hard, though, really hard, when she saw him so often, but she had no intention of letting him know how she felt.

Rather than hurt Abby, she had tried to banish all un-maidenly thoughts from her head and treat Pogie as if she could barely stand the sight of him. The trouble was that he couldn't hide the pain he felt at her snubs and she had relented as far as to treat him as a distant friend. It hadn't helped, of course, and the only way open to her now was to go back to Glasgow or to somewhere even farther away.

'You're very quiet, Kitty.' Fay's gentle voice broke into her reverie.

'I'm sorry – I was miles away.'

'I think not – only a few hundred yards? Am I right?'

'Oh, Fay, is it that obvious? I thought I'd hidden it pretty well.'

'Don't worry, my dear. I don't think anyone else has noticed.'

'Thank goodness. I don't want . . . him to suspect anything.'

'I'm sure he doesn't.'

Gathering up her knitting, Kitty shoved it carelessly into her bag and stood up. 'Anyway, Fay, I've made up my mind to leave. Serving behind a counter in a poky little haberdashery isn't enough of a challenge.'

Her sister-in-law had the sense not to argue. 'Were you thinking of anywhere in particular?'

'Not really. I just know it's the most sensible thing to do. I'd better give myself a quick swill now for Nessie said she'd have tea ready about five.'

'Ah, yes, I forgot you'd been invited to Oak Cottage.'

Jerry came in just minutes after Kitty had left. His face was almost cut in two by a wide grin. 'Mother, Bill Kemp's just asked me if I'd like a job as message boy and I jumped at it. I've to start tomorrow 'cos his last boy's broke his leg and he'll be off for months.'

'But it will still be a temporary job . . . until the other boy comes back?'

'I suppose so.'

'You know, your father always hoped you would stick at your lessons and make something of yourself.'

'Mother, I don't have the brains to make anything of myself.'

'If you'd worked a bit harder at school, Jerry, you could have developed your brain. You're not stupid, I know that.'

'Maybe I'm not but I want to work with my hands.'

'Ask your grandfather if he'll take you on as his apprentice, then.'

'I don't want to be a blacksmith but Pogie's Clarence does. He says he'd rather do that than be an undertaker like his father.'

Fay let him go upstairs now. She didn't want to force him into something he didn't want to do and, in any case, motor cars were fast taking over from horses. It wouldn't be long before blacksmiths and their forges were things of the past.

Her thoughts turned to Kitty. She had been a godsend in helping them to get over Andrew's death and then coaxing them to accept the fact that another baby was on the way. Strangely enough, it had been Henry, dear Tchouki, who had been first to recognise that as a blessing. She, herself, had been unable to banish her feeling of guilt that they had created a new life so soon after their firstborn had been taken from them. It was Kitty who had painstakingly talked her out of that quagmire – not Nessie or Janet or even Abby, though they had all tried.

Poor Kitty, she deserved some happiness but she wouldn't get it unless she put Pogie Laing out of her mind. He still loved Abby as much as ever and he'd be absolutely horrified if he knew how Kitty felt. Thank goodness she had the sense to see that she should remove herself from temptation. They would all miss her when she left, of course, Fay mused, herself most of all.

Some months later, when Henry was helping the committee to plan how the town would celebrate King George V's coronation, he and his family had just returned from their usual Sunday afternoon walk when a motor car pulled up on the street outside. Jerry rushed to the window agog with excitement. 'It's a man coming here,' he squealed, making for the door.

'No, my lad,' his father said firmly. 'I'll let him in, whoever he is.'

Fay tried to hear what was being said but no one came in. 'He's gone back to the car,' Jerry told her, 'and a woman's coming out now . . . and a girl.'

Not having the slightest inkling of the identity of their visitors, Fay had to wait until the kitchen door was pushed open. 'Max,' she cried, in delight, when the tall man walked in. 'And Nora and . . . ?'

'Robina,' supplied Nora. 'We called her after Beenie for she was with me the afternoon she was born and I don't know what I'd have done without her.'

'You'd have managed,' laughed Max. 'Ruby was determined to come out and she wasn't going to wait another minute.'

'Ruby? Is that what they call you?' Fay considered it a vast improvement on Beenie. 'Oh, Nora, I'm so glad to see you again. It's been so long.'

'It's four years since Max's mother's funeral,' Nora said, smiling as her husband ushered Henry and Jerry outside to inspect the automobile. 'Max is like a bairn with a new toy since Mr Miller spoke about it and, now he's been made chauffeur, he thinks there's nobody like him.'

'It's still Mr Miller that's Superintendent, then? Do you get on all right with him and his wife?'

'Oh, yes, they're different altogether from Ledingham – it's her that keeps the accounts and attends to things like that and I was promoted to cook a couple of years ago and she doesn't interfere at all. Even better than that, Mr Miller got a house made for us over the garage – kitchen, parlour, three bedrooms and an inside WC. They fairly believe in keeping up with the times.'

'I'm glad to hear it. And how old are you, Ruby?'

'I'll be thirteen in April,' the girl said shyly.

Fay turned to her daughter who had been standing silently. 'Mara, take Ruby upstairs and let her see some of your books and things.'

When the two girls went out, she said, 'Is Ruby still at school?'

'She's at Peterhead Academy,' Nora said proudly. 'Goodness knows where she gets her brains but she came out top of her class in every subject this year.'

'That's very good.' Fay smiled, rising to put on the kettle, and hoping that Nora wouldn't sense how jealous she was.

The tea made, the table groaning with oatcakes and cheese, home-baked scones, pancakes and shortbread, and dishes of strawberry and blackcurrant jam, Fay called the others to come and eat and, over the meal, Max told them the reason for the visit.

'With me getting promoted, the other two gardeners moved up so there's a job going for a young lad at the bottom of the ladder. I thought about Jerry straight away and he says he wants to work with his hands so I'll put his name forward, with a recommendation. Mr Miller's a fair boss and I think he'd fit in fine.'

By the time the table was cleared again, Jerry was talking as though he had already been hired and Henry had to warn him not to count his chickens. 'No, he's right,' Max assured them. 'I'm near sure he'll get it. Now, seeing we're here, we'd like to go and see Janet for a wee while so we'd best be off.'

The Oak Cottage Home Bakery had been on the go for almost twelve years when Max came to see Janet and he couldn't get over how well she looked. Even more surprising,

221

she was laughing and joking to the people she served – at times it took both women to keep up with the demand for their products. At last, during a lull, she came into the kitchen to talk to her visitors, her face sobering as she remembered that these were the two who had saved her from what could almost certainly have ended in death.

Noticing that her eyes were filling with tears, Nora and Max tried to jolly her along and were thankful that she didn't take long to respond to their light chatter. She was very pleased to meet their daughter and smiled to hear that they had called her Robina after the young girl who had also helped in her escape.

'Is Beenie still there?' she asked.

Nora grinned at that. 'No, you'll never believe what happened to her. It must be about five years ago she got a job as housemaid to the Morrices, the Glen Petra whisky folk, and she hadn't been there long when the son of the house, young Jonathan, came home from Oxford and fell in love with her. By good luck he wasn't one of the love-'em-and-leave-'em kind and he courted her properly before he married her. His father was awful against the wedding but the mother talked him round so Beenie's mistress of a big house on Speyside somewhere, with servants to work for her. I'm happy for her – she was such a nice wee thing.'

'It's always good to hear about somebody having good fortune,' nodded Janet, 'but do you not feel a touch jealous sometimes?'

Nora glanced at Max, who was deep in conversation with Willie. 'Only if I'm really down in the mouth. Max and me get on just fine most of the time and I wouldna change the big lump for all the tea in China. But we should be getting back for a motor can't find its way home in the dark like a horse.'

This last remark being overheard by the two men, there was much laughter before the Dalgarno family went on their way.

In bed that night, Fay said, 'I'm not too happy about Jerry getting a job at The Sycamores, you know. It doesn't hold happy memories for me.'

Henry kissed her cheek. 'Lie down and sleep, my Fairy Fay. The place has completely changed since we were there. According to Max, this Superintendent has made a lot of improvements and his wife's a real gem. And Nora's near as good a cook as Janet. Jerry'll be fine there if he gets the job. Besides, Max'll keep an eye on him.'

'Max is a chauffeur now so he'll be away a lot.' Her husband's frown made Fay add, 'All right, I'm sorry. But I don't want anything happening to Jerry.'

'Nothing's going to happen to him. Goodnight.'

Jerry did get the job. Max was sent the very next day to pick him up in the shiny black Bentley and, after rushing about madly to pack all his clean clothes and make sure she hadn't forgotten anything, Fay stood on the doorstep to wave him a tearful goodbye. Her youngest child, the only son she had left, had gone from her and Mara, having worked in a solicitor's office since she left school, was speaking about looking for a more interesting job, maybe in Aberdeen. If the girl did find what she wanted, she herself would be left with nobody – except Henry . . . Tchouki . . . T H Rae, Town Officer, who would be busy all this week making sure that all the events he had helped to organise to celebrate the coronation of King George V and Queen Mary would go off without a hitch.

CHAPTER EIGHTEEN

Always rather shy and quiet, fifteen-year-old Jeremy Rae had just lately begun to take notice of the girls who also worked at The Sycamores – not that he was interested in any one in particular. He had learned, from listening to the men, that girls magnified everything a boy said into something he had never meant – picking up even one word wrongly then expecting much more than he was prepared to give. With this in mind, when any of the maids spoke to him, Jerry was very careful not to say or do anything that could be twisted into something else.

Although his fellow workers teased him about being 'feart o' the lassies', he took his time about choosing one, watching them at mealtimes, listening to them speak amongst themselves. At the tiniest sign that a girl was a flirt or was foul-mouthed in any way, she was written off in his mind. Even if he heard them making fun of one of the residents, as Mr Miller called them, that was a black mark against them. He, himself, liked to speak to the old men and women who wandered around the flower gardens – it was no hardship to be civil and friendly and they obviously appreciated it. A few of them could even name some of the flowers in the beds he was weeding and discuss what to do about cutting them back or deadheading them or whatever the plants needed. Poor old souls, they must feel it, being in a place like this.

Of course, they were better off than the folk in the County Asylum. People called it the 'Madhouse' or the 'Feel's Place' and rumour had it that, after they'd been there for a while, the inmates started to behave like animals and were treated as such because they had nobody to care what happened to them. At

224

least somebody had been prepared to pay for the residents to be at The Sycamores and there they would be looked after properly. They were allowed to walk where they liked within the high walls if the weather was good, although some did need to be supervised. He had got to know a few of them quite well and was pleased when their faded eyes lit up if he called them by name. He sometimes wondered if he'd be reprimanded for being too familiar with them but Dod Lumsden, the head gardener, had never said anything.

One man, maybe only in his late fifties, had made a point of coming to speak to him at least once every week, obviously glad to have a decent conversation with somebody for it must be difficult to make sense, sometimes, of the other inmates who were all much older. He had said, the first day, that his name was Charles Moonie and that he had been, for many years, manager of the Fraserburgh branch of the Clydesdale Bank, but the rest had come out bit by bit. He had never married, had always lived at home with his mother and her two sisters and had been very happy with the way his life was going. Then, sadly, one of his aunts had died and, shortly afterwards, his mother had also passed away and everything had changed. He had been unable to concentrate on his job and, within a few weeks, he had been replaced by a younger man.

'Everything in me just seemed to be blown apart,' Mr Moonie had confided one day. 'Losing her two sisters so suddenly would have been bad enough for Aunt Maggie without me getting under her feet all day, though she put up with it for some months before it got too much for her. I had no idea how she felt and I missed my dear mother so much that, when she told me to find somewhere else to live, I just went to pieces. That is why our doctor advised her to send me to The Sycamores.'

'But you're much better now, aren't you?' Jerry had asked. 'Your aunt surely wouldn't want you to stay here if there's nothing wrong with you.'

Mr Moonie had seemed uneasy. 'I don't think I want to go

back to her – I am quite happy here. Mr and Mrs Miller are good people who make sure that we are all well looked after and I have no fault to find with the meals. Besides, I can please myself what I do.'

To a certain extent, Jerry had understood how Charles felt but had wondered why such a nice man had never taken a wife. Still, it was none of his business.

Apart from his little chats with the gardener's boy, Charles Moonie had more or less kept to himself since he arrived at The Sycamores. He was different from the other residents – there was no common ground on which to build a friendship. Of course, as he told himself with no false modesty, it was not surprising that one or two of the women saw him as a potential husband. He was, after all, still quite a handsome man, keeping to the custom of his days in the bank by always dressing in a smart dark suit and pomading his greying hair into a sleek blackness. But he had managed to fend off several women over the years and he had certainly no intention of being snared into marriage at fifty-five.

His resolve, however, was forgotten one evening at dinner, when Mrs Miller brought in the latest arrival. 'This is Anna Cairns,' she said brightly, her smile sweeping round the table, 'and I am sure you will all want to make her feel welcome.'

Having intended to speak to the lovely young girl as soon as the meal was over, Charles found that he could not get near her and was about to turn and walk out when he noticed the desperation in her big blue eyes. Guessing that she was terrified of all the ancient wrecks milling round her, he plunged to the rescue.

'Excuse me, excuse me,' he said loudly, as he elbowed his way forward. 'Let me introduce myself,' he smiled when they came face to face. 'My name is Charles Moonie and I'd be honoured if you would take a little stroll with me.'

As if in a daze, she took the arm he offered and he walked her quickly outside. 'I am sorry if I was rather abrupt with you,' he murmured when he shut the thick oak door behind them. 'I could see that you were uneasy with so many old people around you but you have no need to be afraid of me. You are quite at liberty to go back inside any time you wish.'

'If it's all right with you,' she whispered shyly, 'I'd like to take that walk.'

Nothing was said for the next few minutes, during which it occurred to Charles that she was younger than he had originally thought and he was at a loss to understand why anyone could incarcerate such a beautiful girl in a place like The Sycamores. At last, he murmured, 'I have been wondering how old you are . . . Miss Cairns.'

'I'm nearly fifteen and . . . please call me Anna.'

'And you can call me Charles.' He wanted to hear about her background but perhaps she would tell him more when she got to know him better.

It seemed that Anna, too, wanted someone to talk to and, although their next few meetings were accidental, it soon became understood that Charles would meet her at the little stream that wound its way through the grounds, at a point well away from prying eyes. After strolling through the stately sycamores for a while, they would sit on the moss-cushioned grassy bank and talk, like Lewis Carroll's walrus and carpenter, of many things. Charles was astonished at the depth of Anna's general knowledge and felt easier with her than with any of the other girls or women that he had ever known – no barriers, no shyness.

So it went on through the summer and no one missed them during the hour or so they spent together each day. The other residents generally had a nap after lunch and then congregated in the day room for the rest of the afternoon – some of them to play whist, while the others, unable to concentrate on playing cards, chatted with the person seated next to them or, to be more accurate, happily held a conversation with themselves. The female staff, after clearing up and attending to anyone who needed their attention, relaxed in the kitchen, the younger of them discussing the kind of boy they would like to meet, the older women turning over any gossip they had heard.

Willie Rae had been having pains in his chest for some weeks but, being as obstinate as he always was, he told no one, not even his wife. What was the point of worrying her when it was just a touch of indigestion? He'd been lucky being so healthy all his life and he couldn't expect to get off scot-free. He still had all his teeth, he could see to read perfectly well with his glasses on . . . as long as he held the newspaper far enough away. He didn't need a stick to walk with and he would be able to hear a pin drop if Nessie or Janet ever dropped one. He could surely put up with a bit of indigestion now and then?

To their loyal customers' dismay, the Oak Cottage Home Bakery had been forced to close. It was only when Nessie remarked that her legs would hardly take her weight some days that Janet admitted to the constant headaches that plagued her and they agreed to call it a day. Luckily, one of their regulars decided to launch out herself, now that her youngest had started school, so she took over everything they no longer required, including the glass counter, and insisted on paying.

As the weeks passed with nothing much to occupy her hands or her mind, Janet felt old and in the way, although neither Willie nor Nessie had as much as hinted at it. In fact, Nessie often said she didn't know what she'd do without her. But it stood to reason, Janet told herself, they must want some time to themselves, peace in their old age, and she'd been living with them now for . . . how long was it? She couldn't remember exactly but it was a long, long time.

Abby's son Clarence had taken over the smiddy a year or so ago but he was attending to more motor engines than horses lately. He had turned out to be a good mechanic though he'd never had any training for it, which was just as well, for Willie said *he* wouldn't know one end of a machine from another.

Besides, Willie hadn't looked very well for a while – he was sometimes real grey about the gills. He was a proud man, of course, and would never admit to being under the weather. His wife looked like death warmed up at times and all. Janet shook her head at this thought. They were well into their seventies, all three of them, and dying was on the cards for any one of them . . . at any time.

Nessie could see that something was bothering Willie. Several times lately, she had caught him with his hand on his chest, a grain of fear in his eyes, but the old devil wouldn't let her take in the doctor. 'It's just my guts, woman,' he would laugh, every time she suggested it. Janet wasn't her usual self, either. She'd never recovered properly from what that brute Ledingham had done to her.

As for herself, she was nothing like one hundred per cent. It was no single thing – stiff joints, tottery legs and a dull ache below her right shoulder blade. The doctor would think she was off her head if she gave him a list of what ailed her and it couldn't be anything serious anyway.

What a household it was, Nessie thought, wryly. They were three old crocks and it was just a question of which of them would end up having to look after the other two. But, even worse, was the fact that one would eventually be left on their own. Which of them, though? Who would go on to out-and-out senility, their brain useless as well as their body?

This was a most depressing thought and, when it crossed her mind, as it did more and more often as the days went by, she resolutely tried to think about something else.

Samara Rae was quite concerned about her parents but she knew better than to ask anything. They were so touchy these days – liable to snap her nose off for the least little thing – and there were so many old relations to consider. Her grandfather on her mother's side was bothered with his chest – his breathing sounded like the spluttering and wheezing of a traction engine some days. Grandma was unhealthily thin, looking as if she was wasting away to nothing, but she wouldn't admit to anything being wrong.

Granda Willie looked healthier, putting on weight in spite of not eating as much as he used to, and Mara had often caught him holding his chest, on the left side – where the heart was. Nessie – she didn't like being called Grandma for she was only a step-grandmother and she said it made her feel old – didn't look at all well some days, often wincing with pain when she got out of her chair or stood for any length of time, and she took lots of aspirins when she thought no one saw her.

Auntie Janet, as was only to be expected from what had happened to her years before, was in the worst state. She was as fragile as an eggshell, liable to shatter at the least pressure. She didn't speak much now but Mara could recall her saying that she must be a nuisance to everybody, a burden, at which she had reassured the poor woman that nobody looked on her as a nuisance or a burden. It was a blessing that she and Nessie had given up their home bakery. It had been quite profitable while it lasted but it had got too much for them

It must be awful to be old and infirm, Mara thought now, thanking God for her youth and perfect health. Of course, nobody knew what fate held in store for them but she loved to imagine herself, some years hence, with a tall, handsome husband and two or three children. That was the dream she had cherished for some years now and it surely wasn't impossible? She would not expect to live in a grand house – a small cottage would suit her, as long as love was there, and she gave herself up now to mentally arranging the furniture she would have and choosing the colours of the curtains she would make.

Being kept very busy over the summer, Jerry had been relieved that Charles Moonie had not come for a chat for a while – he would hardly have had time to speak to him anyway. It was, perhaps, another week before he spotted the man – an unmistakable figure with his upright bearing and his distinctive trilby at a jaunty angle on his head – walking in the distance with a young girl, both of them talking animatedly.

Assuming that a young niece had come to visit Charles, Jerry gave little thought to the incident but it so happened that he saw the girl on her own the next day much nearer than before – near enough, in fact, for him to have a good look at her. She was about the same age as he was, a good bit shorter than his five feet ten and she was perfect in very way. Her skirt was perhaps rather short and shabby – not the kind of thing one of Charles's relatives would wear. Whoever she was, her hair was long and mahogany-brown, glinting in the sun with flecks of gold, her bosom swelled out above her tiny, tiny waist and . . . the calves of her legs, the parts of their bodies most women and girls never showed, swept down in delicious curves to the tops of her heavy, scuffed boots.

All thoughts of spending time choosing the servant-girl he fancied most went out of his mind. This girl, this total stranger, was the only girl he would ever want. As she came nearer, he could see her face and it only deepened his determination. Her skin was beautifully creamy, her cheeks had very little colour, so she had not been out in the open air much, her lips . . . had parted in a slight smile as she noticed him looking at her.

'Hello,' she said, her voice as soft as the whisper of leaves on the ground. 'Are you the gardener?'

'One of them – the youngest,' He smiled. 'You're surely new here?'

'I've been here for a few months.'

He couldn't understand why he had never seen her before yesterday but what did it matter? 'I'm Jeremy . . . Jerry Rae.'

'My name is Anna. Anna Cairns.'

There was so much he wanted to know about her but he only said, 'I'll show you round the gardens if you like, Anna?'

'That would be very nice.'

Laying down his hoe, he stepped on to the path, then took her from one flower bed to the next, naming each blossom, discussing the types of the petals, the shape of the leaves and why he liked them. She took everything in, nodding seriously but saying nothing. Suddenly, she pointed to the trees on the avenue nearby. 'I know they are sycamores,' she smiled, 'but I don't know what to call these things.' She bent down and kicked up a few of the winged seeds.

Delighted at being asked, he said, 'They're samaras.'

'Samaras? What a lovely name, unusual.'

'That's what my father thought. He worked here years ago

231

and, when my sister was born, he christened her Samara –
though we call her Mara for short.'

'It's a shame to spoil such a pretty name.'

'Mara doesn't mind.'

Hearing feet on the path behind them, they turned round.
'I've been looking for you, Anna,' the young nurse puffed. 'I
didn't know where you'd gone.'

'I'm sorry, Tina. I felt like taking a walk and the gardener's
been telling me about the flowers.'

'You'd better get back before herself misses you. You know
she doesn't like you wandering about on your own.'

Sighing, Anna said, 'Thank you, Jerry, you've been very
kind.' She walked off, smiling.

Tina, the young nurse, lingered a moment then whispered,
'She's an inmate, Jerry, you'd best not encourage her.' She ran
to catch up with her charge.

His spirits were somewhere down around his mud-caked
boots. He had been attracted to Anna the moment he saw her
and he had just been warned to keep away from her. He
dreamed of her that night and, even in sleep, common sense
told him that it was hopeless. No matter why she was in here,
he certainly wouldn't be allowed to court her. In any case, did
he *want* to court her if her mind wasn't in proper working
order? Each time he asked himself this, however, the answer
was always yes, he did.

Tina had been keeping a close eye on Anna for some weeks
now, after she had seen her creeping in furtively by the small
door from the vegetable garden. A few minutes later, Mr
Moonie had appeared and it had dawned on the nurse that the
two had been together. There had been no reason to suspect
that anything out of place was going on but, as the days went
by, she couldn't help wondering. It wasn't seemly for a man of
his age and a young girl to be together so much – anything
could happen, though Mr Moonie seemed a nice enough man.
Even so, she had worried about the situation and, after spotting
Anna with the young gardener that afternoon, it had occurred
to her that here was a way out of the problem. Jerry would be

a far better companion for Anna but it was difficult to think how it could be arranged.

She puzzled over it all night and decided in the morning just to tell the truth. It was always the best way.

After breakfast, she went to the office. 'Mrs Miller,' she began, tentatively, 'I thought I'd better tell you – Mr Moonie's been taking Anna Cairns out walking in the afternoons.' Not wishing to land either of the parties in hot water, she hurried on, 'I don't suppose there's anything in it but . . . well, I just thought . . . it could lead to trouble.'

The Superintendent's wife was frowning now. 'Yes, it is not an appropriate liaison by any means. I shall have to put a stop to it. My husband and I are responsible for Anna's well-being and Mr Moonie's reputation is not . . .' She hesitated, colouring, then said, 'I am afraid that is confidential information and I can say no more on the subject but, even if he is completely recovered from his trouble, I must consider Anna's safety before anything else.'

Now came the tricky bit. Tina was well aware that what she was about to suggest could easily lead to trouble, too. 'I was wishing she had a boy her own age to speak to and then, yesterday afternoon, I saw her speaking to the young gardener and I thought . . .'

'Young Rae? Is that wise? Don't you think . . .' Dolly Miller broke off, obviously mulling it over.

'I've never heard anybody saying anything bad about Jerry, Ma'am, and I told him she was an inmate. I'd put my faith in him not taking advantage of her.'

'In that case, maybe . . . we should encourage them to see each other.'

'Yes, it would be good for her to be with someone of her own age, Ma'am.'

'My husband will probably not agree but what he doesn't know . . .' Dolly tapped her nose with her forefinger.

Tina wondered what was going on. She had gathered from Mrs Miller's confused hesitation that Mr Moonie must have had a problem with young girls – likely why he had been sent to The Sycamores – otherwise she wouldn't have agreed to Jerry seeing Anna, though the girl did need some young company. The thing was, as Tina had just realised, if the poor thing just knew one boy, she might fall in love with him and that would create worse problems. Jerry Rae was a right handsome young lad – all the young lassies eyed him hopefully – and Anna was a beautiful young girl so it would be only natural that he would . . . that they would . . .

Stuck for the word, Tina decided not to bring it to Mrs Miller's attention. Poor Anna had had little pleasure in her life and, even if it led to a sore heart for her, she deserved to get a taste of romance.

Mrs Miller sighed suddenly. 'I must get on with checking the tradesmen's invoices but I suppose it will be all right. Tell the boy that he may stop work at half past five every weekday and spend until six walking with Anna in the grounds. Just make sure that he understands there is to be no familiarity.'

Dolly did not start on her task when Tina went out. She had always felt sorry for Anna, the youngest resident, who had come to them under tragic circumstances. Her father had written first, explaining that his older daughter had witnessed her younger sister drowning and that she blamed herself for not being able to save her.

When Mr Cairns had brought her to The Sycamores, he had been profuse in his thanks that they had agreed to take her. 'My wife has a delicate disposition,' he had informed them, 'and she cannot cope with Anna these days.'

'I would guess that it will be only a short stay,' Dolly recalled her husband saying. 'At fourteen, she will soon get over her shock and be back to normal.'

Mr Cairns had seemed somewhat flustered. 'Um . . . no . . . my wife does not . . . wish her . . . to come home. Could you not agree to her taking up permanent residence?'

Raymond had been shocked at that. 'But surely, Mr Cairns . . . ?'

'I am willing to pay your fees for as long as necessary and any additional expenses incurred, like new clothes, et cetera. I am not short of money and I am sure she will be well looked after here.'

With terms agreed, Anna's father had written out a large cheque. 'I shall pay six-monthly in advance until . . .' He hesitated, embarrassed, and then stated firmly, 'until she marries or, failing that, until either she dies or I do.'

He had turned round then and walked out without going to say goodbye to Anna in the sitting room, where she had been told to wait. It had been very upsetting all round, Dolly remembered. She had almost taken the poor child in her arms when she saw her sitting amongst all the old ladies and men, her face drawn and white, her eyes as round as saucers and dark with fear. The poor soul had not spoken one word for days, but Tina Paul had eventually managed to get through to her and it was more or less understood now that the nurse would keep an eye on her.

Mr Cairns had never come to see how his daughter was and he ignored the two letters advising him that there was no valid reason for her to remain at The Sycamores any longer. A third, more forcibly expressed communication had elicited an immediate response, however. He wrote saying that his son, who was six years older than Anna and at St Andrews University at the time of the accident, had found an extremely well-paid post in Edinburgh. Because of this, he had decided, for the sake of his wife's health, to sell up and take her to live in the south of France. His postscript had added that he would instruct his bank to pay the amount due for Anna every six months.

Shaking her head in her perplexity at how any parents could shut their daughter out of their lives forever, Dolly picked up her pencil to continue checking the bills.

In his capacity as chauffeur, Max Dalgarno was allowed to make use of the smaller car on a Sunday once a month to see that his sister was all right, provided that it was not needed for any other purpose. While he was in Ardbirtle, he sometimes paid a quick visit to the Raes, who were always pleased to have news of their son. Twice in the past few months, he even had Jerry with him, dropping him off and then collecting him a couple of hours later.

Neither of them ever mentioned Anna Cairns. Jerry deemed it best not to, believing it would only upset his mother. And Max, like all the staff, knew why Jerry and Anna were seen together so much, but he had other things on his mind. It was well into 1913, however, before he told his old friend that he was starting a new job the next day.

'That's awful sudden,' Henry commented. 'Where, how and why?'

Max's laugh was somewhat self-conscious. 'I was quite content with my job, really, but Nora kept pushing me to find something better. You know how women are. I wasn't really going to do anything about it but I got speaking to a man in visiting his mother and he was interested to see the Bentley. He was thinking of buying some kind of automobile and was looking for a driver. I just about fell over when he said what he'd be paying – nearly twice what I'm getting now – with a four-roomed house on his estate, just south of Aberdeen on the coast road to Cove. Well, he was needing an answer right away and I knew what Nora would say so I jumped at the chance.'

'And Nora was pleased?'

'She threw her arms round me and kissed me. He's sending a lorry first thing tomorrow to collect our things so it'll be all go the whole day.'

'I'm happy for you,' Fay put in now. 'Tell Nora I wish you good luck and good health.'

'Aye, that's the main thing, isn't it?' Max nodded. 'Well, I'll have to go for we've still a few things to pack. I don't suppose I'll be able to see you so often now but, no doubt, Nora'll be writing to you, Fay, to keep you up to date on what's happening.'

'Yes, we'll keep in touch,' Fay smiled, giving him a warm kiss on the cheek.

Henry went out to the little black Ford with his friend. 'I feel a bit jealous of you, Max,' he admitted as the engine was cranked into life. 'I was perfectly happy till . . .'

'I'm sorry if I've unsettled you but I couldna go without telling you.' Max lowered himself into the driver's seat.

'I'd never have forgiven you if you hadn't come by,' Henry smiled as they shook hands. 'All the best to you and your family, man.'

'Thanks.' The car moved off, rattling loudly, with Jerry waving to his parents from the passenger seat.

Henry could see that Fay was downhearted when he went back inside. 'Max won't be all that far away,' he consoled, although he did feel a touch jealous, 'and he'll likely get the use of a car at the new place and all.'

'I wouldn't care about Max going away,' she said sadly, 'except . . . he won't be there to keep an eye on Jerry.'

Relieved, Henry said brightly, 'You don't have to worry about Jerry. He's quite sensible – not like . . .' He stopped, ashamed at what he had been about to say.

'Not like Andrew, you mean.' Fay shook her head. 'That's what worries me. Even if he was devil-may-care and took risks he shouldn't . . .' she said, blinking away her tears, before going on, 'he had a cheeky resilience about him . . . but Jerry's more sensitive. I don't think he would cope very well if he came up against any kind of trouble.'

'Now, now, my fretting Fairy Fay,' Henry smiled indulgently. 'I'm sure Jerry will face up to whatever fickle fate flings at him.'

His use of alliteration did bring a smile to her lips. 'You are always the optimist, aren't you, my darling Tchouki?'

She stood up to clear away the dirty tea things but he could see that she was no easier in her mind.

As anyone with any common sense would have known, when two impressionable, vulnerable, young people are constantly thrown together, the inevitable will happen sooner or later. Because it was Hogmanay, Jerry had asked Anna to meet him in the gardeners' shed about half past eleven. 'So we can see 1914 in together.'

'But we're not supposed to see each other after supper,' she had murmured, clearly wanting to agree but afraid to break the rules that had been laid down for them.

'Nobody'll know and I want us to be together at midnight. Maybe it'll bring us luck!'

Jerry had gathered from Tina that Anna should not be at The Sycamores now – her brain was as clear as anybody else's. It was only because her parents wanted rid of her that she had been there at all. There was nothing and nobody to stop him being friends with her. Starting the new year together would make that friendship more permanent, could even deepen it to something far more than friendship. Nothing could happen to spoil it.

CHAPTER NINETEEN

At twenty-one, Samara Rae, generally known as Mara, was still very reserved, still shy of strangers. Nonetheless, she found it impossible to ignore the young man who had recently been sitting across the aisle from her in church. At the close of every service for the past three weeks, he had stood up when she stood up, grinning to her as she walked sedately past him behind her parents.

She had given no acknowledgement the first week – it would have been most unladylike since he was an absolute stranger – but she couldn't help responding to his mischievous wink the following week and now she smiled back shyly. Having previously considered going to church a necessary chore, she would now do anything rather than miss even one Sunday. She dreamt of him every night, wishing that she knew his name, wondering where he had come from, what had taken him to Ardbirtle. Yet none of these things really mattered. As long as he still looked at her with those smouldering dark eyes and gave her that wonderful smile, she would be content.

She guessed him to be perhaps a year or two older than she was and a good six inches taller than her five feet six. His brown hair, not exactly curly, had a definite wave in it and was longer than normal, almost resting on his collar. Even knowing she would be too shy to answer if he spoke to her, she wanted to meet him properly and, as it happened, circumstances overtook her reserve. Late for her work in the solicitor's office one rainy Tuesday morning, she ran out of the house, head down, full tilt into the man of her dreams.

'Oh,' she gasped, as his arms went round her to save her falling, 'I'm sorry, I didn't see you.'

'Are you all right?' His voice was soft, his eyes regarded her anxiously.

'I'm fine. I shouldn't have been in such a hurry but I'm late for work.'

'Then I must not detain you any longer.' Having said this, he still did not move. They stood facing each other, aware that the rain was drenching them yet unwilling to part. At last, the young man relinquished his hold on her arms. 'I should have introduced myself, I am sorry. Leonard Ferguson, known as Leo, at your service, or I would have been if I had taken an umbrella with me.' He regarded her with his eyebrows raised. 'May I be so bold as to ask *your* name or is it a secret of the darkest kind?'

His jocular manner made her lose her shyness. 'Samara Rae, known as Mara.'

'Samara? How unusual . . . intriguing.'

When she told him that it originated from the winged seeds of sycamore trees, he said softly, 'I will always think of you as Samara, then. It will remind me of how ethereally beautiful you are. You look as if a puff of wind would blow you away.'

Even the unaccustomed flattery did not faze her. 'I'm much more substantial than that, I'm afraid, and I shall think of you as Leo because you have been like a strong lion for me.'

He pretended to growl and tucked her hand under his arm. 'Will you allow me to walk you to your place of employment, Miss Samara?' Before she could answer, he went on, 'I am being most inconsiderate, however. Your clothes are absolutely soaking. You must go inside and change. I shall wait here for you.'

'I couldn't let you do that,' she smiled. 'My mother would think if very remiss of me if she knew I had left you standing in the rain.'

Opening the house door, she led him in through the porch, chuckling at the amazement on Fay's face when they went into the kitchen. 'This is Leo Ferguson, Mother. He's waiting till I change into dry clothes.'

The young man held out his hand. 'I am delighted to meet you, Mrs Rae.'

His firm handshake did much to banish her fears for her daughter. 'You are soaking wet, too but I can't offer you a change of clothes, I'm afraid. You are much taller than my husband but he does have a spare set of oilskins here and you are welcome to that. It will save you getting any wetter.'

'But Samara should have it.'

'Mara has a waterproof cape she can put on. She was in too much of a hurry to look for it before she went out.'

The girl's first walk with Leo, therefore, was far more mundane than she had dreamt of but she was happier than she had ever been as they sloshed through the water-filled holes in the uneven pavement. Taking advantage of the empty street, he stopped at one point to kiss her and repeated it every time the chance presented itself. Both giggled at the rain running into their eyes and mouths because they were completely at one now and nothing mattered to them except each other.

By the time they reached her office, she was almost an hour late but Mr Kelly's sarcastic rebuke about sleepyheads made no more impression on her than had the rain. She still knew nothing about Leo apart from his name yet she had agreed to meet him the following night for she had no doubt that he was a man she could trust.

*   *   *

Anna Cairns was blissfully happy. From the small beginnings of accidental touching of hands, her meetings with Jerry Rae had graduated to deliberate hand-holding, then arms around waists, then stolen kisses when no one could see.

The kisses themselves had become more ardent until one day she was conscious of his tongue prising her teeth open, which created such a weird, wonderful sensation inside her that she pulled back from him in confusion after a few moments.

'Oh, Anna, I'm sorry,' Jerry muttered. 'I shouldn't have done that. I hope you're not angry with me?'

'Of course I'm not angry,' she breathed. 'I . . . think I liked it.'

For once in her life, she was glad that it was winter. The weather was a good excuse for them to go to their 'love parlour' – Jerry's name for the gardeners' big shed. She hardly knew how she got through each day until it was half past five and she could meet him and 'make love' with him, this being what he called the peculiar kissing. It was the most natural thing in the world to her these days yet he seemed worried that somebody might find out. Anyway, what did it matter if anybody did find out? They were not doing anything wrong . . . were they?

What Charles had done once, some months ago now, had felt far more wrong than Jerry's kisses. She had never been altogether comfortable with the man after he began to touch her, stroking her as if she were a favourite pet, and she had only put up with it because it seemed to give him so much pleasure. Then, that awful day when he got much rougher and invaded the private part of her body, she had tried to fight him off but it seemed that her struggles only served to give him more and more strength. She had hated feeling his hot, panting breath in her face while he pounded into her and it was so painful and disgusting that, when he finished, she had threatened to tell the Millers. He had pleaded with her to forgive him, that he couldn't help himself, that he would never do it again.

She couldn't forgive him but she hadn't told the Millers, either. She had kept on seeing him because she would miss the company and, thankfully, he hadn't broken his promise. She had been quite glad when Tina had told her she was to be allowed to go walks with Jerry Rae. She missed the interesting conversations she'd had with Charles, however, and being able to tell him all her worries. She didn't feel comfortable enough yet with Jerry to do that.

* * *

242

Tina was growing more and more anxious. She kept a chart of the menstrual cycles of each of the female patients under the age of fifty – mainly to be sure of having the necessary cloths ready for them but also because there had been two occasions, some time ago now, when one of the men had been responsible for the fathering of a child. In both cases, the men had protested that the women had been willing or had even instigated the mating, which made no difference really. The thing was, it had to be discovered as soon as possible so that something could be done about it.

She had considered that Anna needed no supervision as far as that was concerned. The girl had been collecting her own cloths for ages but had always let her, as the nurse, know that her 'show' had come but she hadn't mentioned it for quite a while. Tina had no idea how long it had been for she had never thought it necessary to keep a check on the young girl.

The poor nurse was torn apart with the worry of it. She had been so sure she could trust Jerry and he had let her down. Mrs Miller would likely sack her for throwing the boy and girl together. She should have known how it would end but, God's truth, she had done it for the best. The poor girl, as sane as Mrs Miller herself, had been practically isolated in this prison of a place when she should have been mixing with others of her own age. It wouldn't be right to put the blame on Jerry either. How could a young buck like him resist the temptation that Anna must be to him?

Tina sighed deeply. She had to do something, though it might be best to find out if her fears were justified before doing any confessing. Noticing that it was just after ten minutes to six, she went out by the gate to the gardens and walked slowly down the path towards the big shed where the gardeners kept their tools and anything else needed for their work. If anything was going on, that was where it would be taking place.

She was only a few feet away when the door opened and the two sixteen-year-olds squeezed through together, face to face, the boy's lips on the girl's. They had eyes only for each other and, ashamed to be witnessing their love, Tina moved round the side of the corrugated iron construction.

'Till tomorrow, my darling.' That was the girl.

'Oh, Anna, I love you so much. I just wish . . .'

'What d'you wish?'

'I wish we could be married but . . . I know they won't let us.'

'Couldn't we just . . . run away?'

'What would we live on?'

'We could both get jobs. Oh, I'm sure we could manage, Jerry.'

'Where would we live?'

'We'd find somewhere.'

'No, Anna, my dearest, sweetest Anna. It wouldn't work. They'd find us and I'd likely be arrested for luring you away. We'll just have to be content with what we've got. At least we have half an hour together every day.'

There was a short silence – the goodbye kiss, Tina supposed – before the footsteps went their different ways and she let the girl get slightly ahead before hurrying to catch up with her. 'Anna.'

'Oh! It's you Tina? What a scare you gave me.' A short pause and then, 'How long have you been there?'

'Long enough. We'll go upstairs – I have to talk to you in private.'

Once in the cell-like bareness of the girl's bedroom, Tina's heart turned over at the sight of her face – still flushed from what she had clearly been doing a few minutes earlier. She's just an innocent, the nurse mused, a pure innocent . . . and so's the boy. They wouldn't know they'd done anything wrong. Unfortunately, it was up to her to disillusion them – to prise them apart.

'Anna,' she began, softly, 'What were you doing in that shed with Jerry?'

There was no hesitation, although the round cheeks took on a deeper hue. 'We were making love.'

'Do you know what can happen when you make love with a boy?'

244

'It's wonderful,' Anna sighed. 'Have you ever made love with anybody?'

Hardening her heart, Tina said, perhaps more curtly than she meant, 'Making love can result in making a baby, didn't you know that?' The perplexed face gave her all the answer she needed. 'When was the last time you had the curse?'

The perplexity became utter bewilderment and Tina regretted not having taught her the facts of life before letting her loose with Jerry. It had been up to her – this whole business was her fault.

'Anna Cairns is with child, I am afraid, Mrs Miller.' Shuffling his feet, Doctor Watt was clearly uneasy about imparting this knowledge.

The Superintendent's wife stared at him as if he had said something obscene – which he had, as far as she was concerned. 'You must have made a mistake!' she declared, icily. 'How could it have happened?'

Irked at her manner, Dr Watt snapped, 'Surely a woman of your age must know that?' Then, realising how serious the matter was for the Millers who were acting in loco parentis for the girl, he added, 'It was Tina who told me to make the examination so you had better ask her. I will not abort the child if that is what springs to your mind. For one thing, the mother is as sane as I am, as you very well know, and both she and the father are in perfect health.'

He stalked out, leaving Dolly breathing convulsively, her face livid, but, after a few minutes, she rang the bell to summon one of the maids. 'Tell Tina I want to see her,' she instructed the girl. 'At once!'

It was all the nurse's fault. Dear God! What a scandal there would be! Anna's father would likely sue The Sycamores for allowing such a travesty to occur. She and her husband would be thrown out of their jobs when they had done their best to look after those in their care – yes, their very best! And it had taken carelessness on the part of just one lowly nurse to knock the foundations from under them.

Being a fair-minded woman, however, Dolly realised that perhaps it had not been Tina's fault. Maybe Jerry was not to blame either. It *could* have been one of the old men in their basket chairs; always casting lustful eyes at the young maids who were bending down to pick up something from the floor. She had reprimanded Jonathan Gall, ninety last month, several times for stretching out his bony hand to touch a well-rounded bottom and, even worse, for having his hand in his pocket fondling his privates. It must be he who had . . . raped poor Anna.

Tina disillusioned her on this, however. 'It wasn't Jonathan. Mrs Miller. It *was* Jerry Rae, the gardener's boy. But he's a good laddie and they likely didn't know they were doing anything wrong.' Tina ventured a quick glance at her mistress and said, hastily, 'It wasn't his fault or Anna's – it was my fault. If I hadn't thrown them together . . .'

'Yes! It *is* your fault,' Dolly spat out. 'What on earth did you think they would do? Two youngsters ready for . . . they could not help themselves.' Dolly dabbed her damp top lip. 'I have no option, Tina. You have proved that your judgement is not to be trusted and I must ask you to pack your things and leave immediately.'

On the verge of tears, Tina murmured, 'Please don't be too hard on them, Mrs Miller. They're young and in love . . .'

'I shall do what I have to! You are dismissed.'

Saying not another word, the nurse turned away sadly but Dolly called, 'Do not go anywhere near that girl before you leave. She will be confined to her room until we arrange what is to be done with her.'

Before she went in search of her husband to pass on the dire news, it occurred to Dolly that the trauma of a pregnancy and the ordeal of the actual birth might bring on a repeat of the mental breakdown that had brought Anna to The Sycamores in the first place. It would be as well, therefore, to have Tina there to look after her. Praying that she had not left yet, Dolly headed for the staff's quarters, trying to find a plausible apology for the way she had so peremptorily dismissed the young woman minutes before.

Tina was making a last minute check to see that she had left nothing when Mrs Miller knocked and went in. 'Tina, I am really sorry. It was the shock that made me lose my temper. It was not really your fault, my dear. How were you to know they would . . . ?'

'I should have known, Mrs Miller.'

'Do not be so hard on yourself. You thought it would be good for Anna to get to know someone of her own age and you were not to know that the boy would take advantage of the situation.'

'I don't think he meant to take advantage,' Tina sighed. 'I think it was a case of . . . well, I don't suppose he'd ever had any experience of girls and Anna certainly had no experience of boys, so it was a catastrophe just waiting to happen. I should have known.'

'Perhaps you should but I was too hasty. It came to me, after you left me, that Anna will need help to see her through her confinement and who better than you? You have always been a friend to her and she trusts you.' Dolly regarded the nurse hopefully. 'I hope you will overlook my earlier remarks and take on the job? Be a . . . mother figure for her?'

'Thank you, Mrs Miller. There's nothing I'd like better.

'That's settled, then.' Dolly's pleasure at having ironed out this wrinkle faded as she went downstairs. She still had to face her husband's anger.

A hasty telephone call to Anna's father's bank in Edinburgh gave Raymond Miller their address in France and he penned a very cautious letter telling Mr Cairns of his daughter's condition and asking for her to be removed from The Sycamores as soon as possible. It took a week for the reply to reach him.

His fingers were unsure as he opened the envelope, and a quick scan made him thump his desk in frustration. 'Good God! Listen to this, Dolly!' He took a deep breath and read out what Mr Cairns had written.

'As we placed our daughter in your care, trusting you to look after her properly, we set the responsibility for her fall from grace squarely on you. Since I made a contract with you,

247

I shall let my bank continue to send the cheque every six months. I am not, however, prepared to provide for the child who, but for your laxity, would not exist at all. I would suggest that either you make her get rid of it or have the father make an honest woman of her. Failing that, make him provide for it.'

Removing his horn-rimmed spectacles, the Superintendent looked at his wife. 'What kind of man is he? Having lost one daughter, wouldn't you think he would be more loving towards the only one he has left?'

Dolly was lost for words. She had never come across such blatant callousness and what she felt was too foul to say aloud. If the man had been there, she would have . . . sworn at him!

Husband and wife regarded each other helplessly until Raymond said, 'There is only one way open to us, as far as I can see. Get one of the maids to find the gardener's boy and bring him here. I will have to try a bit of negotiating.'

The summons to the Superintendent's office came as quite a shock to Jerry. He couldn't think of any reason for it but he laid his tools down neatly and went inside. 'You sent for me, Mr. Miller?'

'Er . . . yes . . . Jerry, isn't it?'

The youth was surprised by the man's obvious unease but waited silently.

'You have . . . um . . . been seeing quite a lot of . . . Anna Cairns, I believe?'

That was no secret so Jerry said, 'Aye, Tina thought it would be good for her to get to know somebody her own age . . . of the opposite sex.'

'So I believe. Well . . . um . . . it may have been good as an idea but . . . as you are no doubt aware, it has not worked out so well in reality.'

A cold shiver went up the boy's spine. 'What do you mean?'

'I mean that because you let your passions run away with you, Anna is now expecting a child.' Jerry's obvious bewilderment made him go on, 'Did you not know that . . . um . . . what you did . . . could have such a result?'

'No, I didn't know.'

There was no doubt that he was telling the truth and Raymond felt his anger slipping away. 'Well, it seems that neither did Anna but that is exactly what happened. I have notified her father but . . . um . . . he appears to have a heart of stone or no heart at all. He suggested that she gets rid of it but Doctor Watt has said he will not terminate the pregnancy. The other suggestion Mr Cairns made was that you should . . . make an honest woman of her.'

'An honest woman?'

'Are you prepared to marry her and give the child your name?'

Jerry gasped with shock. 'Mr Miller, I would give the world to be able to marry Anna but I can't afford to keep a wife – let alone a child . . .'

'We shall have to come to some agreement then. If you are willing to take the step, that would be the biggest hurdle cleared.'

The other hurdles did not take long to negotiate and, within fifteen minutes, Jerry was walking back to where he had been working. His mind was in a whirl, his legs were shaking but, all in all, he concluded, he couldn't be happier. He was to get an increase in pay, not all that much but at least they were to get their meals and clothes paid for them and they were to have the old lodge at the end of the driveway as a home.

For a moment, his soaring thoughts came to halt. Although he hadn't known why, he had always felt guilty about making love to Anna. He'd had a feeling that it was wrong and exactly how wrong it was had been proved now but, strangely, he hadn't been punished for it. In fact, what he had hoped to achieve some time in the future had been given to him with no strings attached. He and Anna had played with fire and been burned but it had been the best thing that had ever happened to them.

Of the five people closely involved in the forthcoming marriage, two were relieved that they had escaped so easily from what could have meant the end of their careers and two were blissfully happy, although scarcely able to believe their good fortune. Only Tina had misgivings. In her mind, the youngsters were not being punished for the terrible crime they had committed, for it *was* a terrible crime. Instead, they were being rewarded. Not that she wanted the poor things to be made unhappy but it might be better for them if they'd been reprimanded to some degree. It would let them know they couldn't always do what they wanted. There were always other people to consider.

Mrs Miller had relied on her to look after the girl and, by Jove, she would not make a mistake again. Not that it mattered now – it was too late, like locking the stable door after the horse had bolted. She had also to make sure that as few people as possible got to know, to make those of the workers who realised what had happened swear not to spread it about. It wasn't a good advertisement for The Sycamores that the youngest patient had been allowed to get in such a condition – and practically encouraged to do so, some folk would say.

There was one shadow lurking at the edge of Jerry's joy. He knew he should let his parents know about the wedding – and the baby – but he couldn't face his mother's disappointment in him. She had trusted him to behave and he had let her down badly. One good thing was that he wouldn't have to contend with Anna's father as well. Mr Cairns had made it quite clear that he wanted nothing to do with her or her child.

Poor Anna, the boy thought. He was determined to make it up to her for all the love she had missed in her childhood . . . and to shield her from any nasty gossip.

As it happened, a far more serious event took most minds at The Sycamores off Anna and Jerry. The Archduke Ferdinand of Austria and his wife were assassinated in Sarajevo and Britain declared war on Germany on the fourth of August. The chaplain, a young man with no ties, volunteered his services to the army and the marriage, which had been arranged for the tenth, had to be postponed until a new minister could be found. The replacement who eventually turned up was an old bachelor and, having been given no information about the bride's condition, happily performed the ceremony, smiling vacuously at the young couple and their two attendants, the Superintendent and his wife. Anna had asked Tina to be her bridesmaid but she had refused on the grounds that 'it would be out of place'.

No others were present and Jerry told himself that the news of his wedding could safely be kept from his parents until times were more settled. It might be best to wait until after the infant was born. Having a grandchild would surely blunt his mother's anger at him.

CHAPTER TWENTY

1915

New Year's Day was far more exciting for twenty-four-year-old Mara Rae than it had ever been and all because of Leo Ferguson. He had called for her two evenings a week in October, had been accepted by her parents as a suitable suitor and had graduated to coming for her every night during November. Unfortunately, December had turned out to be less favourable for 'walking out'. Gale-force winds and icy conditions meant that they were forced to remain indoors. As a special treat, however, after the bells had rung in the new year and the four of them had drunk a toast to 'health, wealth and happiness', Henry had said they could have half an hour on their own in the parlour.

'But remember,' he had warned Leo, albeit half in jest, 'if you are even two minutes longer, I'll come in to make sure you are not taking any liberties with my daughter.'

'Oh, Father!' Mara protested, her cheeks scarlet with embarrassment.

Her young man shook his head. 'You have no need to worry, Mr Rae. I love Samara, and I will take no liberties, I promise.'

Henry gave him a playful punch on the shoulder as he went past. 'I didn't honestly think you would. Are you ready to go to bed, my Fairy?'

There was rather an awkward silence between the two young people for a moment or two after the door closed, then Mara whispered, 'I'm so sorry, Leo. My father has spoiled everything.'

Leo grinned roguishly. 'Did you want me to take liberties with you?'

Colour flared up in her cheeks again. He added hastily, 'I'm sorry, Samara. I shouldn't have said that. I was only joking.'

She ignored his apology. 'I wouldn't mind if you did . . . take liberties.'

With a quick intake of breath, he slid his arms around her. Thirty minutes had never passed so quickly for either of them and perhaps small liberties *were* taken but none so drastic as Henry had feared. Leo was keeping his promise, breaking off the kisses and caresses before they went beyond the point of no return. At last, very reluctantly, he whispered, 'I had better go, my darling. I do not want to antagonise your father.'

'No,' she agreed. 'It would be best not to.'

Their last kiss was almost Leo's undoing but he managed to slide free of her embrace. 'No, sweetheart, we must stop.' He stood up to show that he meant it.

Giving a small sigh, she also got to her feet. 'I nearly forgot, Leo. Mother said she would like you to join us for a meal tomorrow night – tonight, I mean. That is, if your mother isn't . . .'

'Tell your mother I am delighted to accept her invitation.'

After seeing him out and getting only a quick peck on the cheek, she went back to the parlour to turn out the light – the council had installed gas for them the previous year. It was already twenty-five to one, she noticed, and smiled because there was no sound from her parents' room. As she climbed the stairs, she wondered how long it would be before Leo asked her to marry him. She had hoped that it would be tonight, this special night, but it hadn't happened.

Even though he had to watch his feet in the ruts and humps of ice, Leo was thinking along much the same lines as Mara as he wended his way home. He had originally intended to ask her father for her hand tonight but, during some early talk about the progress of the war, a new concept had arisen in his mind – a concept that would need deep consideration before he committed himself to anything else.

He had made only one friend since coming to Ardbirtle with his father and stepmother four months ago but Samara had more than filled the place previously held by the pals he had

253

left behind in Edinburgh – not that there had been many of them for he had never been a great socialiser. He had been only ten when his mother died and his father had had a succession of housekeepers who had mostly been interested in their employer's financial position and had no time for little boys.

His father had stood out against them for many years but had at last fallen for the blonde, curvaceous Madeline Kerr who was somewhere around forty years of age. It was difficult to tell. Instead of making her objective obvious like her predecessors, Maddy had shown neither interest in his money nor any aspirations towards marriage and her tactics had worked. Within five months she had become the wife of James Ferguson, head of the maternity unit of the General Hospital and heir to the long-retired wealthy stockbroker, John Murdo Ferguson.

His grandfather had died just over a year before, Leo recalled sadly, for he had been very fond of the old man, and while he himself had been left the goodly sum of three thousand pounds, his father had inherited everything else. This had been when Maddy came into her own, pleading and cajoling with her husband to stop working and buy a house worthy of their new status. Still besotted by her, he had not taken long to agree and had, in fact, purchased two properties – one was an impressive mansion in Edinburgh's Morningside and the other, as a holiday home, a not-too-small cottage on the outskirts of Ardbirtle in Aberdeenshire.

Maddy had been delighted with the first, showing it off to her circle of friends, mostly upstarts like herself, and lording it over the servants she had persuaded her husband to employ; but she was not impressed by the second, apart from being able to boast about their 'country house'. It had, however, become a sort of haven for Leo, who had taken up almost permanent residence there since meeting Samara Rae. He had told her nothing about his family and nor had he mentioned his good fortune – he meant to propose to her first. That way, he would know that she loved him for himself, not for his money, and he was quite looking forward to seeing her beautiful face transformed with pleasure when he eventually told her the truth.

Unfortunately, something had occurred that changed his plans. During his last visit to his father in Edinburgh, several women had made scathing remarks in his hearing about 'the rich young men who were afraid to take up arms against the enemy'. The same had not happened in Ardbirtle – not yet, at any rate, but no doubt it would come and Samara, like all the others, would despise him as a coward.

It would break her heart if he left her now, when they had almost plighted their troth, but he would have to go to fight for his country. Samara would understand. Maybe she was already wondering why he had not enlisted.

Jerry was hoping that it was Anna's pregnancy that was making her act the way she was doing. He had known that she was very shy with other people and he *had* kind of expected her to be embarrassed on their first night in bed together but he had *not* foreseen her violent reaction to him. He had been kissing her lovingly, tenderly, which she seemed to enjoy and then his manhood had jumped to attention and everything had changed.

'Take that thing away from me,' she had screamed, jerking her knee up with great force into his groin. 'I know what you're trying to do and I'm not going to let you hurt me.'

He was already out of bed and doubled over in agony so that her last few words did not register in his mind. 'What's wrong with you, Anna?' he muttered as soon as he was fit to speak. 'I wasn't trying to do anything.'

'Yes, you were.' She cowered away from him as he sat down on the edge of the bed. 'I could feel your *thing* boring into me.'

He resented this. His fellow workmates had given him advice before the wedding about what he should do and how he should do it but he'd thought they were joking. His body, however, had shown him that they hadn't been. 'That's what it's supposed to do,' he snapped before the new fear in her eyes warned him to say no more on that subject. 'I'm sorry,

Anna,' he murmured instead, adding beseechingly, ' It's freezing cold out here. Will you please let me back under the blankets? I promise not to do anything you don't want me to do.'

'All right, then.' She whipped back the bedclothes but turned away from him. 'Goodnight, Jerry.'

'Goodnight.'

He was forced to lie with his back to hers, otherwise his erection would make her think he was about to break his promise. He hadn't known that lying so close to her would have that effect on him, not so quickly at any rate, and now the damned thing wouldn't go down.

As Jerry was to find out, his 'thing' had a life of its own, rearing up even before he got into bed alongside his wife every night – also in the mornings when he woke. It was very awkward and sometimes almost impossible to ignore but he fought back the temptation to jump on her and let it have its way. He still loved her, of course, and was pleased with how she coped with her new lifestyle. She had never done any sort of housework before but she kept their little home spotless and showed a flair for sewing, making tiny garments that a trained dressmaker could not have faulted.

Because they were expected to take their meals in the large kitchen along with the rest of the staff, she bemoaned being denied an opportunity to cook for him. What was worse, she was growing more and more childish. Sulking if she did not get her way or stamping her foot.

They had been husband and wife for only seven weeks when she said, as they dressed one morning, 'I wish I knew what was going to happen to me. 'Tina says I'll have labour pains but they surely won't be very bad . . . will they? I don't like having anything sore.'

He was quite aware of that – it was why he had kept his needs under control – but he didn't relish the thought of her wailing at him about pain for the next few months. He had not been told when she was due but, counting back to the day he had given her that first bad kiss, she would just be four months gone with five still to go. That was what he worried about most. How would the actual birth affect her? Would she cope with such a trauma? Would she make the change easily to being a mother with the responsibilities that entailed? Or would she reject the child because of the pain it had made her suffer?

Tina Paul, too, was worried about Anna but not quite from the same angle as Jerry. The nurse knew nothing of her charge's refusal to let her husband have his 'rights' because of the pain it would cause but the far-away look in the girl's eyes warned that all was not well in her brain. Anna had originally been admitted to The Sycamores as a result of a nervous breakdown after her sister's death and was recovering slowly after much special care and treatment. Surely this new experience, a monumental change to any girl's system, would not undo all the good work that had gone before? Surely she wasn't about to lose her mind altogether?

Leo had been gone for almost two months before Mara had received his first letter. She had not recovered from the shock of being told that he had enlisted in the Scottish Horse, though she did feel proud of him for being so brave, and her heart lifted as she read what he had written.

'He'll be home on Saturday,' she told her mother, in great excitement. 'They've been on intensive training – that's why he hasn't written before but I don't care, as long as he's coming home now.'

Fay just smiled, not wishing to spoil her daughter's happiness by asking how long it would be before he had to go back and it was not until she and Henry went to bed that she voiced her worry. 'They haven't seen each other for so long, I just hope they can control themselves. You know, I wish he had married her before he went away.'

'Ach, my Fairy, don't fret yourself about them. They're both sensible adults. She's twenty-four, remember, and he must be nearer thirty.'

'That doesn't matter, not when they're so much in love and we don't want an illegitimate grandchild, do we?'

Tutting his impatience at this, Henry said, 'I don't know about you but I don't want a grandchild at all, illegitimate or otherwise. We're only forty-four.'

She detected a twinkle in his eyes. 'Stop teasing, Tchouki.'

The old, affectionate use of his given name had the somewhat surprising result of arousing him and Mara and Leo were soon forgotten.

Mara intended rushing home as soon as she finished work at one o'clock on Saturday but Leo came to the office at half past twelve.

Mr Kelly looked the tall soldier up and down. 'You'll be Samara's young man, I take it? I suppose I will get no work out of her now so you had better take her away but I want her back here on Monday morning as bright as ever. Off you go, the pair of you.'

Since Mara would not be expected to be home for another half-hour, they took a slow walk across the square into the trees, stopping to kiss as soon as they were screened from other eyes. 'Oh, my dear, sweet Samara,' Leo groaned, 'I've really missed you.'

'Not half as much as I missed you,' she breathed, her heart doing all sorts of acrobatics as his lips sought hers again.

'I was going to wait until we were alone properly but I love you so much I can't wait. Samara, will you marry me? Not straight away, of course.' He stopped and fished in the breast pocket of his khaki tunic, bringing out a small leather-covered box. 'We can be engaged. Look, I bought this in Edinburgh. I hope it fits but, if it doesn't, any jeweller would alter it.'

He lifted her left hand and slipped it easily on to her finger, looking at her in triumph that he had got the size right. If they had not been in a place where someone could come along at any minute, it is doubtful if he could have kept the promise he had made to her father several weeks before. His voice was hoarse and trembling when he murmured, 'This means that we are bound to each other for life now, my dearest.'

'I've felt bound to you since the day we met,' she admitted shyly.

Her parents were delighted to hear their news. 'It's a good thing I didn't use up the drink that was left over at New Year,' Henry crowed. 'It would have been awful if we hadn't been able to celebrate your engagement. Now, when is the happy day to be?'

Mara turned expectantly to her fiancé, her happy smile fading when he said sadly, 'I . . . think we should wait until . . . this war's over. I might be . . . I might not come back and . . . I don't want you ruining your life.'

Fay stepped in quickly. 'It's time we made ourselves scarce, Henry.' She grabbed his arm and almost pulled him through to the kitchen, adding, to save him protesting, 'It's up to them, dear. They have to come to their own decision.'

As Mara could see, Leo had already made his decision, but she couldn't stop herself from trying to talk him out of it. 'I would far rather we didn't wait.'

'I hoped you would understand how I felt,' he whispered, miserably. 'I don't want to tie you to a long life as a widow.'

'But nothing's going to happen to you,' she said, sharply, the very thought of it making her feel sick. 'I'll pray for you every night you're away from me – God won't ignore me.' Her voice broke suddenly. 'And don't you . . . go volunteering for . . . anything dangerous. Think of me first.'

Jumping up, he crossed the fireplace and pulled her to her feet. 'I'll always be thinking of you, my own darling Samara, always, always, but I could not live with myself if I did anything cowardly. I promise not to take any stupid risks, but I have sworn to fight for my country and that is what I have to do – without having to worry about a wife at home, and perhaps a child who would be fatherless if I allowed my personal worries to mar my judgement. Can't you see that?'

'I love you,' Mara said simply. 'That's all I can see.'

'And I love you, with every part of me, you know that, but . . . my darling Samara, don't make it more difficult for me. When I have to go, let it be without any restraint between us.'

She said nothing more, letting his arms enfold her and trying not to think that there might come a time when those strong arms would no longer be there for her.

Some ten minutes later, a gentle knock at the door made them step apart and Fay could tell that Leo's decision had won the day, although Mara's acceptance of it had probably not been given freely.

William Henry Rae's birth had been even more of an ordeal than Tina Paul had expected. Anna's labour had lasted for almost forty-eight hours, her screams increasing in volume and intensity as the clocks ticked on. By the time the infant came into the world, it was not only Anna who seemed to have lost her reason. Jerry, naturally, was in a state of manic disbelief when he learned that he had a son. Was it possible in the short time since he had . . . ? This, however, did not dim his joy at being a father.

Tina, on the other hand, could feel no joy. Something had happened during the birth that had raised a horrible suspicion in her mind and she needed peace to think it over, to consider the implications and, hopefully, dispel the hovering unease. Anna was a demanding patient, however, and for the first week, Tina was at her beck and call twenty-four hours a day.

The demands gradually lessened until, at last, Jerry said that he should manage to cope with his wife to let the nurse have a whole night off. Exhausted though she was, Tina found that she still could not sleep – her mind was too active, too anxious to get at the truth.

Only a month after he went back off leave, Leo's regiment was sent overseas and, from then on, his letters were written at any odd time, whenever he had a moment, and he deliberately kept them light-hearted. He could not tell Samara of the terrible conditions the British 'Tommies' had to endure in the water-logged dug-outs, with the constant gun and shell fire giving them little chance to wash, eat or sleep. Their uniforms were caked with mud, their boots either soaking wet or rock-hard, their faces dark with stubble, their skins itching with ingrained dirt.

No, he wrote of imagined birds singing on verdant trees and lovely, peaceful countryside, when the reality was nothing but devastation as far as the eye could see. He wrote of the camaraderie amongst the men, of evenings spent singing and joking, when, in fact, his companions were different each night, the death toll so high that those left alive were mixed together regardless of regiment or nationality. At times, they were shoulder-to-shoulder with Canadians and the next day it could be New Zealanders or Australians – the Anzacs had taken a terrible punishing too.

He never mentioned the skirmishes, the retreats that usually followed any slight advances gained. He ignored the fierce fighting, the long marches from one battleground to the next, either forwards or backwards, as in the case of Ypres, having to return to recapture a town. He avoided telling her of the comrades he had seen blown to smithereens, of passing dozens of bodies as they trudged, footsore, to engage the enemy again. and nor did he mention the long straggling lines of refugees fleeing from their destroyed homes.

Fortunately, there were some humorous incidents to relate, like the time a corporal was taking a drink from a fast-flowing river and his dentures fell out. He was dubbed 'Gummy' after that. The fact that the poor man had been killed about three days later was irrelevant, unnecessary to repeat. Then there was the little pug that had attached itself to the marching column one day and remained with it for some days. Nobody knew what had happened to it next but Leo left that out.

There were long stretches of time, naturally, when there was no chance to write, not even a short scribble, and he explained these as 'being on the move', leaving Mara to suppose they were being transported by lorries or trucks, instead of Shanks's pony. His powers of prevarication were so strong now that he sometimes thought he should take up writing as a career if he came through the war. *If* he came through – that was the crux of the matter. On his down days, he was sure that he would not but, during his very rare up days, he would picture holding

Samara in his arms again, imagine them standing in front of the altar.

'Do you promise to love, honour and obey her?'

'I do. By God, I do! That's what I'm fighting for.'

He had enlisted to fight for his country but his mind was set on just one thing now – to survive. Dear God, all he wanted was to get back to his fiancée, to love her, to make her his wife. When next he was back on furlough, he wouldn't hesitate. He would marry her by special licence. They wouldn't want any fuss, no big spread, no church ceremony, just the two of them and the two witnesses they would need.

Mara had been worrying about, and praying for, Leo's safety. Newspaper reports were not encouraging and the soldiers, who had been home on leave from France, spoke of terrible slaughter but Leo's letters were always so cheery. He was lucky to be in a place not too badly affected by the war. Maybe it was her prayers that had kept him out of the actual fighting so she decided she would pray even harder now.

She hadn't had a letter for a good while yet it didn't really bother her. His battalion would be on the move again. They were probably well behind the front line, attending to things that had to be attended to. Some men had to do the mopping up and Leo was lucky to be one of them.

'Mara hasn't had a letter for nearly five weeks now,' Fay observed one night, 'but she doesn't seem to be upset about it.'

'She's likely putting a face on it.' Henry shifted slightly. His left hip had been giving him a wee bit of bother this week. 'She surprises me, though. I'd have thought she'd be worried sick.'

'She says she prays for him so I suppose it's good that she has faith in her prayers. I do my bit and pray for him too – and for all the poor men away from their families.'

'Aye, it's a trying time, right enough. There's been a lot of sore hearts already . . . and likely a lot more before this war is finished.'

'There doesn't seem to be any sign of it finishing and it's two years already.'

262

'Aye and maybe two years more. Now, do you think we can go to sleep? I've to get up in the morning, remember.'

Charles Moonie had been very hurt that Anna had not contacted him before she got married. He just could not understand what had happened. It had turned out that she had been pregnant but the child had been born not much more than two months after the wedding. Of course, she had been keeping company with Jerry Rae for about two months before that but they had been so young, so quiet and reserved that rape seemed unlikely and he doubted if they had fornicated at all, during that time, willingly or otherwise. In any case, the actual deed must have been done months before she started seeing Jerry.

Charles's heart missed a beat. He had . . . not exactly raped Anna but he *had* fornicated with her – and she had been unwilling. He had not planned it for he had loved her deeply, still did, but his body had let him down. Like in the old days. Just being close to a girl had made him lust after her and most of the time he hadn't even attempted to deny that lust. At various times before her death, his mother had been forced to pay off at least three girls he had impregnated but it was his Aunt Maggie who had pulled the plug on him. The father of this girl – he couldn't recall her name or even what she looked like for she had meant nothing to him – had come to the house demanding that he marry his daughter but they were common, working-class people and Aunt Maggie had been only too pleased to give them cash to be rid of them.

Unfortunately for him, she had also been only too pleased to commit him to this place. There had been nobody to kindle his lust, not the least little temptation . . . until Anna Cairns put in her appearance.

There was no doubt about it. It was he who had fathered Anna's child, not Jerry Rae.

CHAPTER TWENTY-ONE

Henry was devastated when Willie came one morning to tell them that Janet had passed away peacefully in her sleep. 'I canna stop,' Willie went on. 'I'm on my road to tell Abby and Pogie.'

Henry turned to his wife when his father went out. 'You'll maybe not believe this, my Fairy Fay,' he said, softly, 'but I loved that woman like a mother.'

'I know, my dear, I know.' She, too, had loved Janet – perhaps not as much as she loved her own mother, who had died some years earlier, but pretty close to it. 'It's not my turn to write to Nora but I think I should. I'm sure they'd want to know . . . after what they did for her.' She should have known that it was the wrong thing to say.

'I'll never forgive myself,' Henry muttered, his voice breaking. 'If only I'd noticed we hadn't heard from her for weeks, I could have prevented . . .'

'It wasn't your fault, my poor Tchouki. Even if you'd gone to see her, that devil Ledingham would have fooled you into thinking she was all right.'

'But she'd have told me the truth. I'd have seen for myself . . .'

'He wouldn't have let you see her, and, anyway, he had frightened her out of her wits. She'd have been too scared to say anything.'

'I'd have known, though.'

Understanding that nothing would make him feel any different, she said, 'I'd better not write till we hear when Pogie can do the funeral. Max and Nora might want to come.'

'Nothing would have kept Max away,' Nora Dalgarno told Fay on the morning of the funeral, 'though he's worried sick about his job just now. His boss is seriously ill, not expected to live long, and his nephew, the only heir, says he's not sure if he'll keep on the estate or sell up. I told Max he'd better not ask the day off. If he makes a wrong impression on the man now, he could lose his job whichever way the wind blows and we'd have nowhere to go . . .'

'But Max is a good, reliable chauffeur,' Fay pointed out. 'I'm sure he'd easily get another job. In any case, maybe the nephew won't sell the estate after all. By the way, how did you travel up? Max didn't get the loan of a car?'

'There's only one car now and Max's boss is a cripple, so he hired a man to drive him for the day and we came on the train. The journey wasn't that bad but we'd have been quicker if we could have come by road.'

Giving a quick glance at the clock on the mantelpiece, Fay stood up. 'I made a pot of broth yesterday so I'd better put it on to heat. The men should be back soon if they don't want to be late for the funeral.'

Henry and Max, uncomfortable in their best suits and the collars their wives had starched as stiff as boards, were on their way back from their walk. They had not seen each other for a few years and, because of the circumstances, it had been quite an emotional reunion. Childhood memories flooded back, youthful exploits were smiled over and their fellow workers at The Sycamores discussed. They recalled Janet's many kindnesses to them but not one word was said about her terrifying experience at the hands of the man she had married in all good faith. They knew that, once they started down that path, they were liable to lose control and, on this the last day they could show their respect and love for her, they had to have full command of their senses.

As it turned out, when the pitifully few mourners were sitting at the funeral tea, this was the first subject to arise. Fay did her best to divert Willie when he brought it up, then she remembered that, apart from Max and Nora, Henry and herself, the others had only got to know Janet since she had been taken to Ardbirtle. This resurrection of the tragic incident was too much for the two youngest men who began to weep openly. But Pogie, almost ten years older and well versed in preventing grief from getting out of hand, steered the conversation round to some more recent memories of the deceased woman, who had devoted much of her life at Oak Cottage to helping the Rae family as a whole.

The ordeal, thankfully, did not last too long. Max and Nora had to catch the train to Aberdeen, in time to get the last connection that would take them to Cove.

For some time after the last of the mourners had left, Willie and Nessie sat silently by the fire. Both in their eighty-first year, the commotion of so many people in the house at one time and the strain of trying to appear normal under anything but normal circumstances, had proved too much for them. At last, Nessie gave voice to what she had been thinking. 'I wonder which of us'll be next to go?'

'Losh sakes, woman!' her husband exploded. 'Stop being morbid.'

'It's not morbid, Willie, it's just facing facts. I often wondered, since Janet came here, if you thought more of her than me.'

'What the hell are you on about?'

'I watched you sometimes and it looked like you could tell her things you never told me. Like she was your wife and I was the incomer.'

'Ach, that's daft.' Willie fell silent again, needing time to consider it and, assuming that he didn't intend to discuss it, Nessie rose with the intention of making another pot of tea. She was quite hurt that he hadn't reassured her for it was horrible to think she'd been playing second fiddle to Janet all these years.

While she was on her feet, however, she spotted two bottles still sitting on the dresser – whisky for the men and port for the women – with very little in either.

In a few seconds, she handed her husband a half full tot

glass of whisky – all that was left – and sat down with what had been in the bottle of port – somewhat more than half a much bigger glass – tipping it to her lips like a seasoned toper. Willie was astonished. He had never once seen Nessie take strong drink of any kind before. She hadn't even taken one when everybody else was knocking them back earlier on.

'There's no need to look at me like that,' she exclaimed as she laid down her empty glass, mistaking his expression for disapproval. 'I needed something stronger than tea!'

He shifted uncomfortably in his chair. 'Look, lass, I'll be honest wi' you.'

'I wish you would.'

Her low voice, with a slight catch in it, made him wish he had spoken about this years ago. The thing was he just hadn't thought it was necessary. 'It was you that suggested we should bring her here in the first place, if you mind? I wasna that keen on having a stranger in the house, especially another female. I've ken't some women that nag at a man every hour of the day – you included, for a good few year.' He gave a weak smile, then carried on, 'But you changed, thank the Lord, and you couldna have been a better wife to me. But Janet was an unknown quantity that first day.'

He rose to add some water to his tiny glass to eke out the liquor, then sat down again, took a dainty sip and visibly relaxed. 'That's better! A man needs a bit o' Dutch courage at times. Well, now, I'll get back to what I was saying – though it's about the hardest thing I've ever had to do. At first, although I was heart sorry for Janet, I was a bit scared o' her. I couldna think what to say to her but, once I got to ken her better, I could see she was different from the other women I've come in contact wi'. She never said a thing unless we asked her opinion first and she never criticised me – or you, for that matter. And, when she was fit enough, she helped you in the house as much as she could and she started the bakery and all. Not only that, she helped Abby and Fay wi' their bairns and . . . Oh, Nessie, I can see by your face I'm going at this all wrong.'

267

'I don't think so.' Her voice was icy. 'Your meaning is perfectly clear.'

'No, I dinna mean what you think I mean.' His frustration at being unable to express himself properly was making Willie revert to his old way of speaking. 'Let me try and explain, lass. Aye, I *did* come to love Janet – but just like a friend – then like the sister I never had, a sister I could tell things to – like you said, things I couldna tell you. She was easy to speak to – she didna find fault, she listened and advised and said what she thought but never – never, I say – laid down the law to me. Can you not understand that?'

'I understand I was right all along – you did love her.'

'Oh, Nessie,' he groaned, 'you still dinna understand. I loved her like a sister, I tell you, but I love you like a wife. Like a man should love his wife, though I must admit the years have ta'en their toll on me. The urge is there many a nicht, but . . . the flesh is weak.' He leaned across and took her hand. 'I'm not young and erect like I once was, Nessie, I'm auld and . . . limp.' His eyes twinkled roguishly for a moment. 'The truth is I would if I could, lass, but I canna.'

Nessie swallowed the lump in her throat. 'I'm sorry, Willie. I should have known you would never do anything wrong. Anyway, fancy me worrying about something like that at my age.'

Willie got up and pulled her to her feet. 'No, no, my dear, everybody needs to feel loved – there's no disgrace in that – and, just to prove what I've been saying, come up the stair and I'll squeeze you till you beg for mercy.'

Needless to say, she did not beg for mercy. She savoured his cuddles and kisses and hope rose within her as he caressed her in places he hadn't touched for many a long year. Hope, though, was the only thing that rose and, even if she felt slightly cheated, she was relieved that he went no further. Two eighty-year-olds could never recapture the passion they'd had at forty.

Jerry had meant to go to see his parents when he became a father but his mother's letter made him change his mind. They would be upset enough about Janet's death without him adding to it by springing a daughter-in-law and a grandson on them and, anyway, Anna wasn't well enough yet to be travelling.

Besides, he had something else on his mind. The birth of his baby had not brought the joy that he had expected. After they were given the good news, the older men who worked with him eyed him as if they pitied him and, after puzzling over this for a whole day and night, he tackled the head gardener the following morning. 'Why does everybody keep looking at me like that? You all knew Anna and me had to get wed.' It was not something he was proud of but it was the truth.

Dod Lumsden looked uncomfortable. 'Well, it's like this, lad . . . um . . . how long had you been seeing her afore the wedding? A couple o' month, maybe?'

The young man nodded. 'That's right but what's that got to do with it?'

'You didna ken her afore that?'

'No. Tina thought she should get to know somebody her own age and Mrs Miller agreed to her seeing me.'

Lumsden rubbed his chin pensively. 'Can you mind the first time you . . . made love to her?'

Colouring, Jerry muttered, 'I can't see that it's any of your business.'

'Either it's nae but I still think you should ken . . .'

'I should know what?' A little feeling of unease was hovering round the pit of the youth's stomach now.

'Look lad, somebody needs to set you right aboot things. You see, from the time a man plants his seed in a lassie's belly, it tak's nine month till it's born.' Noticing that the young eyes had clouded, he asked, gently, 'When did you plant your seed in her?'

This being met with a puzzled silence, Dod heaved a deep sigh. 'Godamercy, laddie! You dinna ken what I'm speaking aboot, do you? Well, we'd better leave it there. I dinna want to cause trouble atween you and . . . your wife.'

He walked away, shaking his head and Jerry was left wondering what the man had been trying to say. He and Anna had only known each other for . . . five months at the very most and they'd been seeing each other for at least a month before he gave her that first wicked kiss. He still felt ashamed of it for the boys at school used to say that was what could make the girl have a baby. She hadn't liked it but that's when his seed must have got inside her. Not quite four months before she gave birth. Dod Lumsden had been blethering. Nine months? For elephants, maybe, not human beings!

But he couldn't put the disconcerting information out of his head and, when he went home that night, he asked Anna what she knew about the length of time a baby grew inside its mother.

There was no hesitation. 'What a funny thing to ask. You should know. It took our wee William Henry four months, didn't it?'

It was what he wanted to hear. Dod Lumsden had never had any children. What did he know about it?

Jerry would not have been so sure if he had known how Tina Paul's mind was working. She had been mulling it over for days, had tried to make herself believe that Anna and Jerry must have been meeting in secret months before it had been arranged for them. She wondered if she should tell Mrs Miller but she would only get the blame for not knowing what was going on. She always got the blame – no matter what – and she would likely get the sack for real this time.

Desperate to find confirmation one way or the other, she thought of asking Charles Moonie. Surely he would know if Anna had been meeting Jerry on the quiet. The thing was, since the day he had been told that his walks with Anna must stop, he had been dour and uncommunicative. She had put it down to pique but maybe he thought he was being punished when he had done nothing wrong.

Tina's thoughts stumbled, then picked up speed and skated over something that had been nibbling away at her peace of mind since wee William Henry was born. Each time it had suggested itself, she had pushed it from her, although she knew she would have to face up to it at some point. Not yet. Not today.

Having made her decision, the nurse stood up purposefully. She had set aside at least thirty minutes morning and afternoon to check that Anna was coping with motherhood. The birth had had a strange effect on the girl and her short periods of seemingly withdrawing from the world were growing longer. She would sit staring into space, eyes glazed over, even when her infant was howling for a feed but, as soon as Tina touched her, she snapped back to normal. It was worrying yet Tina always managed to assure herself that things would sort themselves out as time went on.

Fay was concerned about both her children. There had been no letter from Leo Ferguson for an impossibly long time and Mara was going about as if she were just half-alive – not even that some days. The situation did look black but she had to keep her daughter's spirits up. There had been stories of men going missing in combat and turning up nearly a year later, having lost their memory or perhaps being badly wounded and taken to a French or Belgian hospital and being nursed back to health.

'It could happen, couldn't it?' Fay asked her husband one night.

'Aye, Fay, it could happen but I some think we'll need to start being realistic. It'll be all the harder for her when the word does come.'

'I know but I can't bear to be the one to shatter her hopes.'

'D'you want me to say something, then?'

'No, please don't.'

'You know, it just came to me. It would be Leo's father they would tell. He would be the next of kin.'

Fay took a moment to consider this – it was something she had not thought of. Then she said, her voice lifting with hope, '*He* would have let Mara know if anything had happened to Leo. Surely he would?'

'Maybe he doesn't know about her.'

'Leo said he told him they were engaged and he was going to take her to meet them in Edinburgh next time he came home.'

Henry couldn't help noticing that she was using the past tense but he let it go and, in a moment, she said, 'You know, we haven't heard from Jerry for a good while. I hope he's all right.'

'What a woman you are for worrying. If anything was wrong with Jerry, the Superintendent would let us know. He's likely found himself a girl to keep him busy. Better than coming home to see his dull parents.'

'He's only seventeen, for goodness sake.' Her husband's raised eyebrows made her exclaim, 'Yes, I know we were just sixteen when we married but that was different and, besides, he didn't answer the letter I wrote telling him about Janet.'

'Ach, you know what he's like at writing. Stop worrying, for any sake, Fay. He'll come walking in one of these days with a wife and then there'll be a baby. How will you feel about being a grandmother, my Fairy?'

'A lot better than I feel now.'

'In that case, the quicker it happens, the better.

On his daily walk, his constitutional, Willie usually called at Abby's house to catch up on her news, then, after going into the countryside for a mile or so, he looked in on Fay on his way home. Sometimes, he met his son on his peregrinations and stopped for a chat with him. Henry was usually quite glad to stand for a few minutes with his wheelbarrow, besom and shovel at the ready. Their talk was often about the weather, bad or good, but lately it had been about Mara and the likelihood of her fiancé coming back from the war.

This was their topic on the afternoon a few weeks after Janet's funeral and, after standing for a while, Willie accompanied Henry on his round for over an hour while he carried on with his duties. Their lengthy discussion evolved around the question of whether or not Mara should be warned that there was little hope for Leo now.

Willie was mulling this over as he walked back home, his feet dragging with being on them for so long. Poor Mara. She had always been a quiet girl with no interest in boys and he had often wondered if she would ever find a lad. Then Leo Ferguson had come into her life and she had blossomed like a rosebud in the summer sun. He had brought her out of herself – she was livelier, fun to be with and she radiated supreme happiness. But now . . . ?

Willie heaved a long, sad sigh as he entered his own house, hoping that maybe his wife would be able to think of a way round the problem. Having had more experience of life than Fay, she should be able to find the words to tell Mara gently, to help her to cope with the deep sorrow she would feel at the loss of her loved one. 'Nessie,' he called, hanging up his coat and bonnet on the peg in the porch. 'Are you there, lass?' Perturbed by the silence – she hardly went out at all these days – he walked into the kitchen. 'Nessie, are you . . .'

Then he saw her – she was lying on the hearthrug and her face a peculiar bluish-grey. He bent over to touch her forehead, recoiling when he felt no warmth. Oh, no! Dear God, no! But she couldn't be dead! She couldn't be. Leaning forward again, he lifted one of her hands and held it for a few moments but could feel no pulse.

His legs buckling suddenly, he felt behind him for the arm of his chair, plumping down on it just in time. His senses were swimming; his heart was thumping like he had just run a mile at full tilt; his chest was as tight as a drum; he felt sick.

He closed his eyes for a moment but that made him feel even worse. He would have to sit here till he felt better. No, no, he should be going for the doctor. But what use was a doctor to his dear wife now? She was gone!

His heart slowed down gradually, his breathing eased and, though he could still taste the brackish bile in his throat, he was more or less able to marshal his thoughts. He would just sit for another few minutes and then he'd better get somebody. Doctor Hay? Pogie Laing? Henry! He wasn't far away – he'd know what to do . . . wouldn't he?

Willie's tortured thoughts veered abruptly. He hadn't felt as bad as this on the morning Nessie found Janet dead in her bed. Nothing like as bad! That proved he hadn't loved her in the same way as he loved his wife, didn't it? Nessie would be pleased when he told her that. His stomach gave a mighty lurch. Fool that he was! Nessie was dead! His beloved wife of thirty-odd years was dead! Damn it, he couldn't for the life of him remember when he had wed her. For the life of him? He didn't want a life now. They should be going to eternity together.

He took time to consider this. He could easily do it. His cut-throat razor would do the job nicely. He staggered to his feet, swaying a little as he let go the armrest of his chair, but, before he could take even one shaky step, someone knocked on the front porch door. He turned round uncertainly, then decided to ignore it.

Pogie gave another knock, then turned the handle and walked in. Seeing Willie first, tottering on his feet and with a look of great shock on his face, Pogie was on his way across to find out what was wrong when he saw Nessie. 'Good God Almighty!' he exclaimed. It was no profanity, for he was as devout a man as ever walked on two feet. 'What happened, Willie?'

Getting no answer, he bent down to check for a pulse but there was none. Her hand wasn't ice-cold but she had definitely been dead for some time. His first thought was that his father-in-law had killed his wife, after a heated quarrel perhaps, but he was eighty, for heaven's sake, too old to let passion of any kind get the better of him. Straightening up, he stretched out and guided the man gently back into his seat. 'Willie, can you tell me what happened?'

There was no reaction whatsoever for quite a while, then tears welled up in the faded, red-veined eyes. 'She was fine when I went out . . . but that's how I found her when I came back.'

'It looks like she has had a heart attack but we need the doctor to issue a death certificate before I can do anything.'

And so Pogie took over, asking a neighbour to fetch Doctor Hay and trying to calm Willie as he sobbed, 'I wasna here for her . . . I should have been here . . . I bade ower lang wi' Henry. I could have been back earlier, man.'

274

Pogie assured him that it would have made no difference and this was confirmed by the doctor when he had examined the body. 'She died of cardiac infraction, a massive heart attack, about . . .' Halting, he asked, 'How long were you out?'

'I went out about half nine. I'm usually back about twelve but I was speaking to Henry for a long time the day, discussing something we . . .' His voice tailed off and he looked hopelessly from one man to the other.

Pogie stepped forward. 'It's all right, Willie. You were not to know what had happened.'

'No, indeed, Willie.' Having signed the death certificate, the plump little doctor slapped his battered old hat at its usual rakish angle on his head. He had worn it this way since he was a young student and did not care that it made him look a slightly ridiculous figure with his thick white hair flowing from all round it. 'You see, Willie, a person can be as right as rain one minute and drop down dead the next – as in your wife's case. It should be of some consolation to you that she had not suffered. In fact, she had probably been dead before she hit the floor.'

The old doctor had never been known for his tact but his words did go a long way to help the bereaved man. Not only that, after he left Oak Cottage, Hay sought out Henry to inform him of the tragedy so Willie had his son with him before Pogie had finished measuring for the coffin.

For the second time in three weeks, Pogie took over all the funeral arrangements and Abby and Fay promised to organise the catering. Abby also wrote to her two sisters in Aberdeen, telling them of their stepmother's demise 'I know they left home because of her,' she explained to her husband, 'but this would be a good excuse for them to make things up with Father. It wouldn't be like crawling back or climbing down, would it?'

Neither Jeannie nor Bella, however, jumped at the chance of reconciliation with their father. Although Abby had told them that Nessie had changed to being a gentle and caring woman, it seemed they could only remember the harridan she had once been. They still blamed Willie for not protecting them so the only replies they sent were two impersonal printed cards, deckle-edged and black-rimmed, regretting that they could not attend the funeral.

But, proving how different she was, as soon as Kitty got the news, she wrote a long letter to her father from London, saying that she wished she could be there but she couldn't get time off her work. She did make it plain, however, that, if he needed her, she would give up her job to come home and look after him.

Willie, as only to be expected, wouldn't hear of this, asserting firmly that he would easily manage. 'I dinna ken what you're fussing aboot. I'm nae a bairn.'

So Abby conveyed his refusal in a tactful letter.

Nessie's funeral was just as quiet as Janet's. As Fay remarked to Henry when they went home, 'It's really sad, isn't it? People outlive their friends and if they've no family, there's nobody left to mourn for them.'

'At least Janet and Nessie had us,' her husband pointed out. 'We've always looked on them as family.'

It was on the tip of Fay's tongue to say that the two women were closer family than his two eldest sisters – neither of whom she had ever set eyes on – but she did not want to upset him further.

Jerry had been meaning to take his wife and son to meet his parents at the weekend but, again, his mother's letter changed his mind. First, it had been Janet and now Nessie. How could he spring his surprise on them at a time like this? In any case, as the days had gone past, he hadn't been altogether sure if it would ever be a good idea.

For the past two weeks, his wife hadn't allowed him to sleep with her. He had done his best not to come in contact with her when they went to bed but the old mattress they had been given along with the bed sagged in the middle and he couldn't help rolling against her. This was what had caused the friction between them and she had ended up one night by shouting,

'I'm not going to let you hurt me again. It was your fault, I'd to suffer all that pain so you can sleep on the couch in the kitchen.'

Since she had shown no sign of improving, he had decided to postpone their visit to Ardbirtle. His father might not notice anything but his mother's eagle eyes would notice that something was wrong about their marriage. Knowing her, she would try to find out what had happened . . . and he couldn't tell her. He didn't know himself. What had he done to make his wife hate him? And what could he do to stop it?

CHAPTER TWENTY-TWO

After changing her eight-week-old son, Anna Rae sat down in the low chair to feed him. She quite liked the sensation of the actual suckling but she did her best not to let Jerry see her. She hated the way he stared at her bosom when she bared it. It had started one evening a few days after the birth. The baby had dozed off during the feed, as he often did, and, unfortunately, so had she but something alerted her to a slight movement at her side. She had felt sick to find Jerry kneeling beside her, his fingers only a hair's breadth from her oozing nipple. Since then, she deliberately turned her back on him or went into the other room if it wasn't too cold for the child. But he wouldn't be home for hours yet so she was safe enough sitting by the fire.

It was raining quite heavily, with flecks of sleet through it, so she couldn't go out with the old pram Tina had got from somebody. Little William Henry was a contented wee soul, though, and he would drop off as soon as she laid him in the cradle – another item Tina had acquired for her.

After ten minutes, she laid the infant over her shoulder to wind him, then put him to her other breast, his tiny mouth engulfing it as if he hadn't had any sustenance for goodness knows how long. Tired as she always was these days, she still worried about things and her mind settled now on the adulation her son got in the kitchen at mealtimes. All the female staff, from Mrs Miller herself right down to fourteen-year-old Winnie, the scullery maid, fussed over him, cooing and murmuring sweet nothings.

'Ah, my dearie, you're the bonniest bairnie I've ever seen.'
'He's a wee darlin'. I could eat him.'

'He's nae a bit like his father, is he?'

As his mother, she didn't care which parent he looked like for he was absolutely perfect but she didn't want him to be spoilt. Jerry had said calling him after his great-grandfather and grandfather was a safeguard for the future and it hadn't mattered to her. As long as he didn't want to call their son after *her* father who had wanted nothing to do with him, she didn't care.

When she realised that the pull of the little tongue had been stopped for a while, Anna stood up and, before she even got him to her shoulder, he gave a loud burp that made her smile. This was followed by another, more genteel this time, and, as she laid him in the cradle, warmer than the pram, he broke wind with a rumble like an old man. At least he wouldn't be bothered with colic tonight, she thought.

After making sure that he was well covered, she fastened her buttons and sat down again. It was a good chance to catch up on the sleep she had lost worrying about her situation. She couldn't force her husband to sleep in the kitchen forever – he was getting short-tempered already – but he'd do nasty things to her if she let him back into her bed. He swore he wouldn't hurt her but she knew different.

A slight noise from the lean-to scullery at the back intruded on her musings and, thinking that she must have left the outside door open when she came back in from having her dinner, she rose to close it. Finding it as tightly shut as it could ever be, a little prickle of fear ran up her spine. She could have sworn she'd heard something. She turned uncertainly, then gave a sigh of . . . not altogether relief for she couldn't think why he was there. 'You gave me a fright, Charles.'

'The rain was getting heavier so I came inside, I'm sorry. I did knock.'

'It's all right. Come through to the kitchen and I'll make us a cup of tea. Just be careful not to waken the baby. He's not long asleep.'

'Don't bother with tea, Anna, I just want a wee chat with you.'

She sat down, hands in lap, wondering what he'd come to say. She hadn't spoken to him since . . . not since she'd been told to start going for walks with Jerry. Maybe he was annoyed at her for not explaining why she had stopped seeing him. His dark eyes were boring into hers and he seemed to be waiting for her to speak first. 'I hope you're not angry with me?' she managed to get out, long fingers of apprehension clutching at her heart.

His smile held no humour. 'Why should I be angry with you?'

'They stopped me seeing you. They said I should get to know somebody nearer my own age.'

'Did you not enjoy being with me?'

'You know I did . . . except for that one time.'

'And which time would that be, my dear Anna?'

Guessing that he was playing a game with her, she said sharply, 'You know perfectly well when I mean.'

'Would that be the day I . . . made love to you?'

'What you did wasn't making love.'

'No?' His mouth twisted in a sneer. 'It was the only way I could prove my love for you, my dearest girl. Is that not how your *husband* shows his love?'

'Jerry has never touched me like that,' she burst out, wondering where this conversation was leading – it certainly wasn't just a chat.

'He has never touched you like that? Well, that does surprise me! How then, if I may make so bold as ask, do you think that child was conceived?'

She was shivering with terror now. Charles Moonie was up to something and she wished she knew what it was. 'It was a special kiss he gave me once, with his tongue right inside my mouth.'

'What they call a French kiss?'

'I don't know what it's called but I didn't like it.'

'You didn't like what I did to you and I didn't do it again.'

'You tried to,' she whispered, 'several times.'

'Only because I love you, my sweet, ignorant Anna.'

280

'What do you mean, ignorant?'

'You do not know the facts of life, my dear. What Jerry did was only a kiss – nothing more. What I did . . .' He paused. 'Well, we shall leave that for a moment. You say he has never kissed you like that again?'

'No and he hasn't done what you did either. So don't try to make out he's as bad as you are.'

'I would not dream of it, Anna. He has done nothing. He has not even done his duty as your husband.'

The sarcasm caught her on the raw. 'He's a good husband. He loves me and he loves his son.'

The man's expression changed dramatically. Triumphant, he leaned across, grabbed her arm and pulled her to her feet. '*His* son? *His* son? How in God's name can you believe that it is *his* son? It is *I* who fathered that child.'

She gaped at him in disbelief. 'You're off your head, Charles Moonie!'

'I can assure you that I am quite sane. You surely did not think that a kiss was enough to make a baby? What is more, the gestation period – the time it takes for the infant to be ready to make its way out of the womb – is nine months. Nine long months! *Now do you understand?*'

His nose was practically against hers, his breath fiery on her cheek and she realised, with a rush of sickening horror, that he was telling her the truth. Jerry could definitely not be her son's father – there hadn't been enough time. Something snapped in her brain at this point and she lashed out with her foot at the vile creature who was turning her world upside down and shaking out every grain of her happiness.

With a bellow of pain, he put his hands around her neck but a sound from the cradle stopped him in his tracks and he let her go. 'Jerry Rae is not going to bring up my child,' he muttered as he bent over the cradle. With her fists pounding on his back, he pulled the pillow from under the tiny head and pressed it over the infant's face. It wasn't long until the little flailing arms and legs stilled.

The shock of what Charles had done drained all the colour

from Anna's face. She cringed away from him, her eyes vacant. Yet, when he pulled her to him and kissed her hungrily, brutally, she let him carry on, without flinching.

'You can never belong to anyone else,' he screeched hoarsely. 'I had you first so you are mine . . . for ever!'

Although it was possible, even probable, that he had come with the intention of raping the young woman, the murder of the child had robbed the man of his senses. Unable to remember what he had planned, he was forced to release his hold on his other victim and both were panting as they stood with their eyes locked.

Jerry was in the kitchen watching his fellow workers tucking into their supper. His wife was usually here before him with the pram but she hadn't appeared yet, though it was well after six. 'Unable to throw off his apprehension, he pushed back his chair and stood up. 'I'd best go and see what's keeping Anna, Mrs Miller.'

Dolly smiled her understanding. 'Yes, it is not like her to be late.'

Not wishing to show how anxious he was, he set off at a smart pace but, as he neared the old gatehouse, an inner sense urged him to run and he went hell for leather down the short cut from the main building. His lungs were fit to burst when he reached his home but his speeding heart almost stopped when he saw the back porch door standing wide open. Anna always made sure that it was closed properly, to save rats or other vermin getting in.

There was no sign of her when he went inside. 'Anna!' he called twice but there came no reply. Deeply alarmed now, he peeped into the cradle. The baby was sleeping peacefully, which did ease his mind a fraction. Taking time only to straighten the pillow that was edging towards the infant's face, he raced outside again, to search the outhouses – the coal shed, the privy, even the hen-house, but his wife was not in any of them. Almost out of his mind with worry now, he raced back to the big house.

He was in such a state that it took some time for those still in the kitchen to understand what he was trying to say. Then Raymond Miller showed his worth as the Superintendent. He organised several small search parties, with instructions as to exactly which area they were to cover and soon they had all gone. Tina Paul looked at Dolly Miller. 'I'd better be there for that poor wee mite when he wakens up. He'll wonder what's going on. Babies can usually tell when something's wrong.'

Left, more or less, to hold the fort, Dolly decided to make a search of her own. Could Anna be reacting at this late stage to the traumatic time of the birth? She could have regressed to the extremely disturbed girl she had been when she arrived. She might be under the impression that she was still living under this roof, all memory of the past few months expunged.

Some of the inmates Dolly approached looked at her blankly but those who could see that she was upset did their pathetic best to comfort her.

'Anna's a good girl,' observed one woman, nodding her head vigorously. 'She'll come home when she's hungry.' Obviously, she had forgotten who Anna was.

Another, older and even more confused, started singing, 'Will ye no' come back again, will ye no' come back again, better loved ye canna be . . .'

Dolly moved to the next room – Mr Ballantyne might remember her. 'If that's the young lass that baths me of a morning,' the man smirked, 'she'll be off with her lad. She's told me all about him, you know. She's a real one for the boys, that one.'

Frustrated and feeling like shouting at each and every one of them, it dawned on Dolly that she should have asked Charles Moonie first. He had known Anna better than any of them and, if she had run away because of some marital trouble, he might have known where she would have gone to be alone. Sure that he could set her on the right track, she made straight for Charles's door.

When she told him why she was there, however, the ex-bank-manager appeared to be more distressed than she was herself and, guessing how he had felt about the girl, she turned away tactfully.

'Mrs Miller.'

The whispered words made her look back at him. 'Yes? Have you thought of something . . . ?'

'I went to see her this afternoon . . . to talk to her. She was all right when I left.'

'What time was that?'

'Oh, around half past two, I'd say.'

'Thank you, Mr Moonie.'

She was at the top of the stairs when he called out, 'She might be in the potting shed. That's where she used to go with that . . . gardener.'

'Good!' Going down the stairs, it occurred to Dolly that the man had never once met her eyes and he had definitely not been his usual charming self. A coldness swept over her. Had he taken a belated revenge on the girl for marrying someone else? Was she going to find a dead body in the potting shed? With no one to accompany her, she pulled on a coat and ran out.

Charles had been trying to recall the events of that afternoon when Mrs Miller knocked on his door. When he heard what she had to say, he was quite relieved that Anna had disappeared – he had been somewhat afraid that he had killed her, too. But he had been right. He *had* left her in that tiny kitchen, hadn't he? And she must have been alive – otherwise how could she have got out of the house? Maybe she had not taken in what he had done to the child so he would swear that she had smothered it herself and she was in no fit state to deny it even if she were found.

Too late, Charles realised that he should have offered to help in the search. Mrs Miller had probably wondered why he hadn't. It must have been common knowledge that he was very fond of Anna but, hopefully, no one had realised that he regarded her as his own special property. He would have liked to shout it from the rooftops but, as things stood, it was wiser not to.

His heart slowed almost to the point of stopping altogether as a dreadful possibility struck him. Anna had been in a terrible state when he last saw her but, surely, she wouldn't . . . have taken her own life? Could his poor darling, at this very moment, be lying dead somewhere?

Appalled at this thought, his only instinct was to find her before she committed such a terrible deed and, just as he was, in his shirtsleeves and well-worn carpet slippers, he dashed downstairs. He knew a quick way to the potting shed and could be there before Dolly Miller but he wished that he had not mentioned it to her.

Charging blindly through the trees and shrubs, he was unmindful of the branches scraping at his face and hands for he could faintly hear Dolly's slow, sure-footed progress along the gravel path some yards away and he must get in front of her.

He was gaining ground when he remembered that coming this way meant that he would have to cross the burn and the wooden bridge was on the path. He could not waste time changing direction – he would have to jump across. It wasn't really all that wide.

Coming to the rushing water, in spate after the torrential rain earlier in the day, he kept at the same speed as he launched himself into the air but the solid grassy bank had turned into a sea of slimy mud. Perhaps he could have made it if he had been wearing shoes but the soles of his old slippers were so smooth and slippery in themselves that his leverage was gone. By some quirk of fate, his belly flop ended in him striking his temple on the jagged edge of a submerged stone, brought down from the hill by the brown foaming surf. With the full force of his fourteen stones behind his fall, he did not stand a chance of survival.

CHAPTER TWENTY-THREE

The air in the normally warm kitchen was no warmer than the air outside, which increased Tina's fears for Anna. She wouldn't have left the house for long enough to let the fire go out without taking her baby with her. Maybe she had gone out to get firewood and met with an accident of some kind? But the basket in the porch was almost full of the sticks that Jerry brought in every day.

The nurse had fully intended to do something to help Anna while she waited for the infant to wake up, some ironing, perhaps, or housework, but everything seemed to be done. Taking a quick peep into the cradle, she set about getting the fire going again for she didn't want the poor wee mite to catch his death of cold. Once it was crackling merrily, she hooked the kettle on to the swey, directly over the heat. Whatever had happened, Anna and her husband would want a cup of tea when they came in.

It occurred to her then that Jerry might have been in such a state when he couldn't find his wife that he hadn't checked the outhouses thoroughly, if he had checked them at all. Running outside, she went to the privy first but Anna wasn't there. Then she visited the first shed, looking into each of the boxes that had originally held the household items people had given the young couple but they were far too small for anyone to hide in. In the coal shed, she took the old shovel Jerry used for filling the scuttle and dug into the mound of coal. She didn't want to find a body but you never knew.

The next corrugated iron construction was just a repository for rubbish and items too bulky to keep in the house. Like the others, they yielded no clues as to where Anna could be and Tina went back inside.

For a few minutes, she hunkered down and held her hands out to the fire, then she swilled out the teapot with the water that was already beginning to make the lid of the kettle dance. Opening the caddy, she wondered whether to just make enough tea for herself or to fill the teapot right up. She settled for putting in one spoonful – it could be long enough before anyone else appeared, though surely somebody would come to see if Anna had turned up.

As she sipped the welcome warmth into her shivering body, it occurred to her that there had been no sound from the cradle all the time she'd been there and, laying down her cup hastily, she rose to make sure the infant was all right. Finding that he hadn't moved even the merest fraction, she pulled back the cover that was keeping her from seeing him properly and her look of deep concern changed to utter horror as she stared down at the beloved little face, now a deathly greyish shade of blue.

Intent on praying that she would find Anna alive, Dolly Miller heard nothing of what was happening in the near vicinity. If it was a body she found, she would know that Charles Moonie must have killed the girl, though if that was what he had done, why had he told her where to go? Why lead her directly to the scene of his crime? It was puzzling and deeply upsetting and she wished that she had taken time to find someone to come with her.

So cold and wet was she that she contemplated going back to the house to wait for one of the search parties to turn up . . . but she had to know! Head down against the wind, she plodded on. Even if the potting shed was empty, it would be better than sitting in the house alone not knowing anything.

When she reached the fairly large wooden hut, used for the storage of tools as much as for potting, she lifted the latch as quietly as she could but the door gave a loud protesting screech as she pushed it back. Her heart beating wildly for she did not know what to expect, she narrowed her eyes and peered round in the darkness, wishing that she had thought of bringing a lantern with her. At last, however, she was satisfied that there was no one there – alive or dead.

Wavering between relief and disappointment, Dolly took a step towards the door again and then halted in mid stride. What was that sound? Just a small squeak, it could be a mouse or a rat or some other woodland creature. There it was again. Standing stock still, she held her breath. The animal might come out if it thought it was safe.

There was no movement whatsoever and, on the point of leaving, she had one last try. 'Anna?' she murmured, in little more than a whisper.

'Tina?'

The word was barely audible but it gladdened the woman's heart. 'No, it's Dolly Miller. Are you all right?' A slight rustle came from her right and, straining her eyes, she could just make out a figure huddled against the wall. She picked her way across, trying to avoid the various items scattered over the floor but, when she bent down to help the girl to her feet, the poor creature screamed, 'Don't touch me!'

'Did somebody hurt you, my dear? Can you stand up?'

'Don't touch me! Don't touch me!'

Having had much experience of disturbed minds, Dolly decided that it would be best to sit down beside the girl and talk gently to her. The questions could come later – when she was ready for them.

Raymond Miller could see that Jerry was having trouble keeping up with them. 'Look, lad,' he said solicitously, 'why don't you go back and get Dolly to . . .'

But the young man was adamant. 'No, I can't give in.'

'It's not giving in. You've had a shock, you're worried about your wife and you'll be no use to her if you pass out.' Realising that Jerry might pass out on the way back, Raymond added, 'I'll come with you. I should have remembered to bring a storm lantern.' Guiding him away from the others, he called back, 'Carry on without me, I won't be long.'

He was glad he had insisted because the young gardener would have foundered several times as they made their slow way to the big house. 'Dolly!' he cried as they went into the kitchen for there was no sign of her. 'Get some brandy for Jerry, here. He needs it . . . right now!'

There was no reply to this and the two men looked at each other in dismay. 'She can't be in our sitting room, otherwise she would hear me. She must be upstairs.' Raymond raced out and took the stairs two at a time . . . but he couldn't find his wife there either. He came down more slowly, hoping that this was a nightmare and that he would wake up at any moment.

Recognising the despair in his employer's eyes, Jerry said, 'She's gone, too . . . hasn't she?'

'What in God's name is happening?' The Superintendent went to the cupboard and took out a bottle of cooking brandy and two tumblers. 'This isn't the best of stuff but it'll help.'

They said nothing as they sipped, letting the spirits work a miracle, trying to gather enough sense to plan what to do. At last, Raymond said, 'Did you notice Charles Moonie among the searchers?'

Jerry shook his head. 'No but he could have been with another bunch.'

'I don't think he was there when I gave out the instructions. I'll go up and see if he's in his room. He might know something about . . .'

He went out without finishing the sentence but was back in moments. 'He's not there. I've had a queer feeling about that man ever since your wedding. I suppose you knew that he and Anna were . . . very friendly? In fact, I'd say a lot more than friendly as far as he was concerned. I've seen him looking at her as if . . . no, take no notice of me, Jerry, it was probably my imagination.' He opened another cupboard and lifted a lantern from the bottom. 'I'd better get back with this but you stay here and recover your strength.'

Jumping to his feet, Jerry declared, 'No, I'm coming with you. That's two women we've got to look for now.'

'Good lad!'

Before they reached the door, however, it burst open and a wild, blackened figure ran in. 'He's dead! William Henry's dead!' Tina moaned, handing Jerry the small bundle she was carrying and letting Raymond help her to a chair.

The brandy bottle was produced again and, between sips, she told them what she had been doing and how she had found out about the child. When she came to a gasping end, Raymond said, 'Who do you think is responsible for this?'

'I can't think, Mr Miller . . . oh, Jerry, I can't tell you how sorry I am.'

Utterly numbed by this second tragedy, he shook his head helplessly.

'Would it have been Anna herself?'

Raymond's suggestion galvanised the young man into making a reply. 'Anna would never have killed our baby,' he whispered. 'She wouldn't!'

'We've got to face facts,' Raymond said gently. 'She was sent to us in the first place because her parents said she had killed her sister. She was jealous of the attention the younger girl was getting and, if she thought you loved the baby more than you loved her . . . well, jealousy can be uncontrollable. Afterwards, she could have had a flash of normality, realised what she had done and run away.'

'But she was all right – she's been perfectly well for a long time . . . hasn't she?'

The pleading in the young husband's voice tugged at the older man's heart. 'She seemed to be, my boy, but the brain can be inconsistent; in perfect working order for years and then . . . something triggers a total breakdown for perhaps only a fraction of time.' Raymond shook his head sadly. 'I am not saying that *is* what happened, Jerry, but we must consider it as a possibility.'

He turned to the nurse, her face ashen where the coal dust had rubbed off, clasping the glass in her trembling fingers. 'Can

I leave you to . . . look after things here, Tina? I must tell the searchers that Dolly is missing, too . . . and Charles Moonie. He is an unknown quantity in this business.' He made to take the dead baby from its father but Jerry shook his head and clung to it, raising doubts in his employer's mind as to *his* sanity. 'You will have to give him up some time, Jerry. It is not healthy for you to keep holding him. I will put him somewhere safe . . .'

Having laid down the empty glass, Tina saved the situation by turning and whipping the infant from its unprepared father. 'I'll go and put him in your sitting room, Mr Miller. Nobody'll be going in there.'

At that unfortunate moment, the door burst open and four men staggered in carrying the missing women. 'We found them in the potting shed,' Dod Lumsden announced.

'I found Anna first,' Dolly said, proudly. 'She was scared stiff of . . . well, I haven't been able to get anything out of her . . .' Her legs giving way as her feet touched the ground, she reached for a chair and sat down gratefully.

While Jerry was settling his wife into a chair, it struck Raymond that the four rescuers had fallen silent and, glancing round at them, he saw that their eyes were fixed on the blackened Tina and what she had in her arms. Quick as a flash, he dismissed them with thanks for what they had done and, when they were out, the nurse took the opportunity to run through into the Millers' sitting room to deposit her pathetic little bundle on the sofa to save anyone else seeing it.

Then Raymond had a sudden, horrible thought. Those men had seen that the infant was dead and they might well spread it all round the countryside that the young mother had murdered her bairn. Whether that was true or not, he had to make certain that the good name of The Sycamores was not besmirched by scandal. He jumped up and ran out after the four who had just left.

When he returned, in some fifteen minutes, Dolly was feeling more able to deal with things but, even after she told them her story, the others were no wiser as to what had really happened.

It did seem as though Anna, still sitting vacant-eyed and un-responsive, was guilty of smothering her child but neither Raymond nor Tina said so because of Jerry. He had been desperately, but unsuccessfully, trying to get through to his wife and was obviously in a state of near collapse himself.

Then Tina said, 'Mr Miller, it would be best for Jerry to take Anna home to bed but will the police need to question her?'

Dolly opened her mouth to say something but Raymond forestalled her. 'It's all right, Tina. The police . . . um . . . do not have to be told about this.'

Dolly looked shocked. 'A crime's been committed. We must report it.'

'We don't know that a crime has been committed,' Raymond frowned. 'It could have been an accident or . . .' He broke off, shrugging helplessly. 'Moonie may be able to tell us . . .'

His wife nodded vigorously. 'I'm nearly sure he must know who did it. He admitted that he'd been to see Anna this afternoon and, when I said she was missing, he told me to look in the potting shed. I'll go up and ask him to come down.'

'I'm afraid he has disappeared now,' Raymond said, grimly. 'It seems to me that he could have killed the baby and . . .'

'Anna could have seen what he did and run away from him,' interrupted his wife. 'He might be looking for her now.'

Tina shook her head. 'Anna wouldn't have stood by and watched him killing her son. She'd have fought him tooth and nail and he might have tried to kill her and all. That could be why she ran away.'

Jerry sat silently as suppositions and counter suppositions were raised, his eyes large and tortured, his face gaunt but never, by one flicker of an eyelid, did Anna show that she was conscious of what was going on.

By the time daylight filtered in at the sides of the curtains, Anna still had not made a move nor said a word and the other three had also lapsed into silence. They had exhausted all the possibilities and agreed on none. At last, Tina said, 'We're not getting anywhere and Anna really should have some rest.'

Sighing, the Superintendent went over to the girl. 'Anna,' he said slowly, softly but firmly, 'did you smother your baby with his pillow?'

For the first time since she'd been brought in, her eyes clouded with puzzlement, but only very briefly, before she retreated into her cocoon again.

Tina shook her head at her employer. 'That's enough tonight, Mr Miller. Give her time. It can wait till tomorrow.'

Dolly nodded her agreement with this. 'It's tomorrow already, Raymond, and we all need some sleep.' She stood up purposefully. 'You had better go home to your own bed. Anna will be all right here. Tina will look after her. Goodnight.'

The two women went out, supporting the bereaved young mother between them, and Raymond poured another glass of brandy for himself and the younger man. They said nothing for some considerable time, then Jerry murmured, 'I know you think Anna did it, Mr Miller, but I'm sure the answer lies with Moonie. We need to find him before we'll get at the truth.'

The Superintendent leapt up. 'I believe you are right! Come on. He could have hidden in the potting shed after Anna was taken away.'

Handing Jerry a large torch and taking the storm lantern himself, Raymond led the way outside, then said, 'We should stick together. If Moonie has gone out of his mind, it will take more than one to subdue him.'

They scoured both sides of the path as they made for the shed. Then, as Jerry followed Raymond over the little bridge he spotted a large object half submerged in the water some yards downstream. Alerting his companion, he ran along the bank, realising, in the strengthening daylight, even before he reached it, that it was a body – Charles Moonie's body.

It took them some time to carry their heavy burden to the house. Jerry couldn't understand why the man, usually so meticulous about his dress, was in his shirtsleeves and only had carpet slippers on his feet but Raymond said that unhealthy minds did some inexplicable things.

Dolly, however, coming downstairs when she heard the

outside door slamming, was able to confirm that it was how Charles was dressed when he told her where to find Anna. She gave a start at a new thought. 'He couldn't really have known she was there, though, but he must have realised that, if I found her first, she would tell me if he'd suffocated her baby. Yes, that must be it and he's decided to take a short cut to get to her before me.'

Raymond had also been putting two and two together. 'He tried to jump across the burn but his old slippers skidded in the mud and he hit his head on something when he fell in.' He gave an embarrassed cough. 'You know, my first thought when I saw him lying there was that Anna had killed him but it couldn't have been like that. Once she gets over everything, we'll get the real story . . . as she knows it at any rate.'

Jerry had been persuaded to leave his wife in Tina's hands – 'Just till she gets her strength back,' Dolly had said, diplomatically – and to go back to the grim old gatehouse on his own.

Devastated that he wasn't being allowed to talk to Anna, he had a quick nap on the kitchen couch and rose about noon, to spend the rest of the day removing all traces of his beloved son from the house. He stacked the cradle and the pram in the outhouse farthest away from the back porch and then piled in all the tiny clothes, napkins and powder. With everything tidied away, he locked the door and put the key in his pocket. He didn't want his wife to come across them but it was better to keep everything in case they had another baby some time in the future.

It was early evening when Tina Paul came to tell him that the Superintendent and his wife had disposed of the man's body and the infant's somewhere in the grounds. 'They don't want anybody to know. They're scared The Sycamores would be closed down if the authorities hear about it. Anna's given enough of an account to let them know Moonie was guilty and she needs absolute peace and quiet to get over what she's been through – and so do you, my lad. You look all in. Mrs Miller says you can have tomorrow off as well so make the most of it.'

He forced himself to go into the other room after she left him and took off only his shirt and trousers before lying down. He had the whole double bed to himself yet he couldn't sleep properly. He needed Anna and he was afraid that she would never get well enough to come back to him – that he would never hold her in his arms again . . . but surely she would recover. She had to get better!

CHAPTER TWENTY-FOUR

The edge having worn off his initial heart-shattering shock at his son's untimely death, Jerry Rae was to receive equally mind-numbing information from Tina Paul.

At first, she had told him sympathetically that his wife did not want to see him, which was bad enough, but then, as gently as she could, she passed on what she had prised out of Anna herself over the past three days.

His first reaction was to shout, 'It's not true!' But, when she got him to admit that he had done nothing more than kiss Anna – even after they were wed – she reluctantly described the action needed to make a baby. First she used terms she had learned as a nurse and then the more common words he would understand. Despite his slowly dawning look of horror, she added, even more reluctantly, 'And that's what Moonie did – against her will! You must understand that, Jerry.'

In his mind, whether or not it had been done against her will, it had still been done . . . and not by him. He was not the father of the child! He could think no farther than that – not then – and, with a sob, he went into the nurse's welcoming arms. As she knew, he desperately needed comfort from some-where and she was the only one he could turn to. She had been thinking about this earlier and, when he at last drew sheepishly away from her, she murmured, 'Why don't you go home for a while, Jerry? Tell your mother and father what's happened and they'll help you to get over it.'

He shook his head. 'I can't. They don't know anything about Anna. They don't know I'm married. It was all so quick and things happened . . . two deaths in the family within weeks of each other and, not only that, my sister hasn't heard from her fiancé for months. She doesn't know if he's alive or dead. I couldn't upset them any more, Tina. I just couldn't.'

'I'm sure they would want to know. I would if I was your mother. You can't cope with this on your own and it's not me you need. Now, you'll likely think I'm being brutal but there's one more thing you should know. Mr Miller's had some doctors up from Aberdeen to test Anna and not one of them thinks she'll ever get back to anything near normal.' She waited for him to say something but his expressionless face made her wonder if this last blow had been too much for him to handle. There was only so much a human being could take.

At last, he lifted his downcast eyes again, with a look of torture such as she had never seen before. 'Why are you telling me that? What do you want me to do?'

'It's up to you, Jerry, but you're still very young and you've your whole life ahead of you. Why don't you go away and start a new life somewhere else?'

He could scarcely believe his ears. 'What about Anna? You can't expect me to leave her, Tina? I love her. What happened wasn't her fault.'

Her heart going out to him, she said, softly, 'I grant you that but she'll never be a real wife to you again.' Recalling that he and Anna had both admitted that their marriage had never actually been consummated, she added, gently, 'She never *was* a real wife to you, you know that.'

'I was happy the way we were. I love her and that's all that matters.'

'If that's how you feel, I don't suppose there's anything I could say to make you change your mind.' As she left, Tina looked back at him in concern. 'Please, Jerry, talk it over with your family before you decide what to do.'

He stared into the fire for some time after the door closed. He could never leave Anna, no matter what. He didn't care if she didn't want to be a proper wife to him, as long as she got well enough to come home to their cottage and he could see her every day . . . and night. As he visualised this, the first prickle of doubt set in. Would he really be content with that?

Now that he knew the facts of life, could he lie beside her every night and not touch her? His body had needed her before, when he didn't know what was happening to him, but she had rejected him. Could he withstand rejection now? She had protested that she didn't want to be hurt. Had Moonie hurt her? Would he ever manage to banish that man from his mind when he was with his wife? Would the spectre of that monster forcing himself on her ever go away?

The seventeen-year-old realised then that Tina Paul had been right. He needed his family. He needed his mother! She would tell him what to do. She wouldn't judge Anna for letting Moonie into her house when she'd had no choice. She would likely be angrier with *him* for not telling her about his marriage. About the baby . . . her grandson? But he hadn't been her grandson, of course. God, what an awful mess!

Jerry's brain was too active for sleep that night and he sat by the fire going over and over everything that had happened since he had first seen Anna – trying to sort out his true feelings about the events of the last three days. Finally, as the little clock on the mantelshelf struck six, he rose to make himself ready for work. It would be better to keep himself occupied instead of constantly tormenting himself like this.

Pouring some water from the kettle into the old tin mug he had lately started to use and taking the cut-throat razor Dod Lumsden had given him out of its box, he stood in front of the dresser mirror to remove the downy growth from his chin. He had just made two careful strokes when the door burst open and Tina ran in, her eyes almost popping out of her head when she saw what he had in his hand.

'No, Jerry! Don't do it! Not you as well!'

His hand dropped. 'What d'you mean, not me as well?'

She thumped down on the old couch, buried her face in her hands and began to sob hysterically, while Jerry sat down beside her to wait for the storm to pass so that she could tell him what had happened. Some minutes later, with no sign of it abating, he put his arm gingerly round her shoulders. 'You'd better tell me what's wrong, Tina.'

The words were barely out of his mouth when comprehension came. 'No!' he screamed. 'No! Oh, for God's sake, Tina, tell me it's not my Anna.'

Tears still streaming down her cheeks, the twenty-one-year-old looked up into his face. 'Oh, God . . . Jerry . . . I'm sorry.' The words were punctuated by great shuddering sobs and he knew before she told him.

Holding each other for solace, they wept together until they were exhausted, Tina being first to make a move. The kettle Jerry had put back on the swey was singing merrily again, so she rose to make some tea. There was nothing stronger than that to help them.

While they drank the strong, sweet brew she made, she told him what had happened – or what she thought had happened. 'She was awful quiet when I put her to bed last night but she hasn't said much since . . . Anyway, I sat with her till I was sure she was asleep, then I went down to the storeroom to check if anything needed to be ordered. Mrs Miller likes to know before anything goes done. Anna was still sleeping when I went back but she must have risen while I was out and . . . she'd got hold of Mr Miller's cut-throat . . . she must have gone to their private bathroom . . . and she'd been hiding it under the blankets or the pillow.'

The brave face she had put on dissolved in grief again. 'Oh, Jerry! If only I'd thought to check if everything was all right . . . if only I'd looked. But I was really tired, I've hardly had any sleep since the . . . but that's no excuse. I should have thought . . . I should have!'

Knowing what was coming and dreading hearing it, Jerry watched her scrubbing at her eyes with an already wet handkerchief. His hands knotted together by some invisible chain, he could not move. He was completely incapable of doing or saying anything to show the nurse that it was not her fault. In any case, she would probably always feel guilty and it would make no difference what he did.

With an obvious struggle, she managed to overcome her sorrow long enough to tell the young man how she had gone back upstairs after her breakfast with a tray for Anna and, mercifully, kept short the description of the bloody scene that met her eyes when she opened the door.

They sat silently now, their agonised thoughts centring on the beautiful girl they had both loved so dearly – Jerry with no recognition of her frailties, Tina because of them. They would miss her, would always find pity for her in their hearts, for the tragedies she had encountered in her short life. Even sitting apart, each gradually became conscious of the other and let their own misery encompass their companion's.

After a while, Tina murmured, 'I just remembered. Mrs Miller told me to take you back with me, Jerry. She says we can't leave you here on your own.'

He was well aware of what the woman had meant. On his own, he would sit and mope. He would go into a decline and want to end his life, too.

'Come on, Jerry,' Tina urged. 'I'm not leaving unless you're with me.'

He gave in, standing up to get his jacket. What good would it do to kill himself? It wouldn't bring Anna back and it would cause his parents so much heartache.

Raymond Miller laid the letter down on his desk in front of him, wondering if this was how God was choosing to punish him. While he had truly pitied the poor parents for the death of their child, his main reaction to Charles Moonie's evil actions had been worry that it would affect The Sycamores. Would those responsible for the payment of fees take their relatives away? Would the place be ostracised? Would the Board of Governors close it down? Dolly had told him he was worrying for nothing, that none of the incidents had been made public.

'Nobody knows anything,' she had said, 'just that Anna went missing for a while. 'They don't know anything else and, even if they did, the sudden death of an infant is not uncommon and nor is that of a man of Charles's age.'

She was right of course and this morning's tragedy . . . well, no one other than themselves, Tina and the doctor knew what

Anna had done. When he had been called, the doctor had taken one look at the girl, shaken his head and written out the death certificate. 'Poor lass,' he had commented on his way out, 'but it would be as well for you not to tell anybody how she died. Her brain was pretty fragile, as everyone here knew, and they'll just think it had snapped altogether. It does happen, you know.'

He had shaken hands with Dolly then and told her to keep a close watch on the young husband, just in case. Although that had taken place over two hours ago now, Raymond could still recall the gratitude he had felt towards the man. His handling of the situation meant that The Sycamores could go on as usual, that his and Dolly's futures were safe. But everything had changed now!

Heaving a long sigh, he picked up the letter again. An official letter! From the War Ministry! How on earth could those old men in far-off London just snap their fingers and expect people in the north-east of Scotland to do their bidding? Without question? What would happen to the poor residents when the place was commandeered? Would they have to be shifted to the County Asylum . . . the Madhouse?

He was still sitting with the drastic communication in his hand when his wife came into the room. 'Jerry is in a terrible state,' she observed, 'but I don't think he is suicidal, thank goodness.' Getting merely a grunt in reply, she noticed the sheet of paper in his hand. 'What's that? What's wrong?'

He handed it over without a word and watched her while she read it. 'Well, I suppose it had to come,' she said at last, laying it down on the table. 'According to what I've heard, a lot of big houses have been taken over and we're in an ideal spot for training soldiers, surrounded by moors and mountains.'

'Do you not feel angry about it?' Raymond asked, astonished at her calm acceptance of the bombshell. 'It will mean the end for us, as well as for all our guests.'

'Other places will likely be found for the guests,' she soothed, 'and, as for us, to tell the truth, I'll be quite glad to stop working. This last week has been too much for me. I would rather we retired and spent the rest of our lives in peace.'

Taking time at last to consider more fully the eventual consequence of the War Department's order, Raymond felt the tight band round his chest easing. He and Dolly had run this place to the best of their ability for over ten years and made a good job of it but it was certainly beginning to take its toll on them. It would be heaven to lie in bed of a morning with nothing to worry about except the weather; to be able to do what he liked when he liked; to have time to read the newspapers from front page to last with no interruptions.

Taking off his spectacles, he laid them alongside the fateful letter. 'Yes, Dolly, you're right, as always. We have earned the right to take things easy. It will mean a change in our lifestyle, a vast reduction in income . . .' He leaned back in his chair, pleased that his worries had proved groundless. 'But no doubt we shall manage.' His face sobered. 'Dolly, my dear, I don't know what I would have done without you.'

She bent over and kissed his cheek, bristly because he had no razor, or rather, he could not bring himself to use his razor after what had happened. 'I don't know what I would do without you at times either,' she murmured. 'We have made an ideal Superintendent and wife and we did everything we could to shield The Sycamores from scandal, though we need not have bothered. I have no doubt that we will make an ideal retired couple, counting the pennies but getting closer as we grow old. Darby and Joan.' She straightened up now. 'But it is back to the grindstone. There is much work to be done before we can relinquish the reins.'

*   *   *

With her father-in-law visibly getting frailer by the day, Fay had made a point of taking him something to eat every morning and afternoon for some weeks now, apprehensive each time she went in as to what she might find. Willie was inclined to be grumpy – complaining, 'You canna cook like Janet – you're even worse than Nessie' – but she knew that he did appreciate what she did for him. He allowed her to trim his hair, his

302

bushy beard and moustache and even to wash most of his body, though she was very relieved that he always mumbled, 'Just leave me some privacy,' as he placed his big hands over his private parts.

However, there came a time when she had to insist that she washed him there as well, otherwise he would be 'stinking to high heaven', as she put it, trying to smother her own embarrassment as well as his. As he remarked to Henry, who looked in on him every evening, 'That wife of yours has nae shame. She sees bits o' me naebody else has ever seen.'

Although he hated the idea of his wife touching his father in such a way, Henry tried to make light of it. 'She's seen it all before.'

'Oh, aye?' Willie looked at him with a glint of mischief in his eyes. 'And are you and her still . . . ?' He gave a lewd snigger and ended, 'Well, that's fine, then. If you're still doing your duty as her man, I can stop being feared she'll jump on me some morning.'

'Oh, you!' In spite of himself, Henry had to laugh but, on his way home, he didn't feel easy in his mind. As he had heard during his time at The Sycamores, some old men reverted to their lusty youth and his father had been an extremely lusty young man – he, himself, was his thirteenth child. If his mind was running on that subject, his father might try to interfere with Fay. It was a disgusting thought but it had to be considered.

His wife looked up when he went in. 'How is he, then?'

'Fine.'

She laid down the pair of trousers she was patching. 'I can tell something's bothering you, Henry, so you had better tell me. Is he worse?'

'Are you having to wash his . . . wash him all over?'

Knowing what he was thinking, she smiled, 'Every inch. Why?'

'It's . . . um . . . not decent. If you'd said, I could have washed him instead.'

Rather amused at his primness, she teased him. 'Do you not like the idea of me touching his private parts?'

His face flared up with colour. 'No, I don't. It's bad enough to think you're having to bend over him to wash his face and worrying about where his hands are going, without you . . .' He stopped, unable to say the words.

'Without me rubbing up his manhood?' The devil got into her suddenly. 'Would you like me to rub up yours every night, as well?'

'If he reacts the way I'd react to that, it had damned well better stop!'

She looked at him archly. 'Are you jealous, my dear Tchouki?'

'It's got to stop, I tell you! He could easily lose his head and . . . he could . . . interfere with you . . . or worse.'

She burst out laughing at this and he snapped, 'It's not funny!'

'Oh, my darling, stupid Tchouki, of course it's funny. Your father hardly has the strength to lift a spoon to his mouth never mind raise anything else. Besides, he couldn't possibly overcome a forty-year-old woman. I'm sorry I teased you. He's like a baby to me and I wash him in the same way I washed my own babies. And I'll tell you something else, Henry. I soap his most private part, rinse it then pat it dry with a towel and not once – not once, I tell you – has it as much as stirred. He is past being titillated so you have nothing to worry about.'

Detecting a trace of anger in her tone, Henry said, 'I'm sorry, my Fairy Fay. I should have known better.'

But the doubts still lay heavy on him and he brought up the subject of washing with his father again the following day.

'I'm nae wanting you pummelling at me,' Willie declared vehemently. 'Just leave it to Fay. Her hands are maybe cauld but they're a lot softer than yours.'

For the first week after his wife's death, Jerry worked like a slave, doing his best not to leave time for thought, and, with Tina's help and Dolly Miller's, the knife in his heart gradually stopped turning. It was still there but the most unbearable pains came at longer and longer intervals. The uncertainty that hung over the whole place helped him. He was not the only one with no idea of what he was going to do or what would happen to him – not that the patients had really taken it in but they were bound to be affected by it.

The Superintendent had sent letters to all the relatives, advising them of the closure, and, over the next week or two, there had been several people removed to other private nursing homes. Three weeks on, they were still waiting to learn the fate of the remaining two, although it seemed likely that the poor souls would have to go to the County Asylum.

Jerry was feeling rather better this morning, having had a long discussion with Tina and Dolly the previous evening and made his decision overnight. The newspapers were always pointing out that the armed forces required recruits, that the war would not be won until every able-bodied young man volunteered his services. Many had already enlisted, many had been taken – the local farmers had to appeal for exemption for their workers or, much against their will, hire women to replace them. He had mentioned to Tina that he had thought of going into the Gordon Highlanders, that fighting for his country would help him to get over Anna, but he was still only seventeen. 'They'll take you anyway,' the nurse had said, sorry that he would be going away, but glad that he had something to do.

Mrs Miller had encouraged him to do his bit and was allowing him the day off to go to the recruitment centre at Huntly. It would likely be a good while before he actually had to report for training and he had better use the time to go and tell his parents. He was not looking forward to that for he would have to tell them about Anna and the baby too. Little William Henry, so named to please his great-grandfather and grandfather – but who had really been no relation at all.

Coming out of Ardbirtle Station, Jerry Rae's legs were trembling. It had all been so sudden. He wasn't ready for it yet but he had to do it. The recruiting sergeant had welcomed him with open arms, made him sign for the King's shilling and told him to report back at Huntly the following morning. 'Time to bid your folk goodbye,' the sturdy kilted sergeant had said, as though bestowing a great favour.

So it was a case of going to Ardbirtle and writing to Mrs Miller because there wasn't time to go back to The Sycamores. He had spent the journey trying to plan what he would say to his mother. He felt thoroughly ashamed that he hadn't been home for so long, well over a year, and there was so much to tell her. It would be easier since his father would be at work but it was still going to be difficult.

It was much more difficult than he had foreseen. In fact, it was downright impossible. As soon as he went in, his mother exclaimed, 'Goodness, Jerry! Who told you?'

Completely taken aback, he stuttered, 'Who . . . who . . . told me . . . what?'

'You don't know? I was just getting ready to go and see if there's anything else I could do.'

'Anything else?' Feeling stupid, he realised that his mouth was hanging open and hastily pressed his lips together.

'I'm sorry, Jerry, but I'm still all upset. You see, your grandfather passed away yesterday. It was your father who found him, thank goodness, but I'm really sorry he died there on his own . . . and I wish I'd been there for him but I'd to come home to give your father his supper and he was all right when I left him, so he must have died between half past five and half past six. I only had to boil the tatties and heat up the soup and . . .'

The rapid flow of words stopping until she drew breath, Jerry butted in. 'I'm sorry to hear about Granda, Mother, but he was an old man in poor health and it wasn't your fault he died.'

'That's what your father says but it doesn't help. I still feel guilty and now your aunts have pushed me out. Kitty and Abby have taken charge . . . and Bella and Jeannie arrived with the first train this morning though they hadn't been near their father for years and years and years and I'm shut out when it was me that attended to him every day. It doesn't seem right, Jerry.'

'Things often happen that don't seem right,' he muttered. He knew that only too well but this certainly wasn't the time to tell her his troubles. 'Let them get on with it – you've nothing to reproach yourself with. Just sit down and I'll make some tea.'

So strung up that she couldn't help herself, Fay chattered on until he handed her a steaming cup and he had just sat down himself when Henry walked in, his grim face lightening when he saw his son. 'Who told you?'

'I've been through all that,' Jerry said with a slight smile.

'He didn't know until I told him,' Fay sighed. 'I was nearly ready to go to Oak Cottage when he came in and what a sorry welcome I gave him. What's wrong that *you're* back so soon?'

'I couldn't stand the bickering. Bella and Jeannie were trying to lay down the law because they're oldest but Kitty and Abby were giving them what for for neglecting him. I couldn't stand it any longer and Pogie came away with me.' Henry turned now to his son. 'Are you home for a while, lad, or is this just a flying visit?'

Although desperate to unburden himself, Jerry held his tongue, as much in respect for his grandfather as for the effect his tale would have on his parents. 'Just a flying visit, I'm afraid.'

'You'll be here for the funeral, though.' Fay was taking this for granted.

It took Jerry a split second to make up his mind – it was now or never. 'No, Mother, I won't be here.' He held up his hand to stop her speaking. 'I just came to tell you something and I wish to God I could have chosen a better time. I was at Huntly earlier on, enlisting in the Gordons . . .'

'No!' Fay burst out. 'No, Jerry, you can't. You're not old enough. You're . . .'

'I said I was eighteen.'

'But . . .' Fay began but Henry shushed her. 'Has something happened at The Sycamores? I thought you were settled there and you can't walk out the minute something doesn't go right for you. You're nearly a man now, Jerry, and you've got to put up with things, face up to trouble.'

Jerry lowered his eyes. This was an ideal opportunity for him to open his heart to them, to let them soothe away this ever-gnawing agony, but how could he add to the deep pain already etched on their faces? One piece of bad news was more than enough. 'I've been very happy in my work,' he said softly, looking at his father, 'but one man after another was going off to war and I want to fight for my country as well.'

The eruption he feared did not come. His mother gave a little sniff and his father laid his hand over hers. 'No, my Fairy, he's right. It is every man's duty to do his bit.'

'But he's so young,' she wailed.

'He's a strong lad, a brave lad, he'll make a fine soldier. I'm proud of him.'

Jerry was ashamed because his mother's eyes had filled with tears and also because of the ball of emotion that had risen to constrict his throat. Did it prove that he was still a bairn after all?

'When do you have to report?' Henry asked.

'Tomorrow,' the boy succeeded in saying. 'I'd have liked to go back to say goodbye to them all at The Sycamores but there wasn't time.'

Fortunately for all their sakes, the emotional spell was broken by Mara making an appearance. 'You said you'd both be at Granda's,' she accused, then her tone changed when she saw her brother. 'Jerry, who told you?'

The question made the other three give crooked smiles in spite of their heavy hearts.

'Cheer up, my Fairy Fay,' Henry said when they went to bed. 'He'll be all right. He may be quiet but there's strength there and independence.'

'I can't help thinking, though. If anything happens to him, we'll have lost both our sons and I know I couldn't bear it.'

He gathered her in his arms, the same slim body he knew so well. She hadn't changed at all except for the few grey hairs starting to appear. 'Nothing's going to happen to him, my darling. Try to get some sleep. It's been a gruelling day, what with one thing and another, and we've still the funeral to get through.'

There was silence for a minute, then she murmured, 'I wish Mara could hear from Leo. If we could only get one bit of good news, I'd feel a lot better.'

CHAPTER TWENTY-FIVE

On leave after his initial training, Jerry Rae still could not pluck up the courage to tell his parents about his wife and son. In any case, the past few weeks had been so hectic that he had tumbled into bed every night exhausted – no lying awake thinking, nothing except sweet oblivion. So he didn't need his mother's comfort to ease the pain. The pain had already eased a fraction . . . except when he dwelt on it, but enough to let him know that enlisting was the best thing he could have done.

Of course, his father wanted to know all the details of the route marches, the drills, the weaponry they were using and he could speak about that – he was glad to speak about that. He could sense his mother studying him at these times, clearly wondering why he told her nothing of the things she wanted to know.

'Have you made any friends?' she had asked on his first day home.

'No.' How could he? They had no time to socialise.

'Have you met any nice girls?'

'No.' What did she think they'd been doing? Having a holiday?

'Was the food good?'

'Not too bad.' They were so hungry after all the exercise they had taken that they would have eaten anything – one of the horses if it had been cooked and put in front of them.

And so the catechism went on, until he felt like shouting at her to shut up, but he couldn't. She was only trying, like any other mother, to find out what he had been doing and how he had been treated. What on earth would she say if she saw how many of them were packed into each tent? How the ablutions were hardly worth the name? The latrines just dug out trenches? And all this was here in Scotland, a country claiming to be civilised. What would the conditions be when they went to France, to the battlefields? Not long now. He didn't care if he was killed – he was quite hoping he would be – but he couldn't tell her that either.

It was the night before he was due to leave before he said, into a silence that had fallen, 'I should have told you this before but I . . . didn't want you to worry. We're being sent down south when we go back and then it's across the Channel.'

'Oh, no!' Fay exclaimed, her face blanching. 'Not already, Jerry? You're still not eighteen and . . . oh, no!'

'He has to go where they send him.' Henry swallowed, obviously not as calm as he would like to appear.

'They're screaming out for reinforcements,' Jerry pointed out. 'I don't know exactly when we're being shipped, we're never told any details, but the rumour is we go as soon as we've all had our leave.'

Mara had said nothing and he knew she was thinking of her lad but he didn't like to mention it.

They were all up early the next morning, having breakfast when the postman knocked. Nearest the door, Jerry said, 'I'll go,' and after exchanging a few words with the man, he came in and handed a letter to his sister. 'It's addressed to you.'

Colour flooded into her cheeks, hope shone from her eyes but one glance at the envelope made her shake her head and say, her voice dull, 'It's not Leo's writing.'

'At least it's an ordinary envelope,' her father consoled, 'not . . .'

'Would you like me to open it?' Fay suggested.

'No, thank you.' The girl ran her thumb under the flap and pulled out the contents. 'It's from Edinburgh.'

Her parents looked at each other, knowing that she was afraid Leo's father had written with bad news, and Fay repeated, 'Do you want me to read it?' But Mara had already looked at the signature so she added, 'Is it from Leo's father?'

'Yes.' There was silence for a few moments, all watching as

311

her eyes travelled quickly down the page, then she looked up. 'He's alive. He's been there for over two months but he doesn't want to see me.'

Correctly guessing the reason for this, Fay said softly, 'How badly has he been wounded, dear?'

Mara herself looked as if she had been wounded, her eyes round and glittering with unshed tears. 'Very badly, his father says.' She turned the page to read on and then exclaimed, 'He's been blinded, Mother, and he can't bear anyone seeing him. But I must see him. I don't care if he *is* blind. I don't care how badly he's been wounded, I'll still love him.'

She dashed up to her bedroom and they could hear her opening and closing drawers. 'She's not going down there now, is she?' Henry asked. 'Shouldn't she write to his father first?'

Fay shrugged helplessly. 'She had almost given up on him, I know that, and to learn that he's still alive but doesn't want to see her . . . well, I would do the same if I were in her shoes.'

Henry pulled a face at his son as if to say, 'Women!'

Brother and sister walked together to the station, Jerry to take the train north to Huntly, Mara going south to Edinburgh. She looked much better after making her decision and Jerry said, 'I'm pleased your lad's alive.' He almost added, 'and well' but Leo Ferguson was far from well, apparently.

She smiled happily. 'It's not the best of news but, if he still wants me, I'll marry him whatever his other injuries are.'

He felt obliged to issue a warning. 'Don't build up your hopes, Mara. His father said he didn't want to see you and I've heard of some men going home completely changed after being maimed in some way.'

'I don't care. I'll nurse him back to health.'

Jerry's train came first and he kissed her cheek awkwardly. 'I hope everything goes well for you, Mara. I'll be thinking of you.'

Tears sprung to her eyes again. 'Thanks, Jerry, and I'll be thinking of you. Look after yourself.'

As he jumped up the steps, he wished that he had told her

about Anna and the baby. It would let her know that she wasn't alone in her suffering. But at least she would see her fiancé again, though it was doubtful if he'd be pleased about it.

Never having been far from Ardbirtle, Mara had no idea where to go when she arrived in Waverley Station and, when she asked the guard how to get to Cramond – where James Ferguson had bought a new house – he said she should have come off at the Haymarket. She almost dissolved into tears with frustration but a nearby porter, noticing how upset she was, said brightly, 'Ach, lassie, you'll get a bus up on Princes Street that'll take you right there.

The helpful bus conductress told her when to get off but her nerve almost failed her as she came to the house. It was not as big and imposing as she had thought, however – just a solid, squarish villa, looking out across the wide estuary of a river, the Forth, she guessed. She had come all this way so she did not intend turning back now. Opening the gate, she walked up the path at the right side of the lovely, well-kept garden. It was a pullout bell and even one gentle pull was enough to make a loud clang reverberate inside somewhere.

A dainty little maid opened the door and looked at her curiously when she said, 'I've come to see Leo Ferguson, please.'

'Nobody gets to see Mr Leo,' the girl said curtly and made to close the door.

Mara stuck her foot out. She would have liked to say, 'I'm his fiancée.' But perhaps his parents didn't know they were engaged so she said, as confidently as she could, 'I'm sure he'll see me.'

'He can't see nobody – he's blind!' the maid said ungrammatically and with a hint of triumph.

'Yes, I do know he's been blinded,' Mara said patiently. 'His father wrote and told me. Perhaps you could take me to see *him*, then?'

The retired surgeon was much more welcoming than the young servant but not so his wife. 'Leo does not wish anyone to see him,' she declared slowly and deliberately as if Mara

313

were retarded. But Mara held her ground, sensing that the elderly man was on her side and, at last, with a 'Hrrmph!' he turned to the maid.

'Take Miss Rae to Leo's room, Daisy, then make a room ready for her.'

'Yes, sir.' The maid bobbed and went out, muttering, 'This way,' to Mara but her straight back expressed exactly what she was feeling. Just a little way along the corridor, she gave a light tap on a door and, when a tetchy voice said, 'Who is it?' she opened it timidly, as if expecting a telling off for looking in. 'A Miss Rae to see you, Mr Leo.'

Mara let the girl pass her on the way out then walked in herself, having to hold back from running to take him in her arms. He was looking towards her but with unseeing eyes in a face that bore no resemblance to the man she loved. But he was still Leo and had obviously gone through some horrific ordeal . . . and she still loved him. Going forward uncertainly, she murmured, 'Hello, Leo, darling.'

He turned his head away. 'You shouldn't have come, Samara. There's no future for us now.'

'Of course there is,' she said brightly. 'As long as you still love me, nothing has changed.'

'Don't be so bloody stupid! Everything has changed! I might not be able to see myself but I know perfectly well that I look hideous. You don't want to be tied to a freak, do you?'

She bit her lip to keep back the tears. 'You're not a freak, Leo, darling. As far as I'm concerned, you're still the handsome boy who winked at me in the kirk.'

He ran his hand over the angry scars on his face. 'You'll change your mind if you have to look at these every day. I know you will. My stepmother can hardly bear to come near me and I can hear pity even when my father speaks to me. I don't want pity, Samara, his or yours or anybody's! Do you understand?'

In spite of herself, she felt a flash of anger now. 'All I understand, Leo Ferguson, is that you've been sitting there feeling sorry for yourself when you should be glad you're still alive!'

His brows plunged down. 'Still alive?' he sneered. 'That's a laugh! My spine was damaged so I'm paralysed from the waist down and Christ knows what I look like. I am not the young man who winked at you in the kirk. I am not the man who proposed to you and I certainly will not marry you, no matter what you think. Go home, Samara Rae, and find yourself a proper man!'

The tears came flooding out now. 'I don't want any other man, Leo, darling. I just want you, whatever you are, whatever you look like . . .'

'Get out, damn you! Get out! Get out!'

Still weeping, she stood up and walked to the door, hoping that he would call her back but one last glance showed that he had turned his head away.

His father was standing waiting when she went out. 'I did warn you,' he said, shaking his head sympathetically. 'Nobody has been able to make him see sense, not even the doctors and nurses who come in to attend to him. He didn't want you to know – that's why I didn't get in touch with you before – but I eventually realised that you would always wonder what had happened to him and it wasn't fair to keep you in suspense. I see now, however, that it would have been better for you if I had not written.'

'Oh, no, I'm glad you told me. There's bound to be some hope, isn't there? He will improve as time goes on, won't he?'

'The doctors hold out no hope, my dear. There is a large piece of shrapnel lodged near his brain, which is the reason for the change in his personality, and the slightest movement could mean . . . the end for him. I am sorry, my dear, but you will have to face facts. I take it that he does not want you to . . .'

She dabbed at her eyes. 'He told me to go home and forget him but I love him, Mr Ferguson, and I'll never forget him. You told your maid to make a room ready for me so I take it you won't mind if I stay a few days? He might come round with me. He did love me, I know he did.

Mr Ferguson's smile was a trifle sad. 'You are welcome to

stay but are you sure you know what you are doing? I have the feeling that he will break your heart.'

'I'll risk it.'

Most of the servants and workers at The Sycamores left around the same time as the residents. Only Dod Lumsden, two of the maids and Tina Paul stayed on to help clear out the unwanted odds and ends and to scrub the place from top to bottom. At last everything was spotless and it was time for them to go their separate ways before the invasion of the army.

Raymond Miller had bought a small bungalow on the outskirts of Perth, the place of his birth, and he and Dolly were quite looking forward to their retirement.

The two gardeners were to be taking on part-time jobs at houses where the owners could not find, or could not afford to employ, full-time workers. Most of the maids had found jobs not too far from where they lived.

Tina Paul was nursing at Woodend Hospital in Aberdeen, now reserved for Army and Navy cases. She had heard nothing from Jerry Rae and she could not write to him without knowing his service number. The only thing she could do was to pray every night for his safety. If only the war would come to an end, he might find a nice girl and settle down. He deserved some happiness after what he had been through.

'I don't know if Mara's thought things through properly.' Fay looked at her husband, who was scanning the newspaper as he did every evening. She was never altogether sure if he heard anything she said.

'She's been there for six weeks,' Henry said without looking up. 'She must know all Leo's ups and downs by this time.'

'Maybe but I'm not happy about her wanting to marry him. She never says it outright but I don't think he'll ever be a proper husband – if you know what I mean – and she's still only twenty-five. It's not natural, really.'

'I bet her father-in-law to be will have told her exactly what to expect – he was a doctor, wasn't he?'

'A surgeon. But our Mara can be very stubborn when she likes.'

Henry gave a little smile at this. 'Aye, she can, though she's usually quiet and biddable.'

'She loves him, of course, which makes a big difference. A woman in love can ignore any faults or shortcomings in a lover . . .'

'He'll never be her lover, though,' Henry observed, dryly.

Fay sighed gustily. 'That's what worries me. She might get so frustrated, she could start to hate him but she'll be tied to him for life.'

For his life, at any rate, Henry thought but, wisely, did not voice it.

* * *

Jerry had to give in eventually. The other men in his platoon kept teasing him about being scared to go out and meet the girls and he had taken the jibes without a word but there was a limit. They were stationed at Dover and, on this particular evening, six of them had planned to go the local pub for a few drinks, to give them Dutch courage, then go on to the dancehall and had persuaded him to go with them. He had never been in a pub or a dancehall before and he found that the beer did not give him any more self-confidence. The advent of the seven, tall and handsome kilted young men caused quite a sensation amongst the female sex and he sat watching in amusement as each of his comrades swaggered up to the girl who had taken his fancy. Not one was refused and they joined the throng of dancers, the girls howling with laughter about the swinging of the kilts and quite clearly asking if they wore anything underneath.

He was quite enjoying himself. The music was good; catchy tunes that many of the young people recognised and were singing along with. He felt his feet keeping time to the rhythmic beat and he suddenly realised what a sheltered life he had led . . . apart from certain events. He wished that he could dance but he wouldn't have the nerve to ask a girl to be his partner.

Still, it was something he could live without so he shouldn't worry about it.

'Excuse me but do you mind if I sit beside you?'

The soft English voice made him look round. The girl was around the same age as himself, he thought, past his eighteenth birthday now and he quite liked the look of her. She wasn't very tall, maybe five feet one or two, and her thick, light brown hair was tied back with a broad pink ribbon. But he was forgetting his manners. 'No,' he smiled, 'I don't mind at all.'

She smiled back shyly and sat down on the chair next to him. 'I saw your pals had gone off and left you and I'm in the same boat so . . .'

'I can't dance,' he said quickly, to save any misunderstanding.

She grinned now, making her look even more attractive. 'Neither can I.'

The thought of two non-dancers being in a dancehall made them giggle for a moment, then she said shyly, 'I'm Daphne Nelson.'

Having exchanged names, he told her that he came from the north-east of Scotland. The conversation now off to a good start, they chatted happily, learning what they could about each other, until the band came to a rousing close and the dancers started to leave the floor.

Jerry jumped to his feet, not wanting the magic to be broken by the return of his mates. 'Come outside,' he pleaded. 'They'll just tease us if we stay here.'

Daphne needed no second bidding and they walked along the promenade for the next hour, the time flying past at treble its normal speed. Jerry knew, and guessed that his companion also knew, that this could be only a fleeting friendship – it could come to nothing because he would be leaving Brighton in a day or so – yet he had never been so happy. He made no comparison with Anna. She was in the past although he would never forget her. They had still been children – they didn't even understand the workings of their own bodies and were quite ignorant of life. Yet their love had been real and it might have stood them in good stead forever if . . .

Walking back to the billet, Jerry felt no guilt that he had kissed Daphne when he saw her home. He had kept it light, of course. The situation was too fraught with pitfalls to chance letting it develop into something serious. They had enjoyed each other's company and had arranged to meet again the next night.

'The only thing is,' he had told her, 'we might be shipped out at short notice and I wouldn't have a chance to let you know.'

Her smile had been touched with sadness. 'If you don't turn up, I'll know.'

'Well, it won't be because I don't want to see you again because I do. I just wish . . .' He had shaken his head with a sigh and let her go.

Daphne filled his thoughts that night, the softness of her beautiful silky hair, her rosy cheeks, still a little chubby; her rosebud mouth, soft and enticing; her swelling bosom and tiny waist; her buttoned shoes peeping out from under her skirts. Oh, God, if things had been different! If there hadn't been a war, he could have courted her properly. Then common sense told him that if there had not been a war, he would never have met her.

But maybe he would have a few days with her yet. Their departure could be delayed and, even if they were sent across the channel tomorrow, he had taken a note of her address. He would write to her and he would go to see her on the first leave he had.

CHAPTER TWENTY-SIX

The past few weeks had been extremely hard going for all in the house at Cramond, not least Samara Rae. Not only was she fighting against the brick wall that was Leo but she also had his stepmother's animosity to contend with. At first, it had been more or less veiled but no longer. Everything the woman said to her now was heavy with sarcasm or hostility and it had not taken the girl long to see the reason for it. If Leo outlived his father, he would inherit half the estate but, if he died first, his stepmother would get everything. It was as simple as that. She would not want anyone else complicating matters.

Even knowing this, however, Mara could do nothing about it. James Ferguson would not take kindly to a girl he hardly knew complaining about his wife. She felt like asking him to cut Leo out of his will completely but having to explain why would cause trouble. She had, therefore, to 'keep a calm sough', as her grandfather might have said, and to show no ill feeling towards the woman.

She was coming to the end of her tether, however, when Leo gave her a beaming smile one afternoon – not a smile of love or affection, more a smile to acknowledge her presence, but a smile of any kind was a breakthrough. It took another few days before he put out his arm and touched her hand, a brief and feather-light contact but, nevertheless, another step forward. Soon, each day saw another improvement and her spirits soared. His stepmother, naturally, was anything but pleased but what did that matter now? Then one evening, after settling Leo, she opened the sitting-room door to bid his parents goodnight, as she always did, and his father beckoned her in.

'Sit down, Samara,' he smiled. 'Madeline went to bed early with a headache so it has given me the chance to talk to you privately.' Waiting until she was seated, he went on, 'You have done marvels with Leo, my dear, and I know it has not been easy for you.'

She shrugged. 'It hasn't but I don't mind. I love him.'

'Yes, I can see that and it is becoming clearer by the day that he still loves you. My wife has never been altogether happy about having Leo living with us and it is not just because he has been badly wounded. Anyway, she wanted me to send him to a home for disabled servicemen but I would not hear of it. I could not bear to think of him being amongst absolute strangers and that is why I decided to write to you – against his wishes, as you know. I only meant to ask your opinion on sending him away so your reaction was an unexpected gift.

'I thought that, if anyone could get through to him, surely the girl he had loved would succeed and you certainly have! I would not have believed that I would ever see him smile again yet I have heard the two of you laughing sometimes.'

'We like to joke with each other – we always did – but he still has some black spells. Granted, they're not as frequent as they were but . . .'

'Nor so black,' the man grinned, then sobered again. 'I am going to make a suggestion that I want you to consider carefully before deciding. The thing is . . .' He broke off and regarded her seriously for a moment. 'The thing is I do not want you to think I am shelving my responsibility. This will be as difficult for me as it will be for you, I imagine. Still, I had better get on with it. I do not know if you are aware that I still own Corbie Den, the house near Ardbirtle? Madeline does not care for the isolation of it but I have been thinking . . .'

Mara's eyes had lit up. 'You want me to take Leo there? Oh, Mr Ferguson, I can't think of anything I'd rather do.'

'Don't be too hasty, my dear. There are things to be discussed first. For instance, you can't just go and live together . . . you know how tongues wag, especially in a small town like that. What I mean is, if we can get Leo to agree, would you be prepared to marry him? He is a mere shell of a man, remember. He will never be able to fulfil his duty as a husband and you are a young woman, presumably with normal needs. There may come a time when you fall in love with another man and then what would happen to Leo? Either you would go off with your new love and leave him to be put in a home or, more likely knowing you, you would sacrifice yourself, give up any chance of true happiness, under the name of duty.'

'But I'll never love anybody else!' Mara burst out. 'Never!'

'That is what you think at present but time could change your mind.'

'I'll never change and, if Leo is willing, I'll marry him as soon as you can arrange it.'

'If you are still of the same mind in the morning, I will ask our minister to perform the ceremony here. I doubt if Leo would care to be seen in church or in a registry office. Good-night, Samara. Think it over carefully, remember.'

She did not take long to think it over. Despite a tiny voice telling her that she would be meeting her destiny head on, that there would be no turning back, a lovely warmth inside reminded her that marriage was expected to follow an engagement. Marrying Leo was what she had always dreamed of and it would work out for them, of course it would. The cottage on the outskirts of Ardbirtle was, by all accounts, set well apart from any other dwelling places, so there would be no neighbours popping in to upset the apple cart. They would be alone together; she would make her routine around Leo; she would cook only what he liked; she would bestow all her love on him. Surely he couldn't fail to respond to that. Surely they would get back to the relationship they used to have, the fond teasing, the shared jokes, the reciprocated love. It would take time but they had all the time in the world.

Fate was smiling on Jerry Rae for once. The expected move across the Channel had been postponed for at least a month, they were told, with no reason given. Not that he needed a

322

reason. It meant that he and Daphne Nelson could have more time to get to know each other properly.

During the first few days, they arranged to meet at a spot handy for both of them but the slight restraint in her manner to him made him wonder if she wished he had stayed out of her life. Maybe he should have let well alone. He wanted to have her as a friend yet friendship could develop into something more serious and he wasn't sure if he was ready for that yet.

Then Daphne told him that her parents wanted to meet him and the warmth of their welcome, together with the girl's obvious pride in him as she made the introductions, made him realise that she had just been shy before.

They spent every evening together now and practically the whole of the weekends, their blossoming feelings making him almost forget that he was really on borrowed time. By rights, he should have been in France or Belgium, doing his bit to win the war. Instead he was falling deeper and deeper in love with a girl he had known for so short a time.

Unrepentant, however, he let her take him for walks, show him the sights and even teach him to dance – she really could dance. He would have liked to do more than kiss her – he sometimes felt that she wanted more – but he was afraid to try. He had learned, from Anna's experiences, what could happen to a girl if the man got carried away. He had learned, from his own experience with Anna, to hold back his own passions but it was proving much more difficult with Daphne.

Three weeks had passed of the month's reprieve he had been given when he sensed a change in Mr and Mrs Nelson's attitude towards him. They had always been very friendly but now they were treating him almost as if he were part of the family – or as if they wanted him to be.

Then came the night when Rob, Daphne's father, invited him to go to the local with him and his suspicions were proved correct. Not that he minded. It was good to know that the parents of the girl he loved actually approved of him.

He was on his first half-pint of bitter when the man said,

'Lil told me to ask you . . . um . . . if your . . . intentions towards our daughter are honourable.'

Somewhat taken aback, Jerry gave a nervous smile and Rob went on, 'Don't panic, though. It's early days yet so you don't have to commit yourself if you're not sure.'

An instant judgement – he loved the girl, he was fond of her parents – was all it took. 'No, I'm quite sure. I want to marry Daphne if you give your permission?'

Rob burst out laughing now and gave the younger man a thumping slap on the shoulder. 'Give my permission? That's a good un. The wife as much as said I'd to get you to agree even if I'd to hold a gun to your head.' Turning to the man behind the bar, he said loudly, 'We'll have whisky now, please landlord. This kiltie's just asked for my daughter's hand in marriage.'

The landlord, clearly a good friend, shouted out the glad tidings to all and sundry and, in no time, Jerry and his future father-in-law had a row of drinks sitting in front of them. At closing time, Rob had to help Jerry outside and they giggled all the way back to the house, luckily only a short distance.

Probably having guessed that this would happen, Lil Nelson merely gave a resigned smile when they went in, though Daphne showed more concern for her young man. 'Is he all right?' she demanded of her father. 'You shouldn't have given him so much to drink.'

'It weren't me,' Rob sniggered. 'It were Frank's fault. He let the whole bar know and everybody sent us over a whisky.'

Lil frowned. 'You should have known Jerry couldn't manage that. I bet he's never drunk anything more than a pint of bitter before. Aren't I right, Jerry?'

His head spinning to a rhythmic hammering in his brain, his stomach threatening to give up its contents, the youth could only nod. He wasn't sure what was happening, though one thing stood out in his mind. Somehow or other, he had asked for Rob's permission to marry his daughter but it was Daphne he really should be . . . Whatever he should be doing, he couldn't do it now. If he didn't get outside right this very minute, he'd make a proper exhibition of himself.

324

'I'm . . . going . . . to . . . be . . .'

It was Lil who hauled him to his feet, who propelled his rubber legs to the tiny lavatory by the back door, who heaved a sigh of relief when they made it safely.

Once he was allowed back to the sitting room, he was handed cup after cup of strong, sweet tea in an effort to sober him, while Daphne wailed, 'Can't he just sleep here for tonight? He can't go back to his billet like this.'

'He'll have to.' Rob was looking sheepish now, although he was able to hold his liquor far better than Jerry. 'He has to be in by ten, hasn't he? And, if he isn't, he'll be in big trouble. God, I'm sorry. I should've thought . . .'

'So you should,' Lil declared angrily, 'and you're going to make sure he does get back in time.'

Giving Daphne a look of mortified apology – for being drunk, for being sick and for not being able to do anything for himself – Jerry allowed Lil to button him into his greatcoat.

'I hope you've learned a lesson from this,' she said, sharply, jamming his balmoral bonnet down on his head with some force, with its 'Bydand' badge dead front instead of at the side.

'It wasn't his fault,' Daphne pleaded.

Her mother rolled her eyes to the ceiling. 'I know that and you know that and Jerry knows that but there's some people in this house who can never admit to being to blame for anything.'

Rob scowled at her. 'I did. I told you I never thought . . .'

'You never do. Now, get off for goodness sake and get this poor boy back before they put him on a charge or whatever they do.'

'I'll get him back,' Rob muttered, putting the top button of his overcoat through the second buttonhole. 'Don't you worry about that!'

'Should I go with them?' Daphne asked after the two men went out. 'Just to make sure they get there all right?'

'Your father'll manage. He's not as drunk as he looks.'

The blast of cold air increasing the degree of Rob's inebriation, however, it would have been a miracle if Jerry had

325

reached his billet that night at all, if one of the young kilted men who passed them had not recognised him and hooked his arm. 'We'll see he gets back,' he said to Rob. 'Leave him with us.'

'Thanks.' The elder man turned slowly, careful not to lose his balance, and tottered off the way he had come.

And so, not having said a word to the girl herself, Jerry was now affianced to Daphne Nelson and Rob, arriving home a mere ten minutes after setting off on his errand of mercy, got the full force of his wife's wrath for not escorting the boy right to the door of his billet.

Because this was an interval of 'marking time' before they would be plunged into battle, discipline was not so strict, roll call was later and, to make things even better for the young Gordon Highlanders, they were told the next morning that it would be another three weeks at least before they had to leave the white cliffs.

'And God help all the young maidens in Dover,' the sergeant observed with a scowl. 'They'll need to keep their hand on their ha'penny. But I tell you this, if even one o' you silly buggers puts a lass up the spout, I'll take it out on the whole jing-bang o' youse.'

Howls of protest greeted this but he swaggered out of the mess, his kilt swaying in time to the tread of his size twelve boots, polished to such a degree that anyone could see his face in them – if he were brave enough to look.

Nevertheless, it was good news, the very best. These youths, most of them still in their teens, were free from maternal eyes, free from all restraints except the sergeant's threat and, even if they were kept busy drilling and making sure they kept their rifle and bayonet skills sharp, they had every evening free. What else could they do except amuse themselves with the girls?

It had gone well past the amusing stage for Jerry, though. He was in dead earnest now. He had asked Rob's permission – been forced to ask, really, but he didn't mind – to marry Daphne, although he still had to ask the girl herself. He put the question to her that night, not on his knees because the grass was wet, but she hadn't cared. She didn't even take time to consider it, just threw her arms around him and kissed him until he was gasping for air.

He pondered over telling her about Anna and the baby, but it was still too raw too speak about and, anyway, what was the point? What he felt now was far beyond anything he had felt for Anna Cairns, even after they were wed. His love for her had been pity to a large extent and who could tell what she had felt for him? Whatever it was, it was certainly not the love of a normal girl for her husband. Besides, Daphne could never find out about his first marriage. He hadn't told his parents so they could never tell her anything. The only people who knew were the Millers and Tina Paul and Daphne would never come in contact with any of them.

* * *

After the wedding in the house at Cramond, James Ferguson accompanied his son and his wife to Ardbirtle despite Samara's assurances that she could manage Leo by herself.

'If it was a straightforward journey,' the man had pointed out, 'it wouldn't be so bad but you'll need a taxi to take you to Waverley to get the train to Aberdeen and then you've to change at the other end. Once you get to Ardbirtle, you'll need another taxi to take you to Corbie Den and there's luggage to manage as well as an invalid husband. No, it's best that we come with you.'

In the event, as Samara had expected and was quite relieved about, Madeline had opted to have an 'excruciating headache' that day and was unable to travel but the young woman was very glad of her father-in-law's help. She definitely would never have managed on her own.

James stayed with them until he was sure that she was going to cope and he even hired a car to take him to see Henry and Fay, to let them know that his son was far from ready for visitors. Fay's first thought was that he was wrong, that Leo would be delighted to see them, then came the realisation that he was blind and she decided that his father was probably right. It would take some time yet.

James Ferguson made quite an impression on Henry. He had supposed that an ex-top surgeon would look down on ordinary working folk but he couldn't have been friendlier. He visited them quite a few times and he also insisted on staying with Leo for an hour now and then to let Mara go in the taxi to see her parents.

The young bride had to keep reassuring her mother that she would be all right, that she would manage to deal with Leo whatever happened, and Fay could see that her daughter was on heckle pins all the time she was there. It was quite clear that she was not happy being away from her husband.

Before he returned to Edinburgh, James Ferguson endeared himself to Fay by praising Samara and saying that he had every confidence in her. 'She is much stronger than she looks, mentally as well as physically, and she knows how to handle Leo. You and Henry made a good job of raising her and I do not think it will be very long before you will be welcome visitors to Corbie Den.'

Mara now had sole responsibility of caring for her husband for the first time, dealing with his moods and tantrums, easing his aches and pains, allaying his fears of the nightmares that still haunted him. After the first week, she wondered how long she could keep going with only two or three hours' sleep every night but, gradually, as winter gave way to spring, the snow and frost disappeared, the snowdrops began to nod their heads and there were wide patches of yellow and purple as the crocuses put in their appearance.

Everything changed now. Leo thought he could see shadows, not definite shapes, but at least it gave him hope. The soft breezes brought a lightness into the young couple's lives and they spent much time in the gardens surrounding the cottage. The crows – the corbies that gave its name to their home – started to build their nests in the trees, in the same place and same time every year, as the young couple were to discover. A much calmer Leo, his sight continuing to improve, would sit of an afternoon watching Samara as she weeded the flowerbeds, planted seed potatoes and other vegetables in the vegetable patch and generally put their 'estate' in order.

They could converse companionably now and the young woman soon noticed a change in Leo's appearance as well as in his temperament. His facial scars were not so noticeable; the angry redness had faded. She decided that spending so much time in the open air was good for him and so she started taking him outside for an hour or so in the early evenings also. They would listen to the birds chattering to each other, watch them hopping up to the bird tables she filled every day with crumbs and dishes of water, laugh at the blue tits, who would only go into the box with the hole just big enough for them.

It was an idyllic existence and Leo's occasional outbursts were getting fewer and farther apart. Although she knew that he would never get back to being the charming handsome man he had been when they first met, she now had hopes that he would improve even more as time went by.

She had no worries now about leaving him while she went into town on an old bicycle she had found in one of the outhouses to replenish their groceries and any other items that needed replacing. At first, she had come back as soon as she finished shopping but now she took ten minutes to call on her mother, who was always anxious to know how things were going at Corbie Den.

'Can't I come to see Leo?' Fay asked every time but the answer was always, 'He's not ready to see anybody yet.'

Mara sometimes felt guilty about this. Maybe Leo wouldn't mind seeing her mother. Maybe she was being like the blue tits, making sure that no intruders could get in. Maybe she should ask him how *he* felt about it.

* * *

Jerry was grateful that Lil Nelson and Daphne made all the arrangements for the wedding. A special licence had been obtained for the sake of speed and no fuss and the wedding was planned for one week ahead. That would give them fourteen days to enjoy their married state before he was posted overseas. He and Rob took a stroll along to the pub most evenings to be out of the women's way for an hour or so but his last hour was always spent walking with his fiancée.

He had tried to control his increasing passion, even quoting the sergeant's threat, but Daphne just laughed, 'But nobody'll know, darling. We'll be married before I even know myself if I'm expecting.'

He wasn't sure how he felt about this. It wasn't proper for a girl to be so bold but he loved her and her kisses made him want her so much that he couldn't resist any longer.

It was a first time for both of them but, nonetheless, it was marvellously, mind-blowingly, heart-stoppingly perfect. So perfect, in fact, that it was repeated some minutes later and twice every night until their wedding day.

CHAPTER TWENTY-SEVEN

1917

Since arriving in Belgium, Jerry Rae had not often had time to think so a lull in the gunfire and exploding shells came as a welcome reprieve, letting him turn his mind to his darling Daphne. The most beautiful girl in the world. His wife. His father-in-law had insisted on paying for them to stay in a hotel for a week and he had really looked forward to having that time to themselves.

Knowing that their time together would be short – although he hadn't foreseen how short – they let their passions run rampant every time they went to bed until exhaustion forced them to have at least some sleep. And, during the days, they wandered about the town creating memories for the time they would be apart – a time that came only too soon. They had not even had breakfast on the third day of their stay in the hotel when the message came that the battalion was being shipped out that morning and he must report immediately. They'd had no time for a long goodbye – just a quick peck on the cheek in front of the despatch rider and it was over. Perhaps it was just as well. Unlimited goodbyes could stretch out agonisingly. An instant break was easier in the long run.

As relief for a battle-weary set of men who were trying to hold on to a small village they had captured from the Germans, the Gordons were thrown in at the deep end when they finally reached their destination. It had been hard going, one step forward to two steps back, and God alone knew how long they could keep it up.

The acrid fumes of war still hung around them but, if he closed his eyes, Jerry fancied he could smell the delicate perfume Daphne had worn – only for a moment and then it was gone again. There had been no mail yet but he had managed to scribble a couple of short notes to his wife, though it was anybody's guess when she would get them. If he could only have some idea of when he would see her again, it would help him to survive in this hellhole. He would count the days, his spirits rising as the number lessened. Please God, bring this bloody war to an end.

Sadly, the only thing that came to an end was the lull in the firing.

Fay was shocked when she saw Leo and found it hard to believe her daughter's assurance that he had been much worse when *she* saw him first. How any man could have stood up to what he had gone through was a miracle. How any woman could cope with what Mara was faced with every day was also beyond belief.

'My heart went out to both of them,' Fay told her husband that night, 'but they seem happy enough.'

'That's the main thing,' Henry smiled. 'I'll bike over on Sunday afternoon for a wee while. Leo might like a wee chat with a man for a change.'

Despite being forewarned, he was shocked at the pitiful sight his son-in-law presented and found it hard to think of something to speak about. The progress of the war was out of the question. The poor soul wouldn't want to be reminded of the horrors, of the setbacks, the defeats the British army was facing in all quarters. The safest bet was the weather or the garden.

The war, however, was what Leo wanted to hear about, shaking his head at some points but nodding his agreement to others, while Mara lay on the grass beside her husband's chair, smiling fondly as he propounded what his tactics would be if he were the commander-in-chief. Nonetheless, after an hour, she could sense, from Leo's slowing speech, that he was growing too tired and so she got to her feet as a signal to her father to leave.

Thankfully understanding, he, too, stood up. 'I'd better go, Leo, or I'll be getting thrown out.'

Mara saw him off on the bicycle and, when she went back to her husband, she wasn't altogether surprised that his eyes had darkened. 'You could surely allow me to tell my visitors when they should leave?' he barked as she pushed the wheelchair indoors.

'I'm sorry, dear, but I thought you looked tired.'

'If I had wanted him to leave, I would have said so.'

For the rest of the afternoon and the evening, Leo sat in surly silence, barely acknowledging the meal he was given, and Mara wished that her father had stayed away. Her husband was not ready for male company.

She had hoped that Leo would apologise when she made him ready for bed but, even when she was lying beside him, he was rigid and uncommunicative. With a sigh, she turned away, almost regretting having agreed to his father's proposal, but knowing that he was better with her than with his stepmother. In any case, this was just a little hiccup – he would come round tomorrow.

Not much more than three minutes later, she felt his hand on her shoulder. She turned round slowly, guessing that he needed something – a drink of water perhaps or just to be shifted a little.

His hand rose to caress her cheek. 'I'm sorry, Samara. I was an utter brute to you and I don't know why you bother with me.'

Pity for him almost overwhelmed her but it was pity enclosed in a deep, deep love. Whatever he did, no matter how he treated her, she still loved him as much as she had done when he courted her. Even having to look at his wasted body and scarred face every day, she could, at times, see him as he used to be – tall and handsome with an attractive smile and personality to match. 'It's all right, Leo, dear,' she murmured, 'I do understand.'

He tilted her chin up so that he could kiss her. 'I don't think you do, Samara. I grant you I was a little tired but I was enjoying myself for the first time since . . .' He sighed deeply. 'Your father was talking to me as man to man not as a visitor to a crippled wreck. He made me forget what I was. He made me feel whole again until you broke the spell.'

'Oh, Leo, I'm truly sorry. I didn't want you to get overtired – that's why . . .'

'I realise that now and it is me who should be sorry. Can you forgive me?'

'There's nothing to forgive, my darling.' She kissed him tenderly and felt his arms tightening round her.

'Oh, God!' he moaned in a moment. 'This must be purgatory for you. I am useless to you as a husband, absolutely useless.'

'I don't care about that side of things,' she assured him. 'I love you the way you are.'

'You should have married an able-bodied, lusty young man, someone who could give you children to love. You are a born mother, Samara, and I am just your little boy.'

'No, Leo! I never think of you as a little boy. I love you as a man, a real man.'

'A nice try, Samara.'

'It's true! It's perfectly true!'

'Have you never wished that I could make love to you?'

'Stop torturing yourself! I just need to know that you still love me, that's all.'

He fell asleep first and, listening to his steady breathing, she prayed that he wouldn't slip back into the black depths of despair if the improvement he hoped for did not materialise.

Back from the line for a few days' respite, silence reigned as the young Scots eagerly read the mail that had been waiting for them. Jerry got a pile of letters at once from Daphne and sorted them into order by date before looking at what she had written. The first few were mostly about how much she loved him, how much she had enjoyed their three days as man and wife, how much she missed him now. Then the tone changed slightly because she was worried about not hearing from him. He picked up the second last one, hoping that she had received at least the note he had scribbled when they landed in Zeebrugge and had reached only the third line when he gave out a howl of delight.

'I don't know how you will feel about this,' she had written, 'but I am in seventh heaven. I didn't say anything before because I wanted to be absolutely sure but we are going to have a baby.'

He skimmed the rest, hardly taking in the assurances of love, the excitement she felt, how she hoped he would be home in time for the birth.

Waiting until his heart slowed to normal, he read it over again, carefully this time and right to the very end. He *was* glad that he was about to become a father for real – if only he could be with Daphne throughout her waiting time. He would be worrying about her now until he heard that the child had been born and they were both well.

After reading the good news again, he looked at the last letter. She had got his first note, thank goodness, and she said that some of her friends had told her they sometimes had to wait for weeks and weeks for a letter from their men in the forces. So she understood that he couldn't always get time to write but begged him to write as often as he could.

He did his best but he was finding it more and more difficult to know what to write even when he did get time. She would only be upset if he told her of the conditions he was living in, of seeing comrades fall around him like ninepins, of the terror that swept over him when a fresh bombardment began. He could, and did, tell her that they were forging ahead, even if their progress would be more correctly described as 'inching'.

Eventually, thank God, at a cost of hundreds of men, they recaptured one small town that the enemy had earlier wrested from them, and, with so few of each battalion remaining, it was a mixed bunch that put up a careworn, but heartfelt, cheer that the enemy had retreated.

Their spirits rose even further when they were told that each man would be allowed three days' leave, in a rota of perhaps twenty at a time. For most of them, home was too far away even to attempt to reach, so they made plans to have a good old spree in the nearest town that was still standing. Booze and dames, as the Americans said, what more could they want?

Jerry, of course, wanted his own 'dame'. Surely he could chance getting a ship to Dover so he could go and see his wife? Even if they had only one day together, it would be something and she was pretty near her time. He might even be there when the infant arrived – it depended on . . . no, it would be sheer good luck if that was how it landed and he had never been blessed with good luck.

He was one of ten in the second truck that left their position well behind the front line, singing lustily as they negotiated the shell-holes in the road, shouting encouragement to the lines of marching men en route to the battlefield – these were the reinforcements they had managed without but would probably need next time.

Only three were left when they reached Zeebrugge – the others had been dropped off along the way – and they searched for a boat due to depart as soon as possible. After only about ten minutes, they came across a small ex-trawler on the point of leaving for Dover. Their dilapidated appearance won the day for them and they settled down on deck to have a much-needed sleep.

They were awakened, in the grey raininess of the early morning, by the bump against the jetty and sprang into wakefulness immediately, rushing to the side and jumping off as soon as they could. The three young soldiers separated now, heading for various points not too far from the docks. Jerry managed to get a lift on another truck to within quarter of a mile of the Nelson's house and sprinted the rest of the way.

All three of the household had been up since two o'clock. Daphne had felt her first pains in the early evening but had said nothing to her mother – they weren't all that bad. By the time she went to bed, they were growing more uncomfortable and more frequent but she endured them stoically for some hours before alerting her parents.

Rob, trying not to show how scared he was for his daughter,

had gone for the midwife as soon as he had thrown on some clothes. Lil made her usual pot of strong tea for comfort and could do nothing else other than try to reassure the girl. Daphne herself was doing her best not to scream as each shaft of agony came to its crescendo but there came a point when she couldn't help herself and, when Mrs Drake, the stout little midwife, turned up, she encouraged her by nodding, 'That's right, dear. Let 'em rip!'

Now redundant, Rob took himself outside for a smoke to soothe his jangling nerves and he was standing at the garden gate, trying unsuccessfully to light his cigarette with matches that kept fizzling out in the rain, when he heard the running feet. Looking up, he gave a gasp of pleasure at seeing the galloping Scotsman with his kilt swinging in all directions. 'Good God, Jerry,' he exclaimed, holding the gate open, 'you've timed it good and proper, you have.'

'What? What's going on? Is Daphne all right?' Each word was followed by a sharp intake of breath as the puffing Gordon Highlander tried to fill his lungs again.

'She's fine as far as I know,' Rob said, sighing gustily, 'but I'm not allowed to go in now. The midwife's there with her.'

'You mean . . . ? You mean . . . ?

Laughing at his incoherence, Rob nodded. 'The baby's on its way and I don't suppose they'll let you in either.'

'They damn well *will* let me in!' Jerry declared vehemently. 'I've come all this way . . . and I'm the father . . . and·I want to see my child being born!'

'You'll be lucky!' was Rob's retort to his retreating back.

Ignoring Lil's shocked face, Jerry strode straight into the bedroom.

'No, no, now.' Mrs Drake admonished. 'No fathers allowed.'

But Daphne stretched out her arms, beseeching, 'Oh, Jerry, I'm so glad you're here. Please let him stay, Mrs Drake.'

And Jerry stood, holding her hand, as the searing pains racked her body and the stout woman did what she had to do. Two hours passed but still he did not move, still the moans and screams forced themselves out of his wife's mouth and he wanted to push the midwife out of the way and ease his child out himself. But he knew that was impossible – even stupid and dangerous.

At long last, Mrs Drake gave a triumphant cry. 'It's crowning! It's coming! One last push, dear,' and, with a plopping sound, the little body slipped out.

Jerry wanted to close his eyes to the blood and mucus that oozed out along with it but Mrs Drake took the towel Lil was holding ready, wrapped it round the tiny being and handed it to him. 'What is it?' he asked, not having had time to notice the sex.

'Oh, God give me strength!' the woman sighed. 'Never even saw whether he had a son or a daughter. That's fathers for you!'

Thoroughly ashamed of what he termed as his weakness at the sight of the bloody mess, he forced himself not to flinch as he took the little bundle in his arms and Lil came to his rescue. 'It's a boy!'

Pride blotted out everything else from his mind, his chest voluntarily expanding. He had actually fathered a son! What was more, he had watched the birth, seen the crown of the head as it came into view, seen the speed with which the blood-covered, miniature body left its haven and now he was watching the midwife guiding out what she called the afterbirth. He had not known that giving birth was such a complicated and painful process – it was a wonder that any babies ever got born at all.

Now the little midwife claimed the occupant of the towel and sponged it gently in the basin Lil had waiting. Only after he was patted dry with a clean towel did the little creature look human. Red of face and wrinkly but still a human being, with a dashed good pair of lungs.

'I'm glad it's a boy,' Daphne whispered, when the two women went out.

'I hadn't thought about it,' Jerry admitted honestly. 'I didn't care what it was as long as you were both all right.' He looked at his wife in concern. 'You *are* all right, Daphne, aren't you?'

'Never better,' she grinned. 'I never dared to think you might be here and I can still hardly believe it.'

Jerry spent most of his one full day in Dover sitting by his wife's bed because Mrs Drake would not allow her to get up. 'No, no, my lady, a week before you can get on your feet, then up a little longer each day till you're strong enough to stay up. Even then, you have to watch and not do too much. And remember, Father, you must control yourself.'

Mortified at what she was suggesting, Jerry merely nodded. He was happy as long as he could be with his wife, holding her hand and telling her how much he loved her and how proud he was of her and kissing her when he felt like it.

His luck held the next morning. A merchant ship was making ready to leave for Zeebrugge when he arrived at the docks and he gratefully accepted the offer of a spare bunk. He hadn't had much sleep the night before but he lay awake for some time thinking. Not many men were fortunate enough to be witness to the birth of their own child. It was a process kept shrouded in mystery by women – a tightly guarded secret that was seldom divulged to the male sex.

Yet he had been there with his wife. He had seen everything and he would never forget that wonderful, wonderful moment when the tiny person he had helped to create made his entry into the world.

It was a moment he would cherish until the day he died.

CHAPTER TWENTY-EIGHT

Lil Nelson was feeling somewhat annoyed with herself and it was all that Jerry Rae's fault. She hadn't been herself while he was there, what with the birth and all the excitement, but it had dawned on her just after he left. Around the time of the wedding, she had figured that her daughter's monthlies had been due to start on the day of the ceremony but Daphne hadn't come to her as she usually did asking for napkins. She knew Daphne was always as regular as clockwork and had assumed that it was the frenzy of the wedding that had made her period late. But the reason it hadn't come when she expected it to was that the little bitch had been pregnant. Why the hell hadn't she tumbled to it before? The blighter had been at her before-hand.

Lil was in a proper quandary now. However she felt about the filthy brute, she felt duty-bound to reassure the girl at not hearing one word from him. 'Nothing's happened to Jerry. He'll be in the heart of the fighting and they don't get time off to write billets-doux to sulking wives.'

'I know that and I'm not sulking. I'm worried. He's been away for months.'

'The army would let you know if anything happened to him.'

'What if they don't know he's married?'

'Of course they know. He'd to get the Commanding Officer's permission, hadn't he?'

'Maybe he didn't give them our address. He was recalled in such a rush, he could easily have forgotten. And they were sent abroad right away.'

Lil pulled a face. 'In that case, they'd likely notify his parents if anything happened and they'd write to you.'

'I don't know where they live,' Daphne wailed. 'He didn't tell me anything about them – they could be dead, for all I know. Even if they're not . . .' She broke off as another horrifying possibility struck her. 'What if he hasn't told them he married me? They maybe don't know about me at all.'

Lil's patience, already worn thin, snapped at that. 'Pull yourself together, girl! If you keep on like this, it'll affect the baby. Jerry must have let his mother know he was married.'

She was not altogether certain of this herself. He had obviously got what he wanted from Daphne before marriage was ever mentioned – he'd likely had no intention of marrying her at all. The wedding had practically been forced on him – at her instigation, Lil thought wretchedly – and he hadn't really had time to write to his mum and dad. She wished she'd had the chance to let him know how she felt about him, though. Dirty swine, deflowering an innocent girl before he was forced to put the ring on her finger.

She had to watch what she said, though. It was up to her to keep Daphne's spirits up. Whatever Jerry Rae was, the girl was still married to him. 'You're worrying for nothing, dear,' she consoled. 'A whole bundle of letters will turn up one of these days, just you wait and see.'

If only that would come true, there would be peace in the house once more . . . for a while, at least.

A similar scenario was being played out in Ardbirtle. Fay's anxiety for her son was deepening with every day that passed and Henry was more of a Job's comforter than any real help.

'It's been more than six months since we'd a letter,' she sighed one rainy morning, having seen the postman go past without stopping.

Her husband drained his teacup and stood up. 'He's not over there for a holiday, my Fairy Fay. They're fighting against a treacherous enemy and they'll have to be on their guard constantly. No time to write letters home. No time for anything except to mind their backs. I just wish I knew exactly where he was so I'd have an idea of what he's having to face.' He lifted his peaked soft hat from the hook at the back of the door and slapped it on to his head. 'It's time I was off. Just stop worrying. Jerry's fine, I'm sure.'

Fay gave a little snort when the door shut behind him. What did he know about it? If the enemy was as treacherous as he said, it stood to reason that Jerry was in danger and, as his mother, she was entitled to be worried about him.

After washing up and tidying the kitchen, she decided to go to Corbie Den. She needed someone to speak to, to take her mind off . . .

Leo greeted her in a more affectionate way than most men would greet their mothers-in-law but her stomach churned at the thought of Jerry suffering injuries like his. Nevertheless, after an hour there, she had almost forgotten her worries. Mara and her husband were so obviously happy, so obviously in love, even though the miracle they'd hoped for had not taken place. The horrific scars had toned down a little, the gaunt cheeks had filled out, his speech was easier to understand . . . but he had regained less than fifty per cent of his sight and his legs were as useless as ever.

Mara went to the garden gate with her when she left so she was able to admit to her worries about Jerry and, fortunately, her daughter was more sympathetic than Henry had been.

'I know how you feel, Mother,' the girl said gently. 'I was the same when I didn't hear from Leo for so long. I imagined all sorts of things.'

Feeling ashamed at not remembering the long months of waiting before Leo's father had written, Fay couldn't help thinking that it might have been better for Mara if Leo hadn't come back. Yet, looking at her daughter, a pretty young woman still, it heartened her to see the peace in the sweet face, the contentment of being with the man she loved, in spite of what he was now.

*   *   *

Captain Frederick Lindsay felt himself to be in a tight corner. He had taken over as acting adjutant because the battalion's appointed adjutant, John Lawrie, had been killed during the last offensive. And then the CO had been killed too and he was left to carry out a duty for which he was totally untrained. Having been sent in to boost the dwindling numbers on this front – the remnants of various other regiments – they had, thank God, gained their objective but at the cost of so many lives. So far, he knew only the figures for his band of Gordon Highlanders – it could no longer be called a battalion – and, of the sixty-seven who had begun this latest battle, only eighteen remained. It was his job to notify the next-of-kin.

It should have been straightforward to look up Lawrie's records, get each soldier's rank and number and the name and address of the person to be notified in the event of his death and pass on the information to HQ. Should any problems arise, contact the CO – that was how it should be – but it was turning out to be much more complicated than that. Like all the poor beggars who had been wiped out, the records, that Lawrie had kept so meticulously up to date in even the worst possible conditions, had been blown sky-high. And there would be no help from the CO either, now that he too had been killed.

The only thing to do, Lindsay thought, a kind of last resort, would be to talk to the survivors and try to glean some information on their dead comrades. This plan was quite successful, as far as it went. He was given all the names and ranks, some of the numbers from kitbags and personal possessions left behind but hardly anything on the next-of-kin – or should that be next-of-kins since there were forty-nine to worry about? Still, he had done his best and, if he collated the information in alphabetical order and sent on the effects properly labelled, the clerks at HQ should be able to take it from there. Only one thing was nagging at him. It seemed that one of the privates, a Jeremy Rae, had got married just before the battalion was shipped out but no one could give him any details about the wife's whereabouts.

So the telegram and the boy's pathetic possessions would be

sent to his mother who was down as his next of kin. Captain Lindsay did not feel easy about this but, after agonising over it for some time, he decided that the boy's parents would let the widow know. It wasn't his worry now and nor was it his fault. If it was God's will that Rae should die, the Almighty should have made sure that all eventualities had been covered.

Because of the lack of details received at HQ, the information did not reach Ardbirtle until some weeks later.

'You had better look for Henry Rae and give it to him,' the postmaster instructed the young telegraph boy. 'I wouldn't like to think of his poor wife opening it on her own.'

This, then, was why the vital telegram was handed to Henry while he was doing his duty as street sweeper. His stomach churning, his heart barely able to beat, he managed to give the young lad a threepenny tip and sent him on his way. Then, with surprisingly steady hands, he tore open the yellow envelope to confirm what he was already suspecting. Only then, seeing it printed on strips of paper, did he actually believe it. Jerry had been killed in action! His first son had died as a child and his second had died an eighteen-year-old, practically still a child! Now his hands shook, his legs had difficulty in taking him home to tell his wife. His poor Fairy Fay! What would this do to her?

She was stronger than he thought – at least in front of Mara, who had gone in for a few minutes after finishing her shopping. 'I knew something had happened to him,' Fay murmured but there was no tremor in the words, no tears in her eyes.

With her father just standing looking shocked, Mara stepped forward to put her arms round her mother, to console her, but Fay waved her away. 'I'm all right.'

'But, Mother . . .'

'I'm all right, I tell you. Now, go home to Leo, he needs you more than I do.'

Casting one accusing glance at her father, Mara reluctantly went out. His daughter's look prodding him back to life, Henry pulled his wife gently against his chest and they wept for their son together.

It was almost a month later before the parcel arrived and by this time they had more or less come to terms with their loss. Touching his bible, his cap, his badge and all the little trifles he had left behind in his kitbag, brought it all back to them, affecting them even more the second time round. They spent the next hour clasped tightly in each other's arms, recalling the manner of both their sons' deaths, weeping softly but bitterly, then sat for the remainder of the day, one at each side of the fireplace, remembering little incidents in Andrew's short life, as well as in Jerry's.

Before they went to bed that night, Fay wrapped the little package up again and laid it reverently in the left-hand cupboard of the dresser, behind her best china tea set. An onlooker may have assumed that it was being put out of sight to help them to forget what had happened but Fay, at least, knew that it would never be forgotten. It would be taken out regularly in memory of her younger son, the son she had never meant as a replacement for her first born. She had thought, and felt guiltily about it, that she had loved Andrew more than she loved Jerry but that wasn't true. She had loved her younger son every bit as much and would mourn him for the rest of her life.

In the morning, she made her husband go to work as usual, although he hated the idea of leaving her alone. 'I'll be all right,' she assured him. 'I want to be on my own for a while. I'm all churned up inside and I need peace to . . .'

'If you're sure.' Henry felt exactly the same and was dreading meeting people. All his friends, and even mere acquaintances, would want to tell him how sorry they were and he didn't think he could bear it. But he loved Fay too much to deny her the privacy she wanted at this time. In fact, he would shield her, warn well-wishers off going to console her.

Gradually, as always happens, Fay and Henry were drawn back into the daily life of the town and found themselves commiserating with other parents who had lost a son – in some tragic cases, more than one. Two neighbouring families, one consisting of six sons and five daughters, the other five sons and six daughters, had been made closer when all eleven young men were away fighting for their country – the two mothers even compared letters. But, as the war went on, only one of them had the heartache. All five of her sons were killed and her friendship with her neighbour, whose six sons were still alive, turned to hatred.

It was happening all over and no one, even men of the cloth, could explain to the grieving women why God had taken their sons and not others. Fay astounded Henry one evening by saying, 'I'm glad we had only one son to give. If I'd had five taken from me, like Maggie Tyler, I'd either have gone off my head or killed myself.'

'Oh, my Fairy!' he exclaimed. 'I don't think you would. You're made of stronger stuff than that. You'd be like Maggie, putting a brave face on though her heart must be broken – but I bet she gives way when she's in her own house.'

So Fay did her best to emulate Maggie Tyler, keeping up appearances in front of others but giving way to her sorrow when she was alone.

It may have comforted Fay had she known that she had a daughter-in-law and a grandson – they would have given her something to live for – but Daphne, now Mrs Jeremy Rae, had given up trying to find where her husband's parents lived. 'He can't have been killed,' she had wailed to her mother when they were celebrating her infant son's first birthday. 'His mum would have written to me.'

Lil shrugged her bust a little higher because the busks of her corsets were digging into her. 'I think you're right. He's just turned his back on you, that's what. The war's over so he can't be fighting the Germans now. He seemed such a decent young man at first but . . . how could he just walk out on his wife and son? You should write and ask the authorities for an allowance for you and the boy.'

'I'll manage on my own without any help from Jerry or anybody else. As long as you're willing to look after Ollie while I go out to work.'

'You know I am. That child is the light of my life, no matter what kind of father he had.'

It was well into 1920 before Daphne gave up her secret hope that Jerry would come back to her. Only then did she start to lead a normal life.'

'I think we should encourage her to go out more,' Lil told her husband. 'It would be nice if she could find a boy . . .'

'Stop trying your hand at matchmaking,' Rob growled. 'Your first attempt didn't end up too well.'

'It wasn't my fault! How was I to know he'd desert her as soon as she bore his child? Though I suppose I should have realised – after what he did before.'

Rob said no more. His wife was always saying things like that but young Jerry *had* been a decent boy and he wouldn't have walked out on his wife and son. If he had been killed in action, it was possible, going by the post-war accounts of the slaughter and mayhem on the battlefields, that records had been lost or maybe hadn't even been kept. It might be worth writing to the Ministry of Defence or whoever to find out more. They might give out the name and address of his next of kin.

It wasn't up to him though. Lil would go mad if he interfered. She was so bloody positive Jerry was a rotter.

And . . . maybe he was, at that.

PART FOUR

1935-1943

CHAPTER TWENTY-NINE

Henry Rae was beginning to feel his age. The braes were getting steeper, both up and down, and the roads were getting longer. There had been more houses built – whole estates with stupid names like Valentino Gardens, a film star popular long before Ardbirtle had a cinema at all. The old names were best – heroes of the past: Nelson Street, Wellington Road, Kitchener Place, right up to Haig and a few lesser known participants in the war.

His other duties were almost non-existent now. There had been no court case for a long, long time, so no villains to usher in – most of the culprits had only been petty thieves, in any case and the worst crime had been forging a signature on a stolen chequebook. The last public announcement had been the death of Edward VII and the accession of his son, George V. The smart uniform he'd been so proud to wear had then hung in the closet for twenty-five years, with mothballs to preserve it. It certainly had no moth holes when Fay took it out and pressed it for the Silver Jubilee celebrations last year – but the reek of camphor had nearly choked him and anybody who came near him.

He might not get another chance to wear it. The king could live for another ten years yet and he himself was bound to be put out to pasture any day now.

'I've been waiting for the Provost to give me my marching orders,' he told his wife one morning at breakfast. 'It's a whole month past my sixty-fifth birthday.'

Fay looked alarmed. 'But you are still fit enough for the job – are you not?'

His smile was somewhat wry. 'Some days I'm fitter than

others but I suppose I could go on for a while yet.'

'Well, there you are, then,' she said, triumphantly, nodding her silver head at him. 'You know it and I know it and I'm sure the Provost knows it as well.'

'Aye, well, maybe I should just carry on, then.

'No maybe about it. There's no sense in walking into trouble.'

Provost Leslie Main took his place at the council table and looked round the familiar faces, most having been there since he first took his place as an ordinary councillor – donkey's years ago.

'Nae much to speak about the day, lads,' he boomed – his usual manner of addressing them in his mixture of broad Scots and English. 'It has been brung to my attention that our Town Officer, T H Rae or Henry, as most of us ken him, has reached the grand age of sixty-five, as have some of us and all. But his job's a lot mair taxing than ours.' He halted in embarrassment. 'Mair *physically* taxing, I should say. He works wi' his hands but we work wi' our brains. The point is should we retire him? We've certainly nae fault to find wi' his work yet but you never ken, do you?'

'What are you getting at, Provost?' muttered one of the braver souls. 'Are we to retire him or no'?'

Main, kicking seventy himself, scowled at the impudent upstart. Some of these youngsters took too much on themselves. 'If you would learn to have patience, Mester Watt . . .' He stopped to let this sink in. The 'Mester' was intended as an insult since it could be interpreted as Master as well as Mister. 'If you will just be patient,' he went on, 'I will tell you. I propose that we leave things be the now but, if we see the job's getting too much for him, we could *suggest* retirement to him. Mind you, it strikes me we'd ha'e a bit o' a job finding a replacement. It's nae a job to mony folks's liking.'

Mr Watt got to his feet this time to have his say, his round boyish face already red in anticipation of another rebuff. 'I wouldn't say that, Provost. The job's not as bad as it used to be. There's not many horses fouling the roads these days.' A light murmur of agreement from his fellow councillors giving him confidence, he puffed out his chest. 'The law of the land states that the retirement age is sixty-five and there should be no exceptions to the rule.'

This last sentiment was met with loud gasps from those council members who were already past the limit. 'As long as the body's fit and the brain's clear,' said the man on his left angrily, 'I don't see any need to take a man's pride away from him. Henry Rae has given about thirty years' service to the town, if not more, and I propose we employ a young lad to give him a hand. Then we could wait till he says he wants to retire.'

'Seconded!' came a roar from several others.

Leslie Main got to his feet again. 'All those in favour?' He didn't bother to count the waving hands and smirked as he looked at the young troublemaker. 'Carried near unanimously! You'll put an advert in this week's *Advertiser*, Jack? School-leaver required for outdoor work.'

Jack, the editor of the local weekly, took a note of this and then said, 'I shouldna think there'll be much bother about getting a laddie, Provost.'

'No, I suppose you'll get a shoal o' answers so I'll leave it to you to pick oot the best. Noo, if there's nothing else on the agenda, gentlemen, we should catch The Doocot afore it shuts. All those in favour?'

A rousing chorus of 'Aye!' was accompanied by the scraping back of chairs.

The advent of a helper did little to raise Henry's opinion of himself. This was just the thin edge of the wedge and, in a few months, when young Billy had proved his worth, one of the council would be promoting *him* to official Town Officer or maybe they would do away with the job as such and change it to Road Sweeper.

Henry had foreseen some weeks of training the lad, likely getting the height of cheek from him for youngsters nowadays thought they knew everything, but he was pleasantly surprised. The boy was always respectful to him – in fact, it was almost as though he looked up to him – and he was, indeed, a great help. For the first week, they traversed the streets together. Then Billy was given his own 'district' and insisted on doing all the steep hills. They would meet up just after the parish kirk clock had struck twelve, at Henry's house, where Fay had always some kind of soup ready for them and big chunks of the crusty bread she still made herself.

Although extremely shy at first, Billy Webster was soon won round by Fay, telling her that he had been brought up in the Aberlour Orphanage and was now in lodgings in Waterloo Road. She was horrified at this and, without consulting Henry, she told the boy he could lodge with them. It had to be arranged through the proper channels, of course, so it was more than two weeks later before he moved in with a small bundle of clothes, which constituted all his possessions. Fay quickly put this right, buying at least one item of clothing for him each week and assuring him that it was included in what she charged him for his board.

It soon became evident to Mara that Billy worshipped her mother but she felt no jealousy. As she told Leo, 'She looks years younger and she's happier than she's ever been since we lost Jerry. It's doing her good to have somebody like him to look after. I just hope he doesn't get a job somewhere else and leave.'

Her husband shook his head. 'Your mother is a loving soul and, from what you say, I think he's beginning to look on your parents as *his* parents too. I'm sure it would take something drastic to make him leave them.'

Although Mara was easier in her mind about her mother and father, she had an ongoing worry about her husband. His doctor had warned her, before they left Edinburgh, not to expect a long married life. 'Five years at most,' the man had said sadly, yet they had celebrated almost twenty years together a few months ago. It had been hard going for her at times, though Leo had fought against the black moods that took possession of him, almost as if he knew what Doctor Perry had told her and was determined to prove the man a charlatan.

However, since their fifteenth anniversary – at which his father had been present, along with her parents and a few friends who had taken to visiting him – it seemed that he had lost heart. The spells of deep depression, which had grown less and less frequent over the years, had recently accelerated into one or more every day.

He somehow managed to hide them from everyone else – it was she who bore the brunt of his tempers, of his whiplash sarcasm, of the accusations he flung at her about seeing other men when she was out. So far, she had taken his jibes and the swearing by just ignoring them and finding some heavy work to do but it had begun to tell on her. More than one person, her mother most of all, had commented on how tired she looked and she *was* tired – utterly, totally exhausted. It was an effort to rise in the mornings, a bigger effort to stop herself shouting back at Leo and she didn't know how long she could keep going.

She was fully aware that he couldn't help himself and she still loved him as much as ever – in spite of what he said and did. She spoke the truth when she told him she would never look at another man. She would never, ever, meet anyone else that she would want to share her life with. No matter how Leo behaved now, they'd had many long years of almost perfect bliss, much more than she had expected. God had been good to her.

Strangely, it was Henry who got the first hint of change in his son-in-law. He, like Fay, had seen, and been concerned about, the change in their daughter, often discussing what might have caused it, but he had not dreamt of the real reason. Leo had always appeared to be a calm, easy-going young man, accepting his lot stoically and showing his gratitude to his wife for all she did for him. But it had not been like that!

Henry's day had started with Fay complaining of feeling sick and she was no better at noon so, when Mara popped in as usual, he had asked her to stay with her mother for a while to make sure there was nothing seriously wrong with her. 'I'll get Billy to bike . . . no! I'll go myself to let Leo know. Can he manage to make something for his dinner himself?'

'I made a salad. It's on the marble shelf in the larder and I told him to help himself if I was late.'

'That's all right, then. When I get to the end of Waterloo Street this afternoon, I'll see if Jack Rennie'll run me out to Corbie Den. That'll be about two o'clock, or just after, but I don't suppose Leo'll mind.'

He did notice a faint, and quickly stifled, look of what he took to be anxiety for her mother on Mara's face, and wrote it off as natural. He was worried about Fay himself and felt a lot easier knowing that Mara was with her.

It was after two when Jack Rennie drew his Austin up at the end of the long, winding path up to the Fergusons' door. 'You go on up, Henry,' he told his passenger. 'I'll bide here and have a draw of my pipe.'

'I'll not be long.'

'Nae hurry, Henry. Tak' your time.'

Not wanting to keep his friend waiting, however, Henry walked smartly up the garden and walked in without knocking.

'Where the hell have you been till this time?' Leo roared, not turning his wheelchair round. 'I know damn fine you've been with somebody, you slut! I heard the car stopping. Has he got a house you can go to? Do you get a thrill out of making him be unfaithful to his wife? Well? What are you standing there for? Say something, damn you! Tell me the truth! I'm sick to death of your lies so tell me the truth!'

His insides churning with the appalled realisation of what his daughter had been suffering, Henry walked silently forward, taking up his stance in front of the crippled man. He said nothing, just looked at him in disdain.

'Oh, God!' Leo exclaimed, his hands going up to his face. 'I didn't know it was you, Henry! What's wrong? Has something happened to Samara?'

Henry kept his voice and his temper under control. 'Nothing has happened to your wife. I asked her to stay with her mother. She's not very well.'

His anger at being left alone for so long was too much for

the younger man. 'Oh, I see!' His voice dripped now with sarcasm. 'Her mother's not very well so she chooses to leave her disabled husband for hours. That's a bloody fine attitude to take! I could have died and she wouldn't have cared a fig – the whore!'

This proved more than Henry could take and he slapped the other man across the face. 'If this is how you treat her, you selfish bugger, I hope she does find herself another man!'

Even the shock of the slap did not stop the accusations. 'So you encourage her, is that it? Have you been covering up for her for years? I often wondered at a young woman in her prime staying with a wreck like me but she'd been getting satisfaction elsewhere, with her father's help.' He scowled as a new concept struck him. 'Maybe it's been you? Eh, Henry? Is your Fairy Fay getting too old for you. Do you prefer a . . .'

Enraged himself beyond all control, Henry stopped the flow of vindictiveness by punching the sneering mouth. 'And I'm not apologising for that, Leo Ferguson! If you weren't in a wheelchair, I'd have knocked you out! When I think of all the years my daughter has sacrificed herself to look after you and accusations like that are all the thanks she gets, I could kill you! Well, you've fouled your own nest, as the saying goes. I'll go through and get some of Mara's clothes but I'll be back for the rest, don't you worry! She will not be coming back here, I can assure you of that, and you can please yourself what you do.'

He swivelled round, did as he had said and was back in a few moments, carrying a bundle of clothing. 'I have a car waiting for me.'

'Please, Henry,' pleaded the younger man, cringing away, 'I didn't know what I was saying. I'd been on my own for hours, and I'm always scared something happens to me and . . .'

'There's no excuse for the things you said! I feel like leaving you here to rot but I'll send the doctor up. He can maybe arrange for somebody to come in or he could get you into a nursing home.' He went to the door, his legs shaking, his heart thumping dangerously, and strode out, ignoring the sound of

357

weeping as he slammed the door behind him.

When he reached the car, he muttered, 'Don't ask, Jack. Just take me home.'

CHAPTER THIRTY

The past year had been hectic for Henry Rae, in more ways than one. Firstly, in his own family circle, there had been the trauma of getting Mara to settle in. In spite of what Leo had put her through, she swore that she still loved him and was quite prepared to carry on looking after him. Her father did his best to convince her – without giving her the exact details of his fateful afternoon visit – that Leo was past the stage where he could be cared for at home. It was fortunate for all concerned that Doctor Berry endorsed this opinion and, after corresponding with James Ferguson, had had the young man transferred to a very expensive private nursing home near Edinburgh.

Mara's shame at deserting a husband who needed her was eased by the letter she received from his father shortly afterwards, thanking her for all she had done over the years and assuring her not to feel that she had let Leo down. Wanting to be near her ailing mother, she refused his offer of making Corbie Den over to her and acceded to his request that she should not visit his son.

'It would only upset you,' Ferguson had written. 'It seems that the piece of shrapnel that had been lodged near his brain and has slowly shifted over the years, putting more pressure on it. He is past recognising anyone now.'

It was not a satisfactory situation for the poor woman but she occupied herself in looking after her parents and young Billy, who helped by chopping sticks, taking in pails of coal and anything else that needed to be done. It took time but they eventually got into a regular routine.

The old king, George V, died in February, and Mara had to spruce up her father's official uniform for the proclamation of the death and the accession of the Prince of Wales as Edward VIII. There were several events to be organised now for his Coronation but circumstances changed with the news that he wished to marry Wallis Simpson, an American divorcee, who was still married to her second husband.

Opinions about this were divided not only in the Rae household but also all over the country. Henry and Billy backed Mr Baldwin, the Prime Minister, in his stand against such a marriage, while Fay and Mara, romantics both, hoped that the new king would thumb his nose at the cabinet and marry Mrs Simpson when her second divorce was final. In December, Edward settled the controversy himself by broadcasting his intention to abdicate – saying simply that he could not carry out his duties as king without the support of the woman he loved.

So Henry had another proclamation to make and Edward's brother, the Duke of York, came to the throne as George VI. The date of the coronation was not changed so all the souvenirs already made bearing Edward's name had to be sold off cheaply and others made with George and Elizabeth on them.

The whole business had taken a toll on Henry. 'I'm sick of all this rush,' he declared one evening. 'I'm going to retire when the coronation's past.'

He had expected some argument from his wife but nothing seemed to affect Fay these days – good news or bad news, they were all one to her. 'Should we get the doctor in to your mother?' he asked Mara after Fay had gone to bed that night.

She shrugged helplessly. 'I don't know. Father. Some days she's better than others. I think she gets depressed – you know, losing two sons, then my marriage coming to an end, it was bound to tell on her.'

'She was fine for a while, when Billy came first,' Henry reminded her.

'That was because he was somebody young for her to look after. Maybe I should have stayed at Corbie Den and not come here to make her feel she's not needed any more?'

'It's a pity you never had any children, Mara,' Henry said without thinking, 'that would have . . .' Realising his gaffe, he hurried on in embarrassment, 'I mean . . . I'm sorry . . . oh, Mara, I know it wasn't your fault.'

'I would have loved to have children,' she said quietly, 'but things didn't work out that way.'

'No.' After a long pause, he said, 'James Ferguson hasn't written for a while.'

'I'll hear soon enough if . . . anything has changed.'

In one of life's eerie coincidences, the news came the very next forenoon. Mara had swept the kitchen floor, taken the mats out to shake them and was putting them down on the linoleum again when someone knocked at the front door. 'I'll go,' Fay said, moving slowly.

Noticing a car sitting in the road, Mara wondered who it could be but was still shocked when her mother brought in James Ferguson. 'Leo?' she gasped.

'Yes, my dear. I'm afraid he passed away last night, peacefully in his sleep, they told me.'

'I'm glad of that.' Mara couldn't think what else to say.

'I wanted to let you know myself. I wanted to tell you how grateful I was to you, taking him off our hands for so many years.'

'I didn't do it to take him off your hands. I loved him, I still do.'

'Yes, I know, and I am sorry if I have upset you. He was a very lucky man to have you to look after him . . .'

'Not lucky altogether though,' she murmured. 'He was such an upright man, kind and understanding, until . . .'

'Yes, it must have been as hard on you as it was on any of us.'

Fay broke into the uncomfortably long silence that fell now. 'Would you care for a cup of tea, Mr Ferguson?'

'No, thank you. I have left my wife in Aberdeen doing some shopping and I promised to be back in time for lunch.' He stood up awkwardly and held out his hand to her. 'Leo used to tell us how you welcomed him into your home when he was courting Samara. Thank you for that.'

Mara got to her feet. 'I'll see you out.'

She went right to the car with him, wanting to ask a question she did not want her mother to hear. 'When's the funeral?'

His sad eyes dropped. 'They are burying him tomorrow at the nursing home – they have a graveyard in the grounds. I . . . I'd rather you didn't come, my dear. It's going to be painful enough for me as it is.'

'I'm his wife,' she whispered. 'I should be there. I want to be there.'

'Yes, of course you must come. I was wrong there and I am sorry.'

'I understand.'

After asking the details of where and when, she let him drive off. She didn't really know how she felt. She hadn't been expecting it to be so sudden yet his father had said it was for the best – that Leo had been in a dark world of his own ever since he was taken there.

Thankfully, when she went inside again, her mother said only, 'It had to come, Mara, dear.'

'I know.'

That evening, when Billy went out to meet some friends, she told her parents that she was going to the funeral, sure that they would be against it. Henry's mouth pursed in disapproval but Fay rushed in before he could say anything. 'He was her husband, Henry, and no matter what happened between them, if she wants to go, it is not up to us to stop her.'

Mara was glad she had decided to go to the funeral. There had been no lengthy eulogy, no words of praise, until she stood up. 'He was a brave man,' she had begun, the strength of her voice surprising even herself. 'The life he knew before he went into the army was tragically taken from him and, although he once walked proudly and erectly, he spent his last years – so many years – in a wheelchair. I loved him with all my heart and I will always remember him as he used to be, a decent, loving

362

young man any girl would have been proud to have as a husband. I was the lucky one.'

She had turned away then, blinded by tears, but now, on the train home, she felt better than she had done for some time. James Ferguson had taken her for a meal afterwards, mainly to tell her that Leo had left everything to her. She had said that she didn't want anything but, after he told her to take time to think about it, common sense took over. She had often worried, lately, about how they would manage when her father retired. She would have to look after both parents and couldn't take a job so there would just be young Billy's board money coming in – although the council might give her father a small pension. Her inheritance – in the region of ten thousand pounds apparently – would mean that she need never worry again. It was a good feeling!

In the week leading up to the coronation celebrations, Henry was more grateful than ever for Billy's help and, on one wet and windy night, they made the church their last call. Although it was June, it was quite cold outside, and the kirk itself seemed to be even colder. While Billy ran up into the organ loft to make sure that the pipes were in perfect condition for the special service of thanksgiving for the new king and queen, Henry walked slowly up the centre aisle checking that every row of pews was spotlessly clean and the hassocks were all in place.

They had shut the heavy oak door behind them but he could still feel an ice-cold draught gnawing at his feet and he thought of leaving the two choir enclosures and the pulpit area until another night – there was still plenty of time. Yet something made him carry on.

Discovering a hassock missing from one row of pews, he wondered if someone had shifted it. It didn't turn up anywhere else and his hands and feet were actually 'dirling' with cold so he decided to forget about it and check the two stalls where the choir always sat or stood.

'You check the left side,' he instructed Billy, who had made his appearance again, 'and I'll take the right.'

The fifteen-year-old being quicker on his feet, he reached the pulpit first and stopped in amazement at what he saw. He beckoned Henry to join him and they looked down on the beautiful sight of a young girl curled up beneath the lectern with an infant in her arms. She was using the missing hassock as a pillow and was sound asleep.

'What'll we do?' whispered Billy.

Henry scratched his head uncertainly. 'I wonder where she's come from?'

'They'll get a chill if we leave them here.'

'Aye, you're right. We'd better waken her.' He gave a few genteel coughs but the girl didn't stir so he bent down and patted her gently on the shoulder.

She sat up instantly. 'Please don't make us go away,' she pleaded, her blue eyes moist with tears, her cheeks still rosy from sleep.

'It's too cold here for you. Have you nowhere else to go?'

The tears spilled over. 'My father threw me out . . . because of the baby.'

Billy raised his eyebrows hopefully and Henry nodded his agreement. 'You'd best come home wi' us, then.'

'But . . . what about . . . your wife? What'll she say?'

'Fay'll not mind,' Billy said unexpectedly.

Henry didn't contradict him. A baby to look after might be what his wife needed to get her back on track again. 'Everything's going to be fine, lass,' he assured the girl.

Everything *was* fine. There was one more to feed but two more hands to the plough, as the farmers would say. Fay was delighted to have an infant to attend to and young Maggie was only needed to feed him. Pressed to give him a name, she plumped for Henry, who said, 'No, we don't want two Henrys in the house.'

After some thought, Maggie remembered how she had admired the hero in *Little Women* and called her son Laurie.

'But his real name was Laurence,' Mara pointed out.

'I know but I like Laurie better.'

They all did, although little Laurie would have kept on

smiling and gurgling with laughter no matter what he was called.

It was Henry who approached the rather delicate subject of registering his birth. 'It's the law,' he explained, 'and I'll come wi' you if you want. You can wait till he's older before you have him baptised.'

A Registry Office for Births, Marriages and Deaths had been introduced to the town many years before so it was not the church's Session Clerk they had to approach. When the Registrar – George Mavor, grandson of Willie Rae's old drinking crony – asked Maggie for the father's name, she turned to Henry in some confusion. 'I don't want to land him in trouble.'

'Just put in your own name, then,' Henry suggested, and, although Mavor frowned when he learned that she was not quite sixteen, the infant was registered as Laurie Fiddes.

Most of the concerts and parties put on as celebrations for the coronation held no appeal for any of the Rae household but, when Henry said there was to be a dance the next Saturday night, Billy said shyly, 'Would you let me take Maggie? She needs some enjoyment.'

Getting unanimous approval, he put the question to the girl herself and was disappointed that she didn't seem too keen. 'It'll be good fun,' he coaxed her.

'I can't dance,' she whispered tearfully.

'That doesn't matter; we can watch everybody else. Anyway, the last dance I went to, half the people couldn't dance but they soon picked it up.'

Mara altered one of her old summer dresses for the girl, a pale blue shirtwaister, and, to brighten it a bit, she embroidered a few lazy-daisies, white with yellow French knots in the centre, on the left shoulder. On the actual day, she washed Maggie's long hair and brushed it into ringlets, with the result that the girl drew loud gasps of admiration when she came into the kitchen, ready to go.

She looked the picture of health now. Instead of the poor little waif she had been when Billy found her, her face and figure had rounded out, her chestnut hair shone like well-buffed bronze. Her blue eyes had lost their look of fear and worry and she even whistled gaily as she went about her chores, despite Fay's caution that it wasn't ladylike. The blue dress finished the transformation from pretty girl to lovely young woman.

This was the first of many outings she had with Billy, whose well-scrubbed face was now sporting a light coating of fair down on chin and upper lip.

'Shouldn't I be shaving?' he asked Henry one day, as they set off on their daily rounds, his much larger than the older man's now.

'Time enough, yet.' Henry ran his hand proudly over his neatly trimmed beard and thick moustache, both an impressive silver-white. Then, seeing how disappointed the young man was, he corrected himself. 'Aye, I suppose you should be shaving. I'll give you a shot o' my old cut-throat but you'll need to take care. One slip and you could lose your nose.'

They both smiled at that and the three females had great amusement as they watched Billy giving himself his first shave, very carefully. Fay, however, reprimanded her husband later for giving him such a dangerous implement. 'What if he cuts himself?'

'I used to nick myself every day,' Henry grinned, 'and I'm still here to tell the tale. Tell me this, my Fairy. Do you like my whiskers? You've never said one way or the other.'

'Well, I didn't like them at first,' she admitted. 'They tickled when you kissed me goodnight but they made you look real smart in your dress uniform.'

'Aye,' he said, regretfully. He probably would never have a chance to wear it again. 'D'you mind that picture Jack Rennie took to put in the *Advertiser* at the time of George Five's coronation? Even if I say it myself, I was a fine figure of a man then.'

'Indeed you were.'

'Not now, though. My back's getting bowed, I'm tottery on my legs when I'm tired and my brow's got that many wrinkles it's like a sheet o' corrugated iron.'

His wife held out her arm and patted his hand. 'No, no, my Tchouki. You'll always be the handsome young man who came into the druggist shop to get his thumb bandaged. I remember it as if it were yesterday.'

'And I can remember how bonnie you were . . . no, my Fairy Fay, you're still bonnie. Bonnier than any other woman I've ever known.' He pulled her face nearer so that he could kiss her.

Coming in from hanging out the nappies she had washed, Mara said, 'Ho ho! What's this? You should leave the kissing to youngsters like Maggie and Billy.'

'You don't think they're . . . ?' Fay murmured in surprise. 'They're far too young to be kissing.'

Henry gave a loud guffaw. 'No younger than we were, my Fairy, and I've never regretted a minute of our married life.'

'Neither have I,' she assured him but her face showed that she was a little perturbed about their young lodgers.

She was also very much afraid that young Billy would give himself a nasty cut with the open blade when he was shaving and made Mara buy a safety razor for him.

Only about three weeks later, Henry had a nasty shock. He hadn't felt like going to kirk with the young folk and had spent the forenoon pottering about the little garden at the rear of the house. Fay had been the gardener at one time and then Billy had stepped in when she took on looking after little Laurie. But he felt he really should do it himself as master of the house. He was leaning on the hoe catching his breath when Jim Barron looked over the wall.

'I thought I might find you here, Henry.'

'You thought right, then, Provost.' Henry was not too taken with the current holder of the position, who had taken over from Leslie Main about a month before. There was something about him – he was younger, of course, though that didn't necessarily count against him.

'I'm afraid I have some bad news for you. At the council meeting last night, the motion was made that . . . we should . . . ask you to retire.'

'And it was carried unanimously?' Henry smiled.

Barron shifted uneasily. 'Not exactly unanimously.'

'No matter, I've been expecting it. Will young Billy be getting the job?'

The Provost's face, already pink with embarrassment, turned a deep crimson. 'Um . . . not exactly. The feeling was that we need more than one street sweeper to clean the town properly and we will be appointing an overseer and three men, Billy being one.'

Henry gave a relieved sigh. 'As long as he still has a job.'

'Oh, yes, he will still have a job but there is one more thing, Henry. This house was . . . um . . . it came with the job if you can remember that far back?'

'I'm surprised you can remember, Provost.' His sarcasm was lost.

'I don't remember, of course, but it's on record. It was part of your salary and, now that you will no longer be working for the council . . .'

His heart heavy, Henry said, with forced brightness, 'You want me to move out? Is that it?'

'We would like you to vacate the premises as soon as possible.'

'There's more than Fay and me in the house now.' Henry realised that it was probably useless but it was worth a try.

'So I believe and . . . um . . . that is another thing, isn't it? The house was provided for you and your immediate family – not for the waifs and strays you seem to have a habit of picking up.'

'Yes, I see what you mean, Provost, and I assure you that we will leave the house as we found it – in a better state than we found it – but that's neither here nor there. If you give me a date, I'll make sure it is kept.'

The florid-faced man seemed even more uneasy. 'Your retiral date is one week from yesterday and it was agreed that we should give you another week to vacate the house. That lets our overseer take over his post on the first of May.'

Henry held his head erect, despite feeling that his whole

body was caving in, but not one glimmer of a clue to his despair would he give this upstart. 'Very well, Provost. It will be as you say. I will stop working as from next Saturday and leave the house free for the Saturday after that. Good day to you.'

He felt sick when he went inside, his whole body trembling with anger, with fear for the future. 'I've to retire next Saturday,' he told Fay who looked at him speculatively.

'You've been expecting it, though?'

'Aye but I wasn't expecting the rest. We've to give up the house in another two weeks.' Then his voice broke and he sat down with his head between his hands.

'But that's ridiculous!'

'That's what the Provost told me just now. Be out two weeks from yesterday. I should have minded the house went wi' the job.'

'But think of the length of service you've given them. They should have presented you with the deeds – that would have been little enough thanks.'

'Well, well, it hasn't happened like that. We'll just have to shift – lock, stock and barrel – and there's plenty of us to leave the place spotless.'

'I would rather leave it like a pigsty,' Fay declared uncharacteristically.

'No, I don't want to give Jim Barron anything to complain about.'

'Is Billy to get your job? If he is, couldn't we still . . . ?'

She was angrier than ever when he told her what was to happen. 'What about a bell-ringer and court usher? Have they engaged somebody for that?'

'He never said but my guess is they'll do away with that side of the job. Times have changed, you know.'

Neither of them slept a wink that night, agonising over where they could go, but, in the morning, Fay said, 'We had better tell the others. Five heads will be better than two. The trouble is we'll need a house big enough for us all. It would be awful if we had to split up.'

'It'll not come to that, my Fairy,' Henry assured her, although

369

he couldn't think how to prevent it. They could never afford to buy a house and the ordinary council houses were far too small for them. Even if they did offer him one, which didn't appear to be on their agenda, they certainly wouldn't offer him two.

CHAPTER THIRTY-ONE

Despite Henry telling Mara that she shouldn't spend so much of her inheritance, she had bought back Oak Cottage. Willie Rae had left it to his daughter Kitty but circumstances had forced her to sell it a few years later.

When Jeffrey Kelly, Mara's ex-boss's son, told her that the present owners of Oak Cottage had put it up for sale, she knew that this was the answer to her family's problem. Filled with excited anticipation, she had written to her aunt in London – without telling her parents – to ask what she thought of the idea.

Kitty, of course, wrote back to Mara by return, saying that she was really pleased that Oak Cottage would belong to the Raes once again and Mara presented the letter to her parents with a proud flourish. It took a tremendous effort – with young Billy's help – to make them see that it was the best thing for all of them but, succeeding at last, she put the matter in Jeffrey Kelly's hands, stressing the urgency of the matter.

The entry date had been quite acceptable to the Macleans, the fourth occupiers since it was sold, who had been finding it too big. They had been thinking of moving to Aberdeen but hadn't quite made up their minds so the offer of a quick sale with entry within a week made the decision for them.

The house in Mid Street had been cleaned from top to bottom, five pairs of hands making light work of it even in the short time available, and Henry had told Mrs Maclean, 'Leave the house the way it is and don't worry. There's plenty of us to see to things after we're in.'

So the move had been made on the requested date, furniture and all, because the Provost had graciously told Henry to empty the house of all the previous Town Officer's furniture as well as their own possessions. It hadn't taken them long to get everything organised in Oak Cottage to their satisfaction and there was much more room for them all.

Life had been sailing more or less on an even keel since they took up residence. Billy was now courting Maggie quite openly but his dissatisfaction with his job – which had been building up for some time – came to a head in June of 1939. 'I'm tired of being at everybody's beck and call,' he said while they were having supper one night. He looked round the other four but his eyes came to rest on his sweetheart. 'I'm going to join the army,' he said quietly. 'They'll be needing every man they can get if it comes to war.'

'Oh no, Billy,' Maggie exclaimed, her face blanching. 'I don't want you to go. I don't want you to leave me.'

'I'd have liked to marry you first but I've nothing to offer you.'

'I don't need you to offer me anything. I'll marry you as soon as you want.'

He turned to Fay now. 'I'm sorry I brought it up when we're eating. I'll take Maggie for a walk and we'll have a proper talk about it.'

The talk of war had made Fay's stomach judder. She had lost her younger son to a war, her son-in-law as a result of war and she couldn't bear the thought of this young man, as dear to her as Jerry and Leo had been, putting himself in danger but she could say nothing.

The rest of the meal was taken in silence but, when the boy and girl went out, Henry rose to put his arm round his wife's shoulders. 'I can tell what you're thinking, my Fairy Fay, but he'll have to make up his own mind. And Maggie and all – she'll have to think of wee Laurie before she decides anything.'

When her husband went out for his usual fifteen minutes 'constitutional' before going to bed and her daughter had retired early with a headache, Fay confronted her fears. Were they purely for Billy's safety or to save herself from new heartache? But there was Maggie to consider too. If Billy did join up, the poor girl would worry about him – just as she had worried about Jerry and as Mara had worried about Leo. The men never thought of the women they left behind.

Henry had also been thinking. 'I know Billy's brought it all back to you,' he said when he came back in. 'It's the same for me and all but we have to let the laddie make up his own mind.'

'I know. That's what makes it so hard. I feel like I've got no say in anything any more.'

'Maybe Maggie has talked him round.'

'Oh, I hope so!'

He bent down to untie his shoelaces. 'In any case, maybe there won't be a war. A lot of old men in the cabinet making a fuss over nothing.'

She was well aware that he was just trying to stop her fretting yet he had thrown her a lifeline she could hold on to. If she prayed hard enough – as so many other mothers must be praying now – surely it wouldn't happen.

In the morning, Billy told them that he had made a decision. 'Maggie doesn't want me to volunteer but I can't carry on working here so I'm going down to London to see if I can find a better job. I'll give it a month and, if I haven't found anything by then, I'll come home.'

It was Mara who tried to talk him out of this. 'Where do you think you'll find a place to stay? London's not a friendly place like Ardbirtle, you know.'

'I'm not stupid,' Billy said quietly. 'I'm eighteen now and well able to look after myself. I won't let anybody swindle me or take the loan of me and, once I find a job, I'll find somewhere to stay. Then, when I'm on my feet properly, I'll send for Maggie.' His eyes sought hers, the love they shared blazingly obvious.

Fay was afraid to ask about the boy but Maggie said suddenly, her voice just a trifle unsteady, 'I'll be taking Laurie with me. I'm going to carry on my job here till I go, of course – that's if you're still willing to look after him for me, Fay?'

'Of course I am.'

Billy left for work then, prepared to give the obligatory week's notice, which would actually let him leave the following Saturday. Then Maggie went to carry out her duties as cleaner in The Doocot, a job she had held for over a year. Mara was last to go – she did not start until nine o'clock. She had been lucky that old Mr Kelly's son had taken her back into the solicitor's office about eighteen months earlier. She had needed the stimulus of working with her brain, otherwise, as she had told her mother, she would have sunk without trace in a sea of despondency.

Husband and wife looked at each other now, each knowing what the other was thinking. 'It'll maybe never come to it,' Henry said, not altogether convincingly.

'Billy's determined, though,' Fay murmured. 'He'll find a job, no doubt about that, and make a success of it, no doubt about that either. Then he'll send for Maggie and . . . oh, Henry, what'll I do without my darling little boy?'

At that moment, because their attention was off him, the darling little boy had emptied what was left of his thin porridge on to the table and was stirring it round with his spoon.

'Oh, Laurie!' Fay exclaimed but she couldn't help laughing at his pained expression, as if he were completely innocent of any ill. 'Thank goodness we stopped using tablecloths,' she said, as she scraped the goo off the American oilcloth Maggie had bought to save the washing.

Henry studied the toddler pensively for a few moments, mulling over a thought that had just occurred to him and he couldn't understand why he hadn't noticed before. He waited, however, until the little boy was playing outside in the garden before mentioning it to his wife. 'My Fairy Fay, do you not think that wee lamb's awful like Jerry was at that age?'

In the act of laying past the dishes he had dried, her hand halted halfway to the shelf. 'Have you just newly noticed?' she asked, softly.

'So you *have* seen the resemblance?' He sounded pleased. 'Could it be . . . do you think? Could it possibly be?'

374

She shook her still uncombed hair, some more silver strands escaping from their hairpins. 'He can't be Jerry's son, you should know that. It's twenty-two years since he was killed.'

Henry was outraged. 'Do you think I'd forgotten that? What I was thinking . . . well, he could have . . . fathered a bairn before he was sent away and wee Laurie could be that child's son – our grandson. Eh? What d'you say to that?'

'I say it's wishful thinking, old man.' Fay smiled to take the sting out of her words. 'Maybe you can convince yourself but you'll never be able to prove it.'

Over the next few hours, Henry *did* convince himself and he determined to get the proof. He'd have to find out where Maggie's parents lived – one of them could be Jerry's child. Of course, the link could be through Laurie's father and he'd tackle that if he had to. But first things first. It was probably going to be easier to make Maggie reveal her parents' whereabouts than her lover's.

As the days passed, Maggie was puzzled by Henry's determination to learn where her parents lived. The only reason she could think of would be to find out who Laurie's father was since *she* wouldn't tell him. It was nobody's business. In any case, her father had no idea that his younger brother had raped her when he was left in the house alone with her one evening. He had sworn that he would deny it if she told anybody and, if Henry Rae knew, he would go in with guns blazing and there would be a terrible row.

Mara was rather worried about her father these days. He had always been very fond of little Laurie but, this last week or two, he had been more than affectionate – acting almost as if he were a doting grandfather. Her mother, on the other hand, seemed uneasy when she saw him on his hands and knees on the floor with the boy or giving him piggybacks. Of course, she could be worried that he would do himself some harm at his age but it appeared to be more than that.

Maggie was getting a letter from Billy nearly every other day but it was three and a half weeks before the arrival of the one they all secretly dreaded. She read it out to them.

'I've found quite a good job in a hotel near King's Cross as porter and handy man. It's not one of the best places in London but it's far from being the worst. Better still, I've found us a furnished flat. It belongs to the father of one of the waiters here and they seem a real decent family. It's on the third floor, there are two rooms and a shared bathroom and the rent isn't as extortionate as some of them I went after.

'Now for the best news of all. I don't have to start at the hotel till the first of the month so tell the folks I'll be arriving this Wednesday and I'm taking you back with me.'

The gasps made her lift her eyes. 'I'm not going to sleep with him if that's what you all think. He'll have one room and I'll be in the other.'

'Wouldn't it be better to wait until you can be married?' Fay asked, gently. 'Your intentions may be good but the temptation could prove too much.'

'You're saying I might have another illegitimate child? Well, if I did, it wouldn't be because I was taken by force. I love Billy with all my heart.'

Fay shot a quick glance at her husband before saying, 'I know, dear, and he loves you but . . .' She stopped with a sigh. 'Can you tell us anything else he's written?'

The girl looked at the letter for a few moments then burst out, her eyes dancing, 'He's booked the Registrar for Monday. We're to be married the day I go down there so that settles the sleeping arrangements!' She bent her head to read the last few lines, obviously avowals of love, and slid the pages back into the envelope, her cheeks flushed. 'Oh, isn't it great?'

It was Mara, affected by the younger girl's excitement, who reminded her that she would have a lot to do before Billy came for her. 'You'll have to buy a new dress – not a fancy wedding gown but something special so it'll look nice in a photograph for you to remember.'

The two of them chattered on, discussing a style, the colour, the shoe style, whether she should buy a hat, too, while Fay and Henry sat silently, visualising long empty days ahead of them when Maggie and her son had gone.

Billy turned up mid-morning on Wednesday, looking the same as always, and, after showering Maggie with kisses, he turned a cheery grin on the others. 'Are you surprised?' he asked, looking at Fay for approval.

She hadn't the heart to tell him what she really felt – that the event she had hoped would never take place was upon her now – she said truthfully, 'I'm happy for you, both of you.' She held out her arms and, as if it were something he did every day, he threw his arms around her and kissed her cheek reverently.

'I'm glad you're not angry with me for taking them away,' he murmured, far more perceptive than she had thought. 'And we'll come back for holidays – if that's all right with you?'

'Any time and as often as you like,' she whispered, tears starting to edge down her cheeks.

'That's enough of being serious,' Henry said rather gruffly. 'We're all happy, let's keep it that way.'

Having heard the familiar voice, Laurie came bounding in from the garden and launched his sturdy little body at the young man, squealing as he was swung up in the air, 'Billy! Billy! You back?'

Billy grinned. 'Yes, I'm back!'

Maggie, however, had seen the tortured glances Fay and Henry had been exchanging. 'Not for long, though,' she told her son, on the spur of the moment. 'He's going away again in a couple of days and . . .' She hesitated, then stated, to everyone else's amazement, 'And Mummy's going with him. I'll come back for you once we get settled down in our new house in London but you're to stay here for a wee while yet. Fay and Henry and Mara would be awful sad if we all went away together.' She was making a huge sacrifice but it was worth it to see the relief on the two elderly faces.

Fay turned away on the pretext of rinsing out the teapot, while Henry took out his handkerchief and dabbed at his eyes.

377

Mara, more able to cope with the unexpected, just blinked a few times to banish any moisture.

The next two days crawled past for Billy, anxious to start a new life and make Maggie his wife. For Fay and Henry, the time flew by far too quickly, although their sadness was tempered by the thought of having the little boy to themselves for a few weeks. Mara was torn between happiness for the young couple and sadness for her parents – it was as if her emotions were on a seesaw. Maggie, too, had mixed feelings. She would soon be married to the man she loved but she was leaving her darling son behind. Not for long, though.

The parting came, as partings inevitably must, tears were shed, hugs were given and long, heart-rending kisses. The guard's whistle broke the spell and in moments a sad trio were wishing the soon-to-be-wed pair good wishes for the future, and the little boy kept waving until the last carriage was out of sight.

On the way home, Fay remembered something that she had forgotten in the all the excitement of Billy's visit and turned it over in her mind for some time. She could see only one interpretation of it but had to wait until they were in bed before she could ask what her husband thought. 'D'you remember when Maggie was reading out Billy's letter to us?'

'Aye?'

'It was before we knew he'd arranged the wedding and I told her it was too risky to share a house with him?'

'Aye?' The response was sleepier.

'And she said if she had an illegitimate child, it wouldn't be from force.'

'So?' There was interest in this answer.

'Well, I've been thinking about it and I'm nearly sure Laurie was the result of her being . . . raped. What do you think?'

'It sounds like it, anyway,' Henry said, cautiously.

'I think it must have been somebody her father knew and that was why she wouldn't tell him.'

A few moments passed as her husband mulled this over. 'I believe you're right, my Fairy.' Another pause, then he mut-

378

tered, 'I wish I knew where her folks are. I'd get the truth out of them.'

'They don't *know* the truth, Henry. Besides, I think you're wrong thinking one of them is Jerry's child. Put it out of your head, my dear Tchouki, before it twists your mind.'

He certainly did not mention it again but she could tell that he still believed it.

Even Mara noticed something. 'Father's getting too fond of Laurie,' she had said some days later. 'Anybody would think he was his grandfather.'

'He wishes he was – that's the trouble.' Fay shook her head sadly. 'It'll take the heart out of him when Maggie takes that child away.'

Mara made the discovery. She was searching in the dresser for the games she had played, at different times, with Andrew, then with Jerry. They would amuse Laurie too. He wasn't five years old yet but he was as bright as a button and into everything. That's why she had waited till her mother and father took him out for a Sunday walk.

She found two boxes, Ludo and Nine Men's Morris and the strange double-imaged photographs, which looked three-dimensional when seen through a special wooden instrument. That would keep the boy happy for hours at a time if she could only find the viewer. Thrusting her hand right to the back of the cupboard, her fingers touched a package. It didn't feel like any of the games but curiosity made her lift it out. Her heart gave a jolt when she pulled back the wrappings. She should have known her mother would treasure this – Jerry's balmoral bonnet with the antlered head badge – the badge of the Gordon Highlanders.

She had been too engrossed in worrying about Leo for her brother's death to make the impact it should have done and regret made her run her fingers round the headband, a little crumpled now. Laying it flat on the table, she put one hand inside and used her other hand to get rid of the creases. That was how she came across the two documents, folded lengthways so that they could fit into the band – as a stiffener, perhaps.

She flattened the stiff paper and read the first while she smoothed the second. A birth certificate! Her father was right, then. Jerry *had* fathered a child before going overseas or maybe while he was over there. She checked the date – October 1915. Father: Jeremy Rae; Residence: The Sycamores, Near Drymill, Aberdeenshire; Occupation: Gardener. Mother: Anna Cairns; Residence: The Sycamores, Near Drymill, Aberdeenshire; Occupation: Nurse.

Mara's hands were shaking as she picked up the second document – the marriage certificate. This would satisfy her parents, she thought, but it was strange that Jerry had never let them know about it. Then she drew a sharp breath. The birth had come only two months after the wedding! Oh, dear!

She laid the two documents side by side in front of her. She didn't know what to do. If she showed them to her parents, her mother would be dreadfully upset, hurt that her son had kept this a secret from her, and her father would likely be cock-a-hoop that he'd been right all along. Was it right to cause so much distress to one and to give the other the means to justify himself? There was no doubt that he would follow up this information to find the proof he needed. It would be like unleashing a rabid dog and letting it set off on a trail of destruction.

The fact was that William Henry Rae would be coming up for twenty-five, not old enough to be Maggie's father – therefore, Laurie Fiddes was not the grandson Henry Rae thought he was.

But there *was* a grandson . . . somewhere. The question was should she tell or should she destroy the evidence and keep the information to herself?

CHAPTER THIRTY-TWO

'They'll take a while to settle down,' Fay remarked towards the end of August.

'Aye.' Reading his morning paper, Henry was not giving his full attention to her. The headline 'WAR WITHIN DAYS' was alarming – Chamberlain's assurance of 'Peace in our time' had been a hollow promise – but he didn't want to upset his wife by telling her of his fears. It might all fizzle out.

The forecaster, however, had hit the nail exactly on the head. Less than a week later, with Hitler having ignored the ultimatum he had been given, Britain declared war on Germany and those who remembered the last conflict shook their heads when younger men said, with a laugh, 'It won't last long this time.'

Henry and Fay, along with all the others who had lost loved ones in Kaiser Bill's war, were saddened by the thought of all the young men who would be mowed down this time.

'I'm just glad we've nobody they can take,' Henry said, as the Prime Minister's broadcast came to an end. 'The war can't possibly last till wee Laurie's old enough.' As he said it, the thought struck him that Billy Webster was the right age and he was thankful that his wife hadn't realised it.

In November, Maggie's letters began to be more guarded but Fay could read between the lines. 'I think they're having a struggle to make ends meet,' she observed. 'She's speaking about taking a job if I don't mind keeping Laurie for a bit longer. Of course I don't mind but I hope things get better for them, poor souls.'

The note that came with the small parcel at Christmas had Fay in tears. 'She's apologising for not buying anything for us

– they could only afford a little toy for Laurie. Should I send some money to her?'

Henry shook his head. 'I don't think that's a good idea, my Fairy.'

She was determined to do something to help them. 'I'll bake some things for them, then. It'll be a New Year gift so they can't object to that, surely. And I'll maybe buy a new blouse for Maggie and a shirt for Billy.'

Henry smiled affectionately.

Maggie was more forthcoming in her next letter. 'I've got a job as chambermaid in the same hotel as Billy and we're saving to buy our own place. I'd like somewhere with a garden for Laurie but it would take us years and years, so it is out of the question. As it is, it will take us a long time. Everything here is so dear. I'm desperate to see Laurie but I can't afford the fare. Anyway, I know he is being well looked after, though I am sorry you are being left with him for so long.'

'I'm not sorry,' Fay murmured. 'He's a wee angel.'

'He is that.' Henry was even more convinced by now that the child was, if not his grandson, at least his great-grandson, and considered it only right and proper that they were under the same roof.

Mara was quite concerned about her parents. Although Maggie had given them a reprieve – an extension, as it were – they would be absolutely devastated when she took her son away. Thinking about it one night, it occurred to her that William Henry would be old enough to have a family of his own. If she could just learn where he was, she might be able to present her parents with a real great-grandson. All she had to do was trace Anna Cairns, Jerry's widow, and she would learn the where-abouts of his son. It seemed an easy matter until she re-membered that she could not apply to The Sycamores for information. It had been commandeered by the army during the last war and someone had told her that it had been turned into a swanky hotel in the early twenties.

Yet there must be somebody who had worked there who

still lived in the area – maybe even a person who had been interested enough to have taken away all the records of the place before the army moved in. How could she find out?

It was then that she remembered Max Dalgarno, her father's boyhood chum. He and his wife hadn't visited for a long time, though they hadn't lost touch altogether. Nora always enclosed a letter with her Christmas card and there had been no mention of them ever having moved house. Max would know the men who had worked with Jerry and Nora would know the maids and nurses. They might not know where those people were now but it was worth a try.

'I wonder what it is Mara wants to know about Jerry?' Nora took the letter back from her husband and slid it into the envelope again.

'I can't tell you that,' he replied, grinning mischievously. 'I'm not a mind reader.'

'You know what I mean. It must be something really serious. Jerry was killed in . . . 1916 . . . or was it 1917? What would there be to find out after all this time?'

'Who was at The Sycamores that might know something? The only one I can think on would be Dod Lumsden. He was head gardener when Jerry started so he must be retired by this time.'

'Beenie might know something,' Nora said, suddenly. 'She'd stopped working there by the time Jerry started but she might have heard something.'

'That's it, then! Give Mara *her* address.'

'I can't. She flitted about ten years ago and I mislaid her last letter. I've lost touch with her altogether.'

'Well, that just leaves old Dod . . . if he's still alive.'

'Do you remember his address, Max?'

'Not the address but it was the second house along the road to Drymill. She'll easy find it if you tell her that.'

Mara set off on her bicycle the Saturday after she received Nora's letter, which, fortunately, the other woman had had the foresight to get her daughter to address – 'in case you don't want your mother to know you wrote to me.'

It was a lovely day in June, the countryside was looking beautiful and the roadsides were spattered with the yellow, blue, purple and white of vetch, bluebells, foxgloves, star of Bethlehem. Her thoughts, however, were on what may lie ahead. Would the old gardener still be alive? Even if he was, would he know anything? Would his memory be reliable if he did tell her something?

The cottage was easily found and, although Mara's courage ebbed when she lifted the doorknocker, she told herself sternly that it would be daft to give up when she'd come this far. Her knock was answered by a harassed-looking woman a bit younger than herself, an infant in her arms, a toddler at her skirt and another, slightly older, peeping out shyly from behind her. 'Aye?' she said.

Mara smiled encouragingly. 'I'm looking for Dod Lumsden. Is this . . . ?'

'There's nae Dod Lumsden here.'

'He was head gardener at The Sycamores at one time – before the last war, I believe.'

'You should ask Aggie. She's bidden in the hoose next door for well over thirty year. She'll ken if there was ever a Dod Lumsden here. No,' she added, hastily as Mara made to leave, 'she's in wi' me the now. She comes in every morning for a fly cup.' She vanished for a few moments to be replaced by a heavily built woman who eyed the stranger with deep suspicion.

Mara cleared her throat. 'Um, I'm trying to find Dod Lumsden. He worked at The Sycamores before the last war.'

'That's richt. This is the hoose he bade in but he died . . . oh, it must be seven year ago.'

'Oh!

Mara's disappointment was so evident that Aggie burst out, 'His auldest lassie bides in Drymill, though, next the butcher. I canna mind her married name but her first name's Dot. Dorothy, that is.'

'Thank you very much and I'm sorry to have troubled you.'

'It was nae trouble.'

Mara was aware of the woman watching her as she cycled

off but it was only to be expected away out here where they likely hardly ever saw anybody. Her spirits had lifted a little, though the end was not really in sight. This Dot person was not likely to know anything about Jerry, or his wife, but she had to try.

The late gardener's daughter was a cheery, round-faced little woman of round about fifty, who nodded as soon as Mara said her brother's name. 'Jerry Rae? Aye, I mind there was a lot o' speak about him at one time. I was in service in Aberdeen at the time but there was still rumours flying round when I come hame weeks after. You'd best come in, lass.'

She insisted on making a pot of tea before she settled back, with obvious enjoyment, to tell her tale. Her first words, however, warned Mara that she was not about to hear the whole story.

'I dinna think onybody kens what really happened and some folk say one thing and some say another but this is what I heard. There was this young lassie, you see, and the young lad that was under-gardener put her in the family way. He did the decent thing and wed her and the bairn was born just aboot two month on.

'Now, you'll understand, that was a right scandal in them days, even worse than it is now, but there was mair to it than that. Some said he wasna the father at all. They said it was one o' the dafties, an aulder man, but I think they were trying to get a better story out o' it. Whatever, the bairn was born and things were going fine for the young couple, then the lassie disappeared. My father was one o' the search party and when she was found, he helped to carry her back to the hoose. She was in a terrible state, and – this is what made folk wonder – she was never seen again, neither was the bairnie, neither was the daftie and the lad himsel' enlisted in the Gordons and was away in days.

'Of coorse, the story went roon' that he'd found oot he wasna the father and he'd killed the three o' them and ran off.' The woman's hand jumped to her mouth, 'Oh, I'm sorry! I clean forgot he was your brother . . .'

'It's all right,' Mara muttered, her whole body suspended in some kind of acid, which was eating at her very core. 'You'd better carry on.'

'That's aboot it – as far as I ken. Everything was hushed up and then the army took ower the place and that was the end.'

'What do you think happened, though?' Mara asked, desperate to know if her own thoughts were on the right track.

'Well, I wouldna like to say. Maist folk think he'd found out the bairn wasna his and he'd killed the three o' them – yet my father aye said Jerry was a real nice laddie. He believed the daftie had killed the lassie and the infant and then maybe he'd committed suicide and Jerry was that broken-hearted he enlisted. Whatever happened, though, it was a real tragic business, right enough.'

Mara wondered if her legs would hold her if she stood up but she had to get away. 'Thank you for telling me . . . Dot. It has explained something for me.'

Her legs did carry her out to the roadway but her progress back to Ardbirtle was slow and unsteady. As she had said, something had been explained to her but other questions had been raised. Why had Jerry never told them he was married, that he had a son, that they had both died in strange circumstances? Yet she knew now that there was no great-grandson for her to present to her parents. They had been shocked by Jerry's death, but thank God they had no idea of what he must have suffered while he was still alive.

As soon as Mara came in, Fay could tell that she was upset. 'Is something wrong?' she asked, after a while.

'No.' Mara had never told a deliberate lie in her life and she could not do so now, although she camouflaged it to save hurting her mother. 'Not really. I've just heard a really sad story about a young lad who had to marry his girl because she was expecting and then he lost both the baby and his wife.'

'Lost them? You mean they died? Poor boy.'

Mara could not let this misconception go. 'It was worse than that. Everybody thought they'd been killed.'

Fay eyed her daughter uncertainly. 'Murdered, do you mean?'

'Some people think so, apparently, but, as far as I could gather, there was no evidence of that. I think it's just a rumour that got out of hand – bits been added to it over the years.'

'Over the years? How many years exactly?'

'It happened during the last war – 1916 or 1917.' Mara knew for certain that it had been 1916 but sensed that her mother was dangerously near to discovering the person in the centre of the controversial tragedy.

Fay now showed that she was indeed suspecting that it was Jerry. 'Mara,' she said, softly, 'you may as well tell me. You're far too upset for it to have been a stranger – to have been anybody but . . . your brother. Am I right?'

Nodding, Mara rose to take the package out of the dresser and Fay watched in surprise as she pulled the stiff paper from the headband of Jerry's balmoral.

'What is it?' she asked, apprehensively.'

The marriage and the birth certificates were now revealed and the two women tried to find an acceptable reason for them to have been kept secret.

They were both in tears when Henry walked in with Laurie. 'My God!' he exclaimed. 'What's up? Has something happened to Maggie or Billy?'

Fay stretched out a hand to him. 'Sit down, Tchouki, dear. I'll take Laurie through to the kitchen to help me get some supper ready and Mara can tell you something she learned today.'

It was not until the little boy had been put to bed that the three adults could discuss anything and the two documents were spread out on the table. They had been gnawing at possible versions of what might have happened in 1916 for perhaps an hour when Henry muttered grimly, 'I can't understand it. If nothing out of the ordinary had happened, why did they have to hush everything up? There would have been no need for that.'

Mara frowned. 'You think those three *were* murdered?'

'Or took their own lives . . . except the infant, of course.

Somebody . . .' Henry's voice tailed off, as he realised who was the most likely suspect for that.

They sat for hours, going over and over every likely solution, even not so likely solutions, but the only logical suggestion they came up with was that, when Jerry found out that he was not the baby's father, he had gone berserk. Knowing that the natural father was a patient in what was in reality a mental institution, he could have been afraid that the child they had spawned would also be tainted. He had killed all three and enlisted in the army to escape retribution.

Henry was not entirely satisfied with this scenario. 'The Superintendent and his wife were bound to have known what was going on. They'd have reported Jerry to the police. They couldn't possibly have hushed it up. And, don't forget, he came to see us the day he enlisted and was back before he was sent abroad. He never said a word about a wedding or a baby or anything else.'

Mara pulled a face. 'I was remembering, though. It was when we were all at sixes and sevens – if you think back. Janet had died first, then Nessie, then Grandfather and I hadn't heard from Leo for such a long time that we thought he'd been killed. Even if Jerry had wanted to tell us, he probably didn't like to upset you more by saying he'd married one of The Sycamore's nurses because he'd put her in the family way. Then, after it had all gone wrong, he'd been eaten up with guilt and shame at what he'd done.'

'*If* he did it,' Fay murmured sadly. 'I can't think that Jerry would have killed anybody, no matter what they'd done to him. It wasn't in his nature. He never lost his temper, he was always quiet, placid – not like Andrew.'

'I can't help feeling you're right, my Fairy,' Henry sighed, 'though I don't suppose we'll ever learn the truth of it.' His fingers kept returning distractedly to the birth certificate and they half-detected a kind of roughness at the part which gave the mother's occupation.

Mara was more positive. 'And I can't help feeling that there *is* somebody who can tell us – if we can just find him . . . or her.'

388

Henry couldn't sleep that night. He'd had too bad a shock. Apart from learning that his son could have been a murderer, there was something about the whole situation that didn't ring true. It had something to do with the two certificates but he just couldn't think what. And what did it matter anyway?

CHAPTER THIRTY-THREE

Henry was glued to the wireless during the evacuation, although he had no personal reason for concern. The thing was, every poor wretch waiting on those beaches was some mother's son or some woman's husband and he knew what worry about a loved one could do to a person.

The miracle that was Dunkirk finally over, Fay also began to worry. London was being bombed nightly for weeks on end. 'I pray for Maggie and Billy every minute I can,' she told her husband one day. 'From what they say in the papers and on the wireless, it's a wonder anybody's left alive.'

Although Maggie wrote as often as she could, her letters did not give much away. She made light of having to sleep, or try to, in the air raid shelter but made no mention of the devastation they saw every morning, nor of having to clear up the debris from bomb damage to their own and neighbouring houses. Henry and Fay, however, knew that the young couple, like everyone in the capital city, were under bombardments such as had never happened in Britain before yet they kept their horrified fear from each other . . . and from their daughter.

Mara's mind was fully occupied in wondering who else she could contact to solve the mystery surrounding Jerry's marriage. She was certain, beyond all doubt, that her brother was not a killer but she had to find proof of it. She had to hear the truth from someone who had been there, who knew exactly what had happened and why the manner of the three deaths had been hushed up. The best possible source would be the man who had been Superintendent of The Sycamores at the time but he and his wife seemed to have vanished into thin air.

An unexpected note from Nora Dalgarno in the autumn of

1941 gave her at least a smidgen of hope. 'Would you believe I came across Beenie's last letter? It had fallen down the back of the chest of drawers. I wrote asking her if she could tell us anything about what you wanted to know so she might write to you direct. If she writes to me, I will let you know what she says. Hope your mother and father are keeping well. Max is still the same as ever.'

For the next few days, Mara tried to think of some explanation to give her parents if Beenie wrote directly to her but eventually gave up, trusting that something would occur to her if and when a letter did arrive. As it happened, she need not have worried. She met the postman as she went out one morning, while her mother was attending to Laurie and her father was reading his newspaper.

Robina Sangster, as she signed herself, was sorry that she didn't really know anything, just the rumours that were going round the district at the time. 'I never knew your brother,' the letter went on, 'but, knowing your father, I can't think his son had anything to do with the deaths. It was a queer business altogether. The news just sort of leaked out and nobody knew which death came first – or them that did wouldn't say. They had been sworn to silence.'

Mara stuffed the letter into her coat pocket to answer later. She was disappointed but not truly downhearted. Something would turn up yet.

It was two days later when something occurred to her that eased her mind a little. Apparently no one had seen any bodies or any funerals, so . . . what if the baby was still alive? Had somebody taken it in hand to look after him while Jerry was fighting for his country? If so, they must have been left waiting for him to come back – they wouldn't know he'd been killed in action. The War Office wouldn't have notified them. So, Mara thought triumphantly, there could be a twenty-five-year-old man somewhere who was quite unaware that he had two grandparents and an aunt. Her heart slowed down. Where? – that was the question.

Laurie had been fretting – girny, as Henry put it – for a day and a half when Fay decided to call in the doctor. If he had been her own child, she would probably have waited for another day – children went up and down like quicksilver – but he wasn't her own and she was accountable to Maggie for his good health until he could be safely taken to London.

Doctor Bell gave him a thorough examination, sounding his chest, checking his heartbeats, prodding him in a dozen different places to find out if he was in any pain but nothing showed up. 'I just can't think what it is,' the man said, sitting down at the boy's bedside, but keeping his eyes on him. 'He's as healthy a child as I've seen in a long time.'

'But he's not usually as pale as this,' Fay pointed out, 'and he's not one for lying in bed.'

'Mmmphm.' Bell screwed up his nose. 'Well, keep him there meantime. I'll look in tomorrow to see how he is but call me if he gets any worse.'

To save her elderly parents, Mara offered to sit up with Laurie all night but Henry insisted that he wasn't an old man yet and sent both his women-folk to bed.

After the first half-hour, time seemed to take spasms of practically standing still or whizzing past. He would look at the clock and, what felt like an hour later, the hands had only moved a couple of minutes; or else they had moved an hour in what seemed to him to be five minutes. He realised, of course, that he had dozed off for that hour. It was getting more and more difficult for him to keep his eyes open and his mouth was getting as dry as a bone. He stood up to stretch his arms, then, remembering that Mara usually kept a few wrapped boiled sweets in the pocket of her coat to produce to Laurie, he crept into the lobby. He had been half-afraid that Mara had taken her coat into her bedroom, as she sometimes did, but it was hanging on the hallstand as was more often the case.

There were no sweets, unfortunately, but there was an envelope. He wouldn't normally have read anyone else's mail but he had the feeling that this letter was of vital importance

. . . to him. Removing it, he took it back to Laurie's room to read and was puzzled by the signature of the sender. Robina Sangster? The name meant nothing to him but, when he read what she had written, he found that the sender was the girl he had known as Beenie Dickie, young Beenie who had helped Max and Nora to rescue Janet so many years before. But why would Beenie write to Mara? They had never met. They were total strangers.

Henry was wide-awake now, alert to the fact that something was going on that he hadn't been told about. It was clear that Mara was still trying to learn the truth about what had happened to Jerry but how had she got hold of Beenie? In any case, Beenie would know nothing – she had left The Sycamores long before the time . . . of the tragedy.

He spent the next hour and a half mulling over this, going down one avenue and up another, all to no avail, but he was brought out of the past by young Laurie's voice. 'Papa Henry, I'm thirsty and I'm hungry and why are you sitting there?'

Discovering that his dearly loved boy was on the road to recovery, Henry heaved a deep sigh of relief. 'Right then, lad, just you lie there and I'll go and start making breakfast.'

Laurie, however, had no wish to remain in bed and accompanied him to the kitchen. It was a joyous meal, all four eating more than they had done for a couple of days, then Henry said, 'I'll walk along to your office wi' you, Mara. I need to stretch my legs.'

Since he had been sitting all night, Fay took his remark at face value but his daughter looked at him apprehensively. 'What is it, Father?' she asked as soon as they were outside.

He did not hold back. 'Why did Beenie write to you?'

Somewhat disappointed that he had found out, Mara told him what she had done and why. She also told him her latest thoughts on the matter.

'So you think Jerry's son's still alive?' His faded eyes had brightened.

'I can't be sure, of course, but he could be. He'd be about twenty-five.'

393

'Aye.' He pursed his lips for a moment, then burst out, 'If it's true, Mara, I'd be the happiest man alive.'

'I can't think of anybody else that might know anything, though. Can you?'

He shook his head sadly. 'No . . .' but, brightening again, he said, 'But I'll keep on thinking. I might come up with somebody.'

When they reached the solicitor's office, Mara went inside while Henry kept on walking. He had much to think about and he needed to be on his own. His mind returned to his time at The Sycamores, conjuring up pictures of the people who had worked there, the gardeners, the groom, the stable lad. Then his thoughts turned to the female staff, the maids, the nurses. None of them, male or female, would still have been there when Jerry started . . . except Dod Lumsden but Mara had learned that he had died.

Hearing a horn tooting behind him, he realised that he was walking in the middle of the road. He stepped out of the way with a smile but the driver of the butcher's van drew up alongside him. 'Are you wanting a lift, Mr Rae? I'm going as far as The Sycamores if that's any use. The head chef gets all their meat from us and old Pete's fair delighted. The best customer he's ever had.'

'Thanks, Robbie.' With no thought to what his wife would do when he didn't go home for dinner, Henry took advantage of the offer. It seemed providential that he would be taken to the exact spot where all the trouble had been, where his thoughts had been centred for some weeks. He had no chance to plan what he would do when he got there because the young man at his side, whom he had known since he was a wee laddie, never stopped talking.

'I'll drop you at the gate if that's OK?'

'That's just fine,' Henry smiled, adding, in case Robbie wondered what he was doing there, 'I'm going to see an old friend I used to work with.'

'Did you work here at one time? Afore you was Town Officer?'

'That's right – a long, long time ago.'

He watched the van as it turned into the driveway, recalling the day he had seen these gates for the first time with the big brass plaque on them. 'THE SYCAMORES', it had said and, underneath, in much smaller letters, 'Home for the Mentally and Physically Disabled'. It felt like another lifetime. It was another lifetime. The small plate had been replaced by a huge sign saying, 'The Sycamores ***** AA and RAC Recommended'.

Apart from that, little else had changed. The sycamores that still lined the way in, the carpet of their samaras at their feet, had grown a bit taller and thicker and were obscuring most of what lay beyond them. With a sigh, he swivelled round, pleased to see the view was the same as it used to be. The little groups of cottages, built for the people who had worked for the original owners of the estate, were still dotted here and there; the two low hills in the forefront of the white-capped mountains far beyond them; the three willow trees a few hundred yards to the left, their branches arching gracefully towards the stream; the row of stately oaks away to the right, planted there in the dim and distant past by the owner of the time.

He stood for a few moments trying to remember who had stayed in which cottage at the time. He had been the youngest person there, of course, so all the men he had known would likely have passed away.

'Your father hasn't come home yet,' Fay told her daughter at lunchtime. 'I'm getting a wee bit worried.'

'I think he went for a walk,' Mara smiled. 'He's likely met somebody and been taken in for a fly cup. Then he'll have kept sitting and you know how he forgets about time when he's having a good gossip with one of his friends.' She was doing her best to allay her mother's fears but she, herself, was actually more worried. Where could he have got to? What was he doing? Surely he hadn't tried to walk to The Sycamores to try to get at the truth? He was seventy years old, for goodness sake! The old saying was true, right enough. There's no fool like an old fool.

As he walked to the nearest house, Henry prepared the questions he would ask.

1. Do you know where the Superintendent and his wife went when the army took over The Sycamores?
2. What do you know about the tragedy that happened just before that?
3. Can you think of anybody who might know exactly what took place?

Other questions might occur to him as he was speaking.

The first door was answered by a young woman, who said, 'That's funny. You're the second person that's asked me that.'

'That would have been my daughter,' Henry smiled, 'and she spoke to the woman next door as well, I believe?'

'Well, Aggie was in seeing me but, aye, they spoke. We couldna tell her onything though.'

Undaunted, Henry asked his other two questions and then moved to the next house. After he explained that his daughter had already spoken to her, Aggie asked if she had got anything from the person she sent her to. She could give him nothing further on what he wanted so he thanked her and moved on.

After calling at the next four houses without finding out anything useful, his feet were getting sore, he was feeling quite hungry and his tongue was sticking to the roof of his mouth but he was determined not to give in.

Luckily, the next person he spoke to was around his own age and asked him to come in and have a seat. 'You'll have a cuppie now you're here?'

'That would be very acceptable,' he replied.

It was more than acceptable. It saved his life. Along with the tea, the petite little lady produced a plate of girdle scones, a dish of butter and a pot of rhubarb and ginger jam. 'Everything's home made,' she told him, proudly.

After he'd scoffed three (at her urging) of the delicious triangles, she insisted on filling his cup again and only when he patted his stomach and told her he couldn't eat another crumb though her scones were the best he had ever tasted did she say, 'Now, what did you want to ask me?'

He put his first question not really expecting a positive answer and his insides gave a lurch when she said, 'Oh, I mind on the Millers, right enough. They was a nice couple, though their last week or so here wasna so good for them.'

'Were you here then?'

'I was that. Joe, my man, had nae lang finished serving his time in Aberdeen as a joiner and he bought this house afore we were wedded. He was the only joiner for miles – but I'm going ahead o' mysel'.'

Scarcely able to form the words, Henry said, 'You remember what happened? You can give me details?'

'I mind what folk thocht happened but we never heard ony details for it was kept awfu' secret. Of coorse, the rumours began to fly.'

Sick with disappointment, he decided to keep pressing her. She might come up with something she didn't realise was a clue. 'What rumours?'

'Well, it was real queer. You see nothing really come out till after the Millers were left and it was all past. Jerry Rae . . .'

'He was my son.'

'Ah, now I see why you want to ken. Well, he was away to the army and, like I said, the Millers was away and all, afore the first whisper started. I've nae idea who started it but it was about the lassie, Jerry's wife, going missing. There was search parties oot looking for her . . .'

'She'd been killed?'

'Now, now, dinna jump the gun. No, she was still alive when she was found but in a terrible state. Then this other whisper got going. One o' the men patients was found lying in the burn. *He* was dead.'

'The girl had killed him.' Henry couldn't help himself.

'That's what it looked like. They say he'd been trying to kill *her*.'

His brow furrowed in puzzlement. 'So . . . had he been chasing the girl?'

'Naebody kens for sure.' The woman gave a secretive smile. 'Then there was word that the lassie's bairn was dead and all and that made us scratch our heads.'

'I can understand that. And is that all you knew about it, Mrs . . . um . . .'

'I'm just Becky and, no, I ken a bit mair than that.'

'Oh, please, Becky, tell me the rest. I've got to know the truth. I heard that some people think my Jerry had killed them all.'

'Na, na! Jerry never killed naebody. Mrs Miller found the lassie and they took her back to the house and, when my Joe was there measuring for two coffins, the infant's and the man's, he heard Anna telling Mrs Miller that Charles – that was the man's name – he had killed her baby.'

Henry was thankful that he was seated. Becky had taken away his last hope and it was as if his whole body had turned to jelly. 'The baby was definitely dead? It wasn't just a rumour?'

'It wasna a rumour. I tell't you, my Joe made its coffin but we didna ken what had really happened. There was word that this Charles had killed the bairnie to get back at Anna for marrying somebody else and then he'd tried to kill her, to get back at Jerry for taking her away from him. He was one o' the dafties, mind.'

'But what about Anna. Is she still alive? Did she move away?'

'No, no. Joe had to make a coffin for her later on an' all. He wasna tell't how she died, though, so . . .' She shrugged her shoulders then drew in a sharp breath. 'You've gone awful pale. I've been going on and on without thinking. You'll have got an awful shock but at least it's proved your laddie was innocent. He'd nothing to do wi' any o' it. Would you like some brandy to settle you? I usually have a droppie at nicht if I'm tired.'

Henry nodded and the spirits did help to settle him but he

had one last question to ask. 'Becky, do you know why the Millers hushed everything up? Why didn't they report the deaths to the police? If the baby was murdered . . .'

'I believe they didna want the bother it would cause. Whatever way things happened, The Sycamores would have got a bad name and that would've been them oot o' their jobs.' Becky gave a little snort at this point. 'Mind you, it didna last long after that, in any case. The army commandeered it for the rest of the war and the Millers just left withoot telling a soul where they were going.'

Henry was still puzzled. 'I can't understand how none of the men knew at least something of what had gone on at that time. Your husband surely hadn't told any of them what he knew.'

'Only me.'

'I've just thought – would the workers have been paid to keep their mouths shut?'

Becky's sly grin was accompanied by a wink. 'Aye, well, maybe a puckle palms *was* greased.'

Knowing that this was as much as she would admit, Henry got slowly and cautiously to his feet and was relieved that he could actually stand without falling over. 'I had better be going, Becky. My wife'll be wondering where I am.'

'Have you far to go?'

'Ardbirtle.'

'How did you get here? Have you a car?'

'No, I walked a bit then I got a lift in a van.'

'How are you going to get hame, then?'

'I'll walk it.' Henry felt ill at the thought of the long trek ahead of him.

'You'll do no such thing! By the look o' you, you wouldna get half a mile afore you collapsed in a heap. I'll ask Jackie, that's my son-in-law to gi'e you a lift. He's oot at the back wi' his new motorbike and he's dying to try it oot.'

Fay was on the verge of going to the police when she heard a motorcycle stop at the door and, by the time she looked out of the window, Henry was being helped off the vehicle, looking somewhat under the weather. Her first thought, naturally, was that he was drunk, although she had never known him to be drunk in all the time she had known him. She went out angrily to help him inside but the young man gestured to her to let him finish his job.

'My ma-in-law said he's had a bit o' a shock so go easy on him.'

'Thank you for bringing him home,' she remembered to say before he jumped on his steed and roared off.

Looking at her husband, now seated in his chair by the fire, she saw that his face was ashen and he was obviously in such a state of shock that she asked no questions. When he was ready, he would tell her where he'd been and what had happened to him.

CHAPTER THIRTY-FOUR

The more Henry mulled over the information Becky had imparted, the more desolate he felt. Jerry's child had definitely died back there in 1916, naturally or not, so there was no grandson and, therefore, no great-grandson. Despite little Laurie – a sturdy six-year-old now – being the very image of Jerry at that age, he was no relation whatsoever.

That was hard enough for Henry to accept and, all credit to him, it made no difference to his attitude towards the boy but something worse than that was eating away at his innermost fibre. He had sought proof that Jerry was innocent of any crime but he still wasn't sure. Becky's assurance that his son couldn't have killed anybody had to be set against the fact that the Millers had swiftly covered up the whole diabolically sordid affair and had even bribed the joiner and probably several others to keep quiet. They wouldn't have done that if the male patient had been responsible for the two deaths, nor if the killer had been the girl who was Jerry's wife. She had been the last one to go and Jerry was the only one left alive . . . and, therefore, the only suspect.

If the police had been involved, they would have found out whether or not the girl's death was suicide and, if was, they'd have written off the case as nothing further to investigate. She had killed the other two and then killed herself.

But the police had not been informed – that was what he couldn't get over. There had been no investigation. What reason could there have been for that? Surely, even if the guilty party was one of the patients, the good name of The Sycamores would not be sullied. The Superintendent – Miller – could not be held responsible as the insane could not be monitored twenty-four hours a day. On the other hand, Jerry was a paid employee, trusted to behave with propriety, and he must have interfered with the young nurse, made her pregnant and been forced by the Millers to marry her. It was probably this side of things that they successfully hid, afraid that it would be a black mark against them if it was made public – a very black mark.

Unable to sleep with the burden of not knowing weighing heavily on his mind, Henry turned to his other side. It struck him suddenly that there could be another explanation. Jerry had been a personable young man, handsome, quiet and willing to do what he was told when he was told. Could it be possible that Mrs Miller had taken a fancy to him? Her age at the time was unknown to him but he hazarded a guess at between forty and fifty – an age when some women tried to regain their lost youth by having an affair with a much younger man. If that were the case, she would have done her best to shield him.

But that didn't make sense either. The easiest way to take suspicion off Jerry would have been to lay it at the girl's door . . . or the man's. They were both dead and couldn't deny any accusations. But what was he thinking about? He was as good as saying that Jerry *was* guilty. Sighing raggedly, he turned over again.

'What's wrong, Henry?' Fay asked, sleepily. 'You've been tossing around all night. What's bothering you?'

'Oh, my Fairy,' he groaned, 'everything's bothering me. We can't be sure that Jerry was innocent. Maybe he enlisted to run away from what he'd done.'

She groped for his hand and gave it an affectionate squeeze. 'No, my dearest Tchouki, don't get lost down that road. He enlisted because both his wife and his child were . . . dead . . . however it happened. Certainly not by his hands.'

'That's what's bothering me, though. His child – if it was his child – never got past infancy so we have no grandson and no great-grandson. Our Laurie's not ours at all.'

'But we always knew that. We're only his guardians until his mother thinks it's safe for him to be with her in London.

402

That's why, God forgive me, I often hope the war goes on forever and she doesn't come to take him away.'

He put his free arm around her now. 'I feel awful sad when I think I've nothing to show for my life.'

'We've got Mara.'

'She's the finest daughter a man could ever have . . . but she'll never give us a grandson now. Even if she ever does get married again, she's too old to make a son. I'm the last in the line, Fay.'

The catch in his husky voice made her kiss him. 'Last is always best,' she assured him. 'Besides, I love you, my darling Tchouki, as much now as when I was bandaging your poor hand all those years ago.'

'I should stop moaning, for I'm a lucky man. I'll love you, my Fairy Fay, till the day I die – and pray God I go first for I'd be lost without you.'

James Ferguson had been feeling down for a few weeks. The war reports had made him recall the son he had lost because of the last conflict with Germany. And he wondered, as he had so often done over the years, if it would have been better for Leo to have been killed outright instead of lingering on for so long, only part of a man. It was good that he'd had someone like Samara Rae to look after him for most of the time. She was an absolute gem who deserved better than having to care for an aggressive, twisted man with a grudge against the world.

His own wife couldn't hold a candle to Samara. Maddy was a self-centred moaner, who was pleased with nothing unless it benefited her, and it was always he who had to toe the line. Tonight was different. He had stood at a graveside this afternoon, as her body was lowered into the ground, and all he had felt was an immense joy. He had put up with her for almost thirty years but at last he was completely free.

The funeral was attended only by some of her friends and they all wore the same look of boredom on their faces as she had. Once it was over, he had taken the bus into the centre of the city with no idea of what he meant to do but there was always plenty to see in Princes Street. It was just after five yet it was already beginning to get dark and the large stores, whose windows used to blaze with light to attract customers, had the blackouts up, as was demanded of all buildings in this time of strife. It hadn't stopped the crowds, though. Offices were emptying, feet were scurrying here, there and everywhere and the headlights on all the vehicles were shaded with cardboard to conform to the blackout. The bus conductresses were shouting, in their usual quaint patois, 'Come oan, get aff!' as the people waiting to get on board were held back by those trying to get off.

Ferguson sauntered along, drinking in the normality of it and praying that his beloved city would not be flattened by bombs like parts of London had been. He took his time, savouring each step, and, having walked the whole length of Princes Street, he crossed over to go back along the world-famous gardens. It was well past six o'clock now and the shop and office workers had made their various ways home but there were still people on the move.

Uniformed men and women from all parts of the world had been sent to Britain and, next to London, the place they most wanted to see was Edinburgh – a Mecca for sightseers in wartime as much as in peacetime. It was getting too dark to read the flashes on their shoulders as they strolled past him on the lower path between the street and the railway line but he could recognise some of the tongues. French, Polish, Norwegian, Australian, Canadian and, of course, now that the Yanks had come in, American.

James felt tired now, really tired, as if he had walked from John o'Groats to Land's End, and he plumped down gladly on the first empty bench he came to. Atop the huge mass left by volcanic activity in some distant historic era, the castle was silhouetted blackly against the sparse light that was now left in the sky. There had been quartered all the Scottish regiments who had defended the Scottish capital against the English, and other marauders, down through the years. It had always attracted tourists and was well worth a visit – as he recalled from having explored it several times when he was younger, always coming across something of interest that he hadn't noticed before.

His stomach giving a sudden rumble and he wished that he had eaten something after the funeral. He certainly was a foolish old man, as Mrs Gove, their housekeeper, often jokingly remarked when he was trying to do something that involved any exertion. It was good to sit here quietly, though, with nobody to bother him and nothing to go hurrying home for. It would take time to adjust to being his own master, he supposed. A man needed something, or someone, to give him direction, to guide him through the days.

'Excuse me, sir, do you mind if I sit here?'

James looked up and quite liked what he saw – a tall young man in air-force blue, smiling shyly. 'No, no I don't mind.'

'I bet you're like me,' the stranger said. 'You've been walking around so much your feet are killing you. Am I right?'

James grinned. 'I've walked too far, I know that. Haven't done much walking at all for . . . oh, goodness knows how long. Car from door to door, usually.'

'That's the trouble with most people nowadays. There'll come a time when human beings lose the ability to walk and, in a few generations, they won't have any legs at all.'

James couldn't help laughing at that. 'No, I don't agree with you there. How can young men like yourself find a girlfriend if you don't walk around a bit? And, once you've found her, you have to romance her – take her for walks in secluded places. You'll know all about that, though.'

'Not really. I've never been one for chatting up the girls. I'm a bit shy.'

They talked on companionably for fully twenty minutes, then James's stomach gave another loud rumble. 'Oh, excuse me.'

'Have you eaten anything today?' The young man sounded quite concerned.

'As a matter of fact,' James admitted, 'it's been a most unusual day for me. I buried my wife this afternoon . . .'

'Oh I'm sorry to hear that.'

'No need to be. I'm not. She ruled the roost and I'm glad to be rid of her.'

His companion quickly covered up his astonishment. 'Look, I don't think we should sit here much longer. The damp's coming down and it won't do your chest any good. What about having a bite to eat somewhere with me? I'll pay.'

'Indeed you'll not.' James was outraged at the idea. 'I'll pay. I'm nowhere near the breadline yet.'

He rose stiffly and staggered a little as his legs took his weight. 'It's with sitting too long,' he excused himself.

The young man took his arm. 'My dad says, if he sits for any length of time, he has the devil's own job to get moving again.'

Over the next hour or so, James learned that his companion's name was Malcolm Fry, that his mother had died when he was only eight and that his father had looked after him single-handedly from then on. In return, James said that, after his first wife died, he had stupidly married a younger woman who had just been after his money.

Malcolm insisted that James should get a taxi home and he was glad to agree. It had been a taxing day. While they were waiting, he gave the young man his visiting card. 'I'd be pleased if you could come to see me tomorrow, Malcolm. I've a feeling I'll be a bit lonely. Make it about one o'clock when my stalwart housekeeper will have lunch ready. That is,' he added hastily apologetic, 'if you're not doing something else.'

'I'm on a forty-eight hour pass from Turnhouse and I'll be delighted to come.'

'That's settled then – see you tomorrow.' Once inside the vehicle, James waved feebly in response to the young airman's salute, then lay back, feeling every one of his seventy-odd years.

That evening, he thought over the last few hours. He had enjoyed the walk along Princes Street but the interlude with Malcolm Fry had really bucked him up. It had been good to have young male company again and he found himself wishing it was the next day so that they could talk again.

AC1 Fry had spent the night in a boarding house just off the Queensferry Road. It was good to be away from the dozen or so men with whom he normally shared a room – heaven to be able to lie quietly without being disturbed by different levels of snoring and groaning and other natural, but infuriating, noises. He had looked forward to having time to himself yet, by the time he had gone round the castle, walked down High Street as far as St Giles' and then cut through to walk along Princes Street Gardens, he had had more than enough. The first few benches he saw had been fully occupied so his feet had rejoiced to see only one old man on the next seat he came to.

He had thoroughly enjoyed talking to James Ferguson and was looking forward to seeing him again. His overcoat had looked very expensive, probably Crombie cloth, and, when he took it off in the restaurant, he had noticed that his suit, too, had been of the very best quality. A man of means, then – perhaps inherited but more likely to have been earned in some highly qualified position. He would have interesting tales to tell.

James was impressed that his visitor arrived at one minute to one o'clock. Most of the young people he had ever come in contact with had been hopeless with time, late for everything, and usually with no apology or explanation. Mrs Gove had produced a good square meal, nothing fancy but very palatable and filling – thick lentil soup, a dish consisting of potatoes, onions and cheese (a favourite when she had used up their ration of meat), followed by seven-cup-pudding, a favourite of his. They both refused her offer of tea to follow ('Sorry, no coffee.') and adjourned to the sitting room.

'I was thinking last night,' he said, after speaking about the weather and barely touching on the situation in the Far East. The war had no right to intrude. 'Can you drive, Malcolm?'

'I've had a licence for over five years. I never had a car of my own but Dad let me drive him around and sometimes let me borrow his Austin.'

'That is excellent. You will not be averse, therefore, to have the same arrangement with me? I still tootle around Fife, though

I am not too happy to drive into Edinburgh. All that traffic makes me nervous.'

'I'll be delighted to take you anywhere you want . . . if I'm not on duty.'

'Yes, of course, I understand that. I will tell you what I had in mind, if I may? There is someone I have not seen for many years and to whom I would love to pay a surprise call. It is much too far for me to drive and we would need at least one full day to get there and back and allow us some time to talk, although an overnight stay would perhaps be better.'

'That would be fine by me,' Malcolm smiled, 'but maybe we should wait till the weather's more reliable. I'd feel happier if I could have a few short journeys first, anyway, to get used to your car. What is it, by the way?'

James screwed up his face. 'My wife made me buy a Rolls. She was an out-and-out snob, you see. It's fairly old now but still in the best of conditions. If you like, I'll have my garage give it a good going-over, just to make sure that everything is as it should be.'

'That would be a good idea but, to tell the truth, I'll be scared stiff to drive a Rolls. What if I scrape it or damage it?'

'It will repair. Do not worry – I am sure you'll manage. We can go to South Queensferry for a start – that's not far – and then, once you are used to the feel of it, you can have it for an evening. You can impress your lady friend.'

'I don't have a lady friend. I did have but we stopped seeing each other a few months before I was called up and I never met anyone else.'

'You will, lad, you will,' James smiled knowingly. 'A good-looking fellow like you? The lasses should be falling over themselves to get you.'

To Malcolm's relief, that subject was dropped and he was taken out to the large garage at the side of the house to see the Rolls Royce, an impressive vehicle by anyone's standards. The bodywork was a pure shiny black and the trademark figurehead stood atop the bonnet, over the radiator, with, it seemed, her hair and her filmy dress streaming out behind her in the wind.

The inside was even more luxurious. The fascia was in gorgeous walnut, the seats were in a muted green leather and all the gadgets were made of chrome, the gear lever having a padded leather top. The carpets on the floor had a deep pile, deeper than Malcolm had seen in any house, and were in a dark green, which toned in with the upholstery.

'Gosh, Mr Ferguson,' he sighed, 'I'm terrified to even think of driving this.'

'I have every confidence in you,' James smiled. 'You can have as much practice as you feel you need and then . . . and then, you can take me to see my friend – something I thought I would never have the chance to do.'

The months passed at varying speeds for them. For James, impatient to set off on the journey he wanted to make, they crawled. But for Malcolm, unable to rid his mind of reservations about it, they sped past. He did like the old man but felt that their friendship had progressed too far, too quickly. Who else would offer the loan of a Rolls Royce – a Rolls, for goodness sake – to a practical stranger? What was even more unsettling was his reference to a two-day journey. An overnight stay? Did something murky lie behind this? Was James one of those . . . one of those men who preferred other men to women? What was he planning?

However, nothing untoward was said or done on their first little jaunts to South Queensferry. And when they had ventured further afield to Dunfermline one day and round the East Neuk of Fife to St Andrews on another occasion, everything was as proper as it should have been. He was enjoying himself now and so was James by the look of him.

With winter past, the weather grew milder and the trips grew longer and it was only when James remarked that he thought the time was right for the one journey he longed to make that something occurred to Malcolm – and he wondered why he had never thought of it before. 'Where are you getting all the petrol, James? I know Rolls Royces are harder on the juice than any other make of car.'

409

The old man gave a secretive grin, then said, 'I was a surgeon, you see, and having registered as such, I am entitled to as much fuel as I need. I had used hardly any of my petrol coupons before I met you, so I feel within my rights in doing this one last thing.'

He was so clearly serious about this that Malcolm hadn't the heart to tell him his ruse could land him in jail if it were found out – or, at the very least, with a substantial fine to pay. But this trip, to wherever it was, would definitely be the very last, as far as the driver was concerned.

Thus, as soon as Malcolm was told he was due a ten-day pass, they arranged for him to sleep at Cramond on his first free night so that they could set out fairly early in the morning.

The die was cast and time would tell if the young man's fears were justified.

CHAPTER THIRTY-FIVE

Henry was feeling somewhat disgruntled. He had planned to pay another visit to Becky in case something had come back to her – something that might clear his son's name once and for all – but the early morning rain had kept him inside. To be more correct, it had made his wife keep him inside. Fay was always afraid for his chest because his father had died of pneumonia. A little after ten, however, the sky took on a lighter tinge – not 'enough blue to make a pair of breeks for a sailor', as his beloved Gramma used to say, but enough to give body to another of her weather forecasts – 'Rain before seven, sun before eleven.' She had been a right character, his old Gramma. There weren't many like her around today.

The old prophecy had come true and, by twelve o'clock, the sun was streaming into the kitchen, making Henry itch to jump on his bike – struggle on, would be more like it – and pedal off to The Sycamores area.

'And where d'you think you're going?' Fay asked when Henry took his boots out from the cupboard under the stairs. He had never been comfortable in shoes.

'Out.'

'Where to?' she demanded.

'Just out. Can a man not please himself, these days?'

'Not when he's over seventy. I'm not trying to stop you doing what you want to do but I want to know what that is. You spent all day yesterday cleaning your old bike and blowing up the tyres, as if you were going to go out on it, but you're not fit for that, Henry. You know you're not.'

'I'm fit enough if you'd leave me alone,' he growled but slid the boots sheepishly under his chair.

'You can go and meet Mara, if you like, on your feet, though. That'll give you a wee breath of fresh air and maybe take that scowl off your face.'

Unable to argue with her for long, Henry's mouth turned up as he resurrected the boots and tried to put them on. Sitting so long had made his feet swell and he had to loosen the laces a good bit before the opening was anywhere near wide enough. Fay watched, longing to kneel down and help him, but she knew better. She had won one victory; it would be asking too much to try for another.

It took some minutes before Henry, sweating and red in the face, stood up triumphantly, both feet shod, both laces securely tied, but he made a face when his wife held up the jacket she had taken from the peg at the door.

'Anybody would think I was a bairn.'

'And they wouldn't be far wrong.'

But her smile was so loving that his heart beat a little faster – as it had always done and as it always would. Then he detected a mischievous glint in her eyes and knew what she was thinking. 'You needn't look at me like that either for I was going to put on my bonnet to stop my baldy bit getting cold.'

They both laughed at that for it was a standing joke between them. Even the tiniest coin of the realm, the silver threepenny bit, would have a hard job fitting into the bald patch on the crown of his head.

Having buttoned up his jacket, donned his cap and made sure that he had a hankie in his pocket, he opened the door, his bottom lip plunging down when a car drew up in front of him. Not an ordinary car, though – a car such as he had never set eyes on in his entire life. He hadn't even heard the engine of this sleek black vision and came to the conclusion that it must have broken down – right outside his door. He hurried forward to offer assistance to the two men inside.

'If you go down this road and up the next one,' he said to the driver, the younger of the two and wearing an air-force blue uniform, 'you'll see the garage. It used to be my father's smiddy at one time but one of my nephews converted it to a garage in the early thirties.' He turned to the older man now. 'And, if you'd like to come in while you're waiting, my wife will gladly make you a cup of tea or give you something to eat.'

'You do not recognise me, Henry?'

He took a closer look. The set of the head and the style of the walk, as the elderly man crossed the wide pavement, did remind him of somebody; somebody he hadn't seen for a good many years, and, even then, it had only been a few times. It was the cut of the clothes more than anything else that gave the game away. 'You're Leo's father! You're James Ferguson! What are you doing in Ardbirtle?'

James smiled beatifically. 'I've come to see Samara.'

'She'll be home from work in a few minutes. How did you know we were at Oak Cottage? We were in Mid Street when you were up before.'

'I directed Malcolm to Corbie Den first,' James admitted. 'So stupid of me when I should have remembered that it was sold after Leo . . .'

'Did the folk there tell you we were here now?'

'I asked where Samara Ferguson lived now and they told me that she was living with her parents. Then, of course, I had to be redirected again.'

'But I'm keeping you standing. Come in, come in, for any sake.'

Fay's recognition was quicker than her husband's and, after Malcolm had been introduced as 'a young friend of mine', they were all talking as if they saw each other every day. When Mara appeared, some ten minutes later, wondering who owned the expensive car outside, her whole face lit up. 'Mr Ferguson!' She hurried across to kiss his cheek. 'Oh, my goodness, what a lovely surprise. Are you on a touring holiday . . . ?'

'No, my dear, we have come specifically to see you. I feel thoroughly ashamed at not having made more of an effort to keep in touch with you. A card each Christmas is poor acknowledgement for all you did for Leo . . . and for me. Oh, my dear girl, it is so good to see you again.'

Then Malcolm was introduced and they all sat down to a bowl of broth with an oatcake, which was all Mara had time for before going back to work. The meal passed in comparative quiet and it was not until Mara had set off for the solicitor's office – with her father-in-law's assurance that he would still be there when she came back – and Fay and Malcolm had gone into the scullery to wash up, that Henry had a chance to talk privately to their guest. He had been considering it throughout their meal and had decided that James would be the ideal person to give him some guidance on how to find out what had taken place in 1916.

Having guessed what her husband was talking about, Fay took Malcolm out at the back to show him the garden, when they finished the dishes, and then took him through the gate between Oak Cottage and the garage. It had never been blocked up because, as Clarence Laing, Pogie's and Abby's eldest, had said when he took over, 'Best to keep communications open. We never know when we might need each other in a hurry.'

He had pretended that he was thinking of himself but Fay knew that it was she and Henry who were his main concerns. Clarence and Malcolm got on very well, although there were over twenty years between their ages, and presently Henry ushered James out, too, and Fay was free to go in for a seat. She wasn't up to standing very long, nowadays.

When the men came back inside, James said, a little apologetically, 'I hope you do not mind, Fay, if we come back after we have found somewhere to spend the night? I would like to have more time with Samara and we did set off with the intention of returning to Edinburgh to-morrow.'

'For goodness sake, James!' she chided. 'There's plenty of room here for you and I'm sure Mara would be delighted to sit and talk to you till the early hours.'

'My dear lady, I couldn't possibly put you to so much trouble.'

Henry put his oar in now. 'It's no trouble to my Fairy Fay. She just loves looking after people.'

At half past three, Laurie bounded in from school, bombarding Henry with questions about the big motor sitting at the door, but, when he spotted the two strangers, he went to Fay's side and wouldn't open his mouth.

Bemused by the boy's unusual shyness, Henry explained who he was and why he was there, then Fay took him upstairs to help her to make up two extra beds, 'One for Mr Ferguson and one for . . .' She looked enquiringly at Malcolm.

'Just Malcolm, if you please.'

'What's his last name?' Laurie demanded.

'It's Fry. Malcolm Fry.' He was much easier in his mind now that he knew he would have a room – and a bed – to himself. He had been impressed by the size of Oak Cottage and was surprised and somewhat amused on learning that Willie Rae had fathered thirteen children, of which Henry was the youngest.

After Mara came home, Laurie seemed more friendly towards the visitors and ended up on Malcolm's knee, listening to tales of the Royal Air Force, while Fay and Mara set the table and served the supper. Laurie, most reluctantly, was then put to bed, while Fay, Henry and Malcolm retired about nine, all claiming to be exhausted by the events of the day. James, alone with Mara at last, recalled Leo as a small boy, as a schoolboy, as a young university student, while Mara listened enthralled. Leo had never told her much about his youth and she felt more compassion than ever for his father. He must have been terribly hurt when Leo enlisted, giving up the chance of a junior post in the hospital where he himself worked. Then there had been the trauma of the homecoming, followed by years and years of heartache and sorrow that his dreams for his son could never come to fruition.

At last James gave a long sigh of what sounded like relief at having been able to speak about it. 'And then you stepped in, my dear, dear, Samara, to take the burden from me.'

'I didn't consider it a burden,' she smiled. 'I loved him, remember?'

'I am well aware of that and he loved you, deeper than most

men have the capacity to love, and then . . .' He shrugged, his old eyes dimmed even further by unshed tears. 'I, too, love you, Samara, and I will until the day I die, although it was not until I reached my seventieth birthday that I realised I had not done my duty by you . . .'

She shook her head. 'You were under no obligation to me, James. What I did, I did of my own accord, out of my love for Leo, and his love was all the reward I needed.'

He cleared his throat suddenly as if he had made up his mind about something. 'I buried Madeline some months ago. That was the day I met Malcolm and also the day that I planned my visit to you.'

'Why didn't you tell me earlier about your wife? I'm very sorry . . .'

'I wasn't.' His smile was a little lopsided. 'For the first time in years I was able to think my own thoughts, plan what I wanted to do . . . and do it. I am very pleased that I have been able to see you again before it was too late . . . No, don't shake your head. I am an old man . . .'

'The same age as my father,' she reminded him.

'Yes and it will be through your father that I will repay what you did for me.'

'What do you mean? What has he been saying to you?'

'He told me about your brother and how he is sure there is someone who can tell him the truth. I have a car and a driver, who has nine more days before he has to return to his airfield, and I mean to trawl the district around The Sycamores until I find that elusive person.'

'You know, when I came in today and saw Malcolm first, I thought he must be Jerry's son. I thought the baby hadn't died at all but it was just wishful thinking.'

'Samara, I am so sorry. I did not know about the terrible tragedy until today.'

'It's all right, James, but I can't see how you hope to get at the truth when my father couldn't.'

'Possibly I can't but I'll have a damned good try. There are ways of making people delve into their innermost memories.'

'I suppose I shouldn't ask any more,' she grinned, 'though I can't really see you as one of the Gestapo.'

Mara spent some time after she went to bed in thinking over the latter part of the evening. It had been lovely to see Leo's father again and it was no surprise that he was not saddened by his wife's death. Maddy, as Leo had called her, had not been a very likeable person. As for this quest he was set on making, he was an old man and, judging by her father's failing health, she doubted if James was capable of carrying out such an investigation. It could mean hours and hours of going from door to door. He would be in the Rolls, of course, which could impress these country people, could loosen their tongues – plus, if she was reading him correctly, he intended crossing their palms with silver. Grinning into the darkness, Mara closed her eyes and was soon soundly asleep.

At breakfast the following morning, James said, 'I think I'll have a tour round Aberdeenshire now I'm here. You don't mind driving me for a few days, do you, Malcolm? It's new ground to you too, isn't it?'

'I'd love to do a bit of exploring.'

After everyone had left, Henry was very quiet and, when Fay asked him what was wrong, he just said, 'I thought James might have asked me to go with them. I know what he's up to, you know.'

'He's not up to anything. He just wants to see a bit of the countryside and it's lovely at this time of year.'

Henry let her have the last word, although he had a strong suspicion that she did know what James Ferguson meant to do. Of course, he wouldn't succeed either . . . except that he was in a position to offer bribes or, as he would likely put it, rewards for information. Still, if he did learn something, it wouldn't matter how it was done, would it? All Henry Rae wanted was the truth.

Malcolm could tell that the people James spoke to were doing their utmost to give him the answer he wanted. Possibly the Rolls Royce had something to with it or just the old man's manner. He had a way of coaxing information out of people, as he himself had discovered, and several tiny snippets about Jerry Rae seemed to be emerging, enough to build up a picture of the young lad, a hard worker who, while friendly with everyone, kept himself to himself.

'None of them could find anything bad to say about him,' James commented as they turned back towards Ardbirtle in the late afternoon. 'Not until the tragedy came up – and then opinions were divided. I am very glad that I did not reveal my friendship with the Raes as that could have affected their answers.'

'I thought the way you introduced yourself was brilliant,' Malcolm smiled. 'You look exactly right for an author investigating mysteries.' His eyes twinkled suddenly. 'A little old, perhaps, but you could pass for sixty-five, even sixty, in a poor light.'

'Cheeky monkey,' James said affectionately. 'Well, I have had enough for one day but a good night's sleep and I shall be fighting fit again.'

He fended off Henry's curiosity by saying that he was fit to drop and scuttled off to bed not long after they had eaten.

Having covered the outlying cottages on the first day, in a huge sweeping circle around The Sycamores, they tried the village of Drymill the following day but the few pieces of information they gleaned mainly duplicated what they had already been told.

Towards the end of their third day, even Malcolm was feeling frayed at the edges and James had to admit to defeat. 'We'll finish this street and call it a day.'

At the first of the two remaining houses, a very stout, crippled old lady with straggly, yellowing grey hair opened the door. 'Aye?' she asked but not in the least aggressive as some of the others had been.

James recited his spiel and, at the mention of the 'mystery', she perked up a little. 'You'd best come in, sir.' She led the way into a neat little kitchen with a fire burning in the range. 'Sit you down now and I'll put on the kettle . . .'

418

'Don't bother making tea,' James interrupted. 'We have drunk so many cups today that it feels like a whole ocean is sloshing around inside me. I ask you, please, to cast your mind back to a time in 1916, Mrs . . . um . . . when the trouble at The Sycamores began . . .'

'I'm Rosie Allardyce and I was cook there at the time.'

His aches and pains falling away as if by some miracle, James could not believe this good luck. 'So you will have first-hand information about . . . ?'

'I was there, yes, but . . . I'd best start at the beginning . . . well, what I think was the beginning.'

The two men listened intently, afraid to say anything in case she lost the thread of her story. They learned that Jerry Rae and Anna Cairns had met in the gardens and it had been love at first sight. 'Then they was wed . . . she was in the family way, they said, but I still canna think young Jerry would have done a thing like that. He was still a bairn himsel', really, and so was she. To get on, the infant was born two month after they wed and I wasna the only ane thocht there had been dirty work at the crossroads. Everything was kept quiet but the word went round that Charles Moonie – he was one o' the inmates – had ta'en Anna by force and he was the father, nae Jerry.'

Mrs Allardyce stopped to blow her nose and then, with her large handkerchief returned to the pocket of her flowery apron, she carried on, 'Mind you, nae everybody believed that and it would've been forgotten come time but . . .'

She described the uproar there had been when Anna went missing and the search parties that were arranged. 'It was queer, though, for it wasna one o' the men that found her – it was Dolly Miller.'

James asked, 'What position did she hold at The Sycamores?'

'She was the Superintendent's wife and how did she ken where to look? I'm sure somebody had tell't her and it wasna Jerry – he was one o' them out looking. Then Tina Paul come running in – she was the nurse that had most to do wi' Anna – and she was in an awfu' state. She said Anna's baby was dead and Dolly Miller made the rest o' us leave. I'm sure it

419

was her that covered it up. Mind you, they must've forgot I could hear things and I heard Raymond Miller and Jerry going out again – late that night.'

She looked at James with a helpless smile. 'I wasna really listening but I strained my ears when they come back a good while after. So I heard them telling Mrs Miller they'd found Charles Moonie drowned in the burn.' Noticing their incredulous expressions, she explained, 'There had been a helluva lot o' rain, you see, and he'd been trying to jump across and he'd slipped in the mud.'

Her manner changed now, became more business-like, as if she was about to give a decision that she had long debated over. 'So now we've got two dead bodies – the man's and the infant's – and one hysterical lassie in the Millers' kitchen, screaming she doesna want Jerry to touch her. That's the reason some folk said he killed the three o' them – for Anna was dead in no time at all.'

Something that was bothering James had to be explained to him here 'I cannot understand how, with so many people milling about, no one knows the truth of what happened that night.'

Giving a low chuckle, the ex-cook said, 'The truth is, we got ten pound each from Raymond Miller to keep our mouths shut – it cost him a fortune – but I'd say twenty-five year's long enough to keep a ten pound secret.' She looked at James first, with her eyebrows raised, then glanced at Malcolm, as though asking for their agreement.

'I think that would be about right,' James smiled, his eyes twinkling briefly. 'You say you have never believed that Jerry Rae was responsible for the three deaths so who do you think *was* guilty?'

Her shoulders lifted briefly, then she murmured, 'There's folks swear blind it must've been him. He was the only one left alive – there's no getting away from that – but some blame Charles Moonie. They say he was angry at the lass for getting wed to Jerry and he'd killed the poor wee bairnie to get back at her. She'd've went mad at that and, if she hadn't run off,

420

they'd likely have had a fight and he'd have finished her off and all.'

'What about him, though?' James had to get the proper picture. 'Who do they think "finished him off"?' It was an apt phrase in the circumstances.

'They think he done it himsel' out o' shame. But you canna tell what a man like him would've been thinking, can you? He was a patient there, when all's said and done.' Bending over, she lifted the heavy poker from its stand on the hearth and stabbed at the now barely glowing coals in the range until they burst into flames. 'That's better,' she smiled, replacing the weapon and resuming her recounting of the old rumours. 'The lass, now, Anna. One story went that it was her murdered the infant 'cos Charles Moonie had fathered it and she didna want it reminding her about being raped.'

Mrs Allardyce gave a wicked chuckle. 'Folks might think this is a fine, upstanding community but it's had its share o' passion and rape and adultery as well as murder. We've had near every kind o' crime you could think on.'

'But how could Moonie have murdered Anna?' Malcolm, who had been silently following the woman's every word, couldn't hold back the question. 'You say she was still alive when his body was found.'

'Some say she committed suicide but naebody kens how she did it. That was another thing. Not one single worker, man or woman, is even sure she was the last to go. The deaths could've been in any order, for there was such a commotion going on it was damn near impossible to sort the grain from the chaff, if you see what I mean? I tell you this, I've gone ower and ower it in my mind ever since, trying to figure out what happened and when it happened, but it's still a mystery to me.'

James considered this for several moments before asking, 'Can you think of anyone who may have been witness to what went on inside The Sycamores during the time following the discovery of Charles Moonie's body? That, as far as I can make out, was the crucial period.'

Back in the car, James thumped his right fist on his left

421

palm. 'There must have been someone! The Superintendent and his wife would have been doing their best to hide what had happened, afraid that the good name of The Sycamores would be ruined, and they could not have coped with the hysterical girl, who, according to Mrs Allardyce, was screaming her head off.'

Malcolm slowed down to negotiate a nasty double bend in the road, then said, 'She was screaming that she didn't want Jerry to touch her, which proves that he was also in the room at that time.'

'It does not prove that he was guilty of her death, however,' James pointed out, then added, in a low voice, 'nor does it prove him innocent.'

For the rest of the drive back to Ardbirtle, they sat in silence, each caught up in his own thoughts, but, as they approached the first of the houses, James murmured, 'I don't think we should tell the Raes what Mrs Allardyce said. There is such a diversity of ways to interpret the old gossip, so many different accounts of what happened, when, in fact, no one can place the events in chronological order.

'Yes, I think you're right. No point in giving them more to agonise over.' Drawing up at the kerb, the younger man asked, 'Will we carry on tomorrow or should we give up altogether?'

James blew a noisy breath out through his lips. 'Do you know something, Malcolm? I cannot give up now. I want to know the truth just as much as Henry Rae does and not just because I feel I owe it to Samara.'

CHAPTER THIRTY-SIX

In his room that night, Malcolm read through the pages of notes that he had already taken, mostly guesses from the people James had interviewed and nothing very important . . . or so he had thought at the time. Tonight, in the light of what Mrs Allardyce had said, he realised that there could possibly be something that might tie up with her statement. Even a very small corroboration of a very small fact could lead on to something bigger, more important.

Having an analytical turn of mind, he turned to the end of his notebook and headed the very last page 'PARTICIPANTS'. It would be better to have those actually involved listed on one page and, if the name of a person who had not yet been interviewed cropped up more than once, it could be significant.

As was only to be expected, the most repeated names were Raymond Miller, the Superintendent of The Sycamores, and his wife Dolly. They would be the obvious source of information but, equally obvious, they would disclose nothing even if they *were* traced. Still, Malcolm decided it would be worth keeping them in mind in case all else failed.

It was not until he reached his notes on their last call that he shook his head at his own stupidity. Mrs Allardyce, who had been present in the Superintendent's sitting room for most of the relevant time, had mentioned the nurse, Tina, who had run in carrying the dead infant before Dolly Miller cleared the room. The thing was – and Malcolm felt a tingling in his blood at the thought – Tina would, most certainly, have been left inside. Going by how the ex-cook spoke of her, Tina had been very close to the tragic young mother and had actually been sent to sit with the baby until Anna was found. She must be the only person, other than the Millers, who knew precisely what had happened and in what order.

His heart hammering at his ribs, Malcolm had to contain his excitement until James said, as they were almost finished breakfast the next morning, 'I have been thinking, Malcolm. I am very selfish, taking it for granted that you want to spend your precious leave chauffeuring me around.'

Knowing that the old man was giving him the chance to call off their search, Malcolm shook his head forcefully. They needed to see Mrs Allardyce again, to ask if she knew where Tina was now. 'No, James, let's have one more day here and that still leaves me a few days to go to see my dad.'

Sliding her arms into the sleeves of her jacket as she made ready to go to work, Mara said, 'Where is your dad?'

'He actually comes from Liverpool and works for Lever Brothers but they transferred him to Carlisle last year.'

As soon as they set off in the car, James looked at his driver with great curiosity. 'You were very positive about having another day here. Have you come up with an idea of some kind?'

On hearing what Malcolm had discovered, he, too, was anxious to get on but felt obliged to issue a warning. 'If Mrs Allardyce does not know where Tina is, that is it! We give up. I know you will be disappointed but we can only do so much. I would have loved to be able to give Henry and Fay the proof of their son's innocence but too many years have passed.'

'They are such a nice couple,' Malcolm said sadly, 'and they were meant for each other, weren't they? He isn't much taller than she is and they seem to have the same temperaments.'

'Indeed – warm and affectionate. They welcomed Leo into their family as soon as he started courting Samara and he loved them almost as much as he loved her. They used to make me feel like an old friend when I went to see them – that was while I was on my very occasional visits to Corbie Den.'

'Corbie Den?'

'That was where Samara and Leo set up house. It was sold after he died – she did not want to keep it on.'

'She's a lovely person, as well. It seems a shame that she didn't marry again.'

'I told her at Leo's funeral that she should but she said she would never find another man she would love as much as Leo. It's a pity you're so young,' James laughed now. 'I think she has taken quite a fancy to you.'

Malcolm grinned. 'My boyish charm, eh?'

They said little for the rest of the journey; their thoughts concentrated on what they might learn from the ex-cook.

'Well, I never!' Rosie Allardyce exclaimed when she answered Malcolm's knock. 'I was wondering how I could get hold of you.'

'You have recalled something?' James asked, hopefully.

'Not exactly. I was going ower things in my mind, you see, and I couldna mind if I tell't you about Tina Paul.'

'The nurse,' Malcolm encouraged her.

'So I did mention her, did I?' She sounded quite disappointed. 'You'll have been to see her, then?'

'We need to know where she lives.' James hardly dared to breathe.

'If you'd asked me that yesterday, I couldna have tell't you but I was looking in my dresser drawer last night for a recipe I got at the Guild a while back and what did I find?' She looked triumphantly at both men, whose faces were agog with hopeful anticipation.

Malcolm hazarded a guess. 'A letter from Tina?'

'No, not exactly that. It was a letter from one o' the other nurses. She was the same age as me and we got real pally but, when The Sycamores was tooken ower by the army, Lizzie went to bide wi' her sister in Portobello. She's a widow.'

James shot a troubled glance at Malcolm as if to say that their journey had been for nothing – Portobello being practically a continuation of Edinburgh – but Mrs Allardyce was carrying on. 'We've wrote back and fore to each other ever since and one day she writes and tells me she'd seen Tina Paul in Princes Street, when she was in having a look at the shops. And Tina tell't her she was a caretaker in one o' the offices in Castle Terrace.'

'How long ago was this?' James wanted to know.

'It was her last letter – along wi' her Christmas card. So I would think Tina would still be there but I canna tell you the number.'

'Castle Terrace is not very long.' James couldn't keep his excitement out of his voice. 'We will find her, I am sure.' Slipping his hand into the inside pocket of his jacket, he pulled out a well-padded wallet and extracted some notes.

'Put that away.' Mrs Allardyce snapped. 'I havena done nothing.'

James grabbed her hand and pressed the four five pound notes into her palm. 'Indeed you have, dear lady. You have given me the means to let Henry Rae know the truth about his son – whether it will be good news or bad remains to be seen.'

Her mouth fell open for a moment and then she gave a sly grin. 'So you're nae what you said you were? You were working for Jerry's father, is that it?'

'Henry knows nothing about it but he has been in painful ignorance for so many years that I wanted to set his mind at rest – one way or the other. Now take this and keep the secret for another twenty-odd years.'

Her fingers slowly closed round the money. 'I still dinna ken the right way o' it so maybe you would write and tell me? I'll burn the letter as soon as I've read it and I'll keep my mouth shut till the day I die.'

'I will definitely keep you informed, Mrs Allardyce, and I will be eternally grateful to you.'

After shaking hands with the ex-cook, the two men drove away, James telling Malcolm to stop as soon as they were clear of the houses. 'What do you think we should do now?' he asked a few moments later.

Malcolm did not have to think. 'I'd like to go back to Edinburgh this very minute but I suppose we can't?'

'How would we explain it to Henry and Fay?'

'Maybe we should tell them what we've really been doing?'

'It would spoil the surprise. I visualise us going into Oak Cottage one day and telling them that we have found proof –

426

please God – of their son's innocence. But we still have much work to do. We have to find Tina Paul. No, Malcolm, I say we do some real sightseeing today and go to Edinburgh tomorrow. Then I insist that you go to see your father, otherwise I will feel ashamed for making you use up your precious leave in driving me around. What is more, you will take the Rolls – much easier than the train.'

'But I thought we would start asking for Tina at all the offices in Castle Terrace . . . ? You're not going without me, are you?'

'No, my dear boy, I, too, will keep impatience in check until you return.'

Malcolm telephoned his father from James's house in Cramond the following afternoon to let him know he would be arriving in the evening. 'He says that's great,' he told James later. 'His holidays start tomorrow.'

'It couldn't have worked out better for you,' James observed, turning on the oven to heat the bridies they had bought in Forfar.

'I'm glad,' the younger man admitted. 'I was feeling guilty for not telling him about my ten days' leave. Shall I set the table now or wait a little while?'

'Set it now and get it over. I have just had a brilliant idea. Why don't you phone your father again and say that I have invited him to spend his holiday here? You can collect him and bring him up and . . .'

'Good grief! Dad's not going to believe this. Travelling in a Rolls Royce? He'll never get over it.'

'He is a widower, of course.'

'Yes. I think I did tell you my mother died when I was eight and he had to bring me up on his own. I'm glad I can give him a little pleasure in his life now.'

James nodded. 'Yes, it certainly feels good to be able to help others.'

James was impressed by Frank Fry's open manner and immaculate appearance. Wearing a neat navy suit with white shirt and dark tie, his six-feet-one frame was topped by a thick head of grey-flecked brown hair, brushed back off his cheery face. He was of an age between Malcolm and himself, forty-five to fifty perhaps, but there was no awkwardness in the conversations they had. On the first night, Malcolm went to bed early, exhausted after driving to Carlisle and back, leaving the other two to get to know each other with no help from him.

A bottle of Glayva was produced and, during the next few hours, Frank confessed how hard a struggle it had been to raise a young boy by himself – especially after caring for his dying wife for several months. And James spoke about his first, and only loved, wife, his son and his daughter-in-law.

'We've just come back from visiting Samara,' he added and went over what Henry had told him about *his* son. Then he let slip what he and Malcolm were intending to do and Frank said that he would love to help.

'An extra pair of feet should cut down the mileage,' he grinned.

Thus it was that the three men set off the next morning to make enquiries in Castle Terrace, leaving the Rolls Royce and taking the bus to Princes Street. Frank could not get over his first sight of the castle, a back view, a great dark grey mass looming into the sky behind them as they knocked on doors. Only one side of the street was built on, which meant there were fewer places at which to ask.

The buildings were quite high with steps leading down from the pavement to the basements where the caretakers were domiciled. None of them had any luck as they made their way along and three hearts were sinking as they neared the end. It was James who struck it lucky, for which he was truly grateful. He had wanted to be able tell Henry, 'I discovered the truth.'

Tina Robbie, as she turned out to be, née Paul, asked him what he wanted of her and he told her, not altogether truthfully, 'Three of us are trying to learn something about places like The Sycamores, where you worked at one time.'

'You'd best go and get the other two,' she smiled, 'and I'll tell you whatever it is you want to know.'

In no time at all, she was handing round cups of tea and plates of home-made pancakes and gingerbread and nothing was mentioned until everything had been cleared away again. Then she looked at James, as the leader of the group. 'Who told you where to find me?'

He could sense some reservation in her voice, which was not so surprising really. She had taken three strange men into her house and, having had time to think, she had probably guessed what they wanted to know – a secret she had kept for twenty-five years. A secret she was determined not to divulge, James thought, going by the set of her mouth. 'We did not know exactly where you were,' he said carefully, 'but Mrs Allardyce . . .'

'Rosie?' She smiled a little.

'She worked with you at The Sycamores, I believe?'

'That's right, but how did she know . . . ?'

'Apparently she was very friendly with one of the other nurses who kept in touch with her over the years.'

'Oh, yes, I remember meeting Lizzie in Princes Street one day. I think I did tell her I was working here.' The brightness left her face abruptly. 'She must have mentioned it in a letter to Rosie but why do you need to speak to me when you've seen Rosie? She could've told you all about The Sycamores . . .'

James inhaled deeply. 'If I tell you that I am a friend of Jerry Rae's father, do you understand?'

Her eyes were guarded now. 'I can't tell you anything,' she said, coldly.

'I am sorry to hear that. Jerry's parents have spent many long years wondering what had really happened – whether or not their son was a murderer . . .'

'I can't tell you anything,' she persisted but her lips were quivering.

'That is not true, my dear,' James said softly. 'You are the only one besides the Millers who does know – the sequence of events, the manner of the deaths and why the police were not informed.'

429

'I can't tell you anything,' she repeated.

'Do ten pounds ensure your silence for the rest of your life?' James's voice held a sarcastic sharpness.

Her face a deep crimson, Tina didn't try to deny the bribe. 'A promise is a promise and Mr Miller gave me more than ten pounds – much more.'

'You claim to have been a friend to Jerry so do you not think that his parents deserve to know?'

She burst into tears at that. 'I never thought they would hear about it. Nobody was supposed to say anything. Oh, God, I'm so sorry for his poor mother and father . . . and he had a sister.'

'Yes, Samara. I am her father-in-law.' The increased volume of her sobs let James know this had struck home to her even further.

'You can make reparation now,' he urged. 'You can speak out without fear. What you tell us will only go to Jerry's family.'

'Take this,' Malcolm said softly, offering her an air-force blue handkerchief. 'Once you start speaking, you won't feel so bad.'

She began hesitantly but gathered confidence as she told of her part in the drama. 'And Mrs Miller allowed Jerry to see Anna for half an hour every day, to keep her away from Charles Moonie . . . though we didn't know he'd already raped her – Charles, I mean.'

She told of the discovery of Anna's pregnancy, of Jerry practically being forced into marrying her. 'Mrs Miller and me could hardly believe Jerry had betrayed our trust and, as it turned out, he hadn't touched her – but maybe you'd best understand something here. Charles and Anna were both residents – patients, you know – and they weren't stable enough to face up to what had happened and what was actually happening.'

While Tina stopped to think what to say next, James and Malcolm exchanged an astonished glance. Neither had known that Anna was also a patient.

'Charles was angry at Anna for marrying Jerry and maybe

430

he didn't realise the baby was his but he suffocated wee William Henry in his crib and I think he meant to finish Anna off as well – but she managed to get away from him and ran.'

James nodded his head. 'So it was Anna who struck Charles with a stone or something and rolled him into the burn? So how did she die? Did Jerry kill her?'

'No, no, Mr Ferguson.' Tina was more agitated than ever. 'Charles's death was an accident. He slipped in the mud and struck his head on a stone.' Her hand jumped to her chest as if she were having difficulty in breathing.

'Would you like me to fetch you a drink of water?' Malcolm asked and was on his feet even before she nodded.

'Should we leave her now and come back later?' Frank whispered to James.

'No, she still has not told us the most important thing. I need to know who was responsible for Anna's death.'

After taking a few sips from the tumbler, Tina murmured, 'I'm sorry but this is very difficult for me. I was very, very close to her, you see.'

James patted her back. 'I understand that, my dear, and I truly regret having to bully you like this but you cannot just leave it there.'

'I know and I'm doing my best to think . . . look, I'll have to go back to when Jerry went home and found Anna missing. He didn't realise the poor infant was dead and, when he came to tell the Millers about Anna, Dolly told me to go and sit with . . .'

She stopped again, swallowing her sorrow before whispering, 'It was me that saw he wasn't breathing and I went running to the big house and they had just brought Anna back. Then Dolly, or Raymond, made everybody leave and Anna was still screaming she didn't want Jerry to touch her. She was out of her mind, of course, and I think she thought he was Charles wanting to kill her. Anyway, I was told to put her to bed in the spare room next to mine so I don't know what the Millers and Jerry decided to do.'

James looked at Malcolm. 'So Anna was left alone all night?'

'No, no, I bade with her . . . just in case and it must have been one or two in the morning when I heard Raymond and Jerry going out and I knew they were going to look for Charles. It was maybe an hour and a half later when they carried him in for I heard what they said. When I asked Anna in the morning if it was her that hit him on the head and killed him, she swore to me she hadn't seen him after she hid in the potting shed. I wished I hadn't said anything, though, for she never opened her mouth after that.'

'And what about Jerry?'

'He went home – though I don't suppose he had slept a wink – and Dolly Miller let him have the day off. I think it was the day after that – though my brain's not so clear about this bit – I'd to do my morning round of my list of patients – seeing they were washed and dressed and that kind of thing – and that's when Anna . . .'

Sure now that what was coming was the missing piece of evidence that only Tina herself and the Millers were party to, James held his breath, afraid that one wrong word could put an end to her story.

Her eyes were haunted – as if this last event was the most harrowing to recall – but then, with a tiny sigh, she said quietly, 'That was when she had gone to Raymond's bathroom and taken his cut-throat razor.' The horrified gasps from her listeners seemed to give her a small modicum of satisfaction.

'She slashed her wrists?' James muttered.

'No, she . . . cut her throat. There was blood everywhere.'

They sat as though frozen in a tableau until Malcolm, younger and more resilient than the others, got to his feet. 'I think we deserve some tea.'

The three men learned the end of the story while the hot tea was revitalising them. Tina told them she had seen Jerry with a razor and thought he was about to end his life, too. She told them of the discussion that had taken place and how the decision was made not to tell the police. She told them how Raymond Miller had made up his mind that the only way to make sure that his employees would keep quiet would be to give them money and how his decision had been followed by a short argument as to how much he should offer them. Finally, she told them that Jerry Rae had enlisted in the Gordon Highlanders just days later and left the district altogether.

After this, with her emotions at a low ebb, Tina said tearfully, 'I often thought about him and wondered if he came through the war all right. I used to pray he would find another girl to love and have a few bairns and live happily ever after.'

Although quite aware that she would be upset, James felt it his duty to put her right on this. 'He was killed in action, I'm afraid – about a year afterwards.'

'Oh, my God! Poor, poor Jerry.'

She was dry-eyed now and they left after a few minutes. As Frank said, 'She's probably better to be on her own.'

They then made for Ardbirtle, Frank offering to stay in the car until they told the Rae family the truth.

But James was firm. 'No, you were there at the denouement and you should be present at the actual finale.'

Nothing much was said on the journey north but all three minds were going over what they had learned. It was obvious that Tina had known nothing of the coffins that had been made or, perhaps, James thought, it hadn't occurred to her to wonder how or where the bodies had been buried. Probably there was a small graveyard somewhere in the grounds, as there had been where Leo was buried, but that side of the events had not registered with her.

The nearer they came to Ardbirtle, the more apprehensive James became. How would the Raes be affected by the information they were about to hear? Instead of bringing happy answers to all their questions, as he had hoped to do, he would be reminding the inhabitants of Oak Cottage of the agonies they had gone through at the time of their son's death. And they would learn of the tragedy that was Jerry's marriage which, no doubt, would make then feel even worse.

Although he would be giving them proof of the boy's innocence, he was not the bearer of good news.

CHAPTER THIRTY-SEVEN

James went in first, to explain why he had returned so soon, and saying that he had left Malcolm and his father in the car.

'Bring them inside,' Henry cried. 'Goodness, you don't need me to tell you any friends of yours are welcome here.'

Fay was outside before he had finished speaking and was assuring the other two men that they shouldn't be shy about coming into the house.

After being introduced as Malcolm's father, Frank took a back seat and James stopped Fay from putting on the kettle. 'We have come directly from Edinburgh, where we talked to Tina, the nurse at The Sycamores while your . . .'

'Tina!' Fay exclaimed. 'I remember Jerry speaking about her. She was very good to him, as I recall.'

'Indeed she was – more than you could imagine. I have a long story to tell, a surprising story, and I think, Henry, that we will need something much stronger than tea.'

Glasses duly filled, Fay's with lemonade, James told the tale as succinctly as he could, including as much as he could remember, and, if he missed out the slightest detail, Malcolm would put him right. The events were laid bare in such a way that Henry and Fay were left in no doubt as to what went on and, when the very last tragic incident was told, all five people were in tears.

At last, Henry said, 'So there was really only one murder – the little baby. The man's death was an accident and Jerry's wife's was suicide. Am I right?'

'That is correct,' James replied.

'So our Jerry wasn't responsible for any of the things that happened?'

'Not the least little bit responsible. Now, I know that the news has upset you, brought it all back, but I was duty-bound to tell you.'

Wiping her few remaining tears away, Fay said, 'Of course you had to tell us and we are truly grateful to you, James. At least we know now that our son did not murder anybody.'

'I feel bitter that . . .' Henry hesitated and then went on, 'that the baby wasn't Jerry's.'

Frank sat forward in his chair at this point, as if about to say something, but Laurie came running in from school. 'I knew you were here,' he crowed, making straight for Malcolm. 'I saw the Rolls.'

'My legs could be doing with a stretch,' Malcolm smiled. 'How about coming for a wee walk with me?'

Frank also stood up. 'I could be doing with a walk myself.'

When the door crashed behind the boy, Fay turned to James. 'You'll stop for your supper?'

'You are not prepared for three extra mouths,' he told her. 'I was meaning to go after Samara comes home. I would like to see her again.'

'You're stopping and no argument!' She went through to the kitchen to pare some more potatoes, thankful that she had made enough broth that morning to do them two or three days because the boiled beef wouldn't go round everybody. The family wouldn't get any but at least there were plenty carrots.

His wife out of the room, Henry reverted to the topic uppermost in his mind. 'You know, it was years after the army sent on Jerry's belongings that we came across the two certificates – the marriage one and the birth one. That's what made me try to find his widow and their son – of course, I didn't know the boy wasn't Jerry's son at that time – but, as you know, they were not to be found. Mind you, I'd no idea that Anna Cairns, as her maiden name was, had been a patient, though I did have a strange feeling that something wasn't right. That rough bit on the birth certificate, where the mother's occupation was given, had been changed to read 'nurse'. It would have originally said 'patient' or maybe even 'mental patient' and Jerry must have altered it because the registrar or whoever filled out the certificate wouldn't have risked doing it. Altering legal documents is against the law – as my father was to discover when he tried to get my own birth certificate changed.'

James let him talk on. It would do him good to get everything sorted out in his mind.

'Did anybody say anything bad about the infant? I mean, he wasn't like his mother? He was . . . normal?'

'As far as I know, he was. Tina would have said if he had not been. She had a lot to do with him and his mother. She was very fond of them . . . and of Jerry.'

'Aye, that's some comfort.'

Henry fell silent now but the ensuing silence was broken when Mara came in.

'I'm so glad to see you, James,' she said, kissing his cheek.

'Take him up to your room and listen to what he says,' her father instructed her. 'Laurie and the two men'll be back shortly and you'll get no peace in here.'

Having told his story already, James was more fluent and, with Mara being quicker on the uptake, it did not take nearly so long. She did not weep when he came to the last tragedy but shook her head sadly. 'That poor girl . . . and poor Jerry.' She considered for a few moments and then said apologetically, 'I can't help thinking that it's true what people say – that God works in mysterious ways. Anna hadn't been cured, like they all thought and probably the birth had had a lot to do with her mental state. Then the business with Charles Moonie . . .' She hesitated briefly. 'You'll maybe think this is callous of me but, to my way of thinking, Jerry would have that terrible time fresh in his mind for the rest of his life, plus the awful sights he must have seen in battle. It was probably best that he died when he did.' She looked earnestly at James. 'Do you think I'm awful?'

'Not at all. It is not the way my mind was working but I can see your point. I do not think, however, that you should mention it to your parents. They will be struggling with their feelings for some time yet, I imagine, but they will settle down again and perhaps you can put your point of view to them then.'

She gave a wry laugh. 'And perhaps I had better not.'

The two men returned with the boy just as James and Mara went downstairs. James introduced her to Frank and supper was served. Because of Laurie, the meal was eaten amid light-hearted banter and it was Henry who said, as the two ladies were clearing the table, 'Mara, why don't you take Frank out and show him a bit of Ardbirtle? Malcolm can play a few games of Ludo or something to amuse Laurie and I'll help your mother with the dishes.'

She didn't like to refuse. As she told her mother the next day, she quite liked the look of Frank Fry but had thought it would be difficult to know what to say.

Soon after Laurie was settled for the night, Malcolm excused himself on the grounds of all the driving he had done and went to bed, too, although Fay knew that it was only an excuse. 'What were you playing at?' she accosted her husband. 'Are you trying your hand at matchmaking with Mara and Frank? Maybe they're the right age for each other but I don't think it'll work – they're both too shy.'

The couple *were* very shy and walked along silently for a few minutes and then Mara said, 'We can go back if you'd rather. I'm not a great conversationalist.'

'Neither am I but we can surely find something to talk about.'

She found his grin very attractive. 'Right. I believe you brought Malcolm up on your own? It must have been difficult when you had to go to work as well.'

'It wasn't easy but he was a good boy – always ready to help. We got through.'

'You made a good job of it, anyway. He's a very nice young man. I wish he were a good few years older.' Wishing that she hadn't said it, she gave a laugh to show that she was joking. 'One of these days he'll surprise you by bringing home a girlfriend. How will you feel about that?'

437

'I'll have to say nothing – whatever the girl is like.'

'I'm sure Malcolm will pick a winner.'

'I picked a winner,' Frank said. 'Sylvia was everything a wife should be – a good cook, a good housewife, good with money.' He looked at Mara quizzically. 'What about you? Did you pick a winner?'

'I did. Leo was a lovely man when I knew him first – tall and handsome, good fun, good company – but, unfortunately, the war robbed him of all that. I married him after he was sent home, a total wreck. At first, it wasn't so bad and we had quite a few years of perfect happiness. Then there were some years that weren't so perfect and he deteriorated quite quickly after that – until I couldn't cope any longer. That was when James took him away and put him in a home for disabled servicemen.'

'So neither of us had all that long to enjoy our marriages?' He stopped abruptly when they came to what claimed to be an antique shop. 'Can we go in? It's still open and I love browsing through old things.'

'You'll be at home here,' she giggled. 'It's full of old junk.'

She watched him as he sifted through the piles of bric-a-brac lying on the first small table. He wasn't a bit like his son. They were both tall – around six feet – but he had dark, grizzled hair while Malcolm's was much fairer. The shape of their faces was different too. Even at twenty-five, Malcolm's was still round and boyish, his father's was angular, strongly boned. She had also noticed earlier that Frank's eyes were brown and his son's were grey.

'Does Malcolm take after Sylvia?' she asked when Frank straightened up to go to another table. He gave her a most peculiar look, she thought, and she was about to apologise for being too personal.

'No, he takes after his mother.' His voice was soft. Then, seeing her puzzled expression, he went on, 'I think we should find somewhere private to talk.'

She took him to Petty Park, donated to the town in the late nineteenth century by Alexander Roderick Petty, a local boy

438

who had made good in America. It was quite a pleasant night and they had to go well in before they found a vacant seat – crafted by a local cabinet-maker. 'I had better tell you everything,' Frank began. 'I should really have told you and your parents together but I wasn't sure . . .'

'You're making me very curious,' she smiled, hoping that he wasn't about to confess to an affair during which Malcolm had been conceived.

'As you may have guessed, Sylvia was not Malcolm's mother. She had been told, when she was much younger, that she could never have family so, when her best friend lay dying from a flu that was raging at the time and asked her to take her baby, she agreed. He was just over a year old and he was like a gift from God.'

'Was the mother not married?'

'Yes, Daphne had been married but her husband had to return to his regiment the day after the birth and he never came back. She never knew if he'd been killed or if he had abandoned her.'

'Poor girl. That must have been awful for her but didn't her parents want to take care of their grandchild?'

'Apparently she had fallen out with her mother. Daphne's mother said Jerry was a rotter for having his way with her before they were married and then deserting her and the baby. Sylvia did go to them to make sure it was all right for us to have him and Mrs Nelson said they didn't want anything to do with him.'

'Oh, that's sad. Fancy any parents . . . grandparents . . .' Mara broke off. It was too horrible to think about.

'I kept telling Sylvia that we should try to trace Daphne's husband. We could have applied to the War Office or to the Gordon Highlanders Headquarters . . .'

'My brother was in the Gordons.'

'So I believe. I went to ask the Nelsons if they knew his service number but they wouldn't tell me anything – not even his name. Sylvia knew his name but she wouldn't say either. She was scared we'd lose the boy if I stirred things up so we had to adopt him before he could legally have our surname.'

Mara became aware that he was regarding her cautiously. 'But you did find out his name?' she asked after a moment.

'Not until after Sylvia died and I didn't want to lose my son as well as my wife. In any case, I only knew his name – I didn't know where he actually came from. Being a Gordon Highlander, he was almost certainly from the north of Scotland, the north-east probably, but . . .'

The truth struck Mara then, as clearly as if he had actually said it. 'You think it was my brother?'

'Oh, Mara, I wasn't sure. It was only when I heard James speaking about the Rae family that I had any suspicions. Jeremy Rae . . .'

'Killed in action in 1917,' she finished for him. 'Oh, Frank, it *is* him, was him . . . and oh, God, I'm going to cry.'

He put his arms round her and held her closely, kissing her hair and patting her back, until the soft sobs ceased. 'I'm sorry, Samara. I couldn't find a way to tell your parents but I shouldn't have blurted it all out to you like this . . . on your own. I'm sorry, I'm so sorry.'

She stroked his cheek. 'There's no need to be sorry, Frank. You've made me happier than I've been for a very long time. I've discovered today that Jerry was innocent of any crime and that he did find some happiness after he left The Sycamores.' She jumped to her feet. 'Wait till my father learns he really does have a grandson after all.'

The jubilation in Oak Cottage carried on until well after midnight, Fay and Henry practically jumping their own (small) height with joy, James Ferguson shaking his head in delighted disbelief and Malcolm's happy smile, when he hugged his grandparents, so wide that it almost split his round face in half. Looking on, it seemed natural to Mara that Frank was still holding the hand he had clasped for support while he told the others the momentous news.

Not until they were all exhausted did they go to bed, Malcolm first, then James, then Henry and his wife. On her way out, Fay turned to say goodnight to her daughter and Frank Fry but what she saw made her think better of it.

'What a day this has been,' she exclaimed when she closed the bedroom door.

'Aye, you're right there,' Henry agreed. 'And I'm shit done.'

'There's no need for that kind of language,' she admonished him.

'I'm that damned happy I don't know what I'm saying,' he laughed, grabbing her round the waist and twirling her round. 'I feel like I'm sixteen again, courting you, my lovely, lovely, Fairy Fay. I thought we'd go to our graves with just one daughter to leave behind and now we've got a grandson as well. Who'd have believed it?'

'There's something else you're going to find it hard to believe,' she smiled. 'You're going to have a son-in-law as well, mark my words. Did you not notice Frank holding Mara's hand?'

'No, no, you've been seeing things. They only met this afternoon.'

'And you sent them out together. Your matchmaking did the trick, my dear Tchouki. They make a nice couple, though they're both well over forty.'

Henry was too happy to argue. 'I hope they *are* serious about each other. If they get wed, Frank'll not mind so much about us wanting a share o' Malcolm.'

THE END